A Calm Round of Hours

To Carol,
Happy reading!
Becky

REBECCA MARK

Rebecca Mark

. . . aye, thou shalt see,
Dearest of sisters, what my life shall be;
What a calm round of hours shall make my days.

John Keats
Endymion, Book One

Part One
HONEYLESS DAYS AND DAYS

December 29, 1977
Six Hours

So spake they to their pillows; but, alas,
Honeyless days and days did he let pass;

Isabella, or The Pot of Basil
John Keats

*W*hen the doorbell rang, I was making circles in the blue paints with the wooden end of my brush. I had been mixing for several minutes, trying to find my sky. The doorbell was not annoying. In fact, I welcomed the excuse to leave my work. All day I had had no motivation to do anything, and only about four-thirty had I retired to the green room to paint, knowing that I would have to quit soon to prepare supper. No, the doorbell was not unwelcome.

I put down my brush, pushed my glasses up on my nose, and smoothed the hairs of my eyebrows into what, mirrorless, I thought to be a delicate, arched line. I was not beautiful, but I did not mind, for there would be no one at the door.

Only Iris was there, peering at me and yet to one side with that disturbing, almost eerie stance that the mentally disabled often assume. When we were children, my parents had frequently left Melly and me with her, and I remembered crying and running away from her. We didn't know then that she was slightly different; we just didn't want Mother and Father to leave.

She was carrying a square dish, covered with aluminum foil, which she said was a Jello salad.

"When's the funeral?" she asked.

I told her it was tomorrow and that Mother and I were going. I thanked her for the salad and she left. As she clopped down the sidewalk, I noticed that her legs seemed barely able to support her weight; her huge stomach and breasts, her outdated coat, boots, and hairstyle made her appear older than she was, although Mother said she was only forty-eight. If there had been ice on the sidewalk, she couldn't have come, but it had warmed up yesterday and quite a bit of the snow had turned to slush, which, in turn, had melted. It was cold today, though, with a bitter wind, and the landscape, colored only by drab grays and browns, intensified this harshness.

It was the most desolate time of day, the hour before people turned on their lights and lessened the loneliness of dusk. On winter evenings I liked best to walk home from town or school and see the glow of lit lamps in windows along the way. Then even night seemed companionable.

That was why, I suppose, I turned on the Christmas tree lights in the living room after I put the salad in the refrigerator. I was tired of painting, so I sat down beside the tree and closed my eyes. The house was very quiet, and I could hear the clock ticking on the mantel and water running through the radiators making strange noises. In a few minutes, I would have to put sliced ham in the oven; the potatoes were already there. Then I heard Father's pickup in the driveway. He had been out on the farm all afternoon, working on Enoch Peterson's combine engine. A good man at fixing machinery, Father farmed only about 160 acres now and sublet the rest, but it was enough for a fifty-seven-year-old man.

We didn't have pigs either. This was the first Christmas we didn't have pigs. Mother told everyone, in a sad voice, just as she lamented the fact that they had no male heir to take over the farm.

"And we have no boys to continue in Ned's place," she sighed. "And just think of the investment in those machines! All those machines to sell eventually, and young boys starting out can't afford to buy them unless their fathers help. And this is the first year in—why I don't know how long—almost thirty years—that we don't have pigs. I didn't think I'd ever see the day when we didn't have pigs."

She constantly mourned relinquishing the farm, although they hadn't yet sold it all. I might have been resentful or even nostalgic, but I knew she just liked to talk, never regretting that Melly and I were girls. Moreover, I had liked best when we moved to town, for looking out the kitchen window now was almost the same as it was then. I had glanced out before Iris came, and remembering that view, I saw a gently undulating milo field, gray-brown, with snow neatly preserved between the rows of stubble. On the farm there was a fence around our backyard, then a pasture, but in December most of the countryside looked the same, especially from our back window, since we bordered the edge of town. Besides, I liked best streets with lit windows.

I heard Father come in the back door. He would take off his coat and boots in the green room and then wash his hands. Yes, I heard the water running. I knew I should go into the kitchen, but I had been horribly lazy all day and it seemed almost impossible to move from the sofa. I looked at the mantel clock, and it was ten after five. Since the news had already started, I supposed Father would go into the pink room to watch it.

Other people had mud rooms and dens, but we had the green room and the pink room. When we moved to town, Mother gave me a room to decorate. It was to be a sort of family room/den, a place where Mother and Father could watch TV and read the newspapers. Mother said I could do anything I wanted to with it as long as I preserved the "character" of the room, namely that it was to be a "used" room.

Since I had seen a picture of a beautiful room done in pinks and browns, I decided to test my talents with the room Mother had given me. I picked out a nice brown area rug, soft and rich-looking. The room's drapes, which were beige, I left intact since they hung quite nicely. Mother let me buy a nice brown leather sofa and two big comfy chairs upholstered in a swirly floral pattern of pinks, greens, and browns. For the sofa, I found a few pillows in various shades of pink and brown, and I also recovered in the chair fabric two old pillows that we had down in the basement on the farm. The bookshelves, TV cabinet, and end tables I took from our farm house, and I put an aluminum plant and a hot pink-flowered kalanchoe on my grandmother's smoking stand. The table lamps, beautifully tall with shiny brass pedestals, I also took from the old house. I added all the bric-a-brac that gives a room heritage—the books and pictures, the plates and vases, the enamel boxes and candles—for all this clutter told me that the room belonged to our family and no one else. It always told me that, even though I didn't really live here any longer.

The pink room, I admitted with no apologies, was a small, fully-packed room by most of today's favored trends, which demanded so much bareness and adherence to an anti-dust campaign. I had always thought there was something romantically elegant about brass table lamps, even when one could see dust on their rims. I loved the yellow-tinged incandescent in spite of our energy crisis, the way I looked in my bedroom mirror at night with only my lamps on. I hated the way I looked under fluorescent lights, but perhaps only plain, average people made that distinction.

It was five fifteen now, time to put the ham in the oven. As I passed the pink room, I could hear the TV set quite well, even though the French doors were closed. Father's hearing was not very good and he kept the volume very high. There was a light on in the green room, but the kitchen was dark, so I flipped the wall switch, flooding that room with fluorescent light.

Doing so made me remember saying goodnight to Jack once. He could have picked the front steps or the foyer, dimly-lit places where the outline of my cheek bones under pale night light would have made Jack ache to kiss me. But no, it was the kitchen. I remembered staring at him under the bright light, thinking how dreadful we both looked to one another. I remembered smelling the mosquito repellant we'd put on hours ago, speaking softly to each other, hoping my parents could not hear but knowing how well sound traveled in a quiet house. My eyes were tired; my contacts felt dry and brittle. My face needed a good scrubbing. Staring at Jack, I could see light flecks of dirt around his nose and on his chin. My face was equally grimy, a porous canvas of dirt, perspiration, and long-since-applied makeup. In the movies, I thought, it would be different. The girl's face would be fresh, glowingly rested. She would have long, luxurious hair and perfect vision. And it would be moonlight, not fluorescent light.

When I put the ham in foil and opened the oven door, a great burst of heat rushed unto my face, perhaps filling my cheeks with lovely color. I remembered Vivien Leigh pinched hers to make Scarlet's rosy right before a confrontation with Rhett. When we were children, Melly and I had used red jelly beans for lipstick. I imagined Scarlet O'Hara peering into a mirror, pinching her cheeks, and then wetting a jelly bean to outline her lips. I closed the door.

Jack Bindel was on the baseball team at college. I met him because Susan McHenry was dating a player named Pete Byron, who by sheer coincidence happened to be a childhood friend of Simon St. John. Susan persuaded me to go to one of the games with her, and afterwards the four of us went to Lombardino's for pizza. Since we met in the spring and only a few weeks before the end of the semester, we didn't go out on many dates at school. But it turned out that Jack's hometown was only thirty miles from mine, and so we continued to see each other all throughout the summer, even though we both had jobs during the week. I dated him for a little over five months, the longest I had ever dated anyone. I'd heard he was in accounting now.

The lettuce was still wrapped in plastic when I took it out of the refrigerator. I undid it and hit the head hard on the counter-top a few times. After pulling out the core, I ran water over the lettuce. Then I turned it over, shook the water out, and dried it. The sound of the TV got louder.

"Mother ought to be home pretty soon," Father said, coming into the kitchen. "Whatja got for supper? Tossed salad?"

He was standing there in his overalls and stocking feet.

"Yes," I answered, "and ham and baked potatoes."

"Pretty darn cold out there. Hope Mother don't have trouble startin' the car."

"You fix the—what was it?—combine?" I asked.

"Workin' on it. Have to go to Wauseka to get a part. Want some help?"

I told him no thanks and, although my back was turned to him, I could sense him turn around and leave. Then I heard the doors to the pink room close, the TV becoming fainter. It seemed as if it was harder and harder to talk to my father lately. But then he had always been a quiet man, and I had always felt closer to my mother, who was creative and talkative. I didn't pay much attention to farm machinery, crops, football. Mother always said I was a horrible farm girl. "We are lucky," she would joke, "if Sara can tell the difference between alfalfa and corn."

Jack worked for an alfalfa mill that summer, always complaining about the smell. I couldn't remember smells as I could colors. Perhaps memory was based on what they call the "mind's eye." Moreover, I thought of myself as a painter.

My hands were orange from shredding carrots. I washed a tomato and cut it into pieces, putting sections on top of the carrots and lettuce in three bowls. Then I went to the pantry and found a small onion. I cut off three slices and put the rest in a baggie in the refrigerator. They said if you kept your mouth closed you wouldn't cry. Or if you cut it under running water, but my eyes started to tear.

If they didn't offer me a contract next year, then I'd have a good excuse to leave. "It will look better to stay two years and then leave" was what everyone said. They would offer it to me again, though. Even if my parents would be happy, I knew I had to get away during the summer.

As I heard the garage door go up and then the door open, I put some water on the stove for peas.

"Oh, you've been painting!" Mother hollered from the green room.

When I walked in there, she was sitting down and trying to pull off her boots.

"Here, let me help," I said, walking over. I tugged at one boot, which came off slowly.

"It's so cold out there," she said. "I hope we don't get any snow tomorrow."

I got the other boot off. It was like taking the kids' off at school. When they were young and old, you had to take care of them. Mother did not seem as old as Father, though. She had trouble, however, doing things like putting on panty hose and taking off boots. Her boots weren't dirty, but I washed my hands anyway.

"How do you like that color for the sky?" I asked, nodding over to my palette.

"Oh, I do. It's very bright—jungle blue, right?"

As I agreed, she hung up her coat in the closet. I told her that supper was almost ready.

"You're so much help, precious," she said.

I went over and gave her a hug. She was several inches shorter than I was and seemed to get shorter every time I came home. Our backs humped over, our stomachs protruded, our breasts sagged.

Yet there she was in her stocking feet, a short, slightly overweight, round-backed woman, fifty-six years old, and I loved her.

"I'll put this away," I said, taking from her the sack she had picked up. "You go and put on your slippers."

When I reached the kitchen, I realized I'd forgotten to set the table. I quickly dropped some peas in the boiling water, put away the groceries, and began to take plates and glasses out of the cupboard.

I crossed to the round maple table in the bay window alcove. Looking at Mother's mural of our family history on the adjacent wall did not give me the complacent feeling that it usually did, so I turned all my attention to the top of the table where there were two calendars: one, last year's, and the other was a new one Mother had received for Christmas. She'd started marking birthdays in the new one before she had to go to work this morning. I opened the 1978 calendar to January. "Agnes's Birthday" was marked on the 20th. February and March were clear, but I noticed that Easter was at the very end of March. Dan's birthday was April 3rd. Before I turned to May, I recalled from the school calendar that my birthday fell on a Friday this year. Yes, I was right: May 19th was on a Friday. The last day I had to report to work was the following Tuesday, the 23rd. Since I needed to set the table, I put the calendars on the countertop and got out the placemats just as Mother came into the kitchen.

"What'd you do today?" she asked.

I told her I'd been lazy. She asked me what she should do, and I told her she could fill the water glasses. Then I remembered Iris.

"Oh, I almost forgot," I said. "Iris brought over a Jello salad. It's in the fridge."

"How thoughtful of them," Mother said.

When she finished filling the water glasses, she got the salad out. I went over to look at it with her. It was orange with miniature marshmallows on top. Some of them had stuck to the foil, producing a few crater-like gaps in the marshmallow-dotted surface. We said nothing to each other, but I sensed each of us was thinking similarly. I wondered if it was just because I didn't like Jello or also because Iris and Agnes had made it that I didn't want any. Their house always smelled strange, like old houses do when they're inhabited by elderly people. Yet Mother said that Iris was only forty-eight.

"We'll put it out for supper," Mother said, taking the dish over to the table. Father would eat some.

I was suddenly upset with myself, not merely because I'd been so listless all day, but because I knew that my discontent, so fixed to my comfortable inertia, was surmountable without applause. I had, as they say, "everything to live for." Iris did not—at least by most standards—and yet here I was, silently belittling her salad.

"You cannot imagine," Dr. Clarke said one day, "real hunger. None of us can. We know what it's like to be hungry, but what is the fear like that comes from knowing that you may never get a morsel of food? Sometimes we see photos of children with bloated stomachs, and we're reminded that hunger and starvation do exist. But we turn the page and the photos disappear. Now suppose," he paused, lit a cigarette, and looked directly at me, "I were to give each of you a hundred bucks for being such good students." He stopped. To pause was his only tactic as a lecturer. Then he added, in his monotone, "Well, some of you might deserve only ten bucks."

I smiled because I thought it prudent to smile at his humor. The girl next to me, who was studying notes from another class, looked up to see what was happening. He was looking right at her now with that awful stare that made you feel he was going to stop his lecture and start talking about you: *Now Miss Jones here, who studies her psych notes during my class and barely picks up a word or two of what I say, at least that's what her exam scores tell me, she'd be lucky to get five bucks! Actually, she doesn't deserve five cents, but I'm a generous man. I've got to reward her for the little effort that she does show, however small that may be.*

He didn't say this, of course. But it always seemed as if he knew all your petty and egotistic desires, the limitedness of your understanding and the inhumanity of your thoughts. It seemed as if he monitored all my actions. When he stared at me, I thought he knew everything about me. In actuality, he didn't even know my name. One day I went into his office to ask him about the books on our reading list. And he didn't recognize my face! He'd been staring at me for six weeks twice a week, and he didn't even know I was in his class.

Now he was talking about the example from the text, something about a Persian rug. A hundred bucks wouldn't buy a Persian rug. I missed what he had said about the money he was hypothetically handing out, but I understood his point: it was easier to imagine a Persian rug in my living room than a starving child eating food. It was true: probably none of us would give the money to a worthy cause; we would all spend it selfishly.

I liked this idea of imagining, although it was slightly confusing. I defined it by getting a picture in my mind, a mental image. It was interesting that we most commonly defined it in terms of the visual. Perhaps musicians defined it differently. Someone had said, "liquid architecture." It was all so perplexing if I thought about it too long. Yet I was also intrigued by the notion that we verbalized thought, that the words flowed through the consciousness as writers say they do, like a stream. At least, when I thought about thinking I felt conscious mostly of words or word-pictures. To get a mental image, I summoned a word and then a picture of a word. It was almost simultaneous, I felt, but the silent word came first.

Larry Holt was sitting in front of me. I could summon lots of word-pictures about him. I liked to think about him making love to me. Lying in bed, I could imagine lots of sexual adventures, and sometimes it seemed as if my body could even feel the penetration.

Dr. Clarke was staring at me again. *"Sex, that's all you've got on your mind,"* I alone heard him say. *"How do you know?"* I shot back with my eyes. *"You don't even know my name."*

He really said something about the ladder of abstraction. I glanced at my watch. Larry Holt dated a very attractive Theta, and Jack was also dating a Theta. I wished I knew if they were sleeping together. When I dated him, which was over a year ago, Jack had told me he wanted to marry a "pure girl." But then he believed in God and things like that.

Iris had to be a virgin, although I couldn't know for sure. I only knew that she was forty-eight, never-married, unattractive, and mentally disabled. It must be dreadful to go through life not being loved by someone—not being loved, that is, by someone who knew you as a nubile young woman or someone who loved you, either knowing or imagining your youthful beauty, when years had transfigured that youthfulness. Agnes loved Iris for companionship, not beauty. I imagined that she loved her with an odd mixture of pity and relief, knowing that, because she herself (Iris's maiden aunt) was unloved and old, if nature took its course, she would live until death under the caring watchfulness of Iris, who was, I sensed, really anticipating Agnes's death, waiting to see what life would be like when there was only Iris, not Agnes and Iris, who, though they were two, had somehow long ago lost their identities as far as the rest of us were concerned.

Father came into the kitchen just as I was slashing my spoon into the margarine to season the peas.

"Supper's almost ready," Mother said to him. Then she asked him what the weather was doing.

"Not bad," he answered. "No snow forecast. Now you know I can go with you tomorrow if you want me to."

"No, Sara and I will be okay. The highways are clear, and if we don't get any snow, we shouldn't have any problems. You've made your commitment to Wayne a long time ago and there's no need to back out now because of this."

I put the pan with peas on the table and we sat down and began reaching for the food. Everything looked good except for their salad.

"How was work today?" I asked Mother.

"Fine, maybe a bit slower than most days. Doc tried to empty the hospital, you know, before Christmas, and things haven't picked up much since then. Carol Rosenbaugh came in to have her baby, but it hasn't come yet. You remember her? They moved to Padua several years ago—before Melly was in high school. Carol was younger than both of you, wasn't she?"

"Yes, I think so," I said. "I can't really remember her very much. Didn't she have an older brother who was Melly's age?"

"Yes," Mother answered, "his name's Dennis. I heard he farms down in the valley by Brodertown."

"Wasn't her mother, Ida, a Booth?" Father asked. "Seems to me her parents were Irv and Elsie Booth."

"Heavens, I don't know!" Mother said exasperatedly, as if she knew none of the small town genealogies. "That was years before I moved to this town and married you. I do remember hearing about the Booth girls, though."

"Yep," he continued, "now I remember. Ida was one of 'em. There was three of 'em all together: Ida, Virginia, and—let's see—Rosie, I think, Booth. All of 'em pretty girls too. Ida married Rosenbaugh a couple years 'fore you come to town. Right after the war was over. Irv and Elsie passed away during the war, and the two youngest sisters went to live with their grandparents over by Hawk. I think Rosie married a Jensen, Albert Jensen."

"Peggy Berck's half brother?" Mother asked.

"Yep, ol' man Jensen died young and then the wife married Marlin Hoplander. They had Peggy and Rudy, who lives in Tennessee now."

"Why was he called ol' man Jensen," I asked, "if he died young?"

Father paused to think about this, and finally he said slowly, which was the way he always talked, "I didn't mean we called him that. I just meant to distinguish between Albert and his father. It's the way us folks talk, Sara."

I wanted to say *"we folks,"* but I knew I couldn't change him after all these years and that I just had to put up with it. I was feeling somewhat guilty, anyway, about Iris and the salad and my lazy day. And what with the funeral tomorrow, it wouldn't be right to start complaining or correcting. I had almost forgotten about the funeral. It was the least thing I wanted to do, but there wasn't any getting out of it. I wondered if I would feel sick sitting in the funeral home as I did when my grandmother died.

It seemed as if, when I thought long enough about my heartbeat or my breathing, I felt death was imminent. It was worse at night when I went to bed and wasn't sleepy and had to lie there by myself. It was then those thoughts came about dying during the night. *"And if I die before I wake"* it went. Such a horrid prayer for children. And virgins like me.

They were talking now about Pauline Copley and Dick Sanders. She was a nurse aide at the hospital and he was editor of the *Sentinel.* Pauline's husband drove a school bus and farmed some, and they had three small children. Mr. Sanders was also married, but he was much older than Pauline. At least fifteen years older, I estimated. No one understood, Mother was saying, what he saw in her.

I remembered seeing her in the hospital reception area when I went to pick up Mother before Christmas. It was true. Looking quite haggard for only being in her thirties, she was wearing one of those awful nurse pantsuits whose top had a seam running down the middle of the front and, rather than enhancing the bust or waist, as clothes should, it bunched out in the middle. Her hair, beauty-parlorishly teased, had been generously sprayed, which did nothing for Pauline except make her look much older. She was chewing gum, with gusto and noisily, when I saw her.

"She's just watching the clock," Mother was saying, "and when it's just about twelve, she jumps in her car and zooms off. They say she goes downtown and meets him at the *Sentinel* office. It's just horrible the things that go on in this town now days."

Father and I both laughed, for Mother was always summing up the state of morality with the word *horrible*. She didn't know quite what to make of the sexual revolution; she simply felt that adultery and pre-marital sex were wrong. The fact that such transgressions formed one of the sturdiest bases for one of her own faults, gossiping, she never bothered to consider.

"To change the subject," Mother continued, "have you decided yet when you're going back, Sara?"

"I thought I'd start back early in the afternoon on New Year's Day," I answered. "Right after church and lunch—if that's okay with you two."

She told me that sounded fine and then added, "If we get home in time tomorrow from the funeral, why don't we go to the market and you can get some things to take back?"

I told her that was fine. I could get some canned goods and things like toothpaste and toilet paper, which I always needed.

Father was eating the Jello now, and Mother told him that Iris had brought it over.

"Always think of us, don't they?" Father commented.

"Yes, they certainly do. If it's one thing I'm thankful for," she said, "it's that we've always had good neighbors."

Natalie said, "Good fences make good neighbors," quoting Frost, of course, as though Emma Aspen and I were so unlettered as to miss the allusion.

We didn't know quite what to make of Natalie most of the time, but we appreciated her all the same, we realized later, even on the day she started dividing up our room with string.

"Good gracious, Nat!" Emma exclaimed when she walked into our room. "We're not supposed to put tape on the walls. They just painted them last summer. We'll—you will—have to pay a fine now."

"I'll pay the fine," she said calmly, boxing in her bed and closet with string.

"Why on earth are you doing this?" Emma yelled. "You're crazy!"

"Good fences make good neighbors," she repeated calmly.

"I give up. Be a fool. Just don't, don't put any string around mine—my. . . my. . .bed," Emma stammered, becoming so frustrated that the words bottled up in her throat.

When she spoke this way, her voice quivering and the words slightly muddled up, we all knew she was very upset. Natalie, on the other extreme, always cloaked her fury in some bizarre act of madness, never losing the composure for which she was famous. It might have been different if they had not been disgusted with each other. Then Emma and I could have enjoyed this latest bit of craziness; we could have laughed at Nat, who would have welcomed our attention. Natalie knew she was different from the rest of us, but she always chose to be that way. I usually chose to be homogeneous, doubting I would have been happier choosing as Natalie did.

Emma flew out of our room and I guessed she went down to Susan McHenry's room because in a few seconds there was Susan in our doorway to see for herself Nat's latest antics.

"It should be psychedelic yellow, Nat," she commented, "so you won't trip on it in the dark."

"I'm going to let Sara paint it," she responded. "You have my permission, Sara dear," she directed me, "to paint the fence. I think chartreuse might be appropriate. You know, the color of whores in ancient Greece. Quite appropriate."

"Paint that coat rack too, Sara," Susan said. "Now that it's in the middle of the room it needs to be a bright color so you won't bump into it at night."

Susan was doing what Emma and I would have been doing if it had all been a joking matter. But Natalie and Emma had been mad at each other, and I was precariously positioned in the middle where one sympathetic comment toward Natalie or one toward Emma would earn me the wrath of the other.

Now Susan was shouting over the intercom that the newest use for macramé was being demonstrated in Room 30. Natalie had finished her fencing job and was sitting smugly on her bed reading *Madame Bovary*.

I told her I was going to the library and then class, grabbing my sweater and books. When I passed Susan's room I saw Emma in there, so I knew I couldn't go in and explain to Susan how it was a nice try, but she'd probably made things worse. Being scolded by me wouldn't have fazed Susan, though, since she liked having something to say or someone to mother, and she loved defending Emma when it meant doing her best to ridicule Natalie, which was never difficult. I often wondered whether it took genuine guts to act as Natalie did, constantly exposing herself to mockery, or whether it had become so natural to be different that being different was easier than being the same.

I didn't really need to go to the library, but I had a half hour to kill before class. I had wanted to read in our room, but Susan's intercom announcement would have made studying there impossible, especially since it was right after lunch and lots of girls were in the house with nothing better to do before their first afternoon classes than to go see our room. It must be a curious circus in there now, I thought.

Outside it was lovely, so much autumn on the ground and in the trees, making me remember all the bittersweet songs about falling leaves and September. Why were the accents of autumn songs always disconsolate? It was the approaching death of the year—that much was easily grasped—but it was a death to be followed by rebirth. All things individual seemed linear, while nature itself was cyclical—a cruel consolation for the individual. This October day made me a little sad. I didn't feel anger toward Emma or Natalie, only a little weariness.

I walked up the steps to the library and pushed open the door. Hank Locke was in the lobby talking to Pete Byron. Damn them both, I thought. Hank was sure to see me. Yes, even from a distance I noticed his eyes brighten in anticipation of our encounter.

Coming over to me, he said hello, and I greeted both of them, deciding to walk past them and find a corner to hide myself in. Damn them both, I thought. If they hadn't been acting so childish, I could have stayed in the room. They forced me to go to the library where Hank Locke would pester me to death.

"Where're you runnin' off to?" he shot at me as I attempted to escape.

"Gotta study," I muttered, hurrying toward the stairs.

"Hey, Pete," I heard him say, "I've got to talk to Sara so I'll catch you later."

I had just reached the stairs when he caught up with me. There was no escaping now.

"Why are you in so big a hurry, Sar?" he asked me as we started climbing.

"I haven't read the assignment for my semantics class at one, and I've gotta hurry and glance over it before class." I could sense the dreaded question was coming and that my mind would be blank for an excuse. We had reached the top of the second floor. "See you later," I said, heading for a back corner of the library.

"Wait a minute, Sar," he said, following me. "Say, how'd you like to see a movie this Friday night?"

"It's Natalie's birthday," popped out, "and we've got a little party planned. All girls. It's a surprise. Sorry. Look, I've really gotta run now. Bye."

I turned and walked quickly into the stacks and found an empty desk. He hadn't followed me. One thing to be thankful for. I opened my book to Chapter 8 and began reading.

Actually, I had almost finished reading the assignment, but I didn't expect to be able to concentrate on finishing it now. I kept thinking about Natalie and Emma. I had to congratulate myself on the birthday bit. It was convenient to have Natalie as a friend, since no male would believe a bunch of girls celebrating Emma Aspen's birthday. I'd have to tell Natalie about her party, although there was little chance Hank could find out. I never could have thought of an excuse for Saturday night too. Thankfully, he hadn't asked.

Emma said to me, "You're utterly cruel. Just tell him you don't want to go out with him. Why keep leading him on?"

"Leading him on!" I almost screamed. "If he just weren't so dense! How can he possibly not know that I don't want to go out with him after the way I treat him. I'm not even friendly to him.

I never initiate a conversation. I always try to get away from him as fast as I can. He has got to be the stupidest person on earth to keep this up."

"He just thinks you're shy," Emma explained. "Everything you do reinforces what the other guys have told him about you. He's madly in love with you and he can't bear to imagine you aren't wild about him also. You've simply got to spell it out for him, face to face."

We were sitting in our room after dinner, and now Natalie said, "He's a mathematician. I'd go out with him. You could give him a second chance at least. He might be good in bed."

They didn't understand. Natalie felt no guilt about manipulating men; Emma, none about being manipulated by them. I had given Hank Locke a chance. I'd gone out with him only to suffer three of the most miserable hours of my life. I couldn't bear to do it again. They had no right telling me what to do.

"He can't even call me by my correct name!" I yelled. "It's Sara, not Sar!"

"He calls me Em," Emma said with a little empathy. "And no one in the whole entire world has ever called me that."

Since it was impossible to concentrate on the reading assignment, I decided to leave the library. But I wasn't sure if it would be safe, as Hank might be lolling around the main entrance waiting for me. Still, I felt as if I couldn't stay in the stacks another minute. I gathered up my things and headed for the stairs. No sign of Hank. I ran down the stairs and got in line to have my books checked. Again, no sign of Hank. I superstitiously hoped that if I only looked straight ahead I'd be safe. To glance around meant breaking the spell, the materialization of Hank Locke.

Not looking back, I headed quickly for the art building, my favorite place on campus, a dilapidated structure that twenty years ago housed some sciences. Now there was a huge new science hall, a dreary, antiseptic-looking, almost windowless space. I didn't think they'd be able to pawn it off on the art department thirty years from now, for no one would ever want to paint or sculpt in there. No, I felt certain we'd never give up our building. They never seemed to put any improvements into it except those needed to meet the fire marshal's standards. They just let us do whatever we wanted to in the building, which often meant beating it up. You could spill a little paint on the floor and not have to worry about cleaning it up.

I headed for the top floor. There were four floors in all: the basement, my least favorite place; the ground floor, where most of the offices and classrooms were, and the two upper floors, where there were more classrooms and a large lecture hall as well as rooms in which we could work. I had several projects going on right now. I was working with stained glass, painting china, making two African-inspired masks, and doing a watercolor. The masks and watercolor were on the fourth floor, my favorite floor, where there were three enormous rooms. Since the door to 303 was locked, I got out my key to open it.

Inside it was very bright because the room ran from east to west on the south side of the building, with huge windows spanning all the outside walls. Walking over to the table where my things were, I studied the watercolor. I hadn't spoiled it yet. Maybe this one would be good, I hoped.

Suddenly I realized that it was probably getting late and that I should be hurrying to class. I locked the door behind me and walked over to 301, whose door was half open, which meant someone must be in there working. I decided to pop my head inside to say hi. When I opened the door farther, though, no one was there. Probably in the restroom, I guessed.

I glanced over to the table where I had left my masks, but

there was nothing by my spot except some scissors, some feathers, a few pieces of felt and leather, and a glue bottle. I walked farther into the room, scanning all the work stations for my masks, but I did not see them by Andy Anderson's or Marie's spots. Jinbok's spot was full of boxes and art supplies, as was Simon's. I looked on the floor and on the shelves along the wall, but I did not see the masks anywhere. I knew it was late and that I had to go to class, so I locked the door and hurried away. On the ground floor I ran into Kathy Rossey and asked her if she was working in 301, but she said no.

"I was just there and noticed that my masks weren't on the table where I left them," I told her. "I've got to go to class now, but I'll be back afterwards to try to find out where they are."

"Maybe they just got moved somewhere," she suggested.

"Nobody's supposed to move anything in that room. You know how we all feel about that!"

As I backed toward the door, Kathy told me she'd look around for me, and I thanked her as I exited the building.

Now I was running. The chimes had started, playing a little tune and then sounding the hour. Damn them all, I thought. Natalie and Emma and Hank Locke and whoever moved my masks. Now I'd be late for class. It was just like this for so much to go wrong: first, the string all over our room and Nat and Emma even madder at each other than before; next, running into Hank; and now, my masks missing. Think of something to be thankful for, I told myself. Think of all the terrible things that could happen. It was silly to let the little things upset me so much. Years from now I wouldn't even remember this.

Dr. Clarke wasn't in the classroom yet, so I was saved the humiliation of his observation that I was late. I found the least conspicuous seat left and sat down.

I said to them, "We're going to make word pictures today. You each get to pick a slip of paper." I held up Nathan O'Brien's stocking cap. "And everybody has to draw a picture using the word on the slip of paper. For example. Jenny might draw a slip of paper that says 'spring' and so she might draw tulips and robins because that makes her think of spring. Danny might pick a piece of paper that says 'sweet' and he might draw a picture of a chocolate-frosted donut because that's what he thinks is sweet. Don't tell anybody what your word is until I say to, because we're going to play a game after we get done."

There were already hands in the air.

"No," I told them, "put your hand down until I'm finished and then I can answer questions. What I want to get across is that the association may be very obvious between your word and the picture you draw. For example, you may get the word 'dog' and so you could draw a picture of a dog if you wanted to. Or you might pick a piece of paper that says 'funny' and you might draw a picture of your dog Fido because he's the funniest thing you can think of. In that case, the association between word and picture would be very personal and not apparent right away to anyone—unless they knew that your dog Fido is a very, very funny dog!"

Benjy Thornton's hand was waving and stretching out. He must have been born impatient, and I always capitulated to this method he had of raising his arm to ask a question, for he seemed to be in extreme distress.

"Yes, what is it, Benjy?" I asked.

"Are we gonna 'ave to guess what words everybody got?"

"You'll find out later. Now I'm going to walk around and you can pick because I want you to get started right away. BECAUSE YOU ONLY HAVE THIRTY MINUTES! That's it. Only thirty minutes, and your picture has to be done."

Two more hands went up and I called on Jenny, who asked if they could pick another slip if they couldn't think of something to draw with the first word. I told her no as I kept moving around the room. Then Laura began protesting, "What if we can't think of something to draw?"

"Oh, you'll think of something. It's not that hard. If you really can't come up with anything, then I'll help you," I stated. "Yes, what is it, Benjy?"

"I lost my brown," he said.

"Then you may borrow from me or someone else."

"Can we get up and borrow other colors too?" Benjy asked.

"**May** you borrow other colors? Yes, you may, but first you have to ask the owner's permission and return them as soon as you finish. Remember, you can't spend all your time hunting for unusual colors or you won't get done in time. You may come up and borrow the colors on my cart, but you must return them."

This happened every time we colored. They fought over the crayons and colored pencils and markers. Inevitably someone lost or broke someone's borrowed item. LeeAnn Webb, the grocer's daughter, had a deluxe set of crayons, a box with over 60 colors, and everyone always rushed to borrow the exceptional colors that she had. I had several unusual colors too, but it seemed as if the children went first to LeeAnn to get the silvers and fuchsias, maybe, I theorized, because LeeAnn was, by everyone's acclaim, the best "artist" in the class and by borrowing from her or stealing a glance at her drawing, they somehow hoped that theirs would be just as praiseworthy.

Perhaps I was guilty of showing too much enthusiasm over LeeAnn's work, but I never exalted her at the expense of belittling the others. If anything, I was guilty of too much encouragement and praise, generally feigned, for everyone's work, and I always sensed the children could detect my pretense when I stumbled for words to express my delight in what was clearly a project done without thought or motivation or any attempt at artistry, for there were for comparison my spontaneous exclamations over LeeAnn's surprisingly creative projects and thoughtful work.

Everyone had drawn a slip of paper and some of the children were beginning to draw. I glanced at my watch, deciding I would give them until 2:55. Betsy Blake's hand was up in the air, so I walked over to her desk.

"I can't get started," she said softly to me.

She was a tiny girl with very fair skin, dark brown curly hair, and tremendous blue eyes. Her problem was not lack of ability, but rather slowness. It took her forever to finish a drawing or project. She was extremely meticulous and strived for a perfection that was beyond my comprehension. But I didn't really understand why she would be asking for help at this point.

She showed me her slip of paper, which said "tall."

"You can't think of anything to draw?" I asked.

"No, I can't draw what I want to draw. It's too hard."

"What do you want to draw?" I asked.

"A giraffe," she whispered.

"Oh, you draw excellent horses," I said. "A giraffe shouldn't be that difficult. Want to see if the encyclopedia has a picture you can look at?"

She nodded affirmatively, and so I hurried to the bookshelves, selected volume G, and quickly found the entry.

"Here," I said, placing the book on her desk. "Maybe this will help. Now get busy because I really want you to finish today. Next week we're going to start making Halloween masks, and we just don't have time to go back and finish today's project."

Of course, I should have let her look up the word *giraffe* to reinforce her alphabetizing skills, but there just wasn't time. Student teaching and all my ed classes hadn't really prepared me for the reality that I'd always be hurrying my students along. Having to create under time limits was quite unfair. Didn't it take Flaubert something like five years to write *Madame Bovary*? And yet there were always a few children who finished in half the time most of them took. Yes, Greg Riley was already leaning back on his chair and gazing at his picture. Just as he caught me looking at him, his arm shot into the air. I knew before I reached him that he would tell me he was finished.

"I'm done," he said, turning his picture at an angle so I could view it better. Greg drew stick people, stick cows, stick barns, and stick tractors. That was his specialty: the farm scene rendered in stick. If he took up art as a profession and became another Picasso, someday we'd be talking about stickism. How would they describe it? *"The proliferation of the modern world from the ever endemic linear perspective."* Many of the other children drew buildings the same way Greg did, but they always colored the representational mass of the building. Greg drew the outer frame-work and indicated doors and windows, but his was always a skel-eton structure, a black and white, or red and white, or brown and white building, white being the color of the paper. I always had the same suggestion for Greg.

"Why don't you color in the barn and trees?" I offered.

Being also a little lazy, Greg, giving a heavy, disgruntled sigh, always dreaded my suggestion. To fill in the barn with red was a lot of work.

"I can't even tell what season of the year it is," I continued. "Maybe it's supposed to be summer because your trees are out-lined in green, but come on, Greg, trees don't really look like that. You could make your picture be in autumn by putting lots of fall colors into your trees—browns and golds and oranges. You'd let me know it was summer if your trees were all green. Remember one of the neatest things to do when creating trees with colors?

A stunning effect you can achieve with crayons is to apply them very, very heavily, rubbing one on top of another. Look, turn your color around and use the blunt end and fill in your trees with lots of little bits of color. Press really hard and fill it all in. Now, suppose you used pink and white. What would that tell me about your trees?"

He gave me a quizzical look. "A pink tree?" he asked.

"When are trees pink? Don't you have any cherry or apple trees on your farm?"

"Nope, we don't got none of 'em."

"Well," I began, "since your picture is the result of your imagination as it sees the real world, even if you don't really have any cherry trees on your father's farm, if you wanted to, you could still put a tree full of beautiful pink and white blossoms into your picture. Then it would be spring in your picture. That's the neat thing about art. What you create doesn't have to be what really is. You're in control of things. You can make the world look however you want. Now, why don't you surprise me and do something to those trees?"

As Greg reached for his box of crayons, I turned my attention to two boys who were arguing over the use of a light blue crayon. I told one of them to check with LeeAnn to see if she had a crayon he could borrow, reminding him to tell her thank you and return the crayon when he was finished. Doing this made me think that there must be an easier way to teach the concept of sharing. It was unfortunate we were not born generous, that we had to learn to think of needs and desires other than our own. Sadder still was that we shed so seldom this innate self-centeredness. I tried to think of something I had done willingly which was not ego-serving, and I could not think of a damn thing.

Then I felt guilty about imposing my opinions on the children. Perhaps I really was stifling Greg Riley's creativity by telling him to make the trees look the way I would make them look. And yet I was trying to teach him a technique, a way of using his medium.

"What do you do?" he asked.

"I teach art in an elementary school," I said, "first grade through sixth."

"That must be interesting," he said.

"I teach art," I said, "in an elementary school, first grade through sixth."

"I always wanted to do something like that," he said.

"In an elementary school," I said. "Some people say 'grade school.' Some say 'grammar school.'"

"In the East, where I'm from, we say 'grammar school.'"

"I'm from here," I said. "And it's not hard. It's stupid to think being an art teacher is a noble profession."

"Is any profession noble?" he asked. "We work to make money. Some of us are fortunate to like what we do and some of us have to put up with it. I gather you like what you do?"

"Yes," I said, "mostly it's effortless; it pays regularly; it fills time; it offers an excuse when I'm too lazy to 'do something creative.' There's only one thing that troubles me."

"What's that?" he asked.

"Well," I began, "I should feel a sense of satisfaction in helping children to express themselves creatively, but how can anyone teach 'art'? It's such a nebulous, all-encompassing term."

"But it's defined for you," he replied. "When you're teaching a bunch of kids, you don't have to worry about whether a bicycle seat stuck on the wall is art or not, do you? You can't delve into questions of aesthetics with them. You just announce the project—making Valentines—hand out the red paper and doilies and glue and let them go at it."

"Yes, it's easy," I said. "It's stupid to think being an art teacher is a noble profession. By the way, what's yours?"

"My noble profession?" he asked. "It's nobility. Charles Prince, that's my name. What's yours?"

"Sara Keatson," I answered. "Pleased to meet you, Charlie Prince. Is that Charlie, as in Prince Charles?"

"No, it's Prince, as in Charlie Prince. What's yours?"

"Sara Keatson," I answered.

"As in Diane?" he asked.

"No, as in Sara," I said. "Sara Keat-SON."

"I like it. It's nice," he said.

"What's yours?" I asked.

"Kevin Hershey," he said.

"As in chocolate bars?" I asked.

"Matter of fact, you're right," he said. "I'm from the East myself. Hershey, Pennsylvania. It's where they're made. What do you do here?"

"I teach art in an elementary school," I said, "first grade through sixth grade."

"That must be interesting," he said. "Do you have any plans for lunch?"

"No," I answered, "not yet."

"Terrific! Would you do me the honor of joining me for lunch?"

"I'd love to," I said. "That would be nice."

Kevin Hersey was a lawyer. No, he was a journalist. *You're in control,* I had told Greg Riley. Perhaps he should be an architect. Peter Hershey, architect. I always wanted to have someone named Peter fall in love with me. Peter Prince? The alliteration spoiled it. Peter Hershey was better.

"Matter of fact," Peter said, "you're right. It's where they're made."

"In an elementary school," I said, "first grade through sixth."

"I always wanted to do something like that," he said.

"Why did you choose architecture?" I asked.

"Well," he began, "my father wanted me to stay in the business, but I couldn't envision the prices of sugar and cocoa beans being my foremost concerns day in and day out from now until eternity. Chocolate's okay to eat once in a while, but who wants to spend their whole life in it?"

"I know some kids," I said laughing, "who'd jump at the chance to spend an hour in a chocolate factory."

"You must really like children," he said.

"Yes, I really like what I do. There's only one thing that troubles me."

"What's that?" he asked.

"Well," I began, "I should feel a sense of satisfaction in helping children to express themselves creatively, but how can anyone teach 'art'? It's such a nebulous, all-encompassing term."

"I know what you mean," he said. "You say 'art,' someone thinks painting or picture. The Louvre, Rembrandt, the Sistine Chapel frescoes, a smocked, bearded chap with palette in hand on the Left Bank. Is that what you mean?"

"Exactly," I said. "When people hear the word 'art,' they almost always think of the visual arts first. And art is removed from them. It's up there, far away, long ago. The Oriental world has long considered flower arranging one of the most revered arts. Their shoka arrangements represent the relationship between man and the universe. Who's to say that the *Mona Lisa* is a better manifestation of art than a bunch of lilacs in a glass jar? When you stop to think about it, flowers and foliage are great media. You've got color, texture, form, fragrance, and a lot of freedom. The only problem is their transience. So how do we define 'art'?"

"Say it is that which brings beauty into the world," he said.

"I think it has to be more," I said. "Say that it ennobles man, that it gives our comic existence dignity. Or say that art is an act of love, that it is therapeutic."

"I guess I face the same problems as an architect," he said. "You can praise a building for its design, the way line and form blend with function, the whole Wright tenet, you know, with the critics always singling out certain buildings as great, whatever that means. With architecture, art often goes along only for those who can afford it. Now forgive me. I'm going on and on with all this nonsense. Why don't you tell me I talk too much?"

"No, I enjoy listening to you," I said. "And I think you're right. Don't you think I have an obligation to pose the question of what art is and what it means, even if they're only little children? I suppose most of them will go through life never really thinking about it. Maybe they'll be good husbands and wives and mothers and fathers and citizens and taxpayers. Maybe Greg Riley will be a rich farmer someday and go off to Florence so he can 'see art.' Do you think art merely exists, or does it exist for some reason?"

"Both, I think," he said.

"That's the easy answer," I said.

"You talk too much," he said, "and about such weighty matters. I'm getting weary trying to concentrate on this discussion we're having. Let's talk about something else."

"Okay," I said, "what do you want to talk about?"

"You," he said. "Did anyone ever tell you you're very attractive?"

I started to decide what kind of answer I was going to make, but before I could say anything at all, he put his finger on my parted lips.

"You talk too much," he said. Then he turned his head to one side and drew his face toward mine. And then he kissed me.

I told them they had five more minutes. Quite a few were

already finished, although Betsy was still working on her giraffe.

"Everyone, be quiet," I said. "Don't tell what your word was. Stay in your seats and be quiet so everybody can finish."

I was a restorer of order, not a teacher of art. The other teachers only asked of me that at the end of an hour I returned to them their pupils, whose desk tops were clean and who were, if not eager, then at least not totally disinclined to begin a math or reading lesson. They expected their classroom to look as it had when they turned it over to me, which meant that all scraps of paper had to be in the wastebasket, all hands clean from paint or glue, all crayons inside boxes inside desks.

I had already had a bad experience once this year. With the fifth graders one day we ran behind schedule, and their teacher, Mrs. Chandler, came into the room as I was rushing around trying to restore order. She surveyed the disarray and confusion, and then she reprimanded me in front of the children. I apologized, and since then I have kept my greetings and words to her at a minimum. Like a hurt child, I harbored the notion that someday I would get even with her. Our vendetta thrived on my fantasies of vengeance, the worst of which had our school janitor, Sven Lindqvist, discovering that she was a potential child molester, the end result being that Chandler, disgraced and dishonored, was felled by her own vile doings.

Of course, as soon as I had devised this malicious script for Mrs. Chandler, I felt rather ashamed of myself. Criticism from her was hardly grounds for public dishonor. I could see perfectly well how absurd my dislike of her was, but realizing so did not erase the animosity I felt, the revenge I craved.

When I was a child, I disliked my piano teacher because she was always after me to keep my nails short, while I, not desiring to be any great pianist, wanted to have long, nicely-tapered pink nails like those of my second grade teacher. I eventually got over my feelings toward my piano teacher, and now whenever I saw her when I was home, I enjoyed saying hello. Perhaps time would obliterate my feelings toward Mrs. Chandler as well.

I helped Mother clear the table while Father retired to the pink room to read the papers and watch TV.

"Are you going to paint tonight?" she asked me.

"Maybe," I said, "not for long, though. I'll probably go to bed early. What time do we have to leave tomorrow?"

"Well, the funeral's at eleven, so we should probably get there by 10:15. That means we should leave about 8:45. Is that all right?"

I told her that was fine and asked her what she was going to wear.

"I thought I'd wear my black wool suit. How about you?"

"Maybe that sort of black skirt and vest with the tiny gray and maroon design—you know, the ones I wear my gray blouse with."

I didn't say anything else, but I was thinking of the time my grandmother had died when I was eleven. We hardly saw Mother because she had to leave right away to be with the rest of her family. Father brought Melly and me home from school early, and then he left to drive our distraught mother to Fairville. On the kitchen table was a note from Mother in which she suggested what to wear to the funeral. It would be the first time either of us had been to one, and I suspected Melly and I would have had an agonizing time trying to figure out what to wear by ourselves. Thinking black was the only appropriate color, we would have been stymied trying to produce solid black outfits out of our wardrobes. I could not even remember what I wore to that funeral.

"I'm going to bake an angel food tonight," Mother said. "That will be nice to take tomorrow."

"Need some help?"

Although she told me no, after she opened the cupboard and began rummaging around for the cake mix, she asked me to find one for her, which I did. As I put the box and an empty vinegar bottle on the counter, she thanked me and told me I could go do my things. Then she hollered to the hallway, "I'm going to use the mixer for a couple minutes!"

"He can't hear you, Mother," I pointed out.

"Well then, run and tell your father that I've got to use the mixer, so he won't think the TV's gone batty."

I hurried down to the pink room. "Father," I said, sitting down on the sofa, "Mother's going to use the mixer for a few minutes." I picked up the newspaper and began searching for something interesting. Then the TV went screwy.

Screwy Louie was Natalie's nickname for Dr. Louis Patternach, who seduced Natalie one morning after she'd been in the sleep lab. I still marveled at the measures Natalie took to ensure this seduction. She paid some other student twenty bucks to call in and say he was sick in order that she and Screwy Louie could be alone together. Afterward, she told Emma and me many of the details, dramatically reenacting the moments prior to the seduction.

"So did you really wear the Obscene Slit?" Emma asked, referring to the prurient negligee Natalie had purchased for the occasion. Upon Natalie's first showing the nightgown to us, Emma had immediately dubbed it the Obscene Slit. No virgin bride had ever shopped as diligently as Natalie had for her sleep lab trousseau.

"Oh God, what'd he do when he saw you in it?" Emma shrieked.

Natalie smiled secretly. "He didn't do much at all. After all, I was in bed with this sheet around me. What'd you think I was going to do? Assume some outrageously sexual pose?"

"Never know about you, Nat," Emma confessed.

"Of course, he was rather aghast when I innocently asked him how a woman's sexual arousals were measured during her dream cycles. His face got immensely red and he hurried out of the room."

"Then what happened?" Emma asked.

"Then I fantasized a simply marvey episode about what would befall and eventually I fell asleep."

To this, those elaborate stories I devised which were always so much better than real life, I could relate.

"So what happened in the morning?" Emma asked.

"Oh, you don't want to hear the funny little intimate details, do you, Emma and Sara dears?"

"You bet your little ass we do," Emma answered, so Natalie told us how she pulled one of the straps of her nightgown down while she waited for Screwy Louie to enter the lab.

"Oh God, Nat!" Emma exclaimed. "I can't believe it! Can you believe her?" she said to me.

I smiled back. Actually the thought had occurred to me that perhaps Natalie might be pulling the wool over our eyes.

"You aren't inventing all this, Nat?" I asked her firmly.

"Heavens no, Sara dear! Could I deceive you? You know I always—"

"Yes," I interrupted, "you could deceive us and you know it. Now level. Did it really happen this way?"

"Oh better, Sara," she said laughing. "You just had to be there!"

"Well, what'd ol' Screwy Louie do when he saw you?" Emma asked in eager anticipation of the finale.

"He got red. He tried to say, 'Good morning; how'd you sleep?' but his stammer was so bad it took him forever. I was a tad unsure how to proceed, so I just looked right at him—now mind you one of my boobs was almost popping out all the way—and said the most corny thing I could think of: 'I'm very attracted to you, Dr. Patternach.'"

By now Emma and I were laughing at almost every turn in Natalie's tale.

"So what happened next?" Emma asked in exasperation when Natalie was silent for a few seconds.

"Oh, you don't want to know the boring little pornographic details, do you, Emma dear?" Natalie mocked.

"We want to know!" Emma demanded. "And you want to tell us. You just delight in this suspense, Natalie dear."

"Enough of the show, my sweets," she said, getting off the bed where she had been sitting in her bra and jeans with one strap appropriately slipping from her shoulder.

"Ah, Nat," Emma whined, "what happened next? Be a good sport for once in your life. You know how horny I am since Marc's been studying for his MedCATs."

"I thought you had a substitute player," Natalie replied coyly. "What's Simon St. John been doing around here all the time? I thought he was consoling you during your loss."

"Very funny. I only know Simon through Sara and Susan, and we're just friends, Natalie dear, so don't go spreading rumors about me and Simon because it's not true and you know it," Emma said, her voice betraying that she was hurt and worried.

"I like you, Emma," Natalie said solemnly. "I like you and Sara. You're my best friends, whatever that means. You two accept me even when I'm a real bitch, which is most of the time. So don't give me this b.s., Emma, because you know how jealous I am of you. After all, you're *tres jolie* and every guy on campus lusts after your body. And Sara—"

"And you like me," I chimed in, "because no one on campus lusts after my body!"

They both laughed.

"I like you, you All-American Wallflower," Natalie said to me, "because you're so nice and smart, even if you are hard to get to know. And you know you're not really unattractive, you silly little thing!"

Way to make a gal feel real good, Nat! I guessed I might be prettier than Natalie, and yet when she said something like that I really felt homely and unwanted. I had asked for her comment anyway, but now I still felt close to tears, but I managed to keep them hidden. I almost faked a smile, telling myself that Natalie could admit her jealousy of Emma's beauty, never mine.

"And so here's the conclusion, dear sisters," Natalie said, putting on her shirt. "I've got to study, so let's make it short. When I told him I found him very attractive, it was as if I hit oil. His passion gushed forth, he flung himself on me, caressing my breasts, smothering me with kisses all over my body, discovering the Obscene Slit's slit, stroking my thighs. In short, we screwed. He was pretty good. Afterwards I dressed, went to the third floor of the library, and watched the cleaning lady mop the floor. See you later, kiddoes."

With those final words, she left the room.

"Can you believe her!" Emma exclaimed.

"She's something else," I said. "I suppose it really happened, but I guess we'll never know for sure."

"Unless we ask Dr. Patternach. It would've been great to have been a little mouse over there to observe the whole affair."

After I agreed with her, she asked me what I was going to do and I told her I'd probably go to bed early because I was tired.

"You do sorta look it," she said, another comment that caused my ego to deflate even more.

When I asked her what she was going to do, she said, "I guess I'll read a little," and she plopped down on her bed with *Glamour*.

Before I left our room to wash up, Emma looked up and said, "Sara, about what Nat said, you mustn't let her get you down. You know how she is—remember how Susan and you and I talked about it once? God, you're a hundred times more attractive than she is!"

"Thanks," I said. "Sometimes I wonder if I'm hooked on a self-fulfilling prophecy decreed by Natalie: Hail, Sara, the All-American Wallflower."

"Nonsense," she countered. "Nat'll do anything to be different and cute and dramatic and the center of attention. She's just trying to be witty with that slogan. Be glad you're a wallflower and not a sexually degenerate kook like her."

"But why can't I be perfect like you?" I pleaded facetiously.

"Oh, bullshit," she said, perhaps a little pleased. "Now scoot!"

On the way to the bathroom, I thought about how sad it was the way we depended on each other so much to like—certainly evaluate—ourselves. But then I admitted that no one lived in a peopleless void, and so perhaps this dependence on each other was inevitable. "You are dull," Natalie silently told me, and I never really wanted to prove otherwise to her. What was being dull? And was it wrong to be dull? Did being shy contribute to dullness? Still, this cult of trying to be better was despicable. "I am better than you" was what each of us always wanted to affirm. And of course a sorority house was the perfect place for self-evaluation! It was lamentable the way my self-esteem depended so much on one-upmanship. I wondered whether there were any truly non-narcissistic people in the world.

I was getting so comfortable on our pink room sofa when I heard the phone ring.

"Sara," my mother called from the kitchen, "it's for you." When I got there, she whispered, "It sounds like long distance."

After I said hello, a male voice said, "Hi, Sara! This is Pete Byron. How're you doin'?"

"Fine," I answered, very surprised to be talking to Pete Byron. "How was your Christmas?"

"Pretty good. Susan wanted a diamond, of course, so we had to look, but we're just looking and thinking right now, I guess."

"How's Susan?"

"Fine, just as chipper as always. She and her sister said to say hi."

When I asked him where he was calling from, he told me he stayed late at his office in Des Moines and was using the WATS line. He also mentioned that he spent Christmas Eve with Susan, Louellen, and their dad, and then he asked me how long a vacation I had.

"Not long enough. I'm going back to Mount Morris Sunday afternoon, and school resumes on Monday."

"But I bet you had at least a week off, you lucky devil. Some people shouldn't complain."

"Missed your calling," I teased. "El ed's the life. Get a nice long vacation come about the end of May too."

"You don't need to rub it in," he said. "Now one reason I'm calling is that a bunch of us are getting together in Des Moines on New Year's Eve. We're going out to eat and then discoing. Want to join us?"

"Gee," I began, "it sounds like fun, but I don't know though. It's kinda a long drive for me and you can never tell about the weather," and then, deciding I had better not go, I added, "and besides, I'd really love to except I promised an old high school friend I'd try to stop by her house for a party she's having. Thanks for thinking of me anyway."

"Sure, I understand," he said. "This was very short notice anyway. But the real reason I called was to make one more proposition. How does Easter look for you?"

"Easter? What do you mean?"

"How much vacation do you get?" he asked. "Because some of us are planning to go out to Colorado skiing. Now you don't have to say whether you'll come or not this very minute. Just let me know if you're interested or not, and if you want us to keep in touch with you as things develop. It'll only be for that four-day weekend because most of us who're planning to go don't get much time off."

When I told him that I got Good Friday and the Monday afterwards off, he told me that was perfect, so I then asked him who all was planning to go.

"We've got lots of people," he began, "who are interested. Do you know Carl Benson and Rafe Johnson? They were Sigs too but older than us. Emma and Marc. Natalie if she can scrap the money together. Vicki Becker doesn't think she'll be able to make it. Bruce Adams and Jenny. Jenny's brother David—did you know him? He was also three years older than us, like Carl and Rafe. Also, a couple guys that I work with say they might be interested."

"Sounds like a big group," I said.

"Yes, it should be a great time, but we need more girls, so please think about coming. Susan said to tell you that Hank Locke has NOT been invited. And neither has Simon."

I laughed and then said, "Well, it sounds like fun except I've never been skiing before."

"Neither have I. Susan's never been and I guess, well, about half the people who're going have never been skiing. Don't worry about transportation either. You're just a little bit off I-80, aren't you? So it wouldn't be any trouble to swing by and pick you up."

"You state a pretty convincing case," I said. "I'd like to be kept posted about it."

After I gave him my phone number in Mount Morris and we said good bye, I hung up and basked in the sweet smell of angel food cake. Mother was drying the beaters, her cake tipped upside down on the vinegar bottle.

"Who was that?" she asked.

"A friend from college," I answered, "Pete Byron—you know—Susan McHenry's boyfriend. He was on the baseball team. I think you met him a few times when I was dating Jack."

"Oh, yes," she agreed. "Do you suppose Susan still has those enormous glasses?"

"Probably," I answered, remembering petite, small-boned, dark-haired Susan with the large round frames dominating her youthful face. "Anyway, a bunch of kids from school are getting together in Des Moines on New Year's Eve, and Pete wanted to know if I could join them, but I don't really want to drive all the way there and back. Even if I stayed over until Sunday, that was when I was planning to go back to Mount Morris. It just wouldn't work out. But Pete told me he's trying to get a group together to go out to Colorado skiing over Easter weekend. Emma and Nat and lots of other kids. That kinda sounds like fun, I think. I told him I might be interested."

"Oh Sara," she said with worry, "skiing is so dangerous. Do you think you should try it?"

"They have lessons," I said. "And I'll be careful."

"I know you would be," she said, "but Mother will worry nevertheless."

I walked over to her and gave her a little hug. "I know," I said, "but you shouldn't. I'll take care of myself. Now come on, let's sit down. You've worked hard enough today."

She agreed, and after she left the kitchen, I went to the green room to look at my painting. After I finished it, I wanted to start on something for Melly and Dan. Actually it would be for the baby. As I looked at it, I realized how much I disliked this picture of the tiger. At first I had been enthused about it, but now it seemed so stupid. I felt like forgetting it and starting on the baby's. I had already decided it would be a fairy tale-like sort of picture, one filled with vibrant colors, smiling urchins, and gentle beasts, so intricate in detail that the child, as it grew older, would never tire of discovering its many facets. For that reason, I had decided it would be best not to create some scene from a specific story; rather I would give my imagination free reign. But I was not talented enough to forgo a trip to the bookshelf to gain ideas from other illustrators. I turned off the light in the green room and went to the pink room, where Mother was now reading the paper and Father was still watching TV.

"Are all Melly's and my old books still down the basement in those boxes?" I asked Mother.

"You mean like Nancy Drew and Trixie Belden?"

"Yes, and the ones we had when we were younger too, that you used to read to us from."

"They should be there," she said. "I didn't throw any away because you girls told me you wanted them for someday when you had families of your own. And so when we moved from the farm, they all went into boxes, and they've sat down there in the basement ever since."

Father, who had caught our conversation, now said, "Mother we should hunt them up now. Melly may be wantin' 'em."

"Dad," I said, sharing my mother's smile, "the baby hasn't even been born yet, and it will be a while before one of Melly's activities is reading to her child."

"Well," he said, "I was just thinkin' ahead. It takes Mother and me so long to get things done nowadays that we have to plan ahead."

"Oh, we're hardly in the rest home or the grave yet," Mother said with exasperation. "You make it sound as if we're senile or incapacitated."

"It is a good idea, though," I said to establish an air of harmony. "You know we might easily forget about those books until the kid's all grown up. You might mention it to Melly now because later she might be too busy with other things."

"Yes, you're right, Sara," Mother agreed. "And thank you, Ned, for mentioning it in the first place."

"Father knows best," he said.

Between tilting my umbrella up, to see where I was walking, and then down, to provide shelter, I thought it was a priest coming toward me, but the weather made it hard for me to be certain. It was a little after seven and fairly dark, one of those early spring days which began in uncertain cloudiness, with bouts of weak sunshine, turning to rain around dinnertime. It was an incessant, delicate rainfall, really the nicest kind to walk in. I looked up again and saw his collar. The only human being in sight, he was doing a sort of skip-gallop toward me, holding a newspaper over his head.

"Excuse me," he said when were just a few steps apart, "could you tell me where Van Flint Hall is?"

I stopped walking and told him it was on the other side of campus.

"It figures," he said. "Can you give me some directions?"

"Well," I began, hesitating about how best to direct him, "the easiest way to find it without getting lost would be to go back the same way you came from. See that building there, with the sculptures in front?"

He nodded and I proceeded to give him more directions, adding that there were probably maps inside the Student Union.

"Thanks," he said, "I really appreciate it."

He turned around and began running. I made my way to the art building, dark except for the exterior lights and the first floor entry hall light. After I closed my umbrella, I pushed the old door in and entered. Marie was late again. It was almost four years now, and I still refused to go upstairs alone at night. This building, with its creaks and moans, intensified by the emptiness and the rumors of ghosts, frightened me. I shook my umbrella, opened it, and put it down on the floor. Even late in the afternoon, I usually left the building soon after I sensed I was totally alone.

I went over to the door and peered out. No one was in sight; the priest was long gone. Suddenly it occurred to me how he might not have been a priest at all. It might have been an ingenious cover to trap unsuspecting coeds. He could have stopped me, pretending to ask for directions, and then swiftly flashed a knife or a gun at me. Two years ago there was a long string of assaults and rapes on campus. Then you went out only at night in groups. There were escort systems and a proliferation of classes on self-defense.

I turned and glanced at the stairs. I was suddenly very frightened. It was after seven fifteen and I was sure Marie had said she'd be here at seven. I was late myself getting here, but only by a few minutes. She couldn't be upstairs because there were no lights on, and besides, we always waited for each other in the lobby and then went up together. No one was in sight outside.

Although I tried to calm myself, repeating that Marie would be here any minute, the palpitations of my heart seemed stronger and I knew I was really scared. I began to speculate about someone coming softly down the stairs behind me. My ears were tuned to the slightest sound, although the rain muted so much. For good or bad, I wondered. It had seemed a happy rain on the way over; now it was portentous and eerie. Then I remembered my umbrella. I ran over, picked it up, and closed it. It would be my dagger, my weapon of defense.

I kept my eyes fixed to the glass pane in the door, occasionally turning to glance at the stairs. It was now almost seven thirty. I told myself I'd only wait five more minutes, because Marie was never this late. Then I wished the rain would stop and thought again about how when I left the house it had seemed a sort of Gene Kelly singin'-in-the-rain rain; now it was like the telltale heart, beating down in unceasing torture, intensifying my own heartbeat.

I thought about walking over to Marie's dorm, although it was a long way from here. Suppose the priest/rapist had merely pretended to head toward Van Flint? Perhaps he had circled around and followed me to the art building? Perhaps he was out in the bushes now waiting for me to emerge? An umbrella would be useless against a gun.

I clung to the relative safety of my position at the door, forcing myself to believe that Marie's figure would soon appear in the darkness. I needed to concentrate on a cheerful subject, but I couldn't. I tried to remember if I'd read anything about what was going on in Van Flint tonight; that would mean the priest was for real and not a rapist/murderer. If he had wanted to attack me, he could have done it earlier. It was absurd to think he would wait. There was probably a lecture or seminar in Van Flint tonight; not all of them were highly publicized. He was an awfully young priest, though. I always imagined priests as being rotund old men. But that was absurd too. A young liberal priest would be likely to go to a seminar at a university; the old ones were anti-intellectual, conservative types. I had noticed his bright red hair. He looked Irish, and the Irish were always Catholic. This was absurd too, but the fear that I felt had activated my mind into a frenzied search for the logicality of a young priest on campus in the rain looking for Van Flint.

I glanced at my watch again; it was now seven forty. Marie had never been this late. She must not be coming. With no desire to wait any longer, I'd return to the house and call her. Still, I really needed to work. I told myself I'd wait five more minutes and then leave. I began counting to sixty to see if I could keep time with my watch.

Then I saw a figure approaching, although it was too far away for me to see clearly who it might be. It had a big dark umbrella, though, so I reasoned it was not the priest/rapist/murderer. The head and shoulders, hidden by the umbrella, gave me no clue even as it grew nearer. I gripped my umbrella, trying to convince myself it was Marie. But as the figure approached, I knew it was not Marie. It was too tall and too male-like. All I could see were a pair of blue jeans and a light colored jacket, with one hand stuck in the jacket pocket. Maybe it was Andy or Simon or Jinbok? It was too tall for Jinbok, though. I stepped away from the door and waited by the stairs out of view.

When the door opened, it was Kevin Percy. He came in shaking his umbrella off while I walked away from the stairs.

"Kevin," I said, my voice startling him, "hi."

"Hey there. Sara, right? Didn't expect anybody'd be here."

"I was going to work tonight," I explained. "I was supposed to meet Marie here at seven, but I doubt she's coming. We don't like to work alone in here, and that's why I haven't gone up."

As I was explaining this, I remembered that he'd been here working too a few times when Marie and I were.

"Well, I was going to work too," he said, opening his umbrella and putting it on the floor. "Now that I'm here you won't be afraid to go up, will you? I'm kind of glad you're here myself because this place can be pretty spooky at night. I was only going to stay until about ten."

"Oh," I said, "we were only going to work a couple hours anyway, so that will work out fine. Who knows? Maybe Marie will show up."

"Why don't you put your umbrella out to dry?" he suggested, looking at the closed, damp umbrella in my hand.

"Yes," I laughed nervously and then put my umbrella next to his. As we climbed the stairs, I asked him what he was working on, and he told me several sketches, one especially, which was on the third floor. Then I told him I was going up to four and trying to finish some stuff for the senior exhibit.

"When's that go up?" he asked.

I told him April 23rd and that there wasn't enough time for me to get everything done that I needed to. When we reached the third floor he asked me if I had a job yet.

"Not yet," I said, "but I've had one interview and have a couple more lined up."

"You're in art education, aren't you? Where do you want to teach?"

I told Kevin that it didn't matter that much, that starting in a small town would probably be good. Then he left me, reminding me to holler if I saw any ghosts.

After climbing the last set of stairs, I took out my key, unlocked the door, and turned on the wall switch. Then I moved a chair in front of the wide open door to make sure it would not close. With the door open, I could hear any footsteps on the stairs.

I went over to my mixed media for the show, *Gypsy Girl on an Enchanted Plain,* probably one of the best pieces I'd done. I took out my materials and began working on the background. Creating an enchanted plain was definitely going to be the hardest part. I still had, for the most part, an unclear vision in my mind of what it would be. Thus, I would have to experiment with shapes and colors. The girl was done though, and she was good. I reasoned that even if I botched the background she would still carry the picture, just as Mona Lisa did. It was, perhaps, an inartistic approach to take, but I just didn't have time to deliberate about the background. I began sketching in some strange flowers.

"What did you do?" he asked.

"Oh, lots," I said. "You pick them out, but don't look at the names. That wouldn't be fair. Try to guess."

"Any in this room?" he asked.

"Yes, now don't go too close or you'll see the names."

"That one there," he said, pointing to Marie's abstract. "The red and yellow blob."

"No, silly," I laughed. "You know me better than that. I seldom do anything abstract."

"You're a pretty abstract person," he said.

"What do you mean?" I asked. "What's an abstract person? Define *abstract* in terms of people."

"I was only making conversation," he said. "You know, like you make art."

"I make conversation too," I replied. "It's easier to make than art."

"You must be a very gifted person," he said, "to be able to make both conversation and art."

"I am," I said. "There are very few of us who can do both. Unfortunately, society does not appreciate us."

"No," he disagreed, "I think you're wrong. Society appreciates a good artistic conversation maker."

"Do you make anything besides conversation?" I asked.

"Yes," he said smiling, "I make love to art makers."

I felt a tingle in my pelvis. That was another crazy conversation, but it had ended rather nicely. Abbreviated, it might make a cute greeting card. A boy-figure on the front would say, "I make conversation," to a girl figure at an easel who would said, "I make art. Do you make art?" Inside the boy-figure would say, "Yes, I make love to art makers, and that's ART!" To the card recipient, the message at the bottom could be: Wanna make ART sometime?

Then I thought about personifying ART as a baby. Then it would have to be a "Wanna get pregnant?" card rather than a "Wanna screw?" card. It would be funny if greeting card companies expanded their classification systems so that you could find such headings. Perhaps people would be self-conscious hunting through the "Wanna screw?" section. Actually, I supposed that the use of "Humorous" or "Love" as classifications merely pointed to our society's Puritan desire to cloak sex in euphemism. Still, it was curious how the greeting card industry, while it catered to our good thoughts, condensed our lives: birth, marriage, death, with the holidays thrown in to make a handsome profit. However, there were some splendidly creative cards on the market now.

I decided I would draw up my card design for Natalie to give to Screwy Louie. On the front I would put a girl-figure saying, "I make dreams," and a professor-figure who would say—what? I continued coloring some of the flowers on the enchanted plain while I thought. Then I got tired of trying to think about what Screwy Louie could make. I wanted an erotic fantasy. My enchanted flowers were sexual, intricate, delicate, curved, penetrating the enchanted milky moon air, intensifying the gypsy girl's desire. I wished I could make them show how much they perfumed the night air. Such suffocating, lustful fragrance they oozed.

Dr. Patternach stuttered, but stuttering was not made. Neither were dreams. It depended so much on the syntax.

I heard footsteps climbing the stairs and Kevin appeared in the doorway telling me he had "drawer's cramp." He walked over to the old maroon sofa that we had stolen from the theater department and lay down on his back with his head resting on the sofa arm and his hands locked behind his head: the classic pose of insouciance.

I didn't know him very well. I thought someone told me he lived off campus. Only a sophomore, he was already beginning to make a name for himself in the department, having done some really good work. Jinbok knew him better than anyone else and he was really impressed by Kevin's dedication and subsequent productivity. I remembered our sitting around there one afternoon when Jinbok remarked of Kevin: "He work hard, hard, hard. You guys gotta see what he produce. Mountains! And it's great!"

"If he's so great," said Simon, who was slightly drunk at the moment, "what's he doing in a dump like this?"

"What are you doing here yourself, Simon?" Andy asked.

"Well," he chuckled, "ol' Simon's here 'cause my pappy's dairy farm's forty mile yonder, and this here was the cheapest and closest place to go, and my pappy said he was goin' to send his son to college and by golly he did!"

"You're smashed, Simon," Marie said. "Don't make it sound as if your 'pappy' is some backwoods farmer who lives in a dugout. He probably makes more money than all of us here will ever make. You could have gone to the Art Institute if you'd wanted to!"

"Thank you, Marie, protégé of the renowned Earl Hamlin, the great Earl Hamlin, who spent a month every summer with his good ol' buddy Marc Chagall," Simon said bitterly. "Sure, you and Jinbok and Sara and that Percy kid came here to study under the great master. But tell me, how's it been? Has Professor Hamlin written anything praising your work, your budding genius? Has he ever said any damn thing to any of us? He hasn't even given us guidance, let alone encouragement!"

"Okay, Simon," Marie broke in, "so we all thought it was going to be different when we started. We thought we were all geniuses and that Earl Hamlin would marvel at our great talents and befriend us and take us under his wing and circle us out for special help and recognition. You can't say he doesn't comment on what we do, at least some of it."

"Society isn't constructed," I added, "to make all of us rich and famous. I sometimes think that's what Hamlin's trying to tell us. He's not just aloof; he's sad."

"Oh come on, don't make him out to be a fuckin' saint now," Simon muttered, his gray eyes burning mine.

"I'm not," I countered. "I just meant that maybe he does think some of our work's pretty good and he realizes that perhaps it's just a quirk of fate that he's famous and we'll never be, and so he's just preparing us for what it's going to be like in the real world: obscurity."

"That's a bunch of bull," Simon said. He was tall with dark curly hair, very handsome, and always seemed as if he undressed me when we spoke. "You're just making excuses again, Sara."

"No, I agree with Sara," Jinbok said. "Hamlin is great artist and I feel privilege to have work under him four year. He has helped me and I am grateful." And then he added, grinning, "More help and I be more grateful!"

I glanced over at the sofa where Kevin was gazing at the ceiling. He was sort of a handsome boy, I thought: tall and slender, with a kind of farm-fresh face like John Boy Walton. He made me feel old.

Suddenly he looked right at me. I quickly turned my eyes toward the mixed media and tried to concentrate on the enchanted plain, embarrassed by his catching me giving him such a curious stare. When I glanced at him again, he was looking at me.

"Got any inspiration yet?" I asked him.

"Working on it," he said to the ceiling. "Want to come and see what I'm doing when you need a break?"

Surprised by his offer, I told him sure, feeling excited about being alone with him. I realized how disappointed I'd be if Marie or Andy or Jinbok or Kathy Rossey suddenly showed up. It was silly how frightened I had been earlier.

When I told him I was ready to take a break, he walked over to me and said, "That's very good. You're very good with detail and at creating a sense of atmosphere."

"Thanks," I said, feeling very excited having him so close to me. I stepped away, turning to him to say, "Now you promised to show me your masterpiece." Of course, as the words came out, I realized they could be interpreted sexually, and I had a vision of Kevin Percy unzipping his pants and saying, "Here's the ol' masterpiece," as his penis burst out.

He turned away and shrugged a little. Obviously we had not shared visions.

"It's just a sketch," he said, heading toward the door.

On the third floor, he led me into one of the tiniest rooms, one I never worked in because it was so small and dark. On one table a tall white candle was burning, throwing up its light in romantic, gothic phantasmagoria on the ancient wall.

"Where's the light switch?" I asked, halting by the door.

"The light spoils it," he said, walking toward the table. "I like to work by candlelight."

"That's crazy," I observed. "How can you see?"

"Good enough," he said, going to the window ledge and lighting three more candles along it. "Come on in," he continued. "You're not afraid, are you?"

I laughed, somewhat nervously, and walked over to his drawing table. But instead of joining me, he took one of the candles, which was held in an old brass candlestick, and walked past me to the door. "I've got to close the door," he said. "That damn hallway light spoils it in here."

As the door closed, I felt very frightened again. What did I really know about Kevin Percy? Perhaps he was a frustrated, psychotic individual? Another Richard Speck? He walked over to his closed portfolio and stood staring at it, suddenly remarking that it was cold in the room, as if this observation was the conclusion of a long chain of thoughts. As soon as he said it, I realized that it really was chilly and that I was standing with my arms folded defensively in front, half for warmth, half for protection.

"I tried to turn it on earlier," he said, looking over at the old radiator, "but it's stuck. We could go to another room."

"That's okay," I said. "You were going to show me your sketch. It's getting late and I need to get back to my mixed media."

"Sure," he said, turning the portfolio's cover back. "Actually, I'm working on several sketches right now." Quickly he turned over many sheets of paper, so rapidly that I could hardly make out any of them. Human figures, animals, still lifes, geometric shapes—all whizzed by.

"Wow, you really are prolific," I said.

"What?" he said absent-mindedly, totally absorbed in his rummaging. "See this one?" It was an ink sketch of an animal that looked like a buffalo.

"What is it?" I asked. "A buffalo?"

"Yes, the Great American Beast." He examined it for a few seconds and then hurried on, piling sketch after sketch on top of each other.

"Here it is," he said suddenly, stopping at a rather rough black and white sketch of a nude female figure. Armless, she was posed with her back to the artist at an angle so that just a bit of her face and one breast were showing.

Because I was hesitant what to say, I decided to wait for Kevin to speak, so we both stared at the drawing, with me deciding that it was the beginning of a good sketch. Hers was a slender, yet sensuous figure, reminding me of a defiant Greek goddess. However, her armlessness was so salient that I couldn't envision a fully-limbed woman. Finally I asked, "Another *Venus de Milo?*"

"What?"

Since his sketch had none of the Hellenistic humility of Venus, I decided to forget my comment.

Kevin said, "I didn't like the way the model in class had her arms on her hips." When I asked him where he was going to put them, he answered, "That's the trouble. I don't know exactly where I want them."

We stared at the drawing a few more seconds. Then Kevin stepped away from me and said animatedly, "What would you think if I changed her hair and had her bringing her hair off her back and holding it on top of her head?" He started to put his arms up, but then stopped, saying, "I can't do it, but take your hair with both hands and hold it up."

I did what he said and, looking right at him, asked, "Like this?"

"Right. Now turn around so you're at my angle, the artist's angle."

I began to feel a little ridiculous, but I turned halfway around, and Kevin began giving me rather specific directions as to how I should stand.

Suddenly I dropped my arms and turned around.

"You won't do it?" he implored. "It is cold in here. We could go to another room. You could keep most of your clothes on."

I told him it was getting late and that I had work to do, and wanting to stay on good terms, I added, "Besides, those models in class get paid; I'm billable by the hour too, you know, and I charge pretty hefty fees. You'd get a much better rate with them."

"Okay," he said. "I just really felt like working tonight, and sometimes I don't like how the models in class pose."

"Who posed for your buffalo?" I asked.

"I'm not asking you to get naked."

"Really! Honestly, it is late and I've got lots to do. Goodbye." I turned and walked to the door, part of me wanting to take off my clothes and pose for this good-looking boy, the rest of me frightened, prudish, inhibited. I hadn't shaved my armpits and legs for four days. Never prepared, damn it, I said to myself as I ran up the stairs. And who did Kevin Percy think he was! Art for Kevin's sake—how selfish!

I couldn't stay and work on the mixed media now. I'd have to call Marie and find out when she could work again. I only had a couple more weeks until the exhibit went up. Job interviews and filling out the application forms took all my time. I grabbed my purse, locked the door, and headed downstairs.

There was a faint glow emanating from the room Kevin was in. He hadn't bothered to close the door after I left. *The light spoils it*—how weird! I kept going. On the first floor, I picked up my umbrella, closed it part way, and headed for the door.

It was still raining and chillier now, with puddles all over in the old, lopsided walks. I should have rolled up my jeans, but it was too late now. I began walking back to the house, trying to avoid the puddles, and was almost half-way there when I heard a voice behind me calling my name.

I turned around, expecting for some strange reason to see the priest. It was Kevin Percy running toward me. Of my three options—to walk toward him, to turn and continue walking, or to wait—I decided the one would be too nice, the one too rude, and so I stood, letting the rain sprinkle down. When he reached me, the water dripping off our umbrellas hit the pavement between us, creating boundaries which suggested the separateness and inaccessibility of our bodies. I realized now how close we'd been in the art building, feeling again a sort of frightened anticipation.

"What is it?" I asked.

"I just wanted to tell you I'm sorry if I upset you," he said rapidly. "I know you're busy. It was pretty selfish of me."

I told him it was all right and turned to walk away. I'd only gone a few steps when he called again, "Sara!" I stopped and turned around one more time. My name sounded pretty in the rain. Neither of us stepped toward each other to restore the previous distance of communication. The water hit the pavement around our umbrellas, and we were like two fixed dots on a Yin and Yang diagram.

"Yes?" I responded.

"I'm starved. Do you want to come over to my place for an omelet?"

It was a totally unexpected offer, and I could hardly think fast enough to unravel his motives (Was it a ploy to coax me to pose?) and possible ramifications. The timid part of me wanted to go home and cry because I was such a loser; the brave part wanted to go with Kevin Percy.

"Well, now that you mention it," I said, "I am kind of hungry too. Maybe it's the rain. That sounds okay."

He smiled and his smile was really very cute. I hardly felt two years older.

While we were walking, I asked him if he knew of a seminar in Van Flint tonight, but he didn't, and when I asked him where he lived, he answered, "Not far from here. I rent a room, but it's more like an apartment because I even have my own kitchenette. It's only me in the house and Miss Hartwick. It's her house. She's about eighty, your typical little old lady. She gets around pretty well, though. Where do you live?"

When I told him the name of my sorority, he said, "Oh, I didn't know you were one of those. What house is that?"

"It's red brick with white shutters and a lot of ivy. Over on Concord."

"They all look alike to me. I just haven't paid much attention to them. Do you like it there?"

"Sure," I said, "it's a nice place to live on campus. I've got some really good friends there." It seemed as if my words were insincere, but I didn't know exactly what else to say. It was the truth.

Then Kevin asked me if Marie lived there too, and I told him she lived in Westplain Hall. Having almost reached the Union, I inquired if we were going through it, as I was looking forward to a respite from the chilly rain, but he indicated we were not, leading me to the right toward the field house.

"You have a long way to the art building every day," I observed, wondering what his notions of "near" and "far" were.

"It's a nice walk, though," he said. "I love to go out and walk along the river."

"Yes, that's true," I replied. "It's so lovely when the leaves change color."

"It's nice now too," he said. "Have you been there recently?"

"No," I sighed, trying to amplify my regret. "I've just been too busy."

We were walking toward the tennis courts now and toward the north parking lot. Because the pavement was new, it was easier to walk, although my shoes and the bottoms of my jeans felt drenched.

"How'd you know my name?" he asked suddenly.

"Oh, I don't know," I began. "I suppose I just know about all the art majors. There aren't that many of us, you know."

"True, even with Earl Hamlin."

"Know the great one?"

"I met him. I doubt he knows me."

"Don't feel bad," I said. "He's just not the chummy, chummy type like, say, Walt McHale."

"Yeah, I heard he's really chummy, especially with his female students."

I thought about telling him that Professor McHale had slept with at least a dozen of my sorority sisters (It made Art

Appreciation so much easier!), but instead I asked, "Who'd you hear that from?"

"Simon St. John."

"Don't believe everything he says. Simon is a good friend of my friends Natalie and Pete, and Simon told them he's a Hamlin Scholar, and he's not."

"At least Simon's not so cliquish like some people around here are."

"Me included?" I asked.

"Well, you've got to admit that little senior coterie you've got—you and Andy and Marie and Kathy Rossey and Jinbok and even Simon sometimes—doesn't like to mingle with us underclassmen very much. And somebody told me you dated Simon?"

"We're just all such good friends, well, except maybe Simon who's too competitive. And I only went out a couple times with him. We just all started here together four years ago, and we certainly don't mean to exclude anybody."

We were off campus now and, as I glanced up from under the umbrella, I saw we were walking along a row of mostly small frame houses, any of which seemed as if it could be inhabited by Miss Hartwick. Surely we would turn into one of them soon. Deciding not to comment again about the long walk, I said instead, "You strike me—maybe I'm way off—as the kind of guy who wouldn't give shit about belonging to some little group."

He laughed and said, "I don't know. I guess even loners would sometimes like to feel a little bit of the camaraderie others seem to enjoy so much."

"Jealousy, resentment, loneliness—"

"Hey," he interrupted, "do you have to analyze so much? Don't make it sound so bleak. I was only making conversation."

The words shocked me. *Making conversation!* What do you make? I make love—

"This way," he said, turning the corner. "We're almost there."

I looked up again at the houses. They were all Miss Hartwick houses, circa 1900, white frame with front porches, aluminum lawn chairs or creaking swings, spirea bushes, giant oak and maple trees, tulips along the foundations on the south sides, hydrangeas and hollyhocks by the fences in back, starched white doilies on the big arms and backs of the huge, over-stuffed armchairs, a black and white TV set purchased in the early sixties whose reception was limited to two channels. And a stuffy smell, like Iris and Agnes, from old people waddling about.

I was cold and wet and wished I was at the house getting ready for bed.

"This one here," he said, taking hold of my elbow and guiding me up to one of the houses. "I go in around back."

We came to a narrow access sidewalk, which sloped downward, going to the rear of the house. Kevin went first, with me reluctantly following. The omelet expedition no longer appealed to me in the least. I'd been a fool to consent in the first place.

It was dark with little illumination from the street lights reaching Miss Hartwick's backyard. "We go up," he said suddenly, stopping so fast that I almost ran into him, "through the back porch."

I followed him up about six steps and unlatched the catch on my umbrella while he held open the screen door. It was just a small porch with one overhead light, some old newspapers stacked on the floor, a couple of grimy wicker chairs, and a table with some plants on it.

Kevin unlocked the inside door and we entered what I could barely make out was a tiny kitchen, which didn't smell too bad. He walked across the kitchen and I followed. "I'm downstairs," he said, flipping on the wall switch inside a small pantry area. He practically ran down the stairs. I followed slowly on the rail-less, narrow steps. He flipped another switch at the bottom and a lamp turned on. Then he turned off the stairway light, leaving the ascent dark and seemingly forbidden. I thought again about how little I knew about Kevin Percy.

His apartment, or room rather, was small, cluttered with plants and art supplies and unfinished and finished canvases. It smelled like linseed oil.

"Didn't open a window when I left because of the rain," he said, lighting a huge green candle on an orange crate. He moved an old wooden chair next to the wall and hopped on it to crack open the window. "But we have to have a little fresh air," he muttered. Then he turned on a small electric heater. "Make yourself at home," he said, throwing his jacket on the unmade bed. Then he took my umbrella and opened it by the stairs.

I decided my most respectable action would be to show interest in his work, although I curiously felt little desire to examine the drawings and paintings looming all around me. However, I walked over to a framed back and white ink drawing above a desk. It was some kind of animal which looked like, as I could best describe it, an elongated squirrel. The animal was diminished by an enormous expanse of snowy hills.

"Like my ermine?" he asked, startling me out of my reverie.

"What?" I mumbled.

"I asked if you liked it."

"Yes," I replied, remembering the buffalo. "You like to draw animals, don't you? What is it?"

"An ermine—you know—a type of weasel."

I thought of my mother saying, "Sara doesn't know the difference between alfalfa and corn, bulls and sows!"

Ermine, ermine, ermine ran through my brain, and so I said, "Isn't the fur somehow associated with royalty?"

"I think so," he said, lifting my self-respect. "It's a neat little creature; in winter his fur turns very white so he blends in with the environment. It's God's little touch to preserve the ermine from greedy kings and queens."

Instead of uttering this remark flippantly, he sounded very serious, as if there was something profound about the ermine, and I wondered if he was just fooling me or if he was a Jesus freak. I tried to remember if I'd heard his name mentioned with the campus Bible Beaters.

"Would you like a mushroom and cheese omelet?" he asked.

"Sure, that sounds great." And it did. I was suddenly famished.

Kevin walked to the kitchenette area and I asked him if he wanted any help, but he declined my offer. While he began cooking, he said, "I practically live on eggs. I could have omelets every day of the week, and sometimes I do. Or a couple of nice fried eggs with hot buttered toast to sop up the runny yolks."

My mouth watered. "Too bad they've got so much cholesterol," I said. "They say we shouldn't eat more than three a week."

"Hell, I don't listen to that crap. I eat about twenty five per week, and it won't be eggs that will kill me," he said, breaking six into a bowl.

It was the obvious question to ask and so I did: "What will?"

"A supernova," he said matter-of-factly, as if he had said leukemia. So just for a moment I thought perhaps it was the name of some form of tumor or disease I hadn't heard about.

"What's that?" I asked.

"A big nova," he replied calmly, while he moved the cheese up and down on a grater. "I think this is the hardest part. Ruins the delicate hands of the artiste."

"What?" I asked.

"Grating. It's hard work. Someday they should sell shredded cheese."

A mound of grated cheddar cheese lay on the cutting board

like an unbaled lump of cut hay. Kevin took a plastic container from the dorm-sized refrigerator, scooped out a handful of fresh mushrooms, and dumped them down next to the sink.

"What's a nova?" I asked.

"Tsk! Tsk! Almost a college graduate and you don't know what a nova is."

Of course, I knew he was playing with me now, but I had no idea what a nova was. I could only think of novacaine and had a strange vision of an ermine sitting in a dentist's chair.

"Yes," I said humbly, "after almost four years of college I'm functionally illiterate and don't know a simple fact like what a nova is." (Kevin Percy was beginning to remind me of Natalie.)

"Didn't you ever take astronomy?" he asked.

This did not help. "No," I said, "art ed doesn't leave much time for those fun electives like stargazing."

When butter had melted in the skillet, Kevin poured the egg mixture into it and asked me if I'd like something to drink, milk, tomato juice and beer being the options. After I chose juice, he poured it into two jelly jar glasses.

"So please tell me what a nova is," I said.

Scattering the sautéed mushrooms on the omelet, he said, "Just a bright, bright star. A supernova's very, very bright, a million or a billion or a trillion—I've forgotten which—brighter than the sun." The toast popped up and I offered to butter it, asking for a knife. Kevin got out two melamine plates, and I put the toasted bread on them.

"I've got strawberry jam, if you like?" he offered from his position over the omelet. I marveled that this warm hospitality came from the same person who had earlier expected me to become his model. "Now for the cheese." He scooped it up, sprinkled it on the omelet, and put a fork on each plate. "I've got some napkins around here somewhere, I think," he added, opening the kitchen's one cupboard. "I save them for company." He produced a huge, almost full package; I surmised he had very few guests.

Then he took the omelet pan off the burner and slid the omelet out onto one of the plates, folding it in half. It was a huge omelet, with butter clinging to its crevices and cheese oozing out of the edges. I didn't think I had ever seen a more appealing omelet. He cut it in half and put the one half on the other plate.

"Let's eat on the couch," he suggested, picking up his plate and glass of juice.

We sat on opposite ends of a battered brown sofa, using the orange crate for our glasses and balancing the warm plates on our laps.

"It's delicious," I told him.

Kevin ate ravenously. I wanted to ask him about the supernova, but he seemed so preoccupied with eating that I thought conversation might be inappropriate. Finally, when I saw that he was about done, I asked him how a supernova would kill him.

"It will kill you too," he said. "All of us, the whole planet. We're long overdue for one. They happen every so many billion years and we haven't had one for a while. The odds are against us." He stopped to put his plate on the floor and then went over to the bed and lay down. "You could be eating an omelet and zappo! No more omelet, no more Sara, no more earth, no more anything."

"You really believe this is how the earth will end?"

He shrugged. "Some way, if not the supernova. It was a good omelet, wasn't it?"

"Yes," I agreed, taking my last forkful.

"You want a popper?"

"A what?"

"Oh, I guess not," he said, producing a bottle from somewhere and swallowing a pill.

Oh God, not a drug addict, I thought. I had been beginning to like him, but now I asked, "Want me to help you do the dishes?"

He told me no, that they'd get done eventually. I took them into the kitchenette and rinsed them off, also filling the omelet pan with hot water. It would be time to leave soon. My contacts beginning to hurt, I sat back down on the sofa and asked, "Won't God save us from the supernova like He saves the little ermine?"

"Remember, though, not all the ermine get saved."

"Only the benevolent? Will they be saved from the supernova by a miracle?"

"Maybe, who knows?" he said sleepily. "I bet the whole planet will get blitzed."

"Then everything will be destroyed, including all this?" I asked, gesturing around the room.

He got up and said, "How do I know?"

I hopped up and said, "Well, it's late. I've really got to be going. Thanks for the omelet." I started to put on my still-wet jacket.

"I'll walk you back," he said. "Just let me go to the john first."

"Oh no, you don't have to."

"It's late. I'll walk you back to campus at least. You might get lost."

Since I was beginning to think I might need a guide, I decided not to protest any longer. While he went to the bathroom, I stood by the stairs, no longer curious about looking at his artwork.

On the way back we didn't talk much. I found out that his parents were divorced, his mother lived in Omaha, and his father, who had remarried, lived in Bettendorf, and Kevin didn't know where or how he was going to spend the summer. He walked me all the way to my sorority house, which must have taken at least twenty-five minutes. I was cold, soaked, and tired, but Kevin didn't seem to mind the rain or the prospect of the long walk back. That night I concocted a dream in which Kevin Percy fell in love with me, and we had a short, sweet spring romance. When we parted at the end of the semester, I felt certain I'd meet him again someday, when I was famous, of course.

In reality, I saw Kevin Percy around the art building for the rest of that spring, and we even saw two movies together. A week after the last movie he called again and wanted to know if I'd like to join him on an all-day outing along the river, the thought of which seemed very appealing because the weather had gotten really nice, and everyone seemed caught up in a light-hearted mood. The air was redolent of romance, and the idea of a frolic along the river (the girls in the house who'd been there already said it was heavenly) presaged the best of spring and new love. But I was too busy. I had a job interview on the Saturday he wanted to go, and when he asked about Sunday, I had to tell him that after the interview I was driving home to spend the next day with my parents because I needed to take some of my things home.

"Well, I understand," he said, and after he hung up I wished I would have suggested that perhaps I could cancel my trip home. But it was too late now, and I sensed he wouldn't call again. Finals, and then commencement, were just days away, so there just wasn't any time.

Of course, I saw him briefly a few times in the art department, but we barely said hello. I never saw him again working in the evenings, and I had no idea if his figure ever got her arms. But I kept thinking I'd see him at graduation, and I pictured his roaming the crowds outside the stadium to find me. He'd tell me he was staying in town over the summer, he'd get my home phone number, and he'd promise to give me a call so we could get together.

I admitted I really didn't know him very well. Because we went to movies during our two dates, we didn't spend much time talking, compared to the strange, rainy night in April. But he never materialized at graduation. As we stood outside chatting and taking pictures, I expected him to pop up any minute to offer congratulations or at least to say good-bye. Finally Mother said, "Well, we'd better go back to the house and get the rest of your things loaded," and I knew my chances of seeing him again had dwindled to naught.

Curiously, though, I saw the priest again. It was the day after my last final when I went with Natalie to the hospital to visit Sharon Thomasino, who had had another breakdown. The notion that mental illness really existed was somewhat incomprehensible to me, but there was poor Sharon, living proof that such anguish existed.

She had been out of school a year for treatment and, when she came back at the beginning of this semester, she seemed a lot better, maybe cured. Then a few days before finals, we were all having dinner and Susan McHenry, who was rooming with Sharon, ran into the dining room crying and told our housemother that Sharon had said to her, very calmly, "I have to go to the hospital. Please call my parents."

What really perplexed me about Sharon was that she seemed so normal: pretty, smart, popular. There seemed to be nothing in her background to trigger this malady. Now if it had been Susan, who had lost her mother to breast cancer during our freshman year after several years of surgery, remission, and finally despair, then at least there'd be a reason, but in Sharon's case, there seemed to be nothing tangible as the root of her illness.

And so she went to the hospital, St. Vincent's, either because she was Catholic or because it specialized in mental illness, and Natalie said we should go to see her, and so the two of us went.

Since I hadn't seen Sharon before she'd left for the hospital and since Susan kept stressing how calmly Sharon had made the decision to admit herself, as if she had things under control, I expected the best. But when we saw her, she had changed, and it was not good. She sat up in the bed with her arms folded protectively in front and rocked continuously while we were there. It was her dark eyes, though, that troubled me the most. She stared mostly straight ahead, rarely looking at us, occasionally flicking her eyes nervously at us as if we might hurt her. Her expression was more panic stricken than that of Munch's screaming girl on the bridge. They were the dreadful eyes of madness.

While Natalie and I were trying to carry on a normal conversation, the priest stuck his head into the room, and I knew it was the same priest because of the bright red hair and freckles. "Sorry," he said to us. "I didn't know you had company, Sharon. I'll come back later."

I wanted to run out into the hall and bring him back, my desire so strong that as the minutes passed and the words dropped, I only heard myself pleading: *Don't leave us with this crazy girl. Remember me? That rainy night in April when you were trying to find Van Flint Hall? The night of Kevin Percy and the omelet? That was me you stopped. Sara Daphne Keatson. Don't you see she's mad? We try to talk and the sounds are like dandelion fluff blown about by the wind. She's mad and we can't do anything about it!*

Afterwards Natalie wanted to get ice cream cones, but all the way to Baskin's and back to the house, I didn't say anything about the priest. What did it matter anyway? Moreover, at that point I still thought Kevin Percy would call or make some effort to say goodbye. It was not utterly hopeless. But he never did.

With the funeral tomorrow, I didn't want to go down to the basement tonight. On the farm, I'd always been afraid of the farmhouse basement, imagining that some ghoulish clan lived under the steps and, once you discovered their existence, they held you prisoner and you could never go upstairs again. I had horrible nightmares about the basement folk and refused to go down there alone. Even now, I preferred to be downstairs alone only in the daytime. "I'll take a look at the books tomorrow after we get back," I told my mother. Besides, it was too comfortable on the sofa to move. I snuggled up into a ball and closed my eyes.

It was a nice Christmas, this Christmas we found out about the baby. Dan must have been rehearsing the announcement for weeks. Mother just beamed afterwards when she said to me, "He's the most wonderful son-in-law. I'm so thankful he and Melly have each other. And I hope that you'll find someone just as nice someday."

It was Christmas Eve and we had just finished opening gifts. We were all sitting in the living room except Mother, who was on the floor sorting wrapping paper and bows. Father was just about to go hunt for the sticks we used to roast marshmallows in the fireplace, when Dan stopped him and said, "We've got some special news to tell you, and now seems like just the perfect time. Melly?"

She reached for Dan's hand and looked right at our mother. "We're so excited; we're going to have a baby!"

Mother got up from the floor and rushed over to her, exclaiming, "How wonderful!" as she hugged my sister. I offered my congratulations, and Father said, "Well, well, a baby. I guess that means I'm goin' to be a grandpa."

When I asked when she was due, Melly answered, "Around the end of July. My obstetrician pinpoints the due date as July 23rd." Then she reminded Dan about the champagne, and after he got it, all of us, except Melly, who informed us that she'd given up alcohol during her pregnancy, had a glass to celebrate. I asked more questions about what other medical advice she had to follow, and our mother chided me for being nosey, although then she inquired about the baby's room.

"We're going to use the bedroom we're currently using as a study," Melly said. "After school's out, Dan's going to panel the basement, put in a ceiling, tile the floor, and then we'll move the study down there."

"She doesn't think I can do it," said Dan, a high school music teacher, "but I keep telling her the do-it-yourself market is really big these days, and they make everything so simple even a bumpkin like me can handle it."

Then Father offered to help, and Mother began lamenting that they would have liked to have known about the baby before Christmas so that they could have gotten a gift such as a bassinet, stroller, or highchair. Mother insisted that they should go out shopping so that Melly could pick something out.

"Oh Mother, you're just too generous!" Melly said, giving her a hug. "I think it's really going to be fun fixing up the room and buying things, but you must remember there's no big hurry. We've got almost seven more months, and even then the baby won't need a highchair for a while!"

"What color are you going to paint the baby's room?" I asked.

"Blue or pink," Melly replied, "just won't do, although Dan thinks if we paint it blue that's got to influence the baby—something like it'll get 'boy vibes' from the walls. So I think we decided on pale green or maybe light yellow."

"Or perhaps blue?" Dan said softly and sincerely, getting a look of disapproval from my sister.

And that was how it was. We talked for quite a while about the baby's room, and it was grand to listen to all the plans they had and share in their excitement. Mother declared she was going to crochet a green and yellow afghan and offered to do a mural. I made plans to do something also. Father insisted we had Melly's and my old highchair down in the basement, but Mother declared that they'd given it away long ago to Ed and Wilma Effenbrauer, who wanted to use it when their grandbabies came to visit. Now Ed was dead and Wilma lived in the rest home, and Mother confessed she'd never even thought about the high-chair when Ed passed away and Wilma went into the home. Then both of them tried to remember if there'd been a sale before the Effenbrauer place was sold, which they calculated to have been about four years ago, and Mother decided there must not have been one because if there had been one they surely would have gone and seen the old highchair, if it was still there.

Of course, Father was still not sure this was what had really happened to the highchair, but when Mother asked him, "Well, do you remember us arguing about if we should lug a highchair with us when we left the farm?" Father seemed to remember then there being no highchair either to discard or move, and therefore he accepted Mother's account.

In the course of the discussion, they had to talk about where the Effenbrauer's daughters were living now and about whether it was Wilma Effenbrauer or Dottie Anders who Doc said didn't have much longer to live. Then we debated the merits of lino-leum versus tile floors, and each of us gave our opinions about whether we liked light or dark paneling, with the result that light won for a basement.

And of course we talked about names. Melly liked Amanda for a girl and Nathan for a boy, while Dan listed Jodie and Carson as his favorites. Then we all had to know where he's gotten Carson. "Nowhere in particular," he said. "I just like it. It has distinction."

I asked Dan if he was named after anybody in particular and if he knew about Melly's name. He thought perhaps he was named for a great grandfather named Daniel, and he knew Melanie was named after our paternal grandmother. Then I told Dan that I was named for my two great aunts on Mother's side, Sara and Daphne. Melly's middle name, Ferris, was Mother's maiden name. We thought that tradition was nice, especially when a woman took her husband's name and there was a chance her family name would die out because of no male heirs. We had one male cousin on Father's side of the family, Thomas Keatson, who was still in college. Provided Tom married someday and had a son, the Keatson surname would not cease. Melly thought she'd like to use Keatson as a middle name for either a girl or boy, and Dan seemed agreeable to this.

Then we all said the suggested names out loud to test them for ease of pronunciation and melodic quality, discovering that both male choices had identical rhythms. Then we noted that Jodie produced the same effect. Only Amanda was different because of the extra syllable. Melly, who was a junior high language arts teacher, pointed out that my name consisted of three trochees like three of the suggested names.

"DA da DA da DA da, SAR-a DAPH-ne KEAT-son," she said to illustrate, "but Amanda is iambic, while Keatson and Weaver are trochaic."

At this point, Father declared that he believed all these da da's didn't matter much and that it was time to go to bed and seven months from now he'd be happy and we'd all by happy with whatever name was chosen. It was a long speech for our father, but we took his advice and went to bed.

Before I fell asleep, I thought about all the things we had talked about and how the coming of a baby necessitated so much preparation. Our conversation had been tied to these things, the outward aspects of pregnancy and child rearing. We didn't talk about the momentousness of rearing a child, declare our feelings about how it learns to hate and love, analyze the situation from a

Freudian or Piagetian or Christian perspective. We talked about simple, respectable things: basements and highchairs, first and middle names, due dates and diapers. I supposed most families stayed on this ground also.

I admitted I was jealous of Melly, but it was not a bitter, sadistic envy. I was happy for her because she was happy, because she had Dan, who loved her and was also elated about the baby. I doubted all the importance given to sibling rivalry. Melly and I must have had a very mild case. I was jealous only because I wanted someday what she now had, and I was not worried that that someday would never come.

Right before graduation, Natalie had said to me, "Up until this point, I always felt there was the chance that someday I'd be famous. Emma, you know, doesn't give a damn about fame, but I do, and so do you. I suppose you could divide the world into those of us who want fame and those who are content to be anonymous forever. Now I'm scared because I don't think I'll succeed."

I had never expected Natalie, of all people, to admit defeat so soon. I sympathized with her anxiety. She was going to work for the phone company immediately after graduation, hoping to make a dent in her student loans. Emma was going, first, to Europe, and second, to graduate school because those were the fashionable things to do. When Emma finished grad school, for lack of something better to do, she'd marry Marc White or whoever else happened to be around at the time. It was easy to put Emma's puzzle together, but I had only vague ideas about Natalie's future. Emma and I had had great portions of life handed to us on silver platters; Natalie had always had to scrape and dig and fight. I guessed perhaps that was why she was freer and braver. I was bequeathed fears and responsibilities and guilt and, hardest of all to ignore, tradition.

When the chimes sounded for dinner, I put my book down and ran a brush through my hair. Emma was on her bed reading a magazine.

"I'm famished," I said. "There's lasagna tonight. Are you coming?"

She told me she wasn't very hungry and continued to read.

"Aren't you going to go down?"

"Oh damn it, Sara," she snarled. "Who cares whether or not I eat?"

"Did you sign off?"

She rolled her eyes and muttered, "Who cares whether or not I crossed my name off that stupid list?"

"Well, be prepared for another lecture at meeting." Our sorority house had a lot of stupid rules, but letting our cooks have a head count for dinner was not unreasonable.

All through the meal it seemed as if I became hungrier and hungrier, so that when coffee was brought out and Susan asked where dessert was and our housemother announced that it'd been switched to tomorrow night because we were having faculty guests then, a great disappointment descended upon all of us. I really wanted something sweet. There were cookies in my closet, but how could I justify to Emma my consuming them after lasagna?

Through coffee, I plotted my options. I could wait until she left the room and then sneak some cookies. Or I could be forthright about it: stroll into the room, comment about the terrific lasagna, take the cookies out of the closet, and brazenly consume two or four in her presence. "Want some cookies?" I could ask her. They were chocolate with peanut butter filling, which Emma loved. Or I could invite Susan and some others up for cookies. But I was greedy about my cookies; I needed to know they were always on the closet shelf for hunger pangs. I knew that I actually ate less as long as I knew I had these backups on reserve.

Without dessert, dinner ended quickly. As I headed toward our room, I hoped Emma would be gone, but she wasn't. At first I didn't see her because she was on the floor parallel to her bed doing sit-ups. She seemed startled when I entered. This was the first time I had ever seen Emma engaged in physical exercise. She was one of those girls who had a fabulous figure without working on it.

I took three cookies out and started munching on them, resolving to eat less for the remainder of the week. "Want any cookies?" I asked.

She declined and walked out of our room, telling me before she left that she didn't feel well and was going to rest. I headed down to the basement study room, where I spent about the next three hours until Natalie walked into the room and came over to my table. "You're home early," I whispered.

"It's awfully slow over there," she said of the library, where she had a part-time job. "Nobody's there because it's so cold outside, so I got off early. I need a cigarette. Come into the smoking room and talk to me for a bit."

The smoking room was deserted; only the heavy odor of cigarette smoke hung like a noxious mist. I sat down on one of the soiled chairs, and Natalie sat on an old wooden chair at the study table. I yawned and thought about lung cancer. Natalie inhaled deep breaths of smoke and stared straight ahead at the wall we'd painted turquoise, orange, and hot pink as pledges.

"I'm tired," I began. "Didn't you have a test today?"

She nodded, I asked her how it went, and she said okay. I began wishing I'd had my file so I could work on my nails.

"Sara," she said solemnly, "this whole thing's so damned rotten."

Ordinarily such comments were commonplace with Natalie, and I responded by ignoring her, but tonight seemed different. I started to push my cuticles back. Finally I asked, "What's rotten?"

"Just about everything."

"Did you flunk the test?"

"Oh, Sara, Sara, Sara," she moaned.

I thought about getting up and leaving. Often I thought about how life might be happier without having to interact with Natalie.

"I'm tired," I said, "and I've got a lot to do, so get to the point."

"The point, dear Sara, is that there is no point. Why we were all born female was utter chance, but we suffer all our lives for it."

I started to pick up my books. "Have you been up to the room yet?" I asked her. She seemed surprised by my question and then shook her head, as I walked toward the door.

"Wait a minute, Sara. Don't go yet. She made me promise not to tell anybody, but I've got to tell you. It's more envy than affection between Emma and me, but you've got so very little envy in you. That's why you should know."

You're wrong about that, I thought, but I said nothing. She turned her eyes away from mine and looked at the wall again.

"Emma's period is two weeks overdue," she said, "and you know she's always very regular."

"Oh" was all that came out of me, and then I stumbled on, "Has she said anything to you about what . . . I mean, I guess it's still early, right?"

"I saw Marc White today," she said, staring at the wall and blowing up her cigarette smoke. "The most goddamn sonafabitch in the world. He was laughing. Laughing, mind you! I wanted to walk up to him and ask him if he realized the hell Emma's been going through." Then she laughed abruptly. "I wanted to grab hold of his little pecker and pull as hard as I could."

"Has she told him yet?"

"Of course not."

"Two weeks is not that long," I said. "Maybe she didn't count right."

"For you, Sara dear, it is—"

"Spare me, Nat," I interrupted. "This is no time to be cute. I'm sure she was using something?"

"Of course they were using protection, but nothing's one hundred per cent effective anyway, not even the Pill."

"I know. It's just that Emma always seemed too smart to get pregnant."

Natalie crushed her cigarette stub in the Holiday Inn ashtray on the table. "I'll go up with you," she said, picking up her coat and scarf. We walked to the room together in silence. Someone was typing in the dining room, but otherwise the house was pretty quiet. The door to our room was closed.

"Thanks for telling me, Nat," I whispered as we opened it. The room was dark and Emma was in bed.

There were forty-six of us, thirty-one girls and fifteen boys. I guessed over twenty girls were married now, and one was engaged. One had already been divorced and was remarried. I estimated that the girls had produced about fifteen children so far. One who had not been married had born a baby also. I didn't know much about the boys, only that one of them was a father.

"Do you know when Debbie Haskin's wedding is, Mother?" I asked.

She looked up from the newspaper and said, "I seem to recall it's been set for some time in April, late April, I think. Her picture was in the *Sentinel* about three weeks ago."

I looked down at Debbie Haskin's picture. She looked so young, but then we all did. "How many kids has Carla Sudik got now?" I asked my mother, and she told me that she thought it was two. I looked down at the picture of the girl with wavy hair, black-rimmed glasses, and a crooked smile and tried to imagine her as a mother.

"She has—what do you call it?—an Afro?" Mother commented.

"Really! She must look different. Does Judy Hawthorne live in town?"

"No," Mother answered, "she lives on a farm over by Thornton. She married a Thornton boy."

"What are people like Alva Gorski and Mary Pat Darley doing?" I asked.

"Search me. I suppose they got jobs in Acadia."

"How about Toni Fuller?"

"Oh, she finished beauty school," Mother said. "I hear she has a shop in Winsome. Do you know what they said about her?" She whispered, "They said she had an abortion. Isn't that horrible?"

I didn't know if Mother was referring to the gossips or Toni, but I asked, "Who said?"

"Rose Perkins whose sister works in the hospital in Waterloo. She's the one who told it."

"How could she know for sure?" I questioned. "It's probably just a rumor."

"Well, you know Toni always was a little wild. Her older sister got pregnant in high school, you know."

"Is Donna Olson still in school?" I asked.

"Yes, she's still at Drake," Mother answered. "But I ran into her mother the other day in the five and ten, and she told me Donna was going to graduate in the spring."

"It's about time," I said, remembering Donna as scatterbrained and lazy. "I suppose she's an el ed major?"

"Oh no," Mother answered, "I think she's into marketing or computers or something like that."

This was almost worse. The thought of Dumb Donna making

more money than I did was so discouraging. At least the children would be spared.

"You know Janie Wadsworth lost a lot of weight and had her nose worked on?" Mother commented. "She looks so much better. Gladys Huse told me she's got a boyfriend."

"That's nice," I said, turning to the page with Janis' picture, which was really quite flattering, considering her physique and nose. "What's she do?"

"I think she's a waitress over at the Ramada Inn in Acadia."

I turned back a few pages to look at my picture again. Sara Daphne Keatson. I was the prettiest girl on the page after Laurie Lempso, who was homecoming queen after all. The photographer could have gotten me at a better angle, considering what he'd done with Janis Wadsworth. I definitely wasn't wearing enough eye makeup. New Year's Resolution Number One: Do a better job with eye makeup.

I closed the yearbook, rolled off the sofa, and went to the magazine stand: *Woman's Day, Family Circle, Better Homes & Gardens,* a *Herrschners* catalogue. I searched another bin and finally found a *Glamour.*

I started looking through it at all the close-ups of beautiful models, wondering if their makeup-free eyes were as lovely. Probably. Then suddenly the words "Facial Fix-Up" were blasting at me. There was a large photo of a very attractive female labeled "after" and a tiny photo of a mousy girl labeled "before." *Cindy L.,* I read, *is a medical technician in a fast-paced Philadelphia hospital. She needs a makeup plan which is quick to apply and yet lasts throughout her hectic day.* I skimmed the list of products and processes used on Cindy L. and wondered if their idea of "quick" was different from mine.

Julie K. was on the next page. I decided I liked Julie K.'s "before" better. On the opposite page was Shelli P. I looked at Shelli

P's "before" eyes; they seemed small, sad, and dull. Her "after" eyes were definitely an improvement. I read: *To highlight Shelli's deep-set eyes, Mr. Jacques applied (following moisturizer) a white shadow powder, Virginal by Estee Lauder, extending the shadow high into the brows. Then he applied a thin blend of brown shadow, Tawny Cocoa by Bonnie Bell, on the lower half of the lid. Next, an eye pencil, Smokey Grey by Revlon, is used to trace the natural crease in the eyelid. Dark brown eyeliner accentuates the eye contour followed by extra thick Moonbeam Mascara, both by Ultima.*

I thought I had a tiny, cracked plastic compact of grayish blue eyeshadow and three tubes of hypoallergenic mascara, all of which were so old the mascara had mostly dried up. That was the extent of my eye makeup. I resolved to go to the drugstore before school started and buy a whole lot of new stuff.

"Isn't it about time for the news?" I asked, closing the magazine and turning to face Mother, who awoke with a little start from her light doze, ruffling the papers collapsed in her lap.

"What?" she asked bewilderingly.

"Why don't you go to bed, Mother?" I suggested.

"I will shortly," she said. "I just want to finish this section."

When I glanced at her again, her eyes were closed. Father was still watching TV. I had never seen the show before. This appeared to be the chase scene: two cars were racing around winding mountain roads and the one car was shooting at the other car. I was slightly proud that I didn't watch much TV, having discovered that it was too easy to waste an entire evening in front of the TV set. My schedule at my parents' home was all disrupted, though, and here I wasted so much time. It would be good to get back to the routine of teaching.

One of the cars on the television set plunged off the road and burst into flames. I hoped this presaged the end.

I got up and went into the kitchen and drank two glasses of

water. Supposedly this was good for one's health. Then I went to the green room and looked at my tiger. It was almost five to ten, the wall clock said. *Tiger, tiger burning bright in the fields of the night,* I recited in my mind. I thought I would call this picture either "Burning Bright" or "In the Field of the Light" because it was not night in my picture.

I walked back into the pink room, picked up *Glamour,* and turned once more to "Facial Fix-Up." The last time I had used my dried out mascara was when I went out with Arnie Rinehart, and I should not have bothered.

Georgiana told me he was the most eligible bachelor in town. "I hate to discourage you so much," she said, "but he's the best of the lot. There's a couple unmarried farm boys and the short twirp at the bank, but Arnie's got 'em beat. Until Ken Anderson got married last summer, he was our heartthrob. I went out with Ken once, but Arnie's never asked me out."

"Why do you stay here, Georgiana?" I asked her.

"Well, I'm not looking for a fella yet," she said. "I've got plenty of time. I'm only twenty-five, and the livin's pretty good here. I'm savin' up. Besides, I don't think I ever told you, but my momma and daddy live real close over by Walnut Hill, and my daddy has cancer." Before I could say anything, she continued, "He's been dyin' for five years now. The talk of the whole town. Nobody can understand why he just doesn't shove off, but he keeps hangin' in there. To see him, you'd think he should be six feet under. After college I thought about joinin' the Peace Corps or something like that, but I just can't go far away with daddy so sick. I'm gonna stick around here at least one more year after this one, and then I'll look for a job in the vicinity. I figure after four years I'll need a change of pace. How 'bout you? Are you goin' to stick it out another year?"

"It's only September!" I exclaimed. "Who knows? Maybe they won't even offer me a contract for next year."

"Well," Georgiana said, "I hope you stay 'cause I've enjoyed gettin' to know you." It was so sincere I almost started crying. I'd never known anyone so genuine and unpretentious.

"Thanks, and I'm really glad you're here. You're about my only friend in this whole town."

"Oh, fiddlesticks! That'll change soon. Just wait 'til you meet Arnie Rinehart. If you'd join the choir, you'd meet him real soon."

"Singing's not my thing," I protested. "I just don't have a good voice."

"Oh, we don't care about your voice," she countered. "Edna Gebbersberger can't sing a note to save her life, and folks tell me she's been in the choir for forty years."

After I reiterated the fact that I was not going to join the choir, I said, "Besides, I'm sure you'll devise some sneaky way of introducing me to Arnie."

Eventually I did meet our town's most eligible bachelor after church one morning. (I'd started going to church because it was something to do in Mount Morris and I thought it made me look better.) Arnie was fairly good looking up close: dark hair, fairly dark skin, regular features, blue eyes, a little mustache, and slightly taller than me. I hadn't been able to see how piercing his eyes were from my place in the pews. Georgiana had told me he was in his late twenties, but he looked a little younger. A month passed and I saw Arnie only when I went to church and at a few football games. We exchanged greetings and that was all.

One night in October after Junior High MYF (I'd gotten talked into being a co-leader), Georgiana told me excitedly that she had a date for Friday night. So Arnie had finally asked her out, I thought jealously.

"It's a guy from college," she said. "He went to seminary after we graduated. His family lives in Hawkeye Creek. We dated a little bit at school, nothin' much. We belonged to the same Bible study group. He called me up last night and said he's goin' to be home for the weekend for his brother's wedding and would we like to get together Friday night. He's got a church in Missouri. We exchange Christmas cards, that's all, so it was a real surprise when he called."

"That's terrific! What are you going to do?"

"Go out to dinner at the Holiday Inn in Jasper and then probably see a movie."

"Sounds like a good time. What's his name?"

"Jeff Neibuhr."

I told her that sounded like a nice name and suggested that we should go out shopping and find a new outfit for her to wear. As we walked up the church stairs from the basement fellowship hall, we agreed on a departure time for our shopping trip tomorrow. When we stepped outside, Penny McDaniel and Robin Dahlberg were sitting on the steps. It was very still and a little chilly.

"Hasn't your ride come yet?" I asked them.

When Penny indicated that her father was supposed to pick them up and he didn't appear as we waited with them, I offered to take them home, telling Penny that we'd go directly to her house while watching all the cars we passed on our way. As the four of us piled into my Toyota, I asked Penny where she lived and headed in that direction.

"I like your car," Robin said.

I thanked her and Georgiana asked them if they were excited about the upcoming junior high dance. They muttered "kinda" and "a little" and then Robin asked, "Are you going to bring dates to the dance?"

We both laughed. "If we could find any to bring!" I said. Then

I turned to Georgiana and asked, "Do you think Jeff could drive up from Missouri for our big dance?"

"You have a boyfriend, Miss Wylie!" Robin practically shrieked.

"Oh fiddlesticks! See what you've started," she accused me. "They'll have me gettin' married by Christmas the way rumors fly in this town!"

"What's he do in Missouri?" Robin asked.

As Georgiana answered, Penny interrupted to point out her house. I pulled into the driveway of a long ranch, and Penny exited, thanking me for the ride home. As we waited until she got in safely, I saw her mother wave to us from the front door. Then I headed for Robin's home, following the directions she was supplying while she asked about Jeff, "Do you get to see him very often if he lives in Missouri?"

"Not much," she said. "I saw him a couple times over the summer."

"Really!" I insinuated. "Christmas cards? That's all?"

"Oh fiddlesticks, Sara! You're makin' a mountain out of a mole hill."

Robin asked, "Don't you have a boyfriend, Miss Keatson?"

After I told her I didn't, she said I should meet her neighbor. "He's gonna be a doctor. He's extremely good-looking and very polite and smart."

"Who's that?" Georgiana asked, and I was surprised because I thought she knew everyone in town.

"Steven Clonet."

"Oh," Georgiana said, "you mean Sam Clonet's son?"

"The man who has the cleaners?" I asked.

"Yeah," Robin answered, and then she pointed out her house and the Clonet home across the street.

After she got out and thanked me, I headed toward our

apartments and thought about what dresses and skirts I needed to have dry cleaned. Then I asked Georgiana if she wanted to come in for some coffee or tea, and she said yes.

As we drove through the small business district, there was not much activity: a few cars in front of the bar and Legion Club. On my street, I saw the dim light in my bedroom window, symbol of my dislike for walking alone into a dark apartment at night. I was always glad when Georgiana stopped by after MYF or a football game.

"Forgive the smell," I said as I unlocked the door. "I've been finishing that bookcase. Make yourself at home. I'll turn up the thermostat to get some more heat."

I quickly closed the opened windows in the living room, which still smelled of varnish, and then went to put water on to boil and to take my contacts out. Georgiana had followed me into the kitchen and was taking out two cups. It was crowded in my tiny kitchen with newspapers scattered around and under the bookcase, making maneuvering difficult. I told Georgiana I was just going to have a glass of water, and as soon as her tea was ready, we moved onto the sofa in my living room. Then she began, "I've been tryin' to think of some way to get you together with Arnie Rinehart."

"Oh, Georgiana," I pleaded, "please don't! I really don't care in the least for him."

"Well, I know it can get pretty lonely here, male-wise. Things got so bad for me last year, I dreamed I had a date with Ken Anderson, and he was an engaged man!"

I laughed out loud. I had already imagined making love to Ken Anderson, and now he actually was a married man! I couldn't tell this to Georgiana, though. It was hard to reveal my feelings; probably I would always be reticent. Instead I commented on how Ken and his wife were a nice couple. Then Georgiana told me that this would probably be Ken's last year here, as the basketball team had peaked two years ago and he was sure to want a bigger school. I suddenly realized that if Ken Anderson left we might get a new basketball coach who was young, attractive, and unmarried. Things looked better.

"Your bookcase will be real nice," Georgiana said. "Where are you going to put it?"

After I indicated the wall where I would place it, she said, "That'll be nice. I just love the way you've decorated this place. You should have been an interior designer."

I thanked her for the compliment, and we talked for a few more minutes about teaching and Jeff before she announced that she had to get home. She lived in a basement apartment only two blocks from me and consequently she could walk home.

The next evening we found a new dress for Georgiana in Jasper. Because she made most of her own clothes, Georgiana thought forty-three dollars was too much to pay for a dress, but I convinced her it was practically a bargain. I also made her buy some new shoes, even though she complained about the heels.

"How tall is Jeff?" I asked.

When she told me he was about six-three, I assured her she would have nothing to worry about.

"But they'd be so impractical for school," she whined.

"You don't have to wear them to school," I countered. "You can just wear them to church and on special occasions like this date with the guy you only exchange Christmas cards with!"

She laughed and then paid for the shoes. I felt just a little proud about the part I had played in urging her to buy them. During her date with Jeff, he surprised her by asking her to accompany him to his brother's wedding, thus making Georgiana's weekend the most glorious she had had for ever so long.

It was December before Arnie Rinehart asked me out. I had

given up on having any dates the whole semester, but Arnie sat with us at a basketball game one Friday night, and before I knew it, I had accepted his offer to see a movie the following evening.

I spent quite a while getting ready for my date. I even gave myself a facial in the morning and wore mascara, but my efforts were worthless. Arnie Rinehart turned out to be one of the dullest people I had ever met. Later, though, I thought perhaps I had grown into a dull person and Arnie Rinehart merely seemed insipid because I too was that way. And so I cried a lot after my date with Arnie. Thankfully, Georgiana seemed to accept the fact that we had not clicked, and I saw Arnie only from several church pews' distance during the rest of December.

Mother got up from her chair and announced she was going to bed, reminding me again about our departure time tomorrow. The weatherman was predicting cold temperatures but no snow. He wrote in the temperatures for various cities on a large map of the United States. It was 72 degrees in LA, 69 in Dallas, and 74 in Miami. As soon as the weather report was finished, Father got up and said, "I'm turnin' in too. You want the TV on?"

I told him no and that I was going to bed soon too.

"Good night, sweetie pie," he said. "I love you."

"I love you too. Goodnight."

When he had shuffled out, I picked up *Glamour* and put it back in the magazine stand. I shelved my high school yearbook, fluffed all the pillows, and turned off the lamps. Without the TV on, I could hear water running through the baseboard radiators.

I walked into the green room to look at my tiger once more. I was tired of him. I would finish the sky and color a few of the plants, finish as quickly as I could to start on a picture for the baby. This tiger would definitely go into my "sell" pile. I had five oils, two watercolors, and an acrylic in the sell pile—everything

I disliked. What I liked I kept for myself or gave to my family or friends. For this Christmas, I had sent Natalie the first abstract piece I had ever done. She hadn't called or written yet to say if she liked it. I gave Georgiana a floral watercolor, and she was elated. For my parents, I did an oil painting for the pink room. "Those are the cutest piglets I've ever seen!" Mother had exclaimed.

Having reaffirmed that I liked painting on china almost as much as I did painting on canvas, I gave Melly, Emma, and Susan holiday-themed plates. Earl Hamlin had not thought much of my china painting, though. "It's so easily chipped or cracked or broken," he told me at the senior art show. "Art should have as much permanence as it can. Stick to your oils and watercolors. You do some really good work."

Later on I thought of many things to offer in rebuttal: *Nothing in the world is permanent. Everything is subject to manmade destruction. Think of the paintings and stained glass lost during the world wars. Jackson Pollock's paint is breaking away from the canvas he smeared it on. It's on the floor underneath his paintings!*

My only consolation in this confrontation with Hamlin was that Marie, Andy, Kathy, Simon, and Jinbok had all been present. Because Hamlin never offered the slightest bit of praise to anyone, I became somewhat of a celebrity around the art department for the last few weeks of school. "Why didn't I think of painting on china?" Simon had mocked me. "Anything to get a reaction out of The Great One." Of course, everyone knew he was just jealous.

It was glorious being signaled out, even if this tiny bit of fame was short-lived. Since Kevin Percy and I had once spoken of Hamlin's failure to give praise, I thought it unusual that Kevin never mentioned anything to me. He was a strange boy, definitely not my type.

I looked down at the blue I had mixed. Mother had said it was jungle blue. Perhaps it should be night in the picture, darkness to enhance the burning tiger? No, that might be too ominous since I wanted a Rousseau-like quality, cerulean blue.

I switched off the light and went to my old bedroom where I turned on the dresser lamp, took off my glasses, and looked in the mirror. I seemed plain and middle-aged tired. There was a red rim on my nose where the glasses had been. When I frowned, I seemed very unattractive.

Natalie announced at Thanksgiving that she felt forty-five years old. "In college it seemed as if we were always pretty summer girls in wind-tossed sundresses," she stated, "but six months later we're just like haggard housewives. And we're not even married! God, I've never felt so old!"

"Things'll get better, Nat," I tried to say convincingly, aware of how my own abysmal existence tempered my optimism.

"But not by me sitting on my butt being a go-fer girl all my life," she declared. "Ready for the big shock, Sara dear?"

"You're marrying a millionaire?"

Crushing her cigarette in an ashtray I had hunted up, she got up from my rocker, took a brush out of her purse, and began attacking the wind-knots in her thick dark hair. If she truly had some big surprise, maybe it was good that I'd invited her to spend Thanksgiving at my parents' home.

"After much thought, I decided I'm going back to school to get a practical-type degree which will allow me to ascend the ladder of success," she stated.

When I asked her what kind of degree she was aiming for, she told me, "A degree in business."

"You've got to be kidding, Nat!" I exclaimed. "You've never even taken ANY business courses!"

"I know," she said sadly. "It was a mistake at the time. I blame it all on poor counseling. Unfortunately, that means that before I can get accepted into an advanced degree program, I've got to take Accounting I and all that crap."

"So are you, like, going to go to night school?"

"Oh Sara, Sara, Sara," she whined, "you are so perspicacious. How the hell else could I go back to school?"

"Oh Nat, Nat, Nat," I crooned back to her, "will you stop treating me like a naïve child? I just asked a simple question."

"Sorry, it's an old habit." And then she said, as cynically as she could, "I forgot: you're a professional."

I got off my bed and walked over to the mirror where I could see my reflection as I spoke to her. "I was almost ready to feel sorry for you, Natalie," I said determinedly, "but, damn it, no one can feel sorry for such an insensitive person. Have you ever tried to be genuine in your life?"

She had stopped combing her hair, and we stood staring at each other in the mirror.

"What's genuine, Sara?" she asked. "How can you tell the dancer from the dance?"

"Please don't quote poetry. I've read Yeats too. Don't you understand what I'm trying to say?"

"Oh, I understand. You were being rude, Sara dear, and it's not in your nature to be so. But it is in my nature to be a rude, hateful, inconsiderate crazy ol' bitch. I thought you accepted me for what I am."

"Anyone can declare that they're the most obnoxious of human beings on this earth, Nat. You've got no monopoly on being a bitch. In fact, it's a rather easy role to play. But I don't think it's that easy to be genuinely kind and to treat other people with a little respect."

Turning around to face me, she said, "Well, you've certainly garnered a lot of courage in the last few months. That was quite an eloquent little speech, and I even feel a trifle ashamed. Forgive me, Sara."

I stood looking into her huge brown eyes, conscious of how big her skin pores and nose were, trying to determine if she was sincere. Finally I smiled. "Tell me some more about your plans for school," I said.

I thought about going to school in the summer. Georgiana had already asked me what I was going to do this summer. Emma had written that she hoped to go to Europe, would I like to go with her? She was going with a girlfriend from grad school: *She reminds me so much of you. Very artistic and creative. I know we could have a blast together. First, we'll do London, then Paris, then?* I calculated that if I didn't eat in February, I sold five pieces of art, and my parents loaned me about $300, I could go. I needed to lose weight anyway. I had gained almost three pounds in the last four months. I was getting fat. I got down on the floor and did twenty sit-ups, finally falling back exhausted.

"May we join you?" they asked.

"We'd be delighted," she said. "I'm Emma Aspen and this is Sara Keatson."

"My name is Hans," the light-haired one said.

"And I am Frederick," the darker one said. "You two are American?"

We nodded.

"Do you like our country?" Hans asked, and we told them very much.

"You are students?"

"Recent students," Emma said. "I just finished my master's degree. Sara is a teacher."

"Your English is very good," I said. "Are you students?"

"Yes," Hans said, "we study engineering at university. What do you teach, Sara?"

"I teach art in an elementary school, first grade through sixth."

"That must be interesting," he said.

Emma and Frederick got up to dance, and Hans asked me to dance.

Afterwards we strolled back to the hotel, his arm around me.

"Thank you for a wonderful evening," I said, "It—"

"You talk too much," he interrupted. Then he tilted his head and with his hand drew my face toward him. He kissed me softly. Then he put his arms around me and I put my hands on his shoulders. We kissed again, and again, and again.

A pink crayon had crisscrossed the top of one of the tree trunks, and another trunk top had bold orange and lots of yellow. A third was purple. I was puzzled.

"Is this what you wanted?" Greg asked.

"That's very colorful," I said, "but it's not what **I** want; it's what **you** want. You're the artist. I know we talked about seasons of the year, so what season is it in your picture?"

He thought for a minute. "Everything but winter," he answered.

I almost began to question him, but then suddenly I realized he'd taken me at my word. "Okay," I said, "that's really cool. I love those colors. What are you going to call your picture?"

"You want to know what my word was?"

"No, not right now. I just wondered if you'd given your picture a title."

"Do you want me to?"

"No," I answered, "not if you don't want to."

Marie did only abstracts; she had not done anything representational since high school.

"You'll move farther and farther away from it," she told us, "especially once we get out of here and away from Hamlin's oppressive gaze and the legacy of Wood."

"I don't care shit what Hamlin thinks," Simon said. "In fact, that's about all he thinks anyway—shit."

We laughed, all of us unaware that the door had opened and Hamlin had appeared in the doorway. He took scant notice of us and walked to the coffee pot.

I don't think he heard you, Marie mouthed to Simon, as we watched Hamlin pour a cup of coffee and walk out of the lounge. "I've got to go study," Marie said softly, crushing her cigarette and rising.

"Me too," I said.

"Come on," Simon said, "do you think he heard me?"

"I don't think so," I said. "Even if he did, what does it matter?"

"'Cuz, hey Simon," Marie observed, "you don't care shit what he thinks."

Jinbok walked in and came over to us, saying, "Everybody's leaving? Just when I come?"

"We've got work to do," Marie told him, but Simon got up, put his arm around her, squeezed her shoulder, and told her she worked too hard. Then he began messing with her long auburn locks.

I started for the hall, pretending not to notice them. When I got to the doorway, I turned around and asked Marie if she was coming. Jinbok was pouring a cup of coffee, and Simon's hand had moved to Marie's posterior.

"Go ahead," she replied. "I'll catch up with you later."

I thought about how frequently unsatisfying art was when it was supposed to be uplifting. But perhaps that was because I concentrated too much on product, the end result. I wondered if my students enjoyed it. That was the point anyway: to enjoy the process of creating. I couldn't deny that sometimes it was enjoyable, but not always. Mostly I just wished I had finished. I was more like Greg than I thought. I was a fake.

"Only Mrs. Otto will give you trouble," Georgiana said to me. "She means well though."

Betty Crawford said, "She thinks that just because she has a college degree and most of the other mothers in this town don't, she's an expert on child psychology."

I was stationed in the gym close to the refreshment table. They put Mrs. Beech, the music teacher, and me in the gym because we didn't have classrooms. My normal niche was a table, some shelves, and a small desk hidden toward one back corner of the stage, but for Parent-Teacher Night I was moved to the gym floor to be readily visible. I'd placed a lot of the children's art work on the tables by me and on two easels I'd brought from home. I'd even put some sculptures they'd done on the surrounding floor. Mrs. Beech wore a gold treble clef pin on her cowl, and she had brought along catalogues of musical instruments in case parents of the fifth or six graders inquired about prices. She had taught at the school for about fifteen years.

I hoped, in vain of course, that one of the students' fathers was divorced or widowed. He would be young, melancholy, intelligent, sensitive, a lawyer perhaps. (I knew of all five of the town's lawyers and each of them was married and middle-aged or older.) Perhaps he would be a writer, someone who, having published three or four brilliant novels, had retired to this quaint community in the middle of nowhere. None of his neighbors knew he had stories published regularly in *The New Yorker* under different pseudonyms.

Of course, people like that did not exist in Mount Morris.

Because I had grown up in a small town too, I knew that when the young left their hometowns to go to college they rarely returned. Only those who did not go on to school remained or settled close by. There was a tiny influx of college graduates each year to teach, but other than employment by the school system there were few jobs in Mount Morris to attract the college-educated.

As I introduced myself and shook dozens of hands, I thought of the simulation exercise introduced in college education classes. Mr. B., one of your pupil's fathers, asks you to go to dinner with him to discuss his son's educational progress. You (a) eagerly accept, (b) ask if you can arrange a time at school to meet with him, (c) tell him firmly you're not interested in what he's got on his mind. I had always wished Natalie had taken el ed so she could argue why (a) wasn't a good choice. The fathers of Mount Morris, however, seemed to be happily married types. There were no Mr. B.'s; rather they seemed to be mostly faithful farmers in overalls and caps with seed company advertising.

From the corner of my eye, I saw Mrs. Otto bite into a huge donut and then exclaim, "Oh, look at that marvelous display over there! Come, doctor, we must go see."

Mrs. Beech was talking with the parents of a sixth grader about the virtues of a French horn, so I could predict my confrontation with the Ottos was to be solo. I greeted Mrs. Otto warmly as she came over, and she immediately began telling me how much Miles and Monica enjoyed art class. Then she called over to the refreshment table, "Ot, do come over here right now and meet the children's art teacher."

I smiled sweetly at Dr. Otto as he walked over, licking his fingers and wiping them on a napkin. As I shook his hand, he said, "Happy to make your acquaintance too." He was a balding, potbellied man whose vest looked as if it must have been dreadfully uncomfortable.

"Look at Monica's picture, Doctor," Mrs. Otto said, gesturing to one of the easels. "Remember what she said at dinner? 'Be sure to see my picture, daddy.'"

"Of course," the dentist said, studying Monica's crayon drawing.

"This picture is really very remarkable," I said, "for a second grader. Now where does Monica get her artistic talent? Do either of you draw or paint or dabble in something?"

"I'm afraid not," Mrs. Otto said. "My talents lie musically— hello, Mrs. Beech, we'll be over to chat in a moment—but of course I've always thought that the doctor here must have a trifle artistic bent because of his work casting molds for dentures. It's very exacting work, if you can imagine." I nodded in agreement and she continued, "Now Miles is terribly talented in music and math, but it's Monica who's really got the artistic gene."

I tried to counter with an upbeat comment about Miles' enjoyment of art, but she continued, "He is not always motivated to do his best, unfortunately. I think motivation has so much to do with it, don't you? The doctor and I have always tried to provide a home environment which encourages the cognitive and affective development of the children. So many parents just don't seem to care; they let their kids watch television all day long, and that's such a pernicious influence. The doctor and I closely monitor Miles' and Monica's television viewing, and we try to see that they're exposed to many different cultural activities. Why, both children could read before they started kindergarten. Miles, who's in the fifth grade as you know, recently tested out in the ninth stanine in reading. And oh, it frightens me what he does on standardized math tests! Of course, we've thought about sending him to a school where he'll be better challenged, but where would we send him and still see him frequently? I wouldn't dream of shipping off the children to a boarding school, but that's what one would simply have to do."

Throughout her speech, I nodded in agreement at what I thought were appropriate places. "It is an unfortunate predicament," I said sympathetically.

"The other day the Mrs. was saying," Dr. Otto stated, "that she wished Monica could take drawing lessons. I think you could get a little class of four or five girls together if you have an interest at all in doing it, care to make a little extra cash?"

"Yes," Mrs. Otto chimed in. "When Monica was five she took art lessons from a neighbor woman and she just loved it, but Mrs. Swansek is quite elderly and had to stop giving lessons. Do you know Valerie Swansek?" I shook my head negatively as she continued, "Well, she's really very talented but not in the best of health. More importantly, she knew how to motivate Monica. I'm sure LeeAnn Webb and Jenny Hansen would want to take lessons. And I just know if I talked to Liz Sampler she'd agree to let Whitney be in the class."

Then we talked about the possibility of using one of the classrooms at school, and I voiced my reservations since I didn't have a classroom of my own. Then I offered my apartment as a meeting place.

"That's very generous of you," Mrs. Otto said. "Let's try for the school first. Let the doctor talk to Mrs. Strom. He's on the school board, you know. Now Monica has Brownies on Monday after school, and she has dance lessons in Jasper once a month on Thursdays, so those days would be out. How are Tuesdays for you?"

I told her that would be fine, and she promised to "get the ball rolling." Finally Dr. Otto reminded her that they still needed to talk to Mrs. Beech. As she moved away, Mrs. Otto remarked, "The evening has just flown by, hasn't it?"

I looked at the clock beside my bed before I crawled in. It was

11:14, and tomorrow was the funeral. I rolled over on my side and put my hand on the empty pillow beside me. Mother had said Great Aunt Daphne was ninety-one. She was the mother of four, grandmother of eight, and great-grandmother of two. She had lived a "full life," as they say. She wasn't famous, but I supposed she'd been happy, although I'd been in her presence only about a dozen times. I felt no tears for her passing, which was a little strange since I usually cried buckets for characters who died in books or movies.

"I teach art," I said, "in an elementary school."
"That must be interesting," he said.

I was standing on my chair to reach art supplies on the top shelf when he walked across the stage to my corner spot. I had on a gray wool skirt and a silky-soft pin-striped blouse. I didn't hear him approach because Mrs. Beech was having the fourth graders for music on the gym floor, and they were singing "Green Gro' the Rushes Tho'" rather robustly.

When he said, "Excuse me," I was quite startled, and when I turned around I saw the herringbone jacket first, which was alien to Mount Morris, then the black turtleneck, and next the gray pants. Finally I found the penetrating blue eyes. He looked to be in his early thirties, with thick light brown hair and a charming smile. "You're Miss Keatson?" he asked.

"Yes."

"Coming down?"

"Yes," I said, accepting his proffered hand and stepping as daintily as I could manage off the chair.

"I'm Clark Merrick," he said warmly, looking directly into my eyes. "My son has recently started to school here. Noah Merrick? He's in second grade."

"Oh yes," I said, remembering the sandy-haired boy Betty Crawford had told me about. "I've only had Noah a couple times for art class because I only see each grade level once a week."

"Well, you've already made a hit with my son. He says you're the nicest teacher here."

I laughed nervously. "I'm just getting to know him, but he really seems to enjoy art."

"Yes," he said, "that's why I'm here. I understand you have a small class that meets twice a month, and I was wondering if you'd consider adding Noah to your group. He would really like to take art lessons, and from what JoAnne Otto tells me, you're doing a fantastic job with the group. And Noah plays a lot with LeeAnn Webb because she lives nearby, and so you come highly recommended from the Webb family also."

"It's really been more fun than work. I only have four girls right now: three second graders and one third grader. We meet twice a month on Tuesdays after school at my apartment, which works out really well since I live very close to the school. It's just a short walk."

"Sounds perfect," he said. "I know Noah will be excited. Of course, a lot of seven-year-old boys would think taking art lessons would be a pretty sissy thing to do, but he still wants to do it. Do you think his male classmates might give him a hard time about it?"

"I surely hope not," I said. "He seems like a really well-adjusted child. From what I've observed, it looks like he's already made lots of friends here in Mount Morris."

"Thanks for the encouragement, but I do worry a little," he said, turning his eyes away from me for the first time. "Noah's mother died in November. He seems to have adjusted fairly well because he knew she was very sick, but sometimes I wonder how much he hides. I do think, though, that he accepted her death because it meant an end to her suffering."

"I'm very sorry," I told him.

He turned to look at me again and said, "Well, I'm glad he can join your class. What sort of supplies will he need?"

I enumerated a basic list of materials and suggested an art supply store in Jasper that stocked everything, and then he asked me how I preferred to be paid.

"Why don't we let Noah come a couple times to see how he likes it, and then you can pay me. I charge four dollars a session, or eight dollars a month. Cash or a check is fine."

As he wrote in a small date book, he said, "Your fees are certainly reasonable." Then he smiled at me again, saying, "I hope I've not kept you from your work, but I thought it might be best to catch you at school, and I needed to stop by to see Mrs. Strom."

I told him I was glad that he had come and that I looked forward to Noah joining the class, and then we said good-bye to each other.

After school the next day I asked Georgiana if she knew anything about Clark Merrick.

"Haven't you heard!" she exclaimed. "He's moved back here from Denver since his wife died. He's living with his mother and goin' into practice with Doc Watt. The town's been after a second doctor for ever so long, especially since Doc Watt is gettin' up there. It's just a shame Clark Merrick's come under such unhappy circumstances. The little boy is cute, isn't he? And I heard the father's supposed to be real handsome!"

"He is," I said. "He came to school yesterday and asked if Noah could join my after-school art class."

"Holy hotcakes, Sara! Things are surely lookin' up!"

In the afternoon of the day Clark Merrick came to cart the children home, it started to snow delicately. They were gentle flakes that dissipated as they hit the cleared sidewalks. As we walked to my apartment, Monica Otto and LeeAnn Webb caught them on their tongues.

That afternoon we made old-fashioned Valentines. As they were cutting and pasting, I rolled out some sugar cookie dough I had stirred up the previous night and then let the children cut out heart shapes. After the cookies had baked, we decorated them with white frosting and red-colored sugar, and I made a pot of cocoa.

Afterwards I decided he came deliberately early. The lesson was supposed to end at a quarter to five, but he arrived at four thirty as we were sitting around playing with our floating marshmallows and eating the cookies. When we heard the knock, Monica ran to the window and cried out, "Noah, it's your dad and it's way too early!"

"Your dad has carpool duty today?" I asked him, heading toward the door.

"Yes, miss," he said glumly.

At first I noticed how red his cheeks were and that it had stopped snowing and turned colder. Then I noticed how sad his eyes were despite the smile on his face. "Come in," I said. "We were just having a little snack, but I'll get the children ready to leave as soon as I can."

"You're early, Dr. Merrick," Monica whined, looking at her little pink vinyl watch. "We just sat down to eat our cookies. We still have almost fifteen minutes!"

"Grandma and I told you four forty-five," Noah said, a little angrily.

"I'm sorry," he said. "I had to get gas before I came and it didn't take me as long as I thought it would."

"Would you like some cocoa?" I asked, hoping to placate matters. "Please come in and join us."

"Yes, do come and join us," Monica insisted. "My mother will be terribly upset if I get home too early."

Smiling at Monica's grown-up stance, I took his coat and told him I'd be right back with some cocoa. I hurried into the kitchen and took the skim off the remaining mixture in the double boiler. It was still warm but awfully chocolatey. I stirred it with a spoon, poured it into a cup, and tossed a marshmallow on top.

When I returned, the children were showing him their Valentines. "Here's your cocoa," I said, moving my cup away and saying that I'd get another chair. I hurried to my bedroom and brought my desk chair to a corner of the table.

"These are the cookies we made," Monica was saying proudly. "You may only have one or else you'll ruin your appetite for dinner."

"They look delicious," he said, reaching for one.

"My mommy makes Valentine cookies," LeeAnn said, "except she puts on pink frosting and makes lawyers with strawberry filling in between."

We told her they sounded wonderful, and then Noah asked LeeAnn to whom she was going to give her Valentine.

"I haven't decided yet," she said. "Maybe I'll give it to my grandma like you're going to do."

"I like yours the best, Miss Keatson," Noah said. "Who are you going to give it to?"

He caught me by surprise and I was sure my face colored slightly. "Gee, I don't know," I began. "I really just made it as an example. Maybe I'll send it to my mother."

"It's too bad you don't have a fiancé to give it to," Monica said. "Every Valentine's Day my father gives my mother a gift because that's when they got engaged. One year she got diamond earrings!"

"Cindy Lou Morgan gets a Valentine's Day present every year," Whitney Sampler said. "And she gets an Easter present and a Fourth of July present too."

"That would be terribly boring," Monica commented. "No wonder she's so spoiled."

"This is really a nice apartment," Dr. Merrick said to me.

"Thanks, but I'm afraid it's always a bit messy on Tuesdays for class."

"Did you see all her paintings?" Monica asked him, and he looked around the combined living and dining area, commenting on how nice they were.

"Oh, you haven't seen all of them!" Monica said. "You simply must see all of them." She got off her chair. "My mother won't mind if I'm late. Besides, it won't take that long."

"Well," he said, after taking another sip of cocoa, "I do need to get all of you home, so let's try to hurry."

"First, the kitchen," Monica said, leading all of them there while I began organizing the dishes while she led them through the rest of my small apartment. After the tour, I helped them put on their coats, boots, mittens, and scarves. They left in some confusion, with Valentines hurriedly collected for dispersal, swallowed by the cold and darkening evening.

He called late the following night; it was almost ten o'clock. When I heard his voice, I felt a tingle in my lower abdomen. He called to apologize about being early and to thank me for the work I was doing. That was all. The rest of February passed without my seeing him.

On March 1st he called again, earlier in the evening. He wanted to know if I would consider doing some pictures for his office, which he was going to redecorate. He asked if I could stop by the medical clinic and discuss it with him. We agreed on four o'clock the next Monday afternoon.

The building itself was old; 1897 appeared on the pediment.

Inside it was rather dark and stark with old-fashioned vinyl couches and chairs, a dusty artificial orange tree, a small wooden table and chairs for tiny patients, and the usual magazines: *Time, Good Housekeeping, Progressive Farmer.* On the wall were a Norman Rockwell calendar, courtesy of the drug store, a common-looking black and white clock whose cord extended to an outlet by the floor, and two horrible prints of nature scenes, undoubtedly purchased at Woolworth's. One depicted a fawn drinking from a small pond in an autumnal wooded setting; the other showed a barn on a hill in the spring. It was quite a contrast to Dr. Otto's office, which was bright, modern and inviting, with cute little needlepoint pictures of teeth and toothbrushes and big floral prints on the walls.

After I told the receptionist I was there to see Dr. Merrick, I sat down to wait. There were three other people in the office, none of whom I could remember seeing before.

When Clark Merrick walked into the room, I stood up to greet him, noticing how professional he looked in his white coat. "I'm so glad you could come," he said softly. "It isn't much, is it? I think Doc Watt had it the same in 1930."

"It reminds me of the doctor's office in my hometown," I said. "It's not exactly an uplifting environment. How much work are you going to do?"

"As much as I can," he said, almost in a whisper. "Naturally, Doc Watt sees no need for redecorating whatsoever, so I've got to take it gradually. I'm going to start with my office and examining rooms. This will have to come last."

"I see," I said, somewhat thankful that I would not have to work around the fawn and the barn.

"I'll show you the rooms I'd like your help with," he said, leading me first to examining room 1B. "The first thing I want to do is paint the walls." He took a paint chart from the small countertop opposite the examining table, telling me he'd like my opinion about choosing a color.

"Anything would be in improvement over institution green," I joked, noting that the current wall color matched that of the walls of my dorm freshman year. As we stood looking at the paint samples for a few seconds, I asked, "What choices have you narrowed it down to?"

"What do you think of one of the blues, like this one?" he asked, pointing to 3609, Calamine Blue.

"Oh, that's nice. I think that would be quite attractive; blue is a very relaxing color."

"Do you like 3609 or 3607 better?" he asked, and when I answered 3609, he agreed and circled that color. "Now I have another examining room just like this windowless one. Do you think I should paint it blue too or choose some other color?"

I thought of how we had named the rooms in my parents' home and said, "I'd paint it a different color."

"That's what I thought too. What do you think of this yellowish color?"

"That's nice," I said. "It's not too bright and not too dull. I think it'd be a really good choice."

"Okay, we'll go with this one," he said, circling 2202, Buttercup. "Now, do you think you could provide me with some pictures for these rooms?"

"I sure could try," I said, "but I'm afraid I don't really know what your tastes are like. Do you like abstracts or representational paintings? Do you have any favorite artists?"

"That's hard," he said. "I guess I'm not really that educated about art. I just know that if I see something I like, I like it. I liked all the artwork you had in your apartment."

"All right," I said. "Maybe I can do some things and then you can decide if there's anything you'd like. Right now I do have a few pictures in my 'sell pile,' as I call it, and you could look through those."

"That'd be great. Now let me show you my office. It's in really bad shape right now, but I'm getting new furniture and everything. Its only redeeming feature is its size."

He led me into a large room which contained an old battered desk, two dining room chairs with soiled needlepoint seat cushions, a dusty plastic plant, a TV tray piled with papers, and a small metal bookcase. Leaning on top of the pile of papers was a framed diploma. Books and file folders were stacked on the floor in five heaps. I could see there was a picture on the desk, but I could only see its back.

"Please sit down," he said, taking the other dining room chair rather than the folding chair behind the desk. "The furniture should arrive at the end of the month. I'm getting a new desk, a desk chair, a credenza, some bookcases, two upholstered chairs, a small sofa, two end tables, and two filing cabinets. As soon as I get it painted, Joe Huzak's going to lay carpeting, which will be a tan, brownish-flecked color. This is the material for the sofa and chairs." He reached for a swatch on his desk. It was a small plaid with browns, beiges, and cream colors, with just a touch of rust.

"This will be really nice," I said. "What color are you going to paint the walls?"

"That's what I'm undecided about. Do you think I should go with an off-white, say 1009, or something darker, like this?" He pointed to 1015, Raw Umber.

"What about the window treatments?" I asked, noticing that the drapes were drawn, that they looked dusty and hung poorly, and that the entire office seemed rather gloomy.

"I definitely have to do something about those drapes," he said.

"Well, in that case, maybe I'd go with a color like 1012, which has a little bit more of a cream tone, and you could get drapes or blinds around the color of 1015 and maybe get a cornice in your upholstery fabric, since you have such high ceilings."

"Yes, I like that suggestion." He smiled warmly at me and circled the paint numbers I had mentioned and made notations by them. "I'm going over to Fred's Supply tomorrow and will have them mix these colors. I took down the dimensions of all three rooms so Fred can recommend the right amount. I'm hoping it can't be that hard to paint."

"I guess not," I said. "But do you really mean you're going to do it yourself?"

"I have to. Fred told me Al Samuels does painting, but he's off to Michigan to visit his daughter, and I want to get it all done as soon as I can because the new furniture will be here soon. It's been too long anyway. I'm planning to do it this weekend." He hesitated and smiled. "Which brings me to my next request. Would you be free to help me paint?"

"Oh," I said, tingling and feeling myself blush. "I've never painted before, I mean walls, unless it was a mural because my mother does murals and sometimes I help her. I really don't have any experience just painting walls."

"I figure two heads are better than one," he said, "even if we're both novices."

"Unfortunately, I've got a commitment for Saturday. The church youth group I work with is taking a field trip, but I'm free on Sunday, so I suppose I could try to help you out. Anything to make the world a more beautiful place—that's my motto."

"And this place can stand a lot of beautification," he said, laughing. "I'm glad you can make it. How's 7 a.m. on Sunday sound?"

I gasped, "Oh, you plan to get an early start!"

"You bet," he said, rising from his chair. "I'll swing by and pick you up about seven? And thanks again for coming today. Have a pleasant evening."

After I left the office, I went to Webb's and bought lettuce, carrots, and apples. I passed up the frozen pizzas, crackers, and potato chips. I had lost five pounds in the last two months, but I wanted to make sure I would look smashing in a pair of jeans on Sunday. So I exercised every day, bought some new make-up, ate no junk food during the field trip, and went to bed at 9 p.m. Saturday night. However, I could not fall asleep until Clark Merrick had seduced me.

He was a little late on Sunday. It was 7:20 when Noah appeared at my door, and the boy sat between us on the way to the office. "Guess what?" Noah said. "Grandma's bringing us a picnic lunch at noon. And we're going to eat it inside!"

I told them that would be fun, although I'd been looking forward to being alone with Clark Merrick at the clinic.

The morning was uneventful. After we opened windows and moved some drop cloths around, he had me apply masking tape around doorways and baseboards in the buttercup examining room, while he worked in the calamine blue one. Then he had me put primer around the masked-off areas. To do this took longer than I thought it would. Noah ran between the two rooms to keep us company. I was on the last wall when I heard a deep voice.

"I'm done," he said. "Here, let me finish while you rest." He dropped down beside me and we were very close to each other, so close that I could smell his after-shave despite the strong odor of the paint. I gave him my brush and then stood up.

"The smell's not so bad in the waiting room. That's where Noah is now, and my mom should be here soon."

In the waiting room, I found Noah playing with Tinker Toys. While I was helping him build some kind of tall structure, Mrs.

Merrick appeared at the entrance. I glanced at the wall clock, and it was almost noon.

Her appearance made me nervous. She was a tall, gray-haired, smartly-dressed, aristocratic-looking woman whom I'd seen before in church but had never paid any attention to until I'd met her son, whom I'd never seen at church. I felt as though Mrs. Merrick might see me as an obstrusive element in her family or that she was measuring me against her son's deceased wife. I was glad that one of the first things she said was, "Noah, go and tell your father lunch is here."

As she began taking covered containers out of a picnic basket, I told her I'd help her as soon as I washed my hands. Then I picked up my purse and headed toward the small bathroom down the hallway, but father and son were already inside washing their hands. He told me they'd be through in a minute. As I waited near the doorway, the smell of the soap wafted toward me, competing with the strong odor of the paint, and I heard laughter.

"I'm famished," he said when they emerged, and as they walked by me, he came so close to me my pelvic area tingled again. I knew I was attracted to him sexually, but I also thought I might be falling in love. I hardly knew anything about him, but I sensed he was the man I wanted to spend the rest of my life with.

After I washed my hands, I inspected my face, reapplied lipstick, and brushed my hair, happy that I looked good. I felt a thrilling sense of anticipation, an over-powering need to be near Clark Merrick. It was a sensation I'd never experienced before.

Lunch was pleasant. We sat on a large patchwork quilt in the reception area where all the windows were open. There were turkey and ham sandwiches, potato salad, fruit salad, and chocolate cupcakes. Mrs. Merrick seemed like a nice woman, certainly more educated than most of the women in Mount Morris. I found out that she had been a school teacher and was widowed three years ago. When she left after lunch, she took Noah with her. I had thought she would have wanted her grandson there as a buffer between us, but she said he had to go home with her so that we could finish.

After they left, we worked hard for about an hour more, each of us in the separate examining rooms, and then we moved into his office. Yesterday he had painted around all the woodwork and the walls with primer, so he was ready to apply paint with a roller on the walls. Painting his office took a little over two hours, but we were together and chatted a little while we listened to music on a radio. He asked me about my family, college, and what I was going to be doing this summer. I asked him a few questions about college and Denver, but I felt awkward when I sensed the conversation called for him to talk about his late wife. We finally finished painting and cleaning up about 5:30. We were both tired, but the rooms looked good. I could tell he was very proud of what we had accomplished.

We were fairly silent on the way to my apartment. I tried to start a conversation, but he didn't seem to want to talk. When we got to my place, I said, "Well, Dr. Merrick, thanks for showing me that I can paint on something besides canvas."

"Do you think you could call me Clark?" he asked as he turned off the engine. "You're going to ask me in for a glass of wine, aren't you, Sara?"

"Sure," I mumbled, wondering if things were now happening too fast.

Inside he seemed a changed person, much more joking and relaxed than in the car. I only had one bottle of Merlot, but he said that was fine, uncorked the bottle, and poured us each a glass. Then he sat down on my sofa, while I took my glass and sat on the adjacent chair. As he leaned back and stretched out his feet, he reminded me of Ryan O'Neal in his *Love Story* role. As high schoolers then, my girlfriends and I had fallen in love with the handsome, slightly mysterious yet confident Oliver.

"It's probably silly of me to redecorate that old office," he finally said, "since I don't really plan on staying here the rest of my life." He paused when I said nothing. "But for now it's the best thing to do. I was so depressed in that place. I think my patients got sicker as their illnesses were being diagnosed."

I smiled at this humor and said, "It will really be nice when you get your new furniture and some pictures on the walls. Do you want to look at some of my artwork now?"

"I do want to do that, but I'm exhausted now. Plus I've got surgery tomorrow at eight, and my mom's expecting me home for dinner." When I said I understood, he continued, "So why don't we go out for dinner next Saturday night? I owe you at least one nice dinner for all the work you've done, and then maybe we can look at your work before or after we eat?"

"Okay, that sounds nice," I said, almost unable to believe that he'd actually asked me out.

"Good. What time's convenient for you? Say around six-thirty?"

I told him that would be fine and he put down his wine glass and rose. After I walked him to the door and he turned to say good night, he looked at me so intensely I thought he was going to kiss me. But instead he merely opened the door, saying, "I've heard there's a new French restaurant in Jasper. Imagine a French restaurant in the middle of Iowa! Anyway, if you don't mind driving that far, that's where I thought we could go."

I told him that would be great and we said goodnight.

The week passed slowly. Twice I gave myself facials, and every night I ate lots of fruits and vegetables and did exercises on my living room floor. On Thursday, Georgiana and I went shopping in Jasper, and this time it was I who bought a new outfit, a real silk dress in a rosy color and some new heels. She was just as excited as I was, although I attempted to hide my feelings.

On Saturday I tried to take a nap in the afternoon, but my mind kept rushing from one imagined romantic scenario with Clark to another. After I cleaned my apartment, I started getting myself ready, allowing plenty of time to do my nails and apply my makeup. When I was ready, I looked in the mirror and liked what I saw. I assessed my strong points: slender figure; small, straight teeth; well-proportioned facial features. With the eye makeup, my eyes looked as intriguing as any in a Maybelline ad. My face was glowing, blemish-free. I was as pretty as Emma Aspen, twenty times prettier than Natalie or Susan McHenry.

Clark arrived about 6:40. He wore gray pants, a white shirt, and a navy blue sport coat; his tie was burgundy. I couldn't help contrasting his appearance to that of Arnie Rinehart, who had worn a plaid leisure suit when we went out. After we had greeted each other, Clark said. "You look very lovely."

"Thanks," I said, probably blushing. "You look nice too. Would you like some wine before we go?"

"I made the reservation for 7:15, so we'd probably better take off. I'll take you up on your offer after dinner, if that's all right?"

"Sure, that's fine," I said, picking up my purse and coat. When we were in his car, I asked him if he'd had a busy day.

"No, I was in the office in the morning. I stopped out at the hospital for an hour, and then I did a few errands, came home, washed and waxed the car."

"It looks good," I commented, noticing the shine on the hood and remembering how Dan Weaver had always spiffed up his car before he took my sister out.

"So what did you do today?" he asked.

"Oh, nothing much," I said, realizing with panic that all I'd done was get ready for this date. "I straightened up around my apartment, did a little schoolwork, and that's about it."

"I don't imagine life's very exciting for a young girl in Mount Morris."

I laughed nervously. "Well, it's not exactly Des Moines, but I like what I'm doing, I've made some good friends here, and I've got a job in my chosen field, which is more than some of the people I graduated with can say."

"Did you just graduate from college last year?"

When I told him yes, he said, "I thought so. Sometimes you look even younger though. If you'll pardon my asking, how old are you? You weren't some sort of child prodigy?"

"Oh, no! I'm twenty-two, but I'll be twenty-three in May."

He laughed. "Oh, that doesn't just **sound** young; that **is** young."

I couldn't think of anything to say in reply and I didn't want to ask him how old he was, so I just remained silent, and he didn't say anything either. Finally I asked him what college life was like at a small school like Grinnell. After he told me a little about his undergrad years, he asked me if I'd studied under the famous painter at the U.

"I took two courses from him, but I thought he was just average as an instructor."

"From what I've read, Hamlin's pretty respected as an artist though," he said. "I think I read an article in the *Register* a few weeks ago that said he sold a painting for a quarter million."

"That's right. I read that article too. That's not a bad little price. I always felt that Hamlin never encouraged any of us too much because he realized that not every artist makes the kind of money or achieves the level of fame he has." I wanted to tell him what Hamlin had said about my work at the Senior Art Show, but I felt it would be bragging. So instead I said, "What constitutes art is very difficult to define. What constitutes great art is probably even harder. A lot of artists could do what Earl Hamlin does, but only he's going to make a quarter million on one painting."

"Yes," Clark agreed, "I understand what you're saying. It must be a little frustrating for you."

"Oh, not really. I mean I'm sure you're willing to pay at least a quarter mil for one of my paintings for your office?"

He laughed at my joke and said, "If that's as cheap as they are, I'll take half a dozen."

We talked light-heartedly for the rest of the way to Jasper and throughout dinner. Clark didn't mention his deceased wife or talk much about himself at all. He wanted to know more about my family, and so I ended up telling him a lot about Melly and Dan and the upcoming baby, and my parents and the farm and the fact that this was the first year we didn't have pigs. The food at La Table de Pierre was delicious, and the atmosphere was quiet and unhurried, and we ate by candlelight with a pink rose bud gracing our white-clothed table.

After dinner we walked briefly around some park in the city, but the weather was chilly, so we didn't stay out long and then drove back to Mount Morris. Throughout the evening, Clark hadn't touched me except to help me with my coat, and this reserve baffled me. I supposed it had something to do with his deceased wife and the facts that this was our first date and I was Noah's teacher, but even Arnie Rinehart had held my hand as we watched the movie he'd taken me to.

On the ride home, Clark was silent again, so we rode for a long while without talking. Once he mentioned something about Noah and school, and then he brought up my age again. "So you said you're going to be twenty-three in May. Noah is a Taurus too. His birthday is the seventh. When's yours?"

After I told him the 19th, he said, "Golly, twenty-three! That is young!"

Then he was silent for a while, and I felt as if he was rejecting me because of my age, but I didn't want to say anything like, *One of my grandfathers was nine years older than my grandmother,* so I remained silent too. Then about five minutes from Mount Morris, he asked, "I suppose you have exciting plans for the summer? I bet you're going to see that fellow you've dated in college who's now in law school or business school or, possibly even, med school? You haven't told me who's waiting in the wings for you."

"Oh, there's nobody," I said, encouraged by the fact that he wanted to know. "Really. I'm either going to school or to Europe this summer."

"When I asked you before, you said you hadn't decided yet what you were going to do, but don't you have to make some plans?"

"Sure, but it's still early. I just really haven't decided yet. I think I'll probably go to school, but as I mentioned, a good friend from college is begging me to go to Europe with her. Air fare's pretty expensive, though, and hotels and food, so I'll probably start on my M.F.A. degree. I also want to visit my parents, and as I told you during dinner, I'm going to spend a few days with my sister either before or after the baby comes."

"You'll have a pretty busy summer."

"Do you have any special vacation plans?"

"No," he answered, "not right now. I need to get away, and Noah needs a vacation. Maybe we'll go to southern California for a couple weeks: go to Disneyland and Knott's Berry Farm and the San Diego Zoo. We'll probably spend a lot of time enjoying the beach, just relaxing, you know."

"That sounds like fun. I'm sure an eight-year-old boy would love that sort of vacation."

Then we didn't talk for the rest of the way to my apartment, and I was beginning to feel that the evening would end sadly, that Clark Merrick had reached the conclusion that I wasn't the sort of woman he wanted to see again, and my fear was confirmed when we pulled in front of my apartment and he said, "Look, it's pretty late, and I've got to be at the hospital early tomorrow, so I'll take a rain check on that glass of wine, if it's okay with you. And I can look at your paintings another time, if that's all right with you? I mean, I don't want you to think I'm not interested in buying some, because I am. I may not be able to afford a quarter million, but I do like your work, Sara. It's just that it is rather late."

"Yes, it is," I agreed, although I really didn't. "You can see them another time."

As he turned off the car engine and came around to open my door, I felt numb inside, as if I'd lost Clark Merrick forever. After I unlocked my apartment door, I turned to face him and he seemed a million miles away from me on the stoop.

"I had a really nice time," I began. "Thanks again for the wonderful dinner and evening."

"It was my pleasure," he said. "We'll have to do it again sometime. Take care."

"Yes, you too. Goodnight."

"Goodnight," he said, going down the steps.

As I got ready for bed, I felt too disillusioned to cry. What had I done to turn him off? I thought I'd conversed intelligently and I'd listened carefully when he spoke. I'd made no gauche movements. I'd used mouthwash and deodorant. He'd even complimented my appearance. Oh well, there are other fish in the ocean, I told myself. Other fish . . . .

I didn't hear from Clark Merrick for the next two weeks. With the prospect of a relationship beginning with him, I'd earlier said no to Pete Byron when he'd called about the ski trip to Colorado over Easter, so when Good Friday and a short break from teaching arrived and no call came from Clark Merrick, I telephoned my parents and told them I was coming home for the weekend. Melly and Dan were with his parents, so it was just the three of us and, for me, a lazy, boring, miserable Easter weekend.

I didn't see Clark Merrick anywhere around the town—not the grocery store or drugstore or cleaners or five-and-ten. I tried fantasizing about other men, and I even thought seriously about going to Europe with Emma, but somehow Clark Merrick always ended up back in my dreams.

And then suddenly he did materialize in church the Sunday after Easter. I'd never seen him there before, although I'd seen his mother and Noah a few times. I was already seated when the three of them walked down the center aisle to a pew about five rows in front of the one I was sitting in. I sensed he had not seen me, and I sat through the service wondering if he'd speak to me or what he'd say.

When the choir marched out for the recessional, Georgiana gave me a knowing stare, but I tried to appear nonchalant. After the benediction, I joined into the flow of people merging toward the door and managed to get outside the church quite a bit before the Merrick trio. Then, just as I was about to start down the steps toward Georgiana's car, a woman named Flossie Sandhurst, head of the Christian Education Committee, flagged me down to ask me if I'd be interested in teaching Vacation Bible School. She told me the dates, the grade divisions, the theme, and the teachers she already had secured. By the time I told her I wasn't sure I could do it because I'd probably be in summer school by then, the Merricks had emerged from the church. I told Mrs. Sandhurst I'd get in touch with her as soon as I could, and when I turned around, all three of them were right behind me.

"Good morning," I said.

Clark seemed embarrassed to see me, but they greeted me and Mrs. Merrick asked if I'd had a nice Easter. After I replied, I inquired of their Easter, and Clark responded that it was very nice. *So this is how it's going to be*, I thought: *making inconsequential small talk whenever we happen to meet.*

But then he said, "By the way, I got the furniture for my office, so I've really been keeping busy. Say, maybe after school I could drop by some afternoon and look at those paintings you have for sale?"

"Sure. I'm free any afternoon except Wednesday this week."

"How about Thursday? Around 4:30?"

"Fine," I said as coolly as I could. "Have a good day. I'll see you at school, Noah. Goodbye."

I looked forward to and dreaded Thursday afternoon. Would he ask me for another date? Would he give me some clues to understanding his behavior toward me? Would he tell me the words I longed to hear, that he was falling in love with me?

After school that day, I rushed home and hurried to straighten up my apartment and make myself as attractive as possible, but I ended up waiting for twenty minutes because he was late.

I had nine pieces I was willing to sell. I showed him each one, explained its medium, told him the title and price. He looked at them briefly, said they were all great, and asked me if I'd sell him eight of them. He wanted every one except *Tiger, Tiger Burning Bright*. I had sold two works once before, so I had an idea what a fair price would be, but I'd earlier tested my prices on Georgiana, who was used to scrimping and getting by on very little since she sent half her paycheck to her parents every other month. On the contrary, at least twice a month, a ten dollar bill came in a letter to me, and Mother always said the same thing: *Enclosed is a little something for art supplies.* But even Georgiana had found the prices reasonable. "Fiddlesticks, that's nothin' to pay!" she'd told me sincerely. When I figured out the total amount he owed me, it came to a little under four hundred dollars.

"You're not being fair to yourself, Sara," Clark said. "They're worth much more. I've been to galleries a few times, and I know I could never find anything this good for what you're asking."

"No, really," I began, "they're not even framed, and framing and matting cost a lot. By the time you get through doing that, you'll—"

"Gee Sara," he interrupted, "I can afford it. Don't you know doctors make a lot of money?"

"Well, uh, whatever," I mumbled as he wrote out a check, asking me about framing them as he did so.

I told him about a shop in Oto Creek that did good framing and about a do-it-yourself framing place in Jasper that would cost him about half as much. I told him cloth mats might look nice with the oils and mixed medias and that he'd probably want to put glass over the watercolors and that double or triple mats would look good with them. I suggested that he could take along his paint, fabric, and blinds samples when he chose the frames and mats. I showed him examples of pieces I had in the apartment. I even expected him to ask me to accompany him for the framing, but all he said when I was finished was, "Well, I just don't have time right now to build frames myself, so I'll probably take them to that place in Oto Creek. You've really been a lifesaver in helping me get my office redecorated, and I want you to know that I appreciate all the time you've taken on my behalf. Is it all right if I take the pictures with me now?"

"Sure," I said, "I'll get the phone number for that framer in Oto Creek and then help you get them into your car."

And that was it. When I went back in and looked at the clock, it was 5:20. The whole encounter had taken less than forty-five minutes. My only consolation was a check for eight hundred dollars. I looked at his strong, legible signature on the check and wished I knew what he was thinking. Compared to the agony of being in love with Clark Merrick, even the money, more than I earned in a month, was little relief.

I didn't see Clark Merrick that weekend nor the following week. I was depressed at the thought that he'd gone out of my life for good, and to make matters worse, I got sick. It started on Sunday morning when I woke up. First my ears hurt, and by evening my throat did too. I was sure I was in for a bad cold. By Monday night I was stuffed up and sneezing. On Tuesday afternoon the stomach aches and chills began, and I vomited Wednesday morning. I told myself I'd keep going to school until after Wednesday, knowing how difficult it would be for a sub to handle my classes, but I didn't make it through Wednesday. After I vomited in the teachers' washroom, Mrs. Strom insisted on sending me home, and I had to agree with her.

I stayed out of school on Thursday and Friday, sleeping most of the days. I drank tons of water and orange juice and took cold remedies, but I still wasn't recovered. On Friday night, I was bundled up in a blanket, lying on the sofa in my nightgown and wool cardigan watching *The Incredible Hulk,* when the phone rang.

After I said hello, I was shocked to hear Clark Merrick's voice. "You sound awful."

I told him it was just a really bad cold.

"Noah said you weren't in school yesterday or today, and I was concerned about you."

"I'm getting better. I'm sure I'll be back in school next week."

"I'd like to make sure of that. I'll see you in the office at 9 a.m. tomorrow."

"No, really," I protested, "I'm through the worst of it. I'm taking Contact and drinking lots of fluids and getting plenty of rest. I really—"

"Sara," he interrupted, "I want you in the office at nine sharp tomorrow. It upsets me when people don't take care of their health. If I don't see you there tomorrow at nine, you can expect this doctor to make a house call."

I reluctantly agreed to be there and hung up, feeling oddly ambivalent about his call. I disliked him for showing all this concern now after giving me the brush-off, and yet I liked him for caring about my health, for the sincerity in his voice, for his insistence that I see him. I immediately wondered if he'd want to examine me, and if I'd have to undress and lie on an examining table, the thought of which filled me with sexual excitement. I remembered how Emma told me how much fun it was to "play doctor" with Marc.

Before I went to bed that night, I generously dabbed moisturizer on the tender areas of my nose. In the morning, I shaved my legs and rubbed strawberry-scented lotion over my body after my shower. I put on my prettiest pink bra and panties and selected a V-neck top to wear with my jeans. I deftly used makeup to cover up the slight redness on the sides of my nose. I was in his office at 8:55.

When the nurse called me to one of the examining rooms, it was not one of the two Clark and I had painted.

"Doc will be right with you," she said, and before I had time to comprehend what was about to happen, white-haired Doc Watt hobbled into the room, introduced himself, asked me about my symptoms, and told me to hop up on the table. While I sat there, he looked inside my throat and felt my neck. While he listened to my heart with his stethoscope, I could only wonder why Clark Merrick wasn't doing it. Then Doc Watt checked my throat again, said it was good I still had my tonsils, and wrote out a prescription for "somethin' stronger than Dimetap."

"I think this will help," he concluded. "Get plenty of rest and take the pills as directed. Now scoot on home and take care of yourself."

I walked out of the examining room and office more disillusioned and angry than I'd ever been. Hadn't Clark Merrick said **he'd** wanted to see me? Where the hell was he then? I had gotten all dressed up and come out for a two-minute examination when I should have been at home resting. Now I had to go to the damn drugstore and wait for the damn prescription to be filled.

I just couldn't understand Clark Merrick. I tried to tell myself it was stupid to keep on loving him, but as disgusted and perplexed as I was with him, I couldn't stop fantasizing about him.

I spent the rest of Saturday stuffing myself with Georgiana's homemade chocolate chip cookies, and on Sunday I didn't get out of bed until eleven and didn't bother to take a shower. That was why I didn't open the door when the bell rang a little after five.

"Who's there?" I yelled from my spot on the couch.

"Clark Merrick. I just came by to see if you were better."

The hell I'm better with all your help, I thought. I got up and went to the door but didn't open it. "Yes, I'm much better, but I'm not dressed and I look a mess and I was trying to get some rest, so I'd rather not open the door now. Goodbye."

"Goodbye. Take care!" he yelled.

To hell with your care, I thought.

I went back to school on Monday, and the routine of teaching helped me to keep my mind off Clark Merrick. Only Noah's presence was a reminder of his father.

Then Clark surprised me by calling late one Wednesday evening after MYF. He wanted to know if I'd like to see a movie on Saturday night.

"I'm sorry," I lied, "I have another commitment."

"Oh? Sure, I understand. Well, good to hear you're feeling better."

The next Tuesday he came to pick up the children after art class. By now I sensed that maybe he was interested in me, but because he'd hurt me in the past, I wanted to play hard-to-get. Give him some of his own medicine, I reasoned, resolving to be as reserved as I could.

"May I talk to you a minute?" he asked, while the children were gathering up their things.

I told him sure and he suggested we do so in the kitchen. Once there, he began, "School will be out soon, and the year's just been going by so fast we've hardly had time to talk."

"Well, your schedule is pretty busy," I said, looking directly at him.

"How would you like to go out to dinner this Saturday night? I heard there's a great new Mexican restaurant in Jasper."

"Sorry," I lied, "but I'm going to spend the weekend with my sister and brother-in-law." The moment I said this I told myself I was a fool and that I desperately wanted to go out with him, but the proud, stubborn, afraid me had spoken first.

"Doctor Merrick," came Monica's voice, as she entered the kitchen, "we're all ready. Goodbye, Miss Keatson."

"Well," he said, as we walked toward the front door, "I hope we can make it another time."

You're running out of time, I thought. *I'm only going to be in this town for a few more weeks.*

After they left, I started crying. I hated myself for refusing his invitation. I thought about calling him up and saying that my trip to my sister's had been cancelled, but I was too scared and too mad with myself for the foolish falsehoods. Then I worried about his seeing my car parked by my apartment over the weekend and knowing I'd lied. Maybe I could pretend they came here, I thought, but then their car would be out front. Maybe I could pretend they came to pick me up. What a mess I'd made by telling that idiotic lie when I wanted more than anything to go out with Clark Merrick!

I told Georgiana I had a lot of schoolwork and spring cleaning to do over the weekend and was going to shut myself at home until I got it all done. One lie had led to another, and I really hated lying to Georgiana. I kept my drapes closed all day on Saturday and until about five on Sunday. I didn't venture outside once, not even to get my mail. It was another miserable weekend, but I had only myself to blame.

On Monday I felt good just because the weekend was over. I started thinking positively about the men I would meet at summer school. When I saw Noah Merrick in the hall, I thought about how much older his father was than I. He had to be in his early or middle thirties. When I'd be a perky Mary Tyler Moore forty, he'd be an aging fifty-something.

Then that evening everything changed.

The doorbell rang a little after 5:30. I was listening to Walter Cronkite and eating some cheese and crackers. When, after putting on my shoes, I opened the door, there was no one there, but when I looked down there was a lovely little basket sitting on the step. It was white wicker and had real white and yellow daisies entwined around its handle; the contents were individually-wrapped pieces of fudge and divinity and flower-shaped spritz cookies. There was no card or note to identify the sender, and when I peered around the neighborhood, there was no one to be seen. I was about to go inside when Noah and Clark appeared from behind the tall lilac bushes in my neighbor's yard.

"I bet you can't catch us, Miss Keatson!" Noah yelled.

It was a moment of truth: to run after them with wild abandon or to be reserved, rooted, and miserable. They stood there to the side of the bushes staring at me. I stood rigid, unable to reach a decision.

"Come on, son," I heard Clark say, and they started walking up to my stoop.

When they reached the large concrete step I was standing on, I felt afraid, as if what I would say in the next few seconds would alter my life forever. But I hid my intimidation under a calm guise. "It's a very lovely May basket," I said. "Thank you very much."

"It's for a special person," Clark said, "and Noah's favorite teacher."

"You are," the boy said sheepishly.

"But you didn't follow tradition, Miss Keatson," Clark said. "You're supposed to run after us to try to catch us and kiss us, right?"

I felt myself blush uncontrollably and I laughed nervously. "You had quite a head start" was what I finally said.

"We're right beside you now," Cark said, as if challenging me.

I wasn't going to kiss him, but I bent down and gave Noah a kiss on the top of his head.

"Want to help us deliver Noah's May baskets?" he asked. "Then we're going for hamburgers at the Dairy Queen. How can you pass up a gourmet treat like that?"

"Please, Miss Keatson! Please come!" begged Noah.

I happily said I would, grabbed my sweater and purse, and locked my door. Inside Clark's BMW, which he had parked a few blocks away, were boxes with Noah's May baskets. They were homemade out of multi-colored construction paper with a flower decal in the center of each handle. They appeared to be filled with small packets of M 'n' M's and Tootsie Rolls.

"Grandma never had so much fun," Clark said when I commented on how nice they looked. "Actually, it was a family affair. What night did we begin working on them? I think it was Wednesday."

When Noah told him that sounded right, Clark mused, "Yes, yes, had to give up Farrah to cut and fold construction paper."

"Quite a sacrifice," I replied.

We stopped first at Marsha Johnson's house and Noah made the first of 34 deliveries. It was fun to watch him put each basket down, ring the doorbell, and then scoot away to stop to watch the discovery. When a girl answered the door, he would yell challenges to her and then take off running to the car.

When we pulled up to LeeAnn Webb's house and Noah got out and went up the long drive, Clark moved over to me and said excitedly that he thought Noah had a crush on LeeAnn and he wanted to see what would happen here. "Look, he's hesitating," Clark said to me. "Let's make things fairer." He reached around me and locked the backseat door and my side, coming so close to me that I could smell his after-shave.

When Noah reached the car and couldn't get in, he started yelling at us to unlock the doors. LeeAnn was getting close, so Noah ran around to the other side of the car, but Clark quickly slid away from me to lock the doors on the other side. We were laughing, and so was LeeAnn, who was going around the car now, so Noah took off toward her house. While she began chasing him around the big front yard, Clark moved over again close to me to get a better view of the pursuit, and I thought I was going to faint. Finally, Noah fell down on his knees in sweet surrender; LeeAnn ran up and gave him a kiss on the cheek.

"Ah, victory!" Clark said, sighing. "I wish I could hear what they're saying."

"They're probably doing more panting than talking after all that running," I commented.

Then Noah walked to the car, Clark unlocked all the doors, and Noah fell exhaustedly into the back seat, protesting, "Gee Dad, why'd you lock the doors?"

"You needed the exercise. Besides, I figured you wouldn't mind being kissed by a pretty girl like LeeAnn."

Blushing, Noah pleaded, "Promise you won't lock the doors anymore."

Clark agreed and we delivered the rest of the baskets, getting lost a couple times when we had to locate farms. We ended our adventure at the Dairy Queen, and Clark suggested that we take our food to the park across the highway. We followed this plan, and everything seemed to go wonderfully. As soon as Noah finished eating, he wanted to go down the slide.

"All right," Clark said, "but be careful. We'll be over as soon as we're finished."

The boy ran off, leaving us awkwardly alone. While I was trying to think of something to say, Clark seemed content enjoying the beauty of the evening. Finally I said, "This is the first picnic I've ever been on without bugs. It's pretty great." As he agreed with me, I took a long sip of my malt, both of us watching Noah climb the slide.

"I hope you're free on Saturday," Clark said as he watched his son swoosh down the curved metal. "We've got a lot of work to do for Sunday."

I gave him a puzzled look. Sitting across the picnic table from me, he now directed all his attention toward me. "How about if I cook dinner at your place Saturday night? I'm really a culinary whiz. And then we can plan the games for Sunday."

"Sunday? Games?" I asked.

"Oh, I guess I forgot to tell you. Noah and I were talking about it before we came to your place. On Sunday my mom's backyard is going to be invaded by 35 seven and eight year olds. In other words, it's Noah's birthday party. And I would really love if you could help me through it?"

"Well," I said, hesitatingly, wondering if Clark Merrick only saw me as cheap labor when he needed help with something.

"I know 35 kids sounds like a lot," he interrupted, "but Noah insisted we invite them all. Sara, I'd really appreciate if you came over to help with the party because you're so good with children and my mom's old enough that I don't want to overtire her. Also, I would really like to see you Saturday night. And I lied. I'm not a very good cook, but I can manage steaks, baked potatoes, and salad. So, what do you say? Give me another chance?"

After his words had come out, we were both aware that he was trying to apologize, although it had obviously come out subconsciously. "Okay," I said. "I've got a really free weekend coming up, so that will be fine."

"Great!" he exclaimed, his handsome face bursting into a smile. "Now let's go down the slide."

Noah was sitting at the top when we reached the big old slide, and he yelled, "Catch me, daddy," while he pushed away. Clark caught him at the bottom and swung him up into the air, causing Noah to shriek with delight. After Clark put him down, Noah said to his dad, "Now it's your turn. I'll catch you."

Clark climbed the slide, and when he got to the top and sat down, he shouted to us, "Okay, get set! Here I come!" Then with a big push he came rapidly down the sloping curves. All Noah could do was watch him fly by and take a running land at the bottom.

"That looks really slick," I said when he came back to join us.

"You'll see when you come down," Cark said. "You're next."

"Oh boy! Miss Keatson's going down the slide!" Noah yelled to the deserted park.

"Hey, wait a minute," I protested. "I've got on a skirt."

"Excuses! Excuses!" Clark teased. "Come on, you're going down." Noah took me by the arm and pulled me to the steps. "We'll catch you at the bottom," Clark said.

I started climbing up, conscious of the fact that Clark was at the bottom of the steps watching the movements of my posterior, the ever-increasing revelation of my legs. When I got to the top, I glanced down at him and said, with a touch of sarcasm, "Enjoying the view?"

"You bet."

After this exchange, I felt embarrassed because I had never before initiated repartee with a man about the sexiness of my body. I sat down as daintily as I could at the top, tucking my skirt underneath me. Clark had walked to the end of the slide to join Noah and now he hollered at me to come down.

"It's been years since I've been on a slide this high," I said. "I think maybe they're illegal in most parks."

"Come on down," he said. "I'll catch you." He opened his arms toward me. "Just give yourself a little push."

"Okay. Here goes nothing. Get ready!" I pushed myself away from the very top and went rapidly down the smooth, worn gray metal, the momentum blowing my hair back and my skirt up. At the bottom I felt Clark's strong hands grasp my waist as he simultaneously hoisted me up and braced me from going forward. As I landed, I couldn't help putting my arms around him, and I felt his face next to mine and his lips brush against my cheek in a soft kiss. It all happened so fast that we were apart again in a second, and I was still catching my breath and blushing, sure that Noah had not seen anything.

"Wasn't that fun, Miss Keatson?" the boy asked.

"Wow!" I exclaimed. "That's one fast slide!"

"Do it again," Noah said, but I assured him that once was enough for me.

"One more time down the slide, kiddo," Clark told his son. "Then we've got to go home and see who's brought **you** May baskets."

Noah ran around and climbed to the top. "I'm going down on my tummy," he yelled.

"That's how you'll come down the next time," Clark said to me.

"Sure, you bet."

Clark caught him again and swung him into the air, saying, "I'll carry you fireman's style back to the car," as he swung Noah over his shoulder.

"Please, please daddy! Let me down!" Noah screamed in delight.

After a few steps, Clark let him down and Noah immediately spied a small merry-go-round, insisting we had to go on that before we left. I got on the platform while Clark and Noah started pushing and running. Then Noah jumped on while Clark continued to make the wooden disc spin faster and faster. The greens, whites, and russets of the park whirled around me until I closed my eyes. Suddenly I felt Clark beside me, and when I opened my eyes, I saw he had hopped on and was gripping the bars around me, panting loudly. Quickly he looked up at me and smiled, and his smile was full of happiness and love. We continued to spin around, smiling at each other, as the merry-go-round gradually slowed and the trees, shrubs, white posts of the bridge over Peach Creek, and across the highway Ivan's Standard Oil, the Dairy Queen, and the Larson Brothers' Implement all stopped flowing into each other and became separate entities in our eyes.

"That was fun!" Noah declared. "Let's do this tomorrow night too."

We laughed as we walked toward the picnic table and then car. On the way to my apartment, Noah told me all about the planned festivities for Sunday and what he wanted for this birthday. He was genuinely thrilled when Clark told him I would be there too. "It's going to be the best birthday I've ever had!" he stated.

When we arrived at my place, Clark thanked me for helping

them to have such a fun May Basket Day. "I'll give you a call later," he said, "and we'll get things set for this weekend."

I walked to my apartment in ecstasy, feeling certain that this May was going to be the most wonderful month of my life.

He called the next evening to ask if he could come over about six on Saturday. He told me not to prepare anything, that he'd bring the entire meal.

That week the weather turned warm, and I sunned myself after school on Thursday and Friday. I bravely confided to Georgiana that Clark Merrick was coming over to prepare dinner at my place.

"Holy cow, Sara!" she exclaimed. "I just knew he was interested in you. And he's so handsome and nice and comes from such a good family. After you delivered Noah's May baskets with him, I just had a hunch somethin' was brewin'."

"How'd you know about that?" I asked in surprise, and then I felt a little shame because I hadn't mentioned last Monday to Georgiana.

"Oh fiddlesticks, Sara, you have to know about small towns! You know how it is."

"Yeah," I agreed. "So are we sleeping together yet, or maybe we're secretly married by now?"

"No, no, I haven't heard anything like that," she reassured me. "Your reputation is very good, and he's very respected in this town. Most people will agree there's been enough mournin'. I think most of the town gossips find your romance with him, you know, sort of morally uplifting."

I had to laugh at that assessment. "Oh, Georgiana, what would I do without you!"

I spent all day Saturday getting my apartment cleaned, dashing out to buy a small gift for Noah, and grooming myself. I was ready thirty minutes early. The table was set with a lovely bouquet of white and purple lilacs as a centerpiece, a gift from Georgiana, who roomed in a house whose yard had a row of beautiful lilac bushes. The odor of the flowers infused the room with their lovely, romantic scent. I debated about using candles, and finally decided against it on the assumption that candlelight was too overtly romantic.

Before Clark arrived, I spent several minutes admiring myself in the mirror. I had on a favorite white sundress which made my skin seem more tanned than it was. My long brown hair was softly curled and shone in the sunlight with glints of honey colors. My face was clear and vibrant with newly-applied makeup. I liked my reflection.

Carrying two big paper bags from Webb's, he arrived exactly at six and went straight into my kitchen with me following. "I turned on the oven fifteen minutes ago, like you said to do," I told him.

"Good, I've got the potatoes. The master chef will just put them in."

Then he began taking out the rest of the dinner: a wrapped package which went into the refrigerator, a pint of mint chocolate chip ice cream, which went into the freezer, a bag of greens, also stashed in the refrigerator, a loaf of French bread, and finally several small bags and containers which Clark said were all for the salad.

After he put one of the containers in the refrigerator, he added, "The key to a successful salad is to get everything ready ahead of time so you don't have to wash and chop and grate at the last moment. That way we can sit down and talk and enjoy this excellent chilled Chardonnay."

While he opened the bottle, I got two wine glasses. When I put them down on the counter in front of him, Clark said, "I forgot to tell you that you look really nice tonight."

"Thanks. So do you." After I had said that, I thought it sounded both pushy and corny, but Clark didn't react. He filled the glasses, handed me one, picked up the other, and began a toast, "Here's to charming company and what's sure to be a superb dinner and wonderful weekend."

After our glasses clinked, we headed into the living room where Clark sat down on the sofa and I took the chair next to it. I began asking him about tomorrow's party. He told me more details, and I told him about several games the children could play, most of which were suggestions from Georgiana, who taught fourth grade. After we finished discussing Noah's party, Clark leaned back on the sofa and was silent. I tried to think of something to say, but my mind was blank. Just as I was about to make a comment about dinner, Clark startled me with a very unexpected question: "When are you leaving town for the summer?"

"Let's see," I began. "I think probably on the 26th or so. I want to visit my parents for a few days, and then my sister. My classes start in mid-June."

"I suppose you'll be anxious to be in a bigger town after nine months here."

"In some ways, I'll be glad for the change."

"I don't plan to stay here permanently, but for now it's the best situation for Noah."

"Yes, I know. You told me once before."

"Oh, I did? Ummm." He took his glass of wine from the cocktail table and leaned back again on the sofa. "The other time I was here you sat on that chair, while I sat over here. Let me be honest, Sara. I keep getting the feeling from you that you want to keep our relationship on a 'Miss Keatson/Noah's father' level. And for Pete's sake, if that's the case, then please be honest with me. I don't need your pity and your being nice to Noah just because he's a little motherless boy. If you've got some fellow from college who's going to propose to you this summer, then that's the way it is, but I wish you'd be honest with me."

For a second I was a little upset, but then I got excited because this was the first time Clark had broached the subject of a relationship between us. "All right," I began, "I'll be honest. First of all, you asked me once before if I had a boyfriend 'waiting in the wings' and I told you no, and that was the truth, and I don't know why you don't believe me. Second, as far as getting feelings from you, over the last three months I've gotten a lot of contradictory vibes from you. You say you'll call me, but you don't call. One moment something's great, and the next I don't hear from you for weeks. Remember when I was so sick and you called me up and insisted I had to come in and see you and I felt like hell, but I got myself to your office the next day, and then you didn't even show up!"

Clark leaned forward on the sofa and sat fingering his glass and staring at the wine. "I guess I've got some apologizing and explaining to do," he began. "First, I'm sorry I doubted you when you said you didn't have a boyfriend. I guess I got a little paranoid wondering about the competition. Second, I admit that I have vacillated a little, but I think it's mainly because this dating routine is so new to me, and I keep thinking about how young and beautiful you are and how you must have a beau somewhere who's going to sweep you away and out of my life forever. And I think about how much older I am than you are, and so I've worried about losing you before I even . . . . Well, I have a hunch that when you thought I wasn't interested in you, I interpreted that as meaning that **you** weren't interested in me. Does any of this make sense?"

I nodded. I really was beginning to understand.

"And about the time when you were sick," he continued, "I do need to explain about that. You see, I've been attracted to you ever since I met you at school that very first day. Remember when you were standing on that chair and I walked in to ask about art lessons for Noah? Gee, Sara, did anybody ever tell you you have the best damned legs in the world? Anyway, at first I was interested in you and attracted physically to you, but then as I got to know you, I began to see that you really are a wonderful person, but as I said before, I kept having these doubts that you'd ever be interested in somebody like me who's so much older, and I didn't always handle things well.

"When you got sick, I was really concerned. I started thinking more about you and decided that I wanted to pursue a relationship. Maybe I was even falling in love with you. But I guess I never communicated those feelings to you. I swear when I called you up, I meant to be in the office the next morning, but then the more I thought about seeing you there, I knew it wouldn't be right, you know, with all these feelings I have for you. As a doctor I took an oath to maintain a professional relationship with my patients, and I didn't want our relationship to be that of doctor/patient, so that's why I asked Doc Watt to see you. Do you understand what I'm trying to say?"

"I think so."

"Sara, I want to hold you, hug you, kiss you, make love to you. I don't want to be just Doc Merrick or Noah's father to you."

He fell silent, and I felt like going over to him, but I knew there was one more thing we needed to discuss. "There's something else we have to talk about, something we never talk about," I said softly, stopping because I didn't know how to phrase the subject.

"What's that?"

I hesitated but then said, "Your deceased wife." He seemed shocked when I said it, so I continued, "In all the conversations we've had, you've mentioned her less than a half dozen times. It's as if you can't talk about her. I wonder if you can't talk about her because you haven't come to terms with your grief."

He didn't respond right away, and I didn't know what else to say. My words had sounded like clichés, but it was the truth. Finally he shifted on the sofa and said, "I guess I don't talk about her because it's so painful. I loved her very much. We got married after college, and all through med school she was such tremendous support. I was so damned busy with all the studying and hospital duties that we hardly had time to enjoy each other. But I kept telling myself that after med school I'd have more time and we could do more things together. But being a resident didn't change things. Life just got more hectic, especially after Noah came along. After my residency was over and we moved to Denver and I joined a practice, there still didn't seem to be enough time, but I told myself that in a few years it would get better. But we didn't have a few years. Time is a great stealer, isn't it?"

I nodded and said, "Yes, I'm always wishing there was more time. But tell me more, Clark. I need to know; I want to know."

"Well," he started, "after the cancer was diagnosed, we only had two years, and for two years I have never felt more powerless. Here I was a doctor and I was useless. At first, of course, we thought we'd be able to fight it and win. She took all the chemo and radiation treatments. She'd get a little better, and then there'd be a relapse. For the last three months, she was so drugged to keep the pain at a tolerable level that she wasn't lucid very much of the time. God, it was awful to go into her hospital room and see her lying there. But she was brave up to the end. She kept a calendar in her room, and she told me she was determined to live through October. Even when she was almost comatose because of the drugs, she'd remember to ask what day it was. When November 1st came, I went into her room in the morning and she smiled at me and said, 'I knew I could do it. Now I'm going to live through November.' The next day she died."

Clark looked down and began crying, so I went over to the sofa and sat next to him and picked up the hand that wasn't blotting his eyes. I had tears in my eyes too as I put my other hand on his back.

"I haven't told anybody all that," he said.

"I'm so sorry," I said. "What was her name?"

"Merry Ann," he said as he sobbed. "Her parents spelled it differently, like the merry in Christmas."

After I rubbed his back and shoulders, I went into the kitchen and got a box of tissue, which I put down on the cocktail table. Then I went into the bathroom, blew my nose, brushed my hair, and just sat on the toilet for about ten minutes.

When I went back into the living room, Clark wasn't sitting on the sofa anymore; instead he was in the kitchen looking through the cupboards. He turned around and looked directly at me when I entered. "It's time to start the salad, that is, if you still want me to start the salad?"

I nodded affirmatively as I went over to him, putting my arms around him and giving him a hug. We held each other tightly and he began kissing my hair. "I'm sorry, Clark. I'm sorry about Merry Ann. Thank you for telling me." We just held each other for about five minutes until I finally asked, "What were you looking for?"

"A bowl for the salad."

"That I have," I said, pulling away to retrieve a large wooden bowl from a cabinet below the counter.

While he got the salad ready, I cut and buttered the bread. The steaks, already seasoned, went on the broiler pan into the oven. I poured more wine while he mixed sour cream with chives. We seemed to work as a team so that everything was ready at once.

Dinner was satisfying, and Clark talked more about himself than he'd ever had before. He told me about growing up in Mount Morris as the son of a judge, about college, about med school, about his father's death, and about his date to the junior-senior prom, which got us both laughing hysterically. In turn, I told him more about my family, especially about my mother with her part time job as a hospital receptionist whose real passion was doing murals. We talked about our childhood pets, friends, and activities. For the first time I saw Clark Merrick as a complete human being, not just a handsome man I was attracted to.

After dinner I was loading the dishwasher and Clark was putting leftovers away when the phone rang. "My hands are wet. Can you get it?" I asked him.

From what I could hear of the conversation, it was his mother calling about something at the hospital. After he hung up, Clark said, "Sara, I'm afraid this evening's going to be abbreviated, but let me call the hospital first."

While I started some suds to wash the broiler pan and salad bowls, I could hear his conversation: "Sally? Doctor Merrick. Could you put me through to Mrs. Olson?" Long pause. "Lavinia, this is Doctor Merrick. I hear that Vera Padrowski's there. . . . I see. How far apart are contractions?" Another pause. "All right, proceed as usual. I'll be there as soon as I can. Goodbye."

He walked over to the sink where I was scrubbing the broiler top and put his hands on my waist. "Don't fear," he said. "I've got a plan. As you probably heard, there's a woman in labor at the hospital. I've got to leave now, and it's a little after eight. If she has the baby fairly soon and there aren't any complications and I get things wrapped up there before midnight, would it be okay if I came back over for dessert?"

"Sure," I said, rinsing the pan with hot water.

"But if it's after midnight, we'd probably better forget it because tomorrow's not exactly going to be an easy day," he said.

"Right, we'll need all our energy to handle those 35 kids. Here," I said, taking the towel from him, "I'll dry these things. You need to get to the hospital."

"Thanks for understanding. I'll just leave all the containers here, if that's okay? Hopefully, I'll be back later tonight." He gave me a kiss on the cheek. "I'm sorry I have to go. It's been a good evening and I don't want to go so soon. I feel so good about having talked about everything."

"Me too. Now get going!"

He kissed me again, this time lightly on the lips, and then he left.

I finished cleaning up the kitchen, but it was only 8:30. I wished I knew if he were coming back. I turned on the TV but couldn't concentrate on the show. Finally, I took out my contacts, lay down on the sofa, and closed my eyes, telling myself I'd rest for just a while. I thought about everything that had happened that evening, and I felt so good because I was so much in love with Clark Merrick and knew that he loved me too.

Eventually I fell asleep and didn't wake up until shortly after eleven. There was still a little time. I got up, brushed my teeth, used mouthwash, and fixed my hair and makeup. I turned off all the lights I'd left on except one in the living room. I lay back down again and waited, checking the clock at about five minute intervals. Shortly before midnight, I got up, undressed, washed my face, and turned the bedspread down. He wasn't going to come, but it had still been a good evening, and there was the promise of more wonderful evenings to come.

On Sunday I didn't wake up until eight. I had had a restful sleep despite my anticipation for the day. I lay in bed for several minutes thinking about Clark. Then I hopped out of bed, got ready, and had a light breakfast.

It looked like a gorgeous spring day outside, and the newspaper said we could expect highs in the early 70s, so I decided to wear a pair of navy shorts and leave my sweater at home. I put on a navy and white striped shirt, leaving one more button unbuttoned than I usually did when I wore the shirt to school. I practiced leaning over in front of the mirror to see how much cleavage would show and decided it was just enough to be provocative.

Then I sat down at my desk and wrote comments for the watercolors my fifth and sixth graders had done. It was hard to concentrate on evaluating them, harder still to devise original comments for each student, but I told myself I'd feel good if I got this work done before the party. The coming week would consist mostly of evaluations, conferences, inventorying supplies, and preparing selected artwork for a summer show and for display in the school. I had done the portfolios of only one grade, so I still had five more grades to get through, and the prospect of so much schoolwork just when Clark Merrick wanted to begin a relationship seemed so unfair.

I was about half way finished when the phone rang and it was Clark. "Sorry about last night," he said. "The labor and delivery were difficult. It was a breech delivery, and the baby didn't arrive until almost two."

"I understand. The main thing's that the mother and baby are okay."

"Yes, they're fine, but I'm tired as hell. Actually, I just woke up now, so I guess I got about six hours of sleep, but it doesn't seem like it. I've got to start blowing balloons and helping my mom."

I asked him if he still wanted me about one o'clock or earlier, and he confirmed that one was fine and then added, "Gee, Sara,

I was going to start off by saying something sexy like I wish I was waking up next to you, and all I did was tell you about the delivery and how tired I am. I guess it's still hard for me to say the things I want to."

"I understand," I said. "Now start blowing up those balloons!"

After we hung up, I worked fast for about an hour, eating an apple and some cheese while I continued to write comments. Then I brushed my teeth again and put on my favorite shade of lipstick, China Red.

When I arrived at the Merrick home, a large square farmhouse with dark green shutters and a spacious, white-railed porch, Mrs. Merrick led me through the front hall to the kitchen and out the back door to a smaller porch and an enormous backyard, where Clark and Noah were taping down paper tablecloths. It seemed as if there were a hundred multi-colored balloons strung between the huge maple and oak trees. With Mrs. Merrick's blooming lilacs, pots of red and pink geraniums, and bright yellow marigolds, the roomy yard provided a festive, inviting atmosphere. As I greeted them, Clark threw me some tape and said, "The other three tablecloths are in that box. Can you and Noah finish putting them on? I've got to pick up some ice."

"Sure," I said, taking another tablecloth with a Peanuts characters motif. "Don't worry. We'll finish the tables and then I'll help your mother until you get back."

He left hurriedly, and when he returned we continued to work hard until the first guests arrived a few minutes before two. While Noah was with these classmates, Clark drew me aside on the patio and touched me for the first time that morning, putting his hands on my bare shoulders and kissing me softly on the cheek and then lips.

"You look marvelous and you've been marvelous," he said. "I'm sorry it's been so hectic. Do I look nervous? I'm so scared

Noah's going to be disappointed, and I want so much for him to have a great birthday."

"Relax, Clark. It's going to be fine. Noah is sure to have a wonderful time. From talking to him and your mother, I found out he's been enjoying himself all morning. It's been just as much fun for him to get ready for the party. And what could possibly go wrong?"

"Don't say that! I'd rather be delivering a breech baby than entertaining 35 kids for four hours!"

At this point our conversation ended when Mrs. Merrick brought at least ten more children into the backyard. The next two hours were really fun. The games we had planned went smoothly. Clark relaxed when he saw how much fun Noah and the other children were having. As he played and joked with the youngsters, he reminded me of a coach who's both cherished and respected by his team. We spent so much of the afternoon laughing that the time we had allotted for games flew by.

Then it was time for Noah to open his gifts. All the children sat on the grass in a huge semi-circle around Noah, and it seemed as if they enjoyed watching him open each present just as much as he did. Clark assumed a sort of "Master of Ceremony" role, handing Noah each gift and making witty comments to keep the children doubly entertained. After he handed Noah the last gift, he plopped on the grass beside me and whispered in my ear, "There's nothing to fear. All we've got left is food, and that's the part that's never given me any worry."

"See, I told you there was nothing to get upset about. I've got to go help your mother now," I said as I got up, and while I walked toward the house, I was certain Clark Merrick was following my every movement.

Inside her small but spotless kitchen Mrs. Merrick had food and plates positioned around a kitchen table. There were hot dogs, sloppy joes, potato chips, and carrot and celery sticks. The birthday cake was to be a surprise for Noah. It was on a serving cart in the dining room and would be wheeled out into the backyard after the children had finished eating. I took two pitchers of red Kool-aid out of the refrigerator and outside to the tables, where I began pouring as the children filed out with their plates of food.

Clark, Mrs. Merrick, and I didn't get a chance to eat, as we kept busy acting as suppliers of food and drink and then as coordinators of clean-up. Quickly it was time for cake and ice cream. Mrs. Merrick had made the cake, a very adorable Snoopy sporting eight candles, which Noah blew out successfully on one try. The children just finished dessert as parents began arriving to cart them home. A few children who lived in the neighborhood wanted to stay and play with Noah, but Mrs. Merrick scooted them out about six twenty.

Clark and I returned to the neighbors' yards three borrowed picnic tables and benches, took down the few remaining balloons which the guests hadn't claimed, tied up the garbage bags, and essentially got the yard and patio back to normal. Then Mrs. Merrick insisted we eat, and so Clark and I sat down in her cozy den in front of two TV trays. While we ate, we watched the last segment of *Sixty Minutes* and Noah played with some puzzles he'd gotten. Then I helped Mrs. Merrick do some dishes, although there weren't many because the children had used paper plates and cups.

When I returned to the den, which reminded me of my parents' pink room, *All in the Family* was almost over, and Noah and Clark were on the floor having puzzle races. I played with them for a while, and then Mrs. Merrick brought in cake and ice cream for all of us. After we ate that, we carried Noah's presents up to his room, which Clark told me had been his old room.

A twin bed with a navy blue bedspread was on the wall opposite the door, and there were a dresser, a desk, two nightstands, and several bookshelves of worn maple. Stuffed animals, books, and miniature cars, trucks, and John Deere machinery were everywhere. On the walls were posters of Colorado and two pictures Noah had done at school. We piled the new toys in one corner and then went back to the den where we watched more television until nine o'clock, when it was time for Noah to get ready for bed. Before Mrs. Merrick took him upstairs, he hugged me and told Clark that it was the best birthday he'd ever had and that he was happy I had been there too.

When they left the room, Clark smiled at me and motioned for me to join him on the sofa. I sat down close to him and he put his arm around my shoulders. "Your worries were completely unfounded," I began. "Everything went so nicely. I really had a great time too. Thanks for asking me to be here."

"I really appreciated all your help, Sara. I couldn't have done it without you."

"And you should be very proud of Noah. He's a really terrific eight-year-old boy."

Clark leaned toward me and kissed my forehead. With his free hand he reached for my right hand and held it. "When can I see you again?" he asked. "How's the coming week for you?"

I sighed, "Only the busiest of the entire school year. That and the next week."

"I've got a lot of appointments this coming week too. Doc Watt is leaving town on Thursday because his grandson is graduating from Luther next weekend."

"Next weekend is really busy for me too. My friend Georgiana is having a coffee Saturday morning for all the el ed teachers and staff, and I'm helping her with it. That evening is the Retired Teachers' Banquet, and I got talked into buying a ticket. And Sunday's Mother's Day."

"Oh gee," Clark interjected, "I'd forgotten all about Mother's Day."

I knew he was thinking that for Noah this would be his first Mother's Day without his mother. I was already planning what I would say to Noah when his class made Mother's Day cards this coming week. I reassured Clark that I'd already thought about this art project and about Noah and that I'd be there to suggest he could make a card for his grandmother. I also told Clark that I was driving to my sister's home early on Sunday and that my parents were meeting us there. We planned to go out for brunch.

"Have you told your parents about me?" he asked.

"Sort of, but not much, just that I'd gone to dinner with you."

"Do they know how old I am?"

"Of course not! I don't even know how old you are!"

"For the record, I'll be thirty-four in September. I guess I'd better check with my mom to see what she'd like to do on Sunday, but maybe we can get together later in the day. Maybe we can also have dinner some night this week?"

I told him everything sounded fine and gave him a lingering kiss. As soon as I did so I was conscious that Mrs. Merrick had appeared in the doorway. Clark let go of my hand but kept his arm around me.

"I'm just going to glance at the *Register*," she said, picking up a section of the newspaper from the ottoman. Then she sat down in one of the leather wing chairs opposite us.

"Well, it's getting late," I said, "and I've got a big week ahead of me, so I'd really better be getting home."

"Don't you want to stay until the end of the show?" Clark asked, although neither of us had been watching. I didn't want to leave him then, but I felt as if it would be impossible to talk with Mrs. Merrick in the room. I hoped she was a speed reader or would begin dozing as my mother often did. I told him I could stay until ten.

Clark didn't say anything; he just smiled and then he began to stroke my shoulder and arm while we stared at the TV set. I couldn't think of anything I wanted to say to him in the presence of his mother, so I just pretended to watch the show. Mrs. Merrick didn't appear to be a speed reader; rather, after a good fifteen minutes she took up another section of the paper. After a while Clark quit stroking me and when I looked at him, his eyes were closed. He appeared to be dozing, so I just sat motionless watching the screen while Mrs. Merrick continued to read. *Why couldn't she, and not Clark, have dozed off?* When the show ended, I sat up on the sofa.

"Well, it's time for me to go," I announced quietly. Clark woke up with a befuddled look on his face. "You fell asleep," I told him. "Remember, you didn't get much sleep last night, so you should really go to bed right now."

"Gee, I'm sorry," he mumbled.

"Thank you for your hospitality, Mrs. Merrick," I said while I rose from the sofa. "I'm really glad I was invited to share in the birthday festivities."

"We should be thanking you," she said. "Your help was immeasurable."

Clark got up from the sofa too and said, "I'll get my car keys to drive you home."

"No, I drove here, remember?"

"I guess I'm not fully awake yet. Let me see you to the door." As we walked to the front entry, I got out my car keys and Clark said, "I feel like a real jerk. How long had I been asleep?"

"Oh, not that long, only about a half hour. And your snoring was really rather gentle," I teased him.

When we reached the front door, I turned to face him and he said, "I'll give you a call, Sara." Then he reached over and kissed me, harder and longer than he ever had before. "Gee, I don't want you to leave. I love you, Sara."

"I love you too, but I've got to go now," I said, and then I left.

Clark didn't call until Tuesday night. He wanted me to come over for dinner on Wednesday, but I reminded him I had Junior High MYF that night, so we settled on Thursday instead, although I made it clear that I wouldn't be able to stay long since I had several report cards to fill out and end-of-the-year reports to finish.

Dinner that evening was pleasant. After I helped Mrs. Merrick with some kitchen clean-up, Clark and I played catch and then four-square with Noah. Next we played a board game with him, and then I announced that I had to get home. Mrs. Merrick stayed in the den while Noah came to the front door with us.

"I wish you didn't have to go so soon," the boy said. "When will you come again?"

"I don't know," I responded. "I'm really busy with the end of school, but before I leave town I want to have you and your father and grandmother over for dinner."

"I didn't know you were leaving," Noah said. "When are you going?"

"Probably the end of this month right before Memorial Day weekend. I haven't really decided yet."

The child seemed crestfallen. I was about to reassure him that I'd be back at the end of summer when he surprised us by blurting out, "But I thought you were going to marry my dad!"

My eyes turned to Clark, who knelt down next to his son. "Noah," he began, "Miss Keatson—Sara—and I haven't known each other that long. We want to get to know each other better, and she'll be back here next fall."

"And," I chimed in, "I'll visit this summer, and you can come and see me at the university. It's not like I'm going away forever."

"My mom did!" he yelled angrily, and then he ran up the stairs.

I turned to Clark, saying, "I'm so sor—"

"There's nothing to be sorry about," Clark said quickly. "Look, I want to go to him now. Would it be all right if my mom took you home?"

I assured him it would be, and he ran to the den to get his mother, and when they both returned to the foyer, he said, "I'll call you later tonight, Sara," and then he headed upstairs.

Mrs. Merrick and I talked about gardening on the way to my place until we were almost there, and then she said, "Sara, Clark asked me if I thought it was all right if he started seeing you, and I told him yes, because I like you and it's obvious that he's very interested in you. My son is an honest and trustworthy man, and he's a devoted father, so I hope you can see that for the sake of Noah he's going to proceed very cautiously."

"Yes," I agreed, "I understand, and I think that's wise. Thanks for the ride home. Good night."

It was nine-thirty when the phone rang.

"Everything's fine," he said. "We had a long talk. It was good for both of us. He understands that you're going to school this summer because you have career goals you want to achieve. I told him that we'd visit you in Iowa City, and that hopefully you'd be able to come here to see us." After I told Clark that what he had said was perfect, he continued, "Gee, I guess I really feel the same way Noah does. I don't want you to leave town. But I know you've made plans to start grad school, and I think that's great. I really do, but I'll miss you."

"I'll miss you too," I said, knowing that it really was true love because the thought of not seeing him for a few weeks had already left me bereft.

The next three days were very hectic. I had promised

Georgiana I'd bring cinnamon rolls to her coffee, so I got up at six on Saturday to bake them. The gathering went well, but by the time I helped her clean up, it was two in the afternoon. I hurried home, did more schoolwork, and then got ready for the Retired Teachers' Banquet.

This event was held in the Lutheran Church fellowship hall and was prepared and served by the Luther Ladies League. It was typical small town banquet fare, but I enjoyed talking with Georgiana and some of the other teachers I'd grown closer to over the school year. The only dreadful part of the evening was the program. The speakers were so boring I constantly caught myself yawning and wanting to close my eyes. Fortunately, the program was not overly long and I was home a little after ten.

When the phone rang about ten-thirty just as I had finished washing up, it was Clark.

"I've tried calling you every half hour since nine," he explained. "I didn't know how long your banquet would last."

"Too long," I said.

"It's pretty late, but I thought maybe I could come over for a nightcap."

The instinctual part of me wanted to see him, but the rational part told me I was too tired. I knew I had a long drive tomorrow, and so I had to tell him the truth. He understood and reminded me that we'd made plans to see each other tomorrow evening.

For some reason after I hung up, I didn't fall quickly asleep. Perhaps I was too excited about seeing him tomorrow, about having the chance to be alone with him. I took the other pillow from my bed and put my arms around it, pretending it was Clark.

Despite the long drive I had to my sister's home and then back to Mount Morris, I enjoyed seeing my parents and Melly and Dan. Melly was quite pregnant now, and all of us couldn't help but remark how she seemed to glow, to exude warmth and maternalness. Our mother seemed to have a wonderful Mother's Day also, so my time away from Mount Morris seemed justified.

It was a little before six when I opened my apartment door. Clark had said he'd be by about 6:30 and that we'd go out for a light supper. I was just freshening up when the phone rang. It was Clark calling from the hospital.

"Sara, I'm sorry," he began, "but I'm tied up here. A ten-year-old boy from outside McDowd Junction was driving his father's tractor when it tipped over, pinning one leg underneath. I need to ride in the ambulance with him to Des Moines. We're going to leave in five minutes, so I'll call you later."

After I hung up, I was so disappointed, but I knew from the tone of Clark's voice that he was really worried about the boy. It was about nine when the phone rang again; this time Clark was in Des Moines at the hospital. He had thought perhaps the boy's limb could be saved, but that wasn't the case. He sounded very tired. "Arnie's about ready to head back now," he said. "There's nothing for me to do here, so I'm coming back with him. I know it's getting late, so I'll call you tomorrow."

After we said good night, I thought about the boy. He was just a couple years older than Noah. I sensed how Clark must have felt when the boy's leg had to be amputated. Growing up, Melly and I had never been allowed to drive tractors or other machinery. I thought about Elvis Winston, a classmate who'd lost an arm in a combine accident. Then there was Janie Wadsworth's cousin, a pretty fifteen-year-old girl whom we'd met one summer at the pool. A month later we heard she'd been killed when the tractor she was driving tipped over on her. Tears welled up in my eyes for the nameless little boy who'd lost his leg.

After a few minutes, I thought about Clark Merrick riding back to town with Arnie Rinehart. As the town mortician, Arnie also operated the ambulance service. I wondered if Clark would mention me to him. I was sure Arnie knew Clark had been seeing me. Even though I'd been out on only one date with Arnie, I felt a little smug thinking that he'd lost me to Clark Merrick.

On Monday shortly after I'd gotten home from school, Clark called me wanting to know how my week looked. I told him I was committed to go to Eighth Grade Graduation on Tuesday since there were several eighth graders in the church group I was working with. Georgiana and I had also planned to go to the high school commencement on Thursday evening. Clark asked me if he could escort me to both events, and I accepted. He wanted to take me out for dinner at the local country club on Thursday evening before the graduation ceremony. Wednesday, he said, was his day to play in a golf league whose tee-off times were late in the afternoon. I mentioned that I still wanted to have him, Noah, and his mother over for dinner and next week would be good because Tuesday would be my last day to report to school, with dismissal at noon. We didn't say anything about the upcoming weekend, but I was sure we'd talk about that in the coming days.

Tuesday was sultry, with the temperature climbing into the high 80's. For that evening, I chose a sleeveless pale violet dress which made me look cool when I put it on, even though it seemed as if I was constantly dabbing the perspiration from my face. Clark, wearing a light tan summer suit, arrived at seven. He looked cool as well, although I suspected we'd both be hot in the unconditioned auditorium. He kissed me passionately when I greeted him, whispering, "You look lovely."

Then we drove to Georgiana's apartment, where she was waiting on the front steps. All we talked about on the way to the auditorium was the heat. We had to park several blocks away, as most of the town had come for this annual event. Since this was the first public appearance I'd made with Clark, I was nervous about the rumors that would fly, despite Georgiana's earlier assurance that the townspeople approved of our dating. Clark seemed unconcerned. I was conscious of a few "Look, there's . . . ," but he was oblivious. As we went into the rapidly-filling auditorium, Clark put his hand lightly around my waist as he greeted people. There could be no mistaking that he was my date, not Georgiana's.

At exactly 7:30, Mrs. Beech began playing "We've Only Just Begun," and the eighth graders marched proudly to front row seats. Throughout the ceremony, the auditorium was quite hot, but it was not overly uncomfortable sitting on the backless bleachers and using the mimeographed programs as fans. Clark was very attentive; he did not seem bored or restless or even hot. I thought of how Marc White or Simon St. John would have mocked the entire event, and that made me love Clark Merrick even more.

After the conclusion of the program, the eighth graders formed a long receiving line in front of the stage. As the three of us made our way down to congratulate those whom we knew, we ran into Robin Dahlberg's parents, who invited all of us to drop by their home for a small celebration afterward and, since Clark had gone to high school with Robin's parents, he seemed very willing to accept their invitation. On the way to the Dahlberg home, I found out that Clark and Don Dahlberg had played basketball and run track together. This was another aspect of Clark that intrigued me, and I resolved to ask him more about his adolescent years when the time was appropriate.

Besides a few junior high teachers at Robin's home, I also knew Dr. and Mrs. Otto, who lived across the street. Doc Otto had taken off his suit coat, revealing big rings of perspiration on his white shirt, and I could see little beads of sweat on his round fleshy face. Most of the guests congregated in a small dining room, which had a window air conditioner, and since it was so crowded and noisy, we didn't stay for long.

Outside it was still hot; Clark turned the air conditioner on high as we headed to Georgiana's apartment. After we dropped her off, I asked, "Would you like to come in in for a glass of wine?"

"As a matter of fact, I would," he answered.

Inside my apartment it was comfortable since I'd left the thermostat on a low setting. As I brought the two glasses of wine into the living room, I noticed that Clark, sitting on the sofa, had taken off his suit coat for the first time that evening. I gave him his glass and sat down beside him.

"To finally being alone with you," he said, raising the glass in a toast.

"I hope you weren't horribly bored tonight," I began.

"Oh no, I went through all that myself once. It brought back good memories. And it's a nice tradition to honor our young people for worthy achievements like the history award that Robin earned. Some things about small towns aren't bad."

I agreed with him and we sipped our wine for a few seconds in silence. Then Clark asked, "Would you be available for dinner Friday night? I'd like to take you to a place in Pella."

"That'd be nice," I said, wondering if he'd remembered that once he'd asked me when my birthday was and I'd told him May 19th. I decided not to mention anything about that day to him. In fact, I hadn't told anyone in Mount Morris, not even Georgiana, that Friday was my birthday.

After we agreed on a time, we talked about Noah, who was going to be on a T-ball team that began practice next week and who still had Cub Scout meetings during the summer. Clark revealed that he was one of the "lucky" dads who got conned into chaperoning the pack for a camping trip in July.

I smiled at him and said, "You'll survive."

He put his empty wine glass down on the cocktail table, and I asked him if he wanted more wine, but he said he didn't. Then I asked him if he wanted to watch TV.

"No, I just want to be with you," he said, sliding his arm around my shoulders while moving closer to me. He took my almost empty wine glass and put it on the table. Then he took my hand and reached over to kiss me on the lips. It was another long kiss. Then we just sat for a few minutes with my head resting on his shoulder. He began kissing my hair and my temples and then he gave me several short kisses on the lips.

"I really love you, Sara," he whispered between kisses. I felt his hand stroking my bare arm, and then his fingers were on my neck while we continued kissing. I felt giddy sensations all over as he stroked my neck, and then I suddenly felt him fumbling with the top button on my dress. When he got it and the next button undone, his hand began fondling my breasts while he kept kissing me. Then he kissed me on the neck for a while and began stroking my thigh. Eventually his lips returned to my lips and we kissed for a long time. Then very gently he pulled away from me and put his head on the back of the sofa.

"I suppose I should be going, even though I don't want to," he said. "I know you've got to get up early tomorrow for school."

I didn't know what to say, even though I didn't want him to leave. He got up from the sofa and picked up his suit coat. I got up too and followed him to the door, where he turned and took me in his arms again.

"I'm sorry if I kept you up so late," he said, after he had kissed me again.

"It's all right," I whispered. "Thanks for being my escort tonight."

"Anytime," he said smiling, and then he let go of me and left.

Wednesday was hot again. I thought of Clark all day long and especially of him on the golf course that afternoon. After school I put on my swimsuit and sat outside for an hour while I filled out the last set of report cards.

On Thursday the weather changed. It was much cooler, so I decided to wear a suit that evening. After I'd put on my crisp white suit with a soft rose-colored camisole, I spent several minutes in front of the mirror trying to decide if my skin had tanned any after the previous day's attempt. I didn't think there was much difference, but next to the white linen my skin looked good.

Clark arrived at six. He had gotten a lot of sun yesterday, so his face was tanned and his light brown hair seemed to have a few streaks of gold. His eyes sparkled.

"My gosh, Sara," he said as he kissed me, "you look great."

I thought the same about him in his navy suit and white shirt, with the late-day sun shining in through my western window and playing with the gleams in his hair and eyes.

There was hardly anyone at the country club that evening. Georgiana and I had been there once before as the guests of Mrs. Strom and her husband. Then the dining area and bar had been quite busy, but tonight there were only an elderly couple dining and two men sitting at the bar.

Clark and I sat by an eastern window which, since the building sat on a hilltop, afforded a lovely view of part of the golf course and then the town. The verdant slopes of the fairway, several Canadian hemlocks, budding redbud trees, just-beginning to leaf maples and lindens, and the azure sky made for a postcard vista.

We talked for a little while about golf. I admitted that I had only tried the game once in my life, and Clark suggested that we go out to play together next week. He also asked me if I'd like to go on a picnic on Sunday.

"That sounds lovely," I replied.

Then he told me he was considering the purchase of some land, and he wanted me to look at a couple locations. He suggested we could do that on Sunday too, and then he admitted that he was still working on the redecorating of his office and wanted to show me how it was progressing.

"I told you once before that I wasn't planning on staying here for the rest of my life," he continued, "and I still feel that way, but I've got this hankering to build a house. I've always had the inclination. Merry Ann and I had talked a lot about building a 'dream house' in Colorado, but then she got sick. My mother's house is fine for her, but I feel cramped there. There's only one small bathroom upstairs, the bedrooms are fairly small with tiny closets, the one-car garage is unattached—gee, the house was built in the 1890's, I think. You get the picture? And of course there's a tremendous tax advantage to owning my own home."

I nodded in agreement, feeling more and more excited as he talked.

"So I've been scouting around town and especially out this way by the course for possible locations," he continued. "And I've come up with a couple of possibilities. I've even started to sketch a rough blueprint."

I told him his plans sounded wonderful, and we talked for quite a while about Clark's "dream house," as we ate our dinner. After we had finished eating and were waiting for the check, Clark reached across the table, taking both my hands in his, and stated, "I'll be frank with you, Sara. I haven't always been able to say how I've felt about you, and usually my reticence has gotten us upset with each other. But I've always felt better after I've gotten things off my chest, even though it's hard to say things . . . because, well, I guess because you don't really let me know what you're thinking. So please be honest with me after I get this out."

I promised him I would and he continued, "The other day when Noah blurted out that comment about our marrying, I tried to make light of it and spun off those platitudes about how we don't really know each other that well and all that bunk, as if the thought of marrying you had never crossed my mind. Well, I don't want you to have that impression. I've thought a lot about marrying you. I love you very much. I'm not just looking for a fling with a sexy young girl to satisfy my libido. I'm basically an old-fashioned type guy who believes in marriage and fidelity and commitment. I guess I'm saying all this because I still get the impression that you haven't considered me as a future husband."

"That's not true," I interrupted. "I really do love you, and I've thought a lot about being married to you." I stopped because the waitress was coming toward us with the check. Clark let go of my hands and, after scanning the bill, signed it. When the waitress left, he said, "Then I guess we feel the same way."

"Yes, we do."

"Good," he said with a large smile. "Now we'd better get to that graduation or all the seats will be taken and we'll have to stand."

The ceremony was a montage of light blue and navy graduation gowns, solemn-faced seniors whom I didn't know, huge bouquets of carnations, glads, and ferns decorating the stage, farmers in Sunday suits, women in spring-colored outfits purchased especially for the occasion, excited children dressed for church and reluctant to sit still, a speaker from the junior college, speeches by the valedictorian and salutatorian, messages about striving and building and making the world a better place in which to live, cameras clicking and flashing as each graduate walked across the stage, and finally the benediction and recessional.

Afterwards I spotted Georgiana and Bella Bailey, the high school home ec teacher, and we went up to say hello. I had asked Georgiana earlier if we could pick her up, but she'd insisted on not wanting to tag along.

"One more day of kids!" Bella moaned. "I am surely going to

be glad after tomorrow is over. Tell me, are grade schoolers as wild as teenagers on the last day?"

"Oh, we'll have more than our share of tricks and tantrums and fidgety kids tomorrow," Georgiana replied. "I'm going to miss the little devils, though. I always get teary-eyed on that last day."

After a few more minutes of chit-chat, Clark and I excused ourselves and walked to his car, holding hands on the way there. When we were almost to my place, I said, "There's still some wine left if you'd like a glass."

"You read my mind," he replied.

While I poured the wine, he selected an old Beatles album and put the record on my stereo. We settled down on the sofa with our glasses of wine and talked trivialities for a few minutes. Then he began kissing me and we were locked in embraces for quite a long time. Finally Clark drew away from me and announced that he was going to have another glass of wine. "Would you like one?" he asked.

I declined, and when he came back he put the wine glass on the cocktail table, took off his suit coat, walked over to my wall unit, and began looking through my album collection. "The Beatles were popular for a long time," he said. "I was thinking they weren't your generation, but you've got a lot of their albums. When'd they break up, anyway?"

"I don't remember exactly," I said, "but I think sometime when I was in high school."

"Yes," he pondered, "that seems about right. Oh, here's one this ol' geezer likes. James Taylor. Is that okay with you?"

I told him that was fine; he put the record on and came back to the sofa. I kicked off my heels and snuggled up next to him while he sipped his wine. Then he put his glass down and began kissing me. Soon he was unbuttoning my suit jacket and helping me out of that. Then he found the side slit in my skirt and began stroking my thigh. I was nervous and yet immensely excited. Suddenly I felt his hands on my back underneath my camisole, and then he withdrew them and slipped the straps of that down. As we continued to kiss, he began hunting for a back hook on my strapless bra. After several seconds, he whispered between kisses, "Sara, . . how do you . . . unhook your bra?"

"The hook's in the front," I whispered, and he gave a sort of chuckle.

"Oh," he said, moving slightly away from me, as he brought his hands away from my back to the small rosette piece of material between each lacy cup.

"Here," I said, "there's just a little catch. You pull up."

Then I undid the hook and my breasts fell out.

"Oh Sara, you're so beautiful," he whispered, and then he buried his face in my breasts and began kissing them and my neck. After several minutes, he said between kisses, "I don't suppose . . . you're on the Pill?"

While his question surprised me, I was glad he had asked. I shook my head negatively.

"Do you have any contraceptives here?"

Again I shook my head negatively.

"I do want to make love to you," he said. "Do you want me to?" When I didn't answer immediately, he stopped kissing me, looked me directly in the eyes, and continued, "But I don't want you to get pregnant. I mean, I want to have children with you, but I don't think we should start tonight."

I smiled and said softly, "Me too. I love you, Clark, but …."

"It's okay," he said. "It's late and you've still got classes tomorrow. If Georgiana's right, the kids aren't going to be easy to handle either. So I'll say goodnight, and before I start undressing you again, I'll make sure we're prepared. Just stop me if we go too fast."

"Okay," I nodded.

Then he kissed me again and got up. I felt so disheveled that I didn't get up from the sofa.

"Tomorrow at 6:30," he said, picking up his suit coat. "Love you, Sara." And he left.

The next day I hurried home from school as fast as I could. I took another shower, shaved my legs, put on my prettiest underwear, blow-dried my hair, applied fresh makeup, and put on a new dress, a flattering mini of eggshell voile whose matching slip allowed my skin to appear through the sheer cloth of the upper bodice and sleeves.

Just as I was applying lipstick, the doorbell rang. Clark was early. I quickly ran a brush through my hair to fluff up the curls and then hurried to the door.

"My!" he exclaimed. "You look fantastic! That's a very flattering dress."

"Thanks," I said. "You look very nice too." He had on a light gray summer suit. He gave me a quick kiss and walked into the apartment.

"I know I'm early, but I wanted to give you a little something before we left. Come here and sit down."

I walked over to the sofa and sat down beside him. From his pocket he took a small oblong box wrapped in yellow paper and white ribbon.

"Happy twenty-third birthday, Sara."

"Oh Clark, you shouldn't have!" I protested. "And how'd you know it was my birthday?"

"That night we drove home from having dinner in Jasper, I asked you when it was. I don't know why I remembered May 19th. Well, I guess I knew then that I was falling in love with you and that I'd better commit your birth date to memory. Go ahead and open it."

"It's even wrapped in my favorite color," I said as I undid the ribbon and paper. "Now how'd you know that?"

"I just figured you were a sunshiny, daffodil type person."

Inside there was a lovely gold bracelet with two interlocking gold hearts in the middle, each with a green stone inside. "Oh Clark!" I gasped. "It's gorgeous! I've never seen such an elegant bracelet."

"I'm glad you like it, darling," he said, giving me a loving kiss. "Do you know what the saleslady said about your birthstone? She said that the emerald signifies success in love. Maybe she says that about every month's birthstone, but I fell for it. Here, let me help you put it on."

He lifted up the bracelet and held open the catch, and when I offered my wrist to him, he slipped it in place.

"Clark, it's really lovely," I said again, giving him a kiss. "The emeralds are just beautiful. I don't have any pieces of jewelry with my birthstone. Thank you very much."

"It looks nice on your dainty wrist," he said, holding my hand in his. "And I hope it signifies success in love for the two of us. Actually, this is just half your present. I wanted to get you an engagement ring, but I figured we could pick that out together." Then he kissed me again. "I think I took off all your lipstick. Run and put some more on, birthday girl, and then we've got to be off or we'll miss our dinner reservation."

I did as directed and we left for the restaurant. On the drive there we talked about many different things—current movies, the classes I would be taking, Noah, my sister and her pregnancy, Clark's high school days, the picnic set for Sunday, my cooking dinner for all three Merricks on Tuesday evening, and most of all, the "dream house." Clark had brought along his homemade blueprint. After I'd examined it and he'd given many reasons for its floor plan and for several embellishments in its structure, I wanted to tell him that it was my dream house too.

"Clark," I began, "this isn't just your dream house. It's my dream house too. Really, truly, I love every little detail you've told me and shown me about the house."

"That sounds like a marriage proposal," he said with a grin on his face. "I accept."

I stretched across the car seat and swatted him with the blue-print-like sketch, "Well, mister, if you're going to be so smug, then I guess I'd better mention the swimming pool and tennis courts. You haven't sketched them in anywhere. And of course, I'll need a wall in the breakfast area for our family mural—it's a Keatson family tradition—and a room to paint in. You're not the only one who gets a study! And come to think of it, where are the servants' quarters?"

He was chuckling at my speech. "Anything your little heart desires."

The restaurant was called Fanny's Inn and its décor was country: quilted tablecloths, fresh carnations and baby's breath, white china trimmed with daisies, candlelight. We had the house specialty: prime rib with Yorkshire pudding. The food was delicious, and the atmosphere was perfect for intimate conversation. It seemed as if it was so easy to talk to Clark now. For dessert, we had the restaurant's special dessert, pineapple upside down cake. After dinner we window-shopped in Pella's quaint downtown, and then we drove back to Mount Morris.

As Clark turned off the motor in front of my place, he said, "Since I finished off the wine last night, I took the liberty of purchasing a new bottle for tonight. Hope you don't mind."

Inside he poured the wine while I selected a Carly Simon album. We sat silently on the sofa and sipped our wine, with Clark's arm around my shoulders. After a few minutes, he began kissing me. Finally he asked, "Do you want to make love tonight?"

I looked into those gentle, penetrating blue eyes of his and nodded my head affirmatively.

"Let's get some more wine and go into the bedroom where we can be more comfortable," he suggested.

While I poured more wine into our glasses, Clark began unzipping the back of my dress and started kissing me on the neck and shoulders. Then he turned me toward him, kissed me on the mouth, and told me he loved me. "Forget the wine," he murmured, leading me to the bedroom, where he pulled back the bedspread and propped the pillows slightly against the headboard. He took me in his arms and while we were kissing I felt him slipping my dress down so that it fell to the floor.

"Why don't you take off your pantyhose?" he suggested.

While I took off my shoes, my half slip, and my hose, Clark took off his shoes, his suit jacket, and his tie. Then he came over to me and we embraced again, falling into the bed, where I snuggled up next to him and said, "This isn't fair. You've still got on practically all your clothes." I began unbuttoning his shirt and he quickly undid his belt and took off his shirt and undershirt.

"Before I try, please tell me where the hook on your bra is."

"It's in the back this time," I said.

"Tricky, tricky. I thought so."

He reached around me, undid it, and pulled the straps down. When it was completely off, he began kissing my breasts, whose nipples were hard and receptive. Every nerve in my body seemed animated as he kissed me. Finally he pulled away from me and took off his pants and socks.

"Now we're even," he said, and as he pressed his body up against mine, I felt the hardness of his penis confined in his briefs pushing against me. Then he pulled away and said, "I want you to know, Sara, that I really love you and that I'm never doing any comparing between you and Merry Ann. Maybe when I first met you I did some comparing and contrasting, but now I never do. I won't forget Merry Ann, but now it's just you, Sara. You're all that matters, all that I think about."

"I know," I whispered back.

We kissed some more and his hands began roaming all over my panties and thighs. Then he began pulling my panties down. He had to sit up slightly to get them off completely, and when they had been tossed on the floor, I saw him staring at my naked body.

"By God, you're beautiful, Sara," he said. And then he added after a few seconds, "I guess I'm a little nervous."

His words surprised me. "**You're** nervous?" I questioned. "I'm ner--," and while I said "vous," I realized that I was revealing my inexperience. And then I remembered that I loved Clark and he loved me and we didn't have to pretend anymore. So I said softly, "I've never done this before."

He reached down and kissed me very hard, and then he just held me tightly for a few minutes. He began playing with the necklace I still had on, and then he started kissing me again. I brought my hands down from his neck and started touching the elastic of his briefs. He moved away from me and took them off. When his body came back to mine, I felt his penis pushing into my thigh.

"If it's okay with you," he said, "I'll use a condom when it's time. It's a pretty effective contraceptive, so don't worry."

He kissed me some more and began stroking my thighs a lot. With his legs and hand he gently worked to open my legs, which were clamped together. "Relax, Sara," he whispered. "Take a deep breath."

I did so and kept my legs apart while he continued to massage my thighs with his hands. Finally he sat up and got out of bed. I heard him unwrapping plastic while I lay on the bed with my legs apart like a blank canvas ready to receive his color. Quickly he was beside me and then on top of me. It seemed as if his penis found my labia immediately and he thrust himself into me. He felt so immense and powerful that I couldn't help shrieking.

Clark gave me several short kisses and whispered, "I love you. You feel so good. Are you comfortable?"

I nodded yes, and then he began jerking around inside of me, sending vibrations throughout my body. I was conscious of how hard he was panting and how strong he felt. When he climaxed, it felt as if a volcano had erupted inside of me; a burst of frenzy rippled throughout my body, and I shrieked again. Then it was over and he withdrew from me but held me tightly next to him.

"I love you, Sara," he whispered, and I whispered those words back to him. "Did anyone ever tell you you're absolutely beautiful?"

I looked up at the ceiling, trying to decide what kind of answer I was going to give, but before I could say anything at all, he put his finger on my parted lips.

"You talk too much," he said. With his hand he drew my face toward him. And then he kissed me. And then he kissed me. And then he kissed me.

And then finally I fell asleep to other dreams, all of which I have long forgotten, unlike the one about Clark Merrick, which sustained me for many, many lonesome nights.

Part Two
SOLUTION SWEET

August 23, 1981
Eighteen Hours

Into her dream he melted, as the rose
Blendeth its odour with the violet,--
Solution sweet . . . .

John Keats
The Eve of St. Agnes

he sun rose at five seventeen today, although I was not yet awake. I had no idea what time it was now. The sun had already penetrated the drapes and raised the temperature enough that I found myself sneaking my feet over the side of the bed to escape the sheet and the too-hot atmosphere underneath. The mixture of sunlight and cool air from the air conditioner vent felt good. I was very content. There was no need to get up. If I wanted to, I could wallow all morning in our calamine blue sheets. I turned over on my stomach and went back to sleep.

I had one of those strange dreams in which people from totally different times in my life were tossed together in bizarre scenarios. I was a senior in high school and I had a term paper due for English class. It was one day before the end of the semester and I hadn't started yet. My English teacher was Earl Hamlin, and he came out to the farm to talk to Father and Mother, but all Mother wanted to talk about was the gossip at the hospital. She kept saying, "It's horrible the way that nurse aide carries on."

I was so embarrassed that she was behaving so stupidly in Hamlin's presence. I kept shuffling through note cards on the kitchen table, wondering why Hamlin hadn't noticed Mother's mural and trying desperately to find information on William Morris, but none of the cards had anything to do with him. Melly came in with Amanda on her hip, and I asked her to help, but she said she was too busy.

"I've got to get this paper done to graduate," I pleaded. "I've got an A in the class so far, but if I don't get it done I'll fail."

"I'll find one of my old papers for you to use," she said. "I have a good one on one of the English Romantics. Come on, Mandy, let's go find the paper for Auntie Sara."

Then they both disappeared and suddenly the scene shifted and I was in my old high school gym. I was painting a mural of a tropical landscape for the junior-senior prom. Louellen McHenry, Sharon Thomasino, and little LeeAnn Webb were helping me, but I couldn't concentrate because none of these people belonged in my high school world. Sharon took a paint brush and dipped it into the magenta paint. She sat cross-legged on the floor, and while she rocked back and forth, she swished the brush on the paper. *She's mad,* I thought. *Oh God, what's Earl Hamlin going to think of my talent when he sees this mural?*

Suddenly Emma Aspen and Georgiana Wylie walked up.

"Do you have a date for the prom?" Emma asked.

"I'm going with David," I answered smugly. "We're engaged. Who else would I go with?"

Then everything vanished and I was alone with Emma in our room at the sorority house. All she had on was panty hose, and she was putting round band-aids over her nipples. I was trying to take notes on William Morris, but I couldn't concentrate very well because I was confused about why she had shown up at my high school when I didn't meet her until college. As Emma put on a lovely mallow pink halter style dress, I admired how beautiful she was.

"It's too bad David can't come back for formal," she said, brushing the tight curls of electric rollers into a soft flowing cascade of blond curls.

"Yes," I muttered confusedly. Despite Emma's words I knew something wasn't right. I didn't know David. I desperately wanted him to take me to the high school prom or the sorority formal, but he didn't exist in my life then. That was the one fact in the fantasies of my dream that woke me up.

As if to ascertain that David really existed, I turned over to look at him. His head was turned away from me as he lay on his side. I moved my body so that it fit up against his and kissed him gently on the shoulder. He was still asleep.

I rolled back to my half of our bed and closed my eyes. A lazy hazy crazy day of summer, I thought. Oh, the luxury of Sunday! But there was a lot to do too.

I got out of bed, went into our small second bedroom, which we used as a den, took the ironing board out of the closet, set it up, and turned on the iron. Then I went to the bathroom and next to the kitchen to make coffee. The clock on the oven said 8:35. I was surprised that it was still quite early.

When I returned to the den, the iron was hot. I opened the drapes and then put on the board the sampler I'd embroidered for Georgiana's baby. I began to iron the edge of it, glancing out the window every once in a while. There were already lots of sailboats out on the lake. Their white sails lambently dotted the blue water, creating a scene evoking Monet.

I began pressing the cursive letters of the baby's name, which I'd written in my best script and then outline stitched in Italian blue embroidery thread. Matthew Aaron Neibuhr. M.A.N., I thought. That was nice. I had made the same sampler a couple months ago for Pete Byron, Jr. It was quite a coincidence that Susan and Georgiana had both had baby boys who were born on the same day of the week just a couple months apart.

Then I began to reflect on what we would name our child: David Randall Woodley, D.R.W. II; David Oliver Woodley, D.O.W; William Oliver Woodley? W.O.W.! What had Melly once said about the metrics of names? It had slipped my memory completely. I ironed the choo-choo train and then the tiny black letters which said, "Thursday's child has far to go."

"It's too far to go," David said. "If the weather were nicer, I wouldn't mind, but it's a cold rain. The course will be so wet. I don't even enjoy playing when I'm freezing my buns off."

"That's fine with me," I said. "So do you want to do anything special today?"

He got back into bed. "No, just relax. And screw. Let's stay in bed all morning."

"Okay," I said, snuggling up close to him.

April showers bring May flowers, I thought, as I listened to the patter of raindrops on the windows and to the soft sounds of David's kisses on my neck.

There were twelve of us who went to Colorado over Easter vacation in 1978. Rafe Johnson drove his parents' van with six of us, and the other six went in Pete Byron's Oldsmobile sedan.

At about one o'clock on Friday afternoon, the van stopped for me in Mount Morris. A tall good-looking blond fellow got out, introduced himself as Rafe Johnson, and put my suitcase in the back.

After I climbed into the middle row next to Natalie, Jenny Woodley said from her far back seat, "Hi, Sara. This is my brother David, and you just met Rafe. You remember Bruce, don't you?"

"Yes, I remember seeing you around the house," I said to Bruce. "How does it feel to be close to graduating?"

"Pretty damn good," he said. "I don't think I can take too much more."

We talked about his plans after graduation and about mutual acquaintances from college. Natalie talked more than she usually did when she rode in a car, and she only smoked one cigarette in four hours.

When we stopped for food and gas at a truck-stop near York, Nebraska, Natalie took me aside and announced, "I get David. You can have Rafe, okay?"

"Sure, Nat," I said, remembering not to roll my eyes.

Rafe and David were three years older than Natalie and I. None of us could remember meeting each other at the U. Rafe was working for an insurance firm in Des Moines. He seemed to be an intelligent, good-humored guy. He had curly blond hair, blue eyes, a slight tan, one dimple in his right cheek, a slightly aquiline nose, and a slim, yet athletic, build. Jenny's brother looked a little like her. He was good-looking but with undistinguished features, dark-haired and dark-eyed. He lived in Chicago and was a lawyer. Apparently he and Rafe had roomed together at the Sig house. They talked extensively about people who'd graduated before I'd even started college. They both knew Pete pretty well, and both of them could recall meeting Simon St. John through Pete. They also knew Marc White, who, like Pete, was a pledge when they were seniors. They talked a lot about sports with Bruce and then about investing money and the job market.

It was shortly before we crossed the state line into Colorado that Natalie divulged her biggest scoop of gossip. She began innocently enough. "Well, do you suppose the rest of our party will make it there before us or not?"

"I'm sure we'll get there first," Rafe responded. "Pete said they wouldn't be able to leave Iowa City until two, so chances are they won't roll in until after midnight."

"How will poor Emma get her beauty sleep?" Natalie asked.

Jenny laughed. "Now when have you ever known Emma Aspen to need beauty sleep?" she countered.

"Tell me again what this gal looks like," David said.

"Oh, I know you must have seen her around campus," Jenny said. "Once you've seen her, you're sure to remember her. She's not hard to forget. She's got really thick long blond hair and very blue eyes. She's like Christie Brinkley's twin, right Sara?"

"Yes," I agreed, "she's sort of the epitome of feminine physical beauty."

"Was she Miss Ideal Frosh freshman year?" Rafe asked, and I told him yes. "Now I remember her. Don't you remember her, David?"

"Not really," he answered. "Maybe my memory will be jarred when I see her."

"You know the reason you can't place her," Jenny said, "is because she started dating Marc after you graduated."

"That's logical," David replied.

"Very logical," Natalie piped in. "Now that's something Emma Aspen never had much of—logic. And I'll repeat what I said earlier minus the reference to beauty: how will poor Emma get her sleep?"

"What do you mean, Nat?" I asked.

"I mean, Emma with her little ménage a trois has got to have her hands full, or in this case, her vagina." Everyone laughed as Natalie continued, "You know what she always said about Marc— how he'd like to screw three or four times a night."

"So I don't get it," Bruce said. "What exactly do you mean?" With his befuddled look, he reminded me of a tall John Denver.

"I mean, sweet child," Natalie began, "that when one woman has to fulfill the sexual needs of two virile men, she's not going to get much sleep. You know—sleep sleep. Has she told you much about Barrett, Sara?"

"Who?"

"Barrett Sawyer, her paramour from grad school."

"No," I answered, "I haven't heard anything about him. You mean he's the guy who's Emma's friend from grad school who's riding in Pete's car?"

"Oh Sara dear, you always were so perspicacious," Natalie said sarcastically.

"You mean this Emma has two boyfriends along on this trip?" Rafe asked incredulously.

"Yes," Natalie replied. "It's strange. It's amazing. Come to think of it, it's downright selfish!"

We all laughed again and then I asked, "So what do you know about this guy, Nat?"

"Not much. He's about three or four years older than we are. He's a Ph.D. candidate in English. He's very bright, but it's not like he's in the Writers' Workshop. He teaches freshman comp classes and he's getting ready to start his dissertation. Emma said he just passed some big test so he's not doing anything now except teaching and relaxing before he starts research on his dissertation. His family has money to burn, and so he's going to England this summer to start his research. I've never met him, but I hear he's extremely good-looking."

"Well, well, well," Rafe said, "this is going to be an interesting weekend."

"Never a dull moment with Emma Aspen," I added.

"I can't wait to meet this Barrett guy," Jenny said. "Golly, I probably won't know what to say to him. He's probably super intellectual. Maybe you can talk about art with him, Sara."

"I can't remember what you said, Sara," David questioned me. "What do you teach?"

"Art," I replied. "I teach art in an elementary school. I was an art education major."

"I always wondered what art majors did for a living," David quipped.

"Or psychology majors," Natalie added.

"Doesn't Simon have a great job with an ad agency?" Rafe asked.

"Yes, in Seattle," Natalie replied.

"Well," Jenny said, "I know what I'm going to do as an el ed major."

"Sure," Natalie said sarcastically, "teach darling little brats all day to raise their hands before they open their mouths."

Although I laughed along with the others at Natalie's joke, I felt hurt inside. I suddenly disliked this David for what seemed his supercilious stance and narrow-minded remark about art majors. But I didn't have to worry because Natalie had set her snares on David. I could have Rafe. Or maybe even Barrett Sawyer.

We got to our lodgings very late and consequently did not see the other half of our party until the next morning. But I first saw Louellen McHenry, a miniature version of her sister, because she was sharing a bed with Jenny. With Natalie and myself, there were four of us in one room. Emma and Marc had a room, as did Susan and Pete. The other four guys were together in one room.

Because Natalie and Louellen wanted to sleep in, it was Jenny and I who went down to the hotel's restaurant for breakfast. Rafe, David, and Bruce were sitting at a large table, and we walked over to join them.

"I told you she'd be the first gal up," David said. "Mom and dad always said Jenny was born on a pair of skis."

"You know I love skiing in the morning best of all," she answered. "I just can't wait to get out there. Have you ordered yet?"

"Yep," Bruce said, "but only a minute ago. We saved a menu for you, so hurry up and pick something out and I'll get the waitress over here. I'm pretty damned excited about my first lesson."

"So did you decide to take the lessons or just go out with Jenny?" I asked Bruce.

"I'm going to take my life into my hands and gamble with Miss El-Ed-All-the-Patience-in-the-World Woodley."

"I think you should take the lessons, Sara," David said. "Even though Jenny and I have been skiing since junior high, we can't give you all the tips the instructors here can. Rafe's been skiing once before, and he's going to take the beginning lessons, right?"

"Right on," he answered, giving me a big smile. "Sara, you just come with me and we'll break our legs together."

We all laughed, and then Jenny and I quickly ordered breakfast. Right after the waitress left, Rafe asked, "Did you two see Marc White over at that table by the window?" I turned to look in the direction Rafe gestured toward. There was Marc with a half dozen books spread out around his small table. He looked up and gave me a huge smile.

"I should go to say hello," I said. "It's been a long time since I've seen Marc. Excuse me a second."

As I walked over to his table, I felt a sense of excitement simply because Marc White was one the best-looking males I'd ever known. I thought he was proud and materialistic and intolerant of anyone who wasn't just as WASPish as he was, but I could sense that the rest of our table as well as many diners in the restaurant had their eyes on me as I neared his table, and I felt beautiful as he stood up, put both hands on my upper arms, and gave me a little kiss on the cheek.

"Sara," he said, "you look damned good. It's been too long. Sit down a minute. I really need to talk to you."

"You look great too," I said, taking the chair across from him and looking directly into his piercing blue eyes. "But what's with all these books? This is spring break, isn't it?"

"God, Sara, I don't know what the word *break* means. You know in undergrad I never had to study that hard. I just sort of breezed through with good grades, but med school is something else. Everyone in my class is brilliant and they study all the time. There's just a hell of a lot of facts to memorize. Actually, the goddamn profs expect you to memorize whole books almost overnight. I've had serious doubts about whether I'll ever finish."

"Oh," I tried to sound consolingly cheerful, "I'm sure the first year is the hardest, and after you cross that hurdle the rest gets much easier."

"I've heard exactly the opposite," he responded. "They say it gets worse."

"Well, what can I say? How's Emma? I'm dying to talk to her."

"That's what I've got to talk to you about, Sara. Emma's changed. She's practically flunking out of grad school. In fact, she got one F and two Incompletes first semester. It's all a big joke to her. It's as if she's just attending classes to bide the time until I finish med school and we can get married. At this point, I don't even know if I want to marry Emma Aspen."

"I don't know what to say," I began, not feeling the least bit guilty about not feeling sorry for Marc White. "Have you tried talking to Emma?"

"Sara, you're her best friend, so you know how she is. She just clams up if she doesn't want to talk."

"Well, I'm sorry. I don't know what advice to give you."

He picked up his coffee cup and drank, and we were both silent. Finally he said, "You know where she is right now, don't you? She's in the sack with that Barrett Sawyer. They're up in our room having a grand ol' time. I could walk in on them and she'd deny that they were lovers."

I really didn't know what to say to him now, so I told him I had to go eat my breakfast and that I'd try to talk to Emma. When I got back to our table, everyone had to know about Marc, so I filled them in as best I could, minus the part about his disillusionment with Emma.

After we ate, Rafe and I rented skis and went out for a ten-o'clock lesson. The instructor was a gorgeous redhead who was very encouraging to everyone in the group. It hurt me a little because Rafe seemed so impressed with her, but she didn't flirt anymore with him than she did with two high-school-age boys in our group. By the end of the morning, we had all managed to ski down Knovice Knoll.

When Rafe and I went in for lunch, we saw almost all the rest of the group at a big table. There were Susan, who looked just the same, Pete, Louellen, Natalie, Emma, who looked even more beautiful than when I'd seen her last December, and a tall dark-haired fellow whose hair was much longer than the other males and who seemed much older than we were.

Of course, Emma and I had to hug, and then Rafe got introduced, and finally I got introduced to Barrett Sawyer.

"Emma's told me so much about you," he said with a half-grin on his face and an enchanting flicker in his grayish blue eyes. "It's a pleasure to meet you, Sara."

As we ate the talk was mainly about friends from college and skiing. When we were almost finished, Jenny, Bruce, and David came in, and another round of introductions took place. As we sat and talked, it was amusing to see the changes in Rafe and David in the presence of Emma. It was suddenly as if there were a contest to see who could make her laugh, who could impress her, who could hold the attention of those beautiful blue eyes. Of course, Emma was at her best. With just one intense look at any of the men, one silly comment, one smile, she seduced them all. Finally it was Natalie, who sat silently smoking and answering queries directed to her in monosyllables, who asked, "Where's Marc?"

"We saw him on the slopes," Bruce answered. "He said he could only afford about an hour of skiing and then he'd have to study. Goddamn, he's dedicated! He wanted to know what time we were eating dinner and if he could join us. Of course, we said sure, but we didn't know exactly what time to tell him, so he just said he'd be in the coffee shop studying and to get him before we left."

Then the talk turned to dinner and to possible restaurants, with the result that Pete telephoned to make reservations for seven o'clock at a place Barrett had been to before.

"It's a pity about poor Marc, isn't it, Emma?" Natalie said when Pete got back to the table, and I knew Emma wanted to throttle Natalie, but she didn't say a word.

"Say, Sara," Rafe said, "would you like to take a hike this afternoon? Anybody else want to join us?"

He had mentioned this earlier to me, and we agreed to meet at 2:30 in the lobby. No one else wanted to join us.

Then everyone broke up, most for a quick trip to their rooms, Natalie to the gift shop for cigarettes, David back to the slopes. He seemed to be the most avid skier of our group, even more so than his sister.

The hike with Rafe was invigorating, as he was a fast walker. He seemed like a really nice guy, and I was definitely looking forward to spending more time with him. After we returned to the resort, I took a nap and then showered and got ready for dinner.

That evening there were the twelve of us at a long rectangular table, with Pete and Marc at each head. I sat at Pete's left, with mainly Susan and her sister and Barrett to talk to. I was nervous about talking to him because he seemed so worldly and intelligent.

The name of the restaurant was Fratelli's, and Barrett said it had wonderful northern Italian cuisine. Bruce asked what the hell that was, and Barrett never answered him. Instead, he devoted almost all his attention to conversing with me, ignoring Susan, Louellen, Pete, and Natalie, who sat on his other side, to the point of rudeness. I could hear her, in turn, lavishing all her attention on Rafe, who was seated next to her. Leave it to Natalie to be jealous of me and try to snatch Rafe away, I thought. I couldn't see either Emma or Rafe very well because they were on my side of the table. I guessed Natalie was also upset because David, who sat directly across from Emma, had the pleasure of so much of her attention. And of course, Emma looked stunning in a soft pink sweater dress with a scalloped neckline.

I tried to talk with Pete, Susan, and Louellen, but Barrett kept engaging me in difficult conversations. He wanted to know all about Earl Hamlin and what I thought of his work. I could handle that, but then he got started on Grant Wood.

"I think he was far too underrated," he said. "Artistically, the man was a factotum. He did metal work, architecture, interior design, in addition to his drawing and painting. To me, his work shows such a dichotomy. One has the idealized vision of Midwestern America alongside the acerbity of something like *Daughters of Revolution*. Don't you think so?"

I knew this was going to be tough, but at least I'd studied Wood in college courses. "Yes," I ventured, "I think I know what you mean. You see, personally, I have no neat little definition of what art itself is. I guess it's something I'll wrestle with all my life, . . . if I'm lucky. I like Wood. I'd love to have some of his rural idylls in my home for my own personal enjoyment. I love the way he treats our Iowa landscape in lovely arcs and circles, with the whole effect being so neat, so serene. I wouldn't care to have *Daughters of Revolution* or *American Gothic* in my home, though. They're wonderful pieces of satire—don't get me wrong, I think satire has a place in art—but eventually this little farm girl would get tired of looking at those tight-lipped, thin-lipped women with their sour expressions. Do you understand my point?"

"I think so," he said, putting his arm across the back of my chair and turning almost his entire body toward me. I couldn't remember seeing pictures of Lord Byron, but from what my mind imagined he looked like, Barrett Sawyer was the twentieth century reincarnation: dark, handsome, sensual, philosophic, rakish, the kind of man who made Lady Caroline Lamb go mad with infatuation.

"But I don't share your distaste for those demonic-looking characters of Wood," he continued. "I think I could live very nicely with them. In fact, I'd relish having the D.A.R. stand guard over my bed!" Then suddenly he laughed, took my left hand in his, and started reciting:

"'A thing of beauty is a joy forever: Its loveliness increases; it will never pass into nothingness, but still will keep a bower quiet for us, and a sleep full of sweet dreams, and health, and quiet breathing.'"

During his recitation, the entire table had become silent. With all their eyes upon us, I felt immensely awkward. "I always liked the beginning of *Endymion*," I said to break the silence.

"Goddamn," Bruce said authoritatively, "what the hell are we doin'? Havin' pasta or talkin' loco?"

Everyone except Barrett laughed. He let go of my hand and turned slightly away from me. Then Jenny said, "As you can see, Bruce doesn't appreciate poetry."

"Was that what that was?" he asked.

Then Marc piped in, "Bruce, why don't you ask Emma to recite a little poetry? I like the one about the heart. What is it, sweet? My heart is like an apple tree....Come on, Emma darling."

"Oh, Marc," Emma began to protest.

"Hell, Emma, you're into this poetry recitin' too!" Bruce exclaimed.

"Christ," Marc said, "I thought you all knew. Ever since her acquaintance with Mr. Sawyer, Emma's taken up with Christina Rossetti. And no, Bruce, that doesn't mean they're lesbian lovers."

"Emma, Emma, Emma!" Natalie said with theatrics. "I had no idea!"

"So who's this Christina chick?" Bruce asked. "Her name is kinda sexy."

"She was an English poet," Barrett said haughtily, "one of the finest female lyricists who ever lived. The poem to which you refer, Marc, is entitled 'A Birthday.' The line you find so memorable: 'My heart is like an apple tree/Whose boughs are bent with thickset fruit.'"

"Wow!" Bruce gasped. "That's like so deep. I'm getting a boob image—"

"Did Emma tell you," Marc interrupted to address Barrett, "how we laughed over that poem last night in bed? Oh, I guess not. You take the damn stuff so seriously."

Marc was a little lit, and most of the rest of us were somewhat embarrassed. Susan and I exchanged knowing looks. I knew we were both worried about a full-fledged duel erupting. Barrett was silently aloof. I kept trying to think of some comment to make that would change the subject, but then Natalie got started.

"Tell me, Emma dear," she said, "does this passion for Christina Rossetti's verse extend to other poets? You see, I thought the twentieth century novel and *Glamour* were the extent of your literary interests."

Marc laughed boisterously and said, "Oh Nat, I love you!"

Come on, Barrett, I thought, *defend Emma the way you defended Christina Rossetti,* but he was silent.

"People change," Emma said. "I like Christina Rossetti's poetry. She wasn't perfect; I'm not perfect. No one's perfect. Give me a break, everybody. Let's talk about something else."

"Fine with me," Marc said, giving her a light kiss, as if that gesture could obliterate his rudeness.

"Me too," Bruce said. "Say, did any of you guys see that couple that looked just like Gerry and Betty out on the slopes?"

"What!" exclaimed Jenny. "Come on, Bruce. We never saw—"

"Fooled you!" he cut in. "See, you didn't think I could change the topic so fast. Let's talk about something I know a little something about."

"What's that?" Jenny asked. "Politics? Real estate?"

"Hell no, silly! The only thing that matters in life: sports!"

With that comment, our entrees arrived and the table talk broke down into small groups. I queried Louellen about life in college and her plans to go into the Peace Corps, and I talked with Pete and Susan about their upcoming wedding. Barrett said nothing; he simply ate his pasta. Finally, I thought I should make some comment to include him, so I asked, "How's the linguine with smoked salmon?"

"All right," he answered. I thought he would ask me how my tortellini carbonara was, but instead he said, "I don't like him— Keats, that is. Thank God he died young."

I was worried about getting involved in another mentally taxing conversation about some artist or poet about whom I would be able to find nothing intelligent to say, so I started to ask Louellen about some girls in the sorority, but Barrett interrupted me, "Sara, do you have a favorite writer?"

That question worried me. There was no one whose works I'd read extensively. I was afraid if I said Hemingway or Steinbeck, Barrett was sure to be an expert on them, and I'd end up looking like a moron. It was safer to make him do the talking, I reasoned, saying, "No, no one in particular. I heard you're going to begin work on your dissertation soon. What's your subject?"

"I have not yet decided definitively," he responded, "but I'm rather leaning toward doing something with Ernest Dowson."

When I heard the name, I got worried again because I'd never heard of him. Be ignorant, I told myself, and I said, "I've never heard of him. Tell me all about him."

The short life of Ernest Dowson (he died in 1900 at age 33) took us through dessert and coffee. Barrett was very happy to indulge in a biographic sketch of him, and it was as if his monologue was being read from a text. By the very end of dinner, I knew there were too many things about Barrett Sawyer that I disliked, although I couldn't really put my finger on them. Finally, I decided that, although superficially they seemed to be opposites, the essence of Barrett Sawyer was that he was just like Marc White.

After Pete had collected money from everyone for the bill, David announced, "Let's head out to Joe's. There's a great little band there and wonderful libations, if what I've been told is accurate, and we can burn off some of these calories with a little dancing. Everybody coming?"

"Oh damn," Marc groaned, "there's no fuckin' way I can, although I'd sure as hell love to, man. Emma and I want to go back to the hotel. If all of the rest of you go, you can just drop us off, all right?"

"Us too," Pete said. "I'm still sort of bushed from the drive."

"Yeah, sure," Bruce alluded, "we understand." All of us knew that Susan and Pete planned to burn off their calories with another kind of exercise.

"Oh come on," a red-faced Susan said. "Don't forget, tomorrow's Easter Sunday. Pete has to go to Mass."

"Okay," David said, "so the four of you can go back to the hotel in Pete's car, and the rest of us can take the van."

Quickly Barrett said to me, "Sara, do you want to go with them?" meaning in the van.

While I was excited that such a handsome man was interested in me, it also seemed to me that this was a rude way of asking me to sleep with him. I was both angry at him and dumbfounded, so it took me a few seconds before I could answer. The entire table was silent, as if my answer were the announcement of some long-awaited decision.

"Oh, after all this pasta," I said, "dancing is what I need. What'd you say the place was called?" *Fuck you, Barrett Sawyer,* was what I thought as the words came out. I knew he was crestfallen.

That made eight of us at Joe's, and Barrett was still sullen. Somehow Marc had manipulated things so that Barrett couldn't return to the hotel with them. Soon after we ordered drinks, the band took a break and I got to talk to Rafe, David, and Natalie, who was really quite pleasant without competition from Emma. Poor Louellen, solemn-faced and sober and too spiritually-inclined for our rowdy group, just didn't fit in. At least she was sitting next to Jenny and could talk to her. No one chatted with Barrett, and he didn't speak to any of us.

I danced first with Rafe. David danced with Natalie. Then Bruce and Jenny danced while we sat with Louellen. When they returned, Bruce asked Louellen to dance, and then David asked me. Natalie, of course, grabbed Rafe. The band was quite good, playing a lot of rock, some blues and a little folk and country.

As the song finished, David asked me, "So are you having a good time?"

"Yes," I answered, "no broken legs yet. Knock on wood."

"Want to dance the next one?"

"Sure."

It turned out to be a slow, romantic number. I bet Nat's mad at me, I thought, as David took a hold of me. He smelled nice and seemed so confident. I thought about how long it had been since I was that close to a man.

"You really enjoy skiing," I said. "Do you get a chance to go very often?"

"Not as much as I'd like to. My work keeps me pretty busy.

I'd like to take a week's vacation early next spring and go to some place like Vermont. I've never been to New England."

"Me either. I think it'd be nice to go there someday."

We danced a while without talking. I saw that all the others were sitting at our table. Natalie and Barrett were smoking, and they all seemed to be laughing. Maybe Barrett had finally gotten over Marc's victory and my rejection and was going to act civilized.

"So how do you like Chicago?" I asked.

"I love it. It's a really exciting city. You're never bored there. Have you ever been there?"

I told him I hadn't and he replied, "You'll have to take a trip there. I bet you'd love the Art Institute."

"Yes, I'm sure that would be wonderful." It was easy to talk to David after Barrett: nothing philosophic or aesthetic, just generalities.

"My firm's not far from the Art Institute."

"Really! Do you go there often?"

He laughed and said, "Only when I have to entertain out-of-town visitors like my parents or Jenny and her friends from college."

"Do you two have any other brothers or sisters?"

"No, there's just the two of us. How about you?"

I told him I just had one sister, that she was four years older than I was, and that she was married and expecting her first child in July. When David asked me if she'd gone to the U, I told him that both she and her husband had gone to Simpson.

"Really," he said. "I had a good buddy from high school who went there. He graduated in '73."

"Melly and Dan graduated in '73 too. What's his name?"

"Charlie Brown."

"Really! Like the comic strip?"

"Exactly."

"Well, that will be an easy name to remember. I'll have to ask Melly and Dan if they knew him."

When the song ended, we went back to our table, but before I could even sit down, Natalie hopped up, grabbed my arm, and said, "Do be a dear, Sara, and help me find the Little Girls' Room. We'll be right back."

When we were barely inside the restroom, Natalie said, "I thought we agreed I could have David. What's with the two dances in a row?"

"I couldn't help it, Nat," I pleaded. "He asked me. Besides, you seemed pretty buddy-buddy with Rafe in the restaurant."

"Well, it was pretty obvious Barrett was interested in you, Sara. You had your chance. You know he wanted to go back to the hotel with you and screw you. Sometimes you are so dense!"

"Well, I didn't want to go back with him," I said as I began brushing my hair. "He's really obnoxious. You know, I thought he was going to be sour grapes all night, but he looks like he's become a little more sociable, thank God."

"That's because I told him you're gay."

"What!" I exploded. "Nat, how could you!"

"You really hurt him, Sara. Men as handsome as Barrett have very delicate egos."

"I can't believe you did this, Natalie. How could you possibly tell a lie like that about me? We're supposed to be friends!"

She just stood there looking into the mirror as she applied a fresh coat of bright red lipstick. "Oh Sara, it worked, didn't it? I did it for Louellen. The poor kid was so depressed because Barrett was totally ignoring her. Now at least he's talking. You wouldn't have wanted to have put up with his moodiness all night!"

"Natalie," I said with controlled anger, "you did not tell that lie for Louellen's sake. You did it for yourself because you were jealous that I was dancing with David. I suppose you told the entire table, including Rafe, that I'm gay."

She turned and went into a stall. "Of course not, Sara," she said from behind the door. "I just whispered it to Barrett. I don't think anyone else heard."

"You don't think—oh, Natalie!" I said as I went into the stall next to her.

"What are you so upset about? You just told me you think Barrett's obnoxious, so what the hell do you care what he thinks? You're being so defensive about this, Sara. Maybe you are gay." Then she flushed the toilet.

"Natalie," I said calmly, "you know it was a lie. It was a horrible lie, horrible not just because it was an untruth but because it was a self-serving lie and you refuse to acknowledge that fact and apologize to me."

There was silence and finally I said, "Nat, are you still there?" I quickly flushed the toilet and opened the stall door. She was facing me head on, with her back to the mirror.

"Look, I'm sorry, Sara. I know it was a lie and I guess I shouldn't have told it. I don't think anybody else heard, but just to make sure I'll dance the next dance with Rafe and explain everything to him."

"Oh, thanks a lot," I said as I washed my hands. "How can I possibly trust you, Nat?"

"You can trust me, Sara. We agreed that you could have Rafe. I'm going to do everything in my power to see that you two hit it off. Come on, let's go."

I had no choice but to accept her declaration of sincerity. Back at the table I tried to detect if Jenny or Bruce or Louellen had heard Natalie's lie, but none of them acted any differently toward me. When the song ended, Bruce and Jenny got up to dance, and Natalie quickly asked Rafe. I thought perhaps David seemed a little surprised. The four of us sat in silence, listening to the band and watching the dancers. When the song ended, Bruce and Jenny stayed on the floor. Rafe and Natalie came back, and he asked me to dance.

"Come on, David," Natalie said. "We can't let a terrific Simon go to waste."

David got up to dance with Natalie, which left Louellen and Barrett alone. Poor Louellen, I thought, as I danced the next three dances with Rafe. The third one was a slow number, and he took me in his arms before I knew what was happening.

"This is really turning out to be an exciting weekend, isn't it, Sara?" he whispered in my ear.

"Yes, it is." I wanted to find out what Natalie had told him, but I didn't know how to go about asking. Suddenly he drew me really close and started giving me little kisses on my cheek. I felt him erect and pushing against my body. I guess she told him the right thing, I thought. I closed my eyes until my contacts began to hurt. When I opened them, I saw that Louellen and David were dancing together. They made an odd pair because he was tall and looked a little older than his age while Louellen was barely five feet and looked as if she could be in eighth grade. I bet Natalie's really ticked, I thought. She'll have to tell David Louellen's gay.

When the song ended, we all went back to the table and ordered another round of drinks.

"Aren't you a dancer?" Jenny asked Barrett.

"No, I don't dance. Perhaps I'll call a cab and return to the hotel."

"Oh, there's no need to do that," Jenny said. "We'll probably be going pretty soon anyway. What time is it, Bruce?"

He looked at his watch and said that it was a half past midnight, and Jenny remarked that she didn't know it was that late and that she was exhausted.

"Well," David proposed, "let's finish this round and then head back to the hotel. Everybody in agreement?"

That was fine with everyone, including Barrett. When the waitress brought our order, Bruce asked Barrett what he was drinking and Barrett told him it was an Alaska cocktail.

"I gotta try one of those sometime," Bruce said. "That's a great color."

"I doubt you'd enjoy it," Barrett said. "It can be a trifle bitter."

The rest of us, except David, who was drinking Sprite because he had volunteered to drive, were drinking beer and wine.

"Then, hell, I guess I'd better stick with Bud," Bruce said.

When the next song started, he and Jenny went off to dance. Rafe asked me to dance, but I noticed that David said nothing to Natalie or Louellen. As the song ended, we were next to Bruce and Jenny, and he said, "Hell, I haven't danced with you yet to-night. Shall we, Sara dear?" Rafe took Jenny, and I saw that David and Natalie got up to dance.

Then I rejoined Rafe. It was a slow number and he held me very close and we didn't talk at all. David and Natalie were finally together for a slow dance. They didn't look right together, I thought. Natalie was big-boned and needed a huskier man, someone with a long nose and beard who looked more foreign-born; David was too all-American.

After that dance, we all sat down and drank and just listened to the band. Finally Jenny announced, "Last dance. This is it and then we go, okay?" She and Bruce got up. It was another slow number. Rafe had his arm around me, but he didn't ask me to dance. He seemed tired. David yawned. I knew Natalie wanted to dance with him, but neither one said anything, so we all sat and watched Jenny and Bruce, who, as I stared at them, didn't seem to be an ideal couple either. He was too much of a clown; she was too serious. Perhaps we're all mismatched, I thought.

On our return to the hotel, Louellen sat in back with Jenny and Bruce, who were cuddled together. Natalie had to sit on a cooler on the van floor. Rafe and I got the middle seats, with David driving and Barrett beside him. None of us spoke.

At the hotel, we all made comments about how tired we were. Rafe gave me a peck on the cheek, and then we separated, the four women going to our room and the four men to their room. Our rooms were at almost opposite ends of a long hall. Once inside, we took turns washing up, and all of us were asleep as soon as our faces hit the pillows. Natalie and I never said a word to each other, not even good night.

On Easter Sunday, Pete and Susan went to a morning church service. All of us had earlier agreed to meet for brunch at noon. I didn't even hear Jenny when she got up at nine to meet Bruce and David out on the slopes. I woke up shortly before ten but just lay in bed dreaming up a future romance with Rafe Johnson. I finally got up around 10:30. When I got out of the shower, Natalie and Louellen were awake too. Jenny returned a little after eleven and took a quick shower. After we all got ready, we went down to the lobby to meet the rest of the group.

By noon we all gathered and drove off in the van and Oldsmobile to another place Barrett recommended. There was a lovely buffet complete with ice sculptures and lots of blooming lilies. All of us ate as if we hadn't had food for a week. At least Barrett knew how to pick restaurants, although he complained profusely to the waitress that the blueberry blintzes in the buffet line were cold and hard. Finally, during one of his reprimands to the waitress, Bruce said, "Hell, Barrett, shut your trap and give the gal a break. She's not responsible for no damn blitz bein' cold!"

"They rarely are," he said indignantly, and then he didn't say another word during the rest of the meal. Other than Barrett's silence, the rest of the group was very convivial. Rafe gave me a lot of smiles and patted my knee a couple times. Natalie was quite pleasant, and even Marc had no sarcastic remarks and little bragging to do. Susan and Pete talked a lot about the upcoming wedding and their plans, including buying a house and filling it with kids and antiques, which made for very light and optimistic conversation.

After we returned to the hotel, all of us changed clothes except Marc, who went off by himself to study, and those of us who had to rent equipment did so. We'd all decided to go out together under David and Jenny's guidance. The rest of us, with perhaps the exception of Barrett, who was not very coordinated, could safely be called novices.

I stuck close to Rafe and managed to ski down a moderately steep run. I only fell once but didn't hurt myself at all. Unfortunately, I went down in some dirty snow and got my cap and the back of my hair a little dirty, but Rafe said, "No problem. We can take care of that with a little soap and water," and I imagined taking a shower with him, which was a rather pleasant thought.

Finally David announced that we might be ready for a bigger challenge, but after the lift had taken us up, I knew that I wasn't ready for this run. Louellen and Susan were equally hesitant. After I expressed my apprehension, Susan said, "The view here's terrific, and we girls are just going to stay right here and enjoy it!"

"The rest of you have our blessings to break as many legs as you want," I added.

"I think these women need companionship," Rafe piped in. "I volunteer to stay with them." Then Pete admitted that he didn't want to try the run either.

"That's all right," David said. "The most important things in skiing are, one, to be not afraid, and two, to know your limitations. It'd be foolhardy to attempt this run if you were scared. Is there anybody who does want to try it?"

"I'm going down," Barrett said. "Are you coming with me, Emma?"

I sensed Emma was a little frightened as she said, "Let me think about it a moment."

Then Bruce and Jenny agreed that they'd ski down and David asked, "How about you, Natalie?"

"I'm definitely up for it," she affirmed. "I just wish you'd all decide what you're doing." This put Emma on the spot, and I knew she couldn't disregard a challenge from Natalie, so she agreed to try it.

First, Jenny took off and curved gracefully down the slope. Bruce was anything but poised, but he was relaxed and had a sort of natural athletic ability. Emma went next with Barrett just a stride behind her, so that they were actually almost at one another's sides most of the way down. She wasn't a skilled skier, but she was steady and lucky. Her blond hair few back from her teal blue cap as she whished down, and her lithe blue-clad figure next to Barrett's emerald green ski jacket and pants made such a complementary contrast against the white snow.

"Your turn, Natalie," David said, as she flashed him a big smile and took off. Smiling was unusual for Natalie because she had very large crooked teeth, never having had them straightened as a child. She had told me at Thanksgiving that she was trying to put a little money aside for orthodontia, but that she'd probably be thirty before she got braces and forty before they came off. When she joked like that, it made me feel so sorry for her.

Finally David took off, weaving wide arcs behind Natalie's fairly straight path.

"They make it look so easy," Pete said. "Maybe we should give it a try, Susan."

Jenny and Bruce, just tiny dots, were already safely at the bottom and seemed to be waving up to us. What happened next occurred so fast that I really didn't see it coming or note any causes. There was just Natalie lying slumped over on the snow and screaming in pain.

"Oh, dear God," Susan gasped, "please hope she's not hurt too badly."

At the bottom we learned that Natalie had hurt her ankle. As the ski patrol brought her to us, she was crying and kept repeating how painful it was. Emma was trying to calm her down, and we all offered sympathy and encouragement. One of the ski patrol told us to take her to the emergency room of a nearby hospital. "They don't want crowds in the ER," he said. "Decide which two of you are going to take her there. If you don't have transportation, we can call an ambulance."

We told them we had a van, and they carried Natalie on the stretcher back to the resort's parking lot. After Natalie was put in the back of the van, it was decided that Rafe and I should go to the hospital. David wanted to go too, but we convinced him it wasn't really necessary.

I crouched beside Natalie in the back of the van, held her hand, and kept telling her she was going to be fine. She had calmed down a little, but she said her ankle hurt like hell.

"Think of all those handsome interns in the emergency room waiting to shower you with tender loving care," I said, and she smiled.

"Oh, hell, Sara, they could all look like Robert Redford and I wouldn't give a shit."

"May I have that in writing, please?"

She smiled again and squeezed my hand. Soon we reached the emergency entrance, and Rafe and I got on each side of Natalie and helped her in. The hospital staff was friendly and efficient. She was questioned about her health background, examined, x-rayed, given antibiotics and a pain pill, and finally bandaged. The doctor, a short, balding man in his fifties, said she was lucky, that there were no breaks; she simply had a badly sprained ankle. He told her to keep ice on the ankle and urged her to keep her weight off her foot. We were back at the hotel in just a little over an hour.

When we walked in, we immediately saw Susan and Pete in the lobby. They were on their way to the lounge for hot buttered rum. After they were filled in on Natalie's condition, Rafe asked where everyone else was.

"Bruce, Jenny, and David are still skiing," he responded. "Marc's in the coffee shop studying. Emma went off with Barrett. Let's see, is that everybody?"

"You forgot Louellen, silly," Susan chided. "She's up in your room reading."

Louellen's introversion coupled with her diminutive physique seemed to make everyone else forget that she too was along on the trip.

"Well, the rum sounds great," Rafe said. "We'll be down for some as soon as we get Natalie settled upstairs."

"Hey, the rum sounds great to me too," Natalie said.

"The pill's going to make you fall asleep," I reminded her. "Plus you shouldn't have alcohol with it. You've got to get some rest, Nat."

"Oh mommy Sara dearest," she began to whine, but Susan cut her off, and reluctantly Natalie agreed to go up to our room. We no sooner had the blanket tucked over her and ice packs around her ankle than Natalie fell asleep. Rafe put his arm around me and asked me if I wanted to join him in the lounge, but I told him I wanted to take a quick shower and wash the dirt out of my hair. Rafe promised to check on me later.

I was shocked when, several minutes later, I emerged from the bathroom with only my robe on and my hair turbaned with a towel to see Jenny, Bruce, Rafe, David, and Louellen all whispering while Natalie was still asleep.

"I'm sure glad it was nothing serious," David said to me, as I went over to my suitcase.

"Me too," I answered. "She'll be fine." I began collecting underwear and the clothes I wanted to put on. Then Bruce and Jenny left to get something to eat. I was about to go back to the bathroom to dress when Rafe announced that he and David were going back to their room. After their quick departure, I began dressing. I'd just put on my panties and bra when there was a quiet knock on the door. Louellen put down her Harlequin romance and went to answer.

"It's us again," Rafe said. "Can we come in?"

Quickly I put my robe back on and Louellen let them in. "There's a slight problem," he continued. "We can't use our room right now because Barrett's got Emma in there. Can we use your john and then we'll get out?"

After they took turns using the bathroom, Rafe said, "Sorry you haven't been able to get dressed, Sara. We're leaving now. Come to the lounge when you get ready."

"You too, Louellen," David added.

We agreed and they were almost out the door when Natalie woke up. "What's all the commotion?" she asked. "David, is that you?"

"How are you feeling?" he asked, as he came over to the bed.

"Not too bad. It doesn't hurt right now."

"Wait 'til the pain pill wears off," Rafe said. "Hell, I guess I shouldn't have said that."

"Nurse Sara, when do I get to take another one?" Natalie asked, and I told her not until seven and to try to get some more rest.

"And why don't you try to have a show at a Soho art gallery, Sara. Damn it, I'm not sleepy now!"

"Natalie, I feel really bad about what happened," David said. "I shouldn't have let you attempt that run."

"Oh hell, it wasn't your fault, David. It was just an accident and I was the lucky victim. If you feel guilty, then do me a favor and stay and keep me company."

"I think Sara needs to get dressed," he said.

"Oh, she can go in the bathroom," Natalie replied, giving me a you-better-comply-look.

"Well," Rafe said, "we might as well hang out here for a little while. Our room's occupied at the moment, if you know what I mean."

"Ummmm," Natalie guessed, "Bruce and Jenny?"

"No," Rafe answered, "Barrett and Emma."

"I have a deck of cards if anybody wants to play?" Louellen ventured.

"Terrific!" Rafe exclaimed. "Leave it to little Lou to come through. I've been dying to play some bridge all weekend. You know, Woodley, it's my turn to take you after that double you gave me the last time we played."

"Hell, you're the one who redoubled."

"I hope you girls play," Rafe said while moving the small window table over to Natalie's bed.

Louellen told him she could manage and Natalie said that she'd always wanted to learn. I told him I knew how to play but that I needed to get dressed first. Rafe said that sounded fine, that they'd fill Natalie in on the game's fundamentals until I was ready to help her. Since everyone was agreeable to this plan, I took my clothes and cosmetic bag and went to the bathroom. I dressed as quickly as I could, blew what was left of the wetness out of my hair, and curled it a little. Finally, I applied makeup and put in my contacts. Earlier I'd felt so drab and ugly in Rafe's presence, not even daring to put on my glasses or to start combing my wet hair while he was in sight. When I came out of the bathroom, Rafe was dealing a new hand and I asked, "Who's winning?"

"We've only played one hand," Rafe answered. "It took a while to explain things to Nat. But Lou and I have a 60 leg. And oh, you look nice." He gave me a big smile.

I told him thanks, grateful I had bought a new outfit for this trip: navy cords, a plaid shirt, and a yellow sweater.

"Since I was dummy," Rafe continued, "I ran downstairs and found Bruce and told him he'd better knock before he tries to go into our room."

"Help Natalie out now," David said to me, so I sat down on the bed beside her and counted her points. Rafe passed and David bid a spade. Louellen also passed.

"I bid one of these?" Natalie asked, pointing to her five hearts, and I agreed.

"One heart," Natalie said proudly.

"You have to say two," Rafe corrected, and so she did. Then David responded, "Three clubs."

Natalie had four clubs with the ace, a singleton ace of spades, and fourteen points total. They probably had enough for game, I reasoned, and playing in a suit would be better than no trump.

"I hope I don't get you into trouble, David," I said, "but Natalie's going to say five clubs."

"Five clubs!" she shouted.

"What the hell, I'm doubling," Rafe said, and then David studied his cards for a few seconds, grinned, and redoubled.

"Hell, that was fun!" Natalie exclaimed. "What happens next?"

"You don't have to worry about anything, Nat," I said. "You're the dummy."

Louellen led a small diamond, and I instructed Natalie in laying out her hand. When she'd finished, David said, "Terrific support, Nat!" I knew he'd like her singleton and aces. Rafe and Louellen won the first trick with Rafe's ace of diamonds.

"David can only lose one more," I said to Natalie, "but I'm sure he's got things under control, . . . I hope."

"I don't think I can stand to watch this," Natalie said. "And besides, I've been dying to go to the john. Do be a dear and help me, Sara?"

Although I really wanted to watch David try to make the contract, I helped Natalie into the bathroom. When the door was closed, she said in a quiet but excited tone, "Oh Sara, I think I'm in love! Isn't he just about the most handsome man you've ever seen!"

"David?" I asked, thinking about Marc White.

"Of course, David! I love everything about him. I'm aching to be alone with him. Do me a big favor, Sara, and get Louellen and Rafe out of our room so we can be alone together."

"How am I supposed to do that?"

"Tell Rafe you're dying for some hot buttered rum. He adores you, Sara, so you can easily get him down to the lounge."

"What about Louellen?"

"Take her with you."

"Suppose she wants to stay up here and read?"

"Call her in here so we can explain things to her."

"I'm not going to call her in here," I protested. "She's playing her hand. What are the guys going to think?"

"Oh, we'll think of something. We'll give her a few minutes and then we'll call her in," Natalie said, as she opened Jenny's makeup case and found her mouthwash. She used it and then helped herself to some lipstick. "I hate this blue eye shadow of hers," she said. "Do you have any shadow handy?"

When I told her no, she hopped over to the door, stuck her head out, and called sweetly, "Louellen, when you're through, could you come here a sec?" Then Natalie hopped back over to the closed toilet seat, sat down, flung her head down, and began brushing her thick dark hair. It was one of Natalie's best features. Soon Louellen appeared and Natalie filled her in on the plan, stressing that we should act quickly. I agreed and the three of us returned to the table and bed. "How'd you do, David?" I asked.

"It couldn't have been more beautiful. Made five exactly. That's 400, right, Johnson?"

"Don't rub it in," Rafe said.

"You mean we have 400 points and they only have 60?" Natalie asked.

"Plus we have a game," David said. "We cut off your leg."

"Hell, this is fun!" Natalie gushed.

As David dealt the cards, Rafe asked, "What was the conspiracy in the john?"

"Oh nothing," Natalie said with perfect glibness. "Sara and I just couldn't figure out who was using which towels. Since Louellen has dandruff, we didn't want to get them confused."

I saw Louellen's brown eyes widen under her huge eyeglasses. That was really horrible, Nat, I thought. Someday the gods are going to punish you.

"Don't pick up the cards," Natalie said suddenly to me. "Sara dear, you go play in David's place and he can come over here and coach me. No offense, Sara, but he's obviously the better player and I can probably really learn a lot."

"No problem," I said as I got up. It would be fun to play a hand anyway. After David and I exchanged places, I picked up my new hand and suddenly hated everything about Natalie. I only had two points. "Pass," I said. There was nothing more boring than having to wade through a hand of bridge with an utterly rotten hand. The other three bid, but I could only pass.

Louellen and Rafe won the contract with three diamonds. David told Natalie to double and Rafe redoubled. She'll have to take all five tricks herself, I thought to myself. Surprisingly, she did, with David's help, of course. As Rafe recorded our hefty score, I knew my chance to put Natalie's plan into effect had come.

"After that last hand," I began, "I can tell this seat's no good for me. And ever since I heard the words *hot buttered rum*, my mouth's been drooling. Is anybody up for a sojourn to the lounge?"

Louellen quickly said she'd like to go, and Rafe conceded that, since Lady Luck wasn't with him, he'd love to join us. Then David said, "I haven't eaten anything since breakfast and I'm starved. I hear they've got great appetizers in the lounge, so let's get going, folks!"

I panicked as he spoke and got up from his place on the bed next to Natalie. "Shouldn't somebody stay here with Nat?" I asked, my eyes meeting David's.

"Oh, I thought you were going down too," David said to her while looking at me.

"I just don't feel up to it yet," Natalie responded. "Don't mind me. I'll be perfectly fine here. You all go down and have fun."

I sensed there was a message here I was supposed to decode and act upon. "How about if we send somebody up with some hot chocolate or coffee for you, Nat?" I asked.

Giving me the warmest smile, she said, "Oh Sara dear, that would be divine! Didn't the doctor order a cup of hot chocolate with two big marshmallows? But don't hurry—just take your time. I'll be here resting."

Phase One accomplished, I thought as we left the room. Now all I had to do was get David to deliver Natalie's beverage to her.

In the lounge we joined Bruce and Jenny. David and Rafe ordered potato skins, nachos, Buffalo wings, and fried zucchini. We postponed ordering Natalie's beverage. At first I was afraid Jenny would offer to take it to Natalie, but then I guessed that she was hungry and wanted some of the appetizers. The waitress had just brought our food when Emma and Barrett walked up and joined us. Barrett ordered a cup of tea and was his usual moody self, while Emma seemed very happy.

Just a couple minutes after they sat down, Marc White suddenly appeared over Emma's shoulder and gave her a kiss on the top of her head. The two tables we'd pushed together were very crowded and there wasn't an unoccupied chair at any of the nearby tables, so Marc just stood between Barrett and Emma, drinking out of her wine glass and munching on the appetizers. When the waitress brought Barrett's tea, Louellen suggested that we order Natalie's hot chocolate, and so we did. She and I exchanged a knowing look that said, *Sara, it's your turn now; good luck getting David to take it to her.*

When the waitress returned with the steaming mug of hot chocolate, Barrett, who had grown even more morose in Marc's presence and who had finished sipping his tea while not touching the food, quickly rose and offered to take it to Natalie. I tried to think of something to say but all I could muster was, "You've barely sat down, Barrett."

He seemed surprised that I spoke to him and called him by name, but he said, "I want to do some reading before dinner, so please excuse me. I'll just drop this off and make sure Natalie's all right."

He no sooner left with Natalie's drink and Jenny's key card than Marc plopped down into his seat and said, "Thank God he's gone. Does that guy get off on being anti-social?"

"Well, all I can say," Bruce replied, "is that if he was rushing our house, he'd sure as hell be the ideal candidate for the 'boiler room tour.'"

Then all the men laughed and Jenny said, "That's cruel and besides, I know you don't really do that."

"Sure we do," Bruce said.

"No, you don't," she countered.

"But we do!"

Then they started reminiscing about rushing undesirable freshmen and laughing at the "losers" they could remember. All the men and Emma were laughing, but Louellen didn't even smile, and Jenny kept protesting that they were exaggerating. I sighed; inside I was feeling as if I had the worst friends in the world.

Finally Louellen said, "I think it's unfortunate that people generalize and also that they judge each other so much on physical appearance. Life is unfair, but I believe God put us here to do all we can to make life fairer."

Louellen's words made me realize that one of my worst faults was judging people too hastily. Now here was Louellen, whom I considered to be somewhat dull, a person whose interests seemed confined to Harlequin romances, Third World proselytizing, and scientific research, gently reminding us of our worst habits. I pictured Louellen in some lab trying to find the cure for our most egregious maladies, and at the same time all I could think about was how Susan and Louellen had lost their mother to cancer. I felt my eyes getting a little wet.

Since we were all silent and probably uncomfortable with Louellen's reference to God, there was a lot of sipping and chewing. Finally Jenny said, "I need to wash up before dinner. Are you coming up too, Bruce?"

He agreed, but they'd been gone less than five minutes when Bruce returned to the table. "I thought I'd better warn everybody," he said. "Nat and Barrett are in the sack together. Jenny's going to use our room to wash up. Here's your key card, Sara. If I were you guys, I'd order some more appetizers. So long, everybody."

As he spoke, I noticed Louellen's mouth drop open in disbelief. Emma seemed a little shocked too. Rafe and David exchanged smiles, and Marc, of course, was jubilant.

"Ol' Nat's amazing, isn't she!" he exclaimed. "You know, Sara, I thought ol' Barrett was after you. What the hell happened?"

"Oh," I blurted out without thinking, "Natalie took care of everything. She told him I was gay. Did you know Louellen has dandruff? She probably told Barrett that Emma's got V.D."

All my bitterness came out so quickly that I was angry at myself for the words I had spoken. I was sure I'd surprised everyone. I hadn't meant to embarrass Louellen or Emma, although I didn't really care about Marc. Everyone knew he was a cuckold anyway.

"Sara's right," Louellen said. "Natalie shouldn't make up lies about people."

Then several seconds elapsed before anyone else said anything. It was Marc who spoke first, "Well, I've really got to get back to the fuckin' books. Do you want to come quiz me, Emma?"

She agreed, and after they left, there were just the four of us. I sensed David and Rafe were trying to put all the pieces of Natalie's plot together, but neither one spoke. Finally Louellen asked me, "How can you be friends with Natalie?" I told her I didn't know and then she said, "She just seems so uncaring about everybody except herself."

"Did you know that Nat and Emma were roommates their freshman year?" I asked. "A computer matched them up."

Rafe commented that that seemed amazing, and then we all talked about our freshman year roommates and the people we were close to who graduated with us.

"The number of people who left before graduating," David reflected, "was pretty high. Some got married, some joined the armed forces, some transferred to other schools, and some just left to join the rat race a few years before us." Some had mental breakdowns, I thought, remembering Sharon Thomasino. "Hey, Rafe, do you have any idea whatever happened to Raisley Calvert?"

While he and David did some more reminiscing, Louellen

wiped her mouth, put her napkin down, and slid her chair away from the table slightly. When they had finished talking, she said, "Well, I'm old-fashioned. I know Susan and Pete sleep together, but they're in love and they're going to get married. Natalie told us she was madly in love with you, David, and just because it was Barrett who took the hot chocolate up to her, and not you, **he's** the one she's in bed with. I don't think that's morally right, and I just had to say all this to get my feelings out of my system. Sorry, I'll be quiet little Louellen now."

I was surprised Louellen had revealed the whole plot, but perhaps there was not that much left to figure out. She had spoken what I felt also, but I was too reluctant to admit it, lest I be thought prudish. While she appeared to be very disillusioned, I thought Rafe and David seemed to be merely amused. "It's okay, Louellen," I said. "It's partly my fault for always going along with Natalie."

"Well, I've got a headache and I want to go lie down before dinner, but now I don't have anywhere to go," she said.

"You can always use our room," David offered.

Just as he spoke, Rafe waved to Susan and Pete, who were standing near the lounge entrance. "These look like people we know," Pete said, as they sat down in two of the empty chairs.

"How's Nat feeling?" Susan asked.

"Evidently quite well," David responded. "She's in the sack with Barrett, and now that I think about it, I'm actually glad he's along on this trip."

Susan almost choked on the Buffalo wing she'd bit into. "What!" she shouted.

"Nat and Barrett!" Pete echoed her shock. "I don't believe it!"

"Well, I guess I can believe it," Susan said, wiping the sauce from around her mouth with a napkin. "With Nat, anything's possible! Remember Screwy Louie, Sara?"

I nodded, while Louellen said, "Worst of all, they're in our room. Sara and I don't have anywhere to go. I wanted to take a nap before dinner."

Susan rose quickly. "You can always use our room," she said, "but that's not the right solution. Just leave things to me, honey. Natalie has no right to infringe upon your rights. After all, you're paying for the room too." She seemed so full of motherly protection in her indignation. "I'll give that Natalie a piece of my mind," she continued. "Just give me five minutes, and then you and Sara can come on up."

"This I wanna see," Pete said. "I'll go up with you."

"We're meeting for dinner at seven forty-five," David reminded him. "We'll see you two later."

After they left, we were quiet again. "So we're going to the best pizza place in town?" I ventured, with the hope of a new conversation.

"Absolutely," David answered. "We couldn't leave town without a trip to Mama Spionetti's, or so the concierge tells me."

"I don't think I can stand to even look at food," Rafe said. He'd been the most robust eater of the group. I reminded him that in a couple of hours, he'd be hungry again. Then David motioned for the waitress, we spent a couple minutes figuring out our shares based on the money the others had left, and finally we headed up to our rooms.

When Louellen and I entered, Natalie was lying on her side with her eyes closed. She opened them and asked, "Will you get me a glass of water and my pill when it's time, Sara?" I told her I would and she rolled over to the other side and seemed to fall asleep.

The next hour passed slowly. Jenny came in and lay down. Louellen slept too. I tried to rest, but I never fell asleep. I woke them all about seven fifteen, and after we got ready, we met all the others in the hotel lobby.

The pizza place was noisy, and it seemed as if it took forever to get our order. Barrett directed all his attention to Natalie, who was in extremely good spirits. Marc was happy too, obviously because he had Emma all to himself. Rafe drank a lot of beer, since David said he'd drive, and kept one arm around me most of the time. Pete and Susan were their usual contented selves. Bruce got bombed and told several dirty jokes, but I couldn't hear most of them because of the noise. Jenny and Susan talked a lot with Louellen, and David laughed heartily at Bruce's jokes. By all appearances we seemed to be a very happy group.

It was a little after ten when the waitress brought our bill. Bruce and Jenny announced that they wanted to see *Futureworld*, and David asked Louellen if she'd like to see it too. She said yes, and then Rafe stated that he'd already seen the movie and that it was okay but not really worth seeing twice. That meant I went back to the hotel with the others, who quickly scurried off to their rooms. Rafe asked me if I'd like to go to the lounge for a drink, and it was really the only thing I could do since I didn't know where Natalie and Barrett were going.

In the lounge, I found out more about Rafe's family, his work, and his bad luck playing the stock market. After we'd each had one drink, he told me he had a bottle of champagne in his room and asked me if I'd like to go have a nightcap. I sensed we were both thinking the same thing: this is our last night, our last chance. . . .

"That sounds nice," I said.

In his room, thankfully unoccupied, he poured us each a glass and we toasted a terrific Easter weekend. Then he took my glass and put it down with his on the dresser. His arms went around me as he pulled me next to him and gave me a long kiss.

"Let's lie down on the bed, Sara," he muttered.

It seemed as if we almost fell on the bed, and he stayed practically on top of me for the longest time kissing me. My arm started to ache where it was pinned under his body, and my contacts hurt also. Finally he moved over on his side, and I managed to get my now-numb arm free. He kept kissing me passionately while pulling my shirt out of my cords. Finally I felt his hands on my skin moving up to my bra. Suddenly my right eye began to hurt like crazy.

"I've got something bothering my contact," I told him. "I've got to take it out."

As he let go of me, I sat up and popped the lens out. Instant relief. Then I walked over to the dresser where I'd left my purse.

"Why don't you take both of them out and be comfortable?" Rafe suggested. "I noticed Barrett has some stuff for contacts in the john."

I went into the bathroom, closed the door, and put both lenses back in their case. Then I dabbed the tears in my eye and blew my nose. There was a knock on the door.

"If you want," Rafe said from the other side, "my p.j.'s are hanging on the back of the door. The blue ones. You'd look terrific in my top."

"Okay, I'll be right out," I answered.

What I thought was: This is absolutely ridiculous. Why lose my virginity to Rafe Johnson and then probably never see him again? He didn't love me; I didn't love him. I'd known before we'd left Iowa that I wasn't going to sleep with anyone on this trip, not even Marc White. I unzipped my cords, tucked my shirt back in, and zipped them up again. Then I brushed my hair and put on some fresh lipstick.

I couldn't really tell if Rafe was surprised when I emerged fully dressed because I didn't have my contacts in. He was sitting in bed under the covers with his back resting against the headboard. At least from the waist up, he was naked.

I went over to the bed and sat down beside him. "Look, Rafe,"

I began, "I've really liked getting to know you on this trip, but we only met two days ago. I'm just not the type of person who plunges into relationships quickly."

He was totally passive while I spoke, looking me straight in the eye. He seemed a beautiful Nordic god with his curly blond hair and tanned chest. I knew if he touched me I'd probably succumb to his seduction, but he didn't move.

"It's really late and we've got a long drive ahead of us tomorrow, so I'd best say goodnight," I said and then gave him a gentle kiss, but his lips didn't respond, so I got up quickly and left the room.

Once I was in the hallway it did strike me that if Barrett wasn't in Rafe's room he was probably with Natalie. As I walked toward our room, I decided I didn't care. I was feeling a little down anyway. I unlocked the door and turned on the overhead light in the entry area, saying quietly, "Nat, it's me, Sara. I'm back."

I heard a muffled, "Oh shit." Then I went to use the bathroom, lingering there quite a while. When I walked out into the room, Barrett was pulling his sweater over his head.

"Hi, Barrett," I said.

He didn't respond. I went to my suitcase, got out my robe, gown, and makeup bag and went back to the bathroom. When I emerged this time, Barrett was gone. Natalie was still lying on her back in bed with her eyes closed.

"Do me a favor, Sara dear," she said. "Hand me my nightie."

I took her gown from the back of a chair and gave it to her, asking, "Did you take your pain pill?" She said yes as she put on the gown. It felt funny to get into our bed after Barrett had been there. The white hotel sheets seemed tainted; I thought they smelled like sex, although I had no idea what sex smelled like. At least it was a king-size bed, and I didn't feel any wetness on my faraway space. "I'm sorry I interrupted things," I said.

"Oh, you didn't really," Natalie responded. "Barrett couldn't get it up. Emma says he's frequently impotent; I think she's nuts, but she says it's one of the things about him she finds rather charming. Anyway, I'm tired as hell."

I couldn't fall asleep for quite a while. I lay on my back, not wanting my face to touch the pillow in case Barrett's had been there. Soon I heard Natalie snoring lightly. Back to my amazing fantasy about the fictional Clark Merrick, I decided. I hadn't dreamed about him for a couple months.

Departure time was set for ten fifteen. I woke up at seven thirty, got dressed, packed, and took a walk outside. Then I had room service send up orange juice and an English muffin. Everyone else slept until almost nine, when they woke to the knock on the door and the smell of complimentary coffee with my breakfast. They all wanted me to order food for them, which I willingly did. After I ate, I helped Natalie pack a little since it was hard for her to move about. Susan came by to make sure we were up. By nine-thirty Louellen and Jenny were both ready, but Natalie, who was still in only her bra and panties, was just starting to put on her makeup.

"I'm taking my suitcase down to the lobby, and I'll just stay down there and read," Louellen said. "I want to get a new paperback for the trip back."

"You can go with her if you want, Sara," Jenny said. "Bruce said he'd be by about ten, and I'll stay here and help Nat."

I decided to accompany Louellen down to the lobby. It would be a good chance to read the novel I'd brought along and not even glanced at so far.

In the lobby were David, who was reading a newspaper, and Barrett, whose legs were slung over the arms of a big wing chair and whose interest seemed consumed by some boring-looking tome. We said hello to David, and I sat down nearby while Louellen went off to the gift store. I felt relieved at not having to face Rafe.

Just after Louellen returned with her new romance, we were all distracted by the cries of an infant. Its mother, who was sitting not far from us, kept trying to calm the child, but eventually she ended up walking around the lobby.

"Whom are you reading, Sara?" Barrett asked.

"Edith Wharton," I answered. "*The House of Mirth.*"

"Such a dreadful writer!" he responded immediately. "There is such a dearth of tolerable female novelists, and Wharton is definitely not one of them."

"Barrett," I said as calmly and icily as I could, "are you aware that Louellen and I have been offended by your use of the deprecating term 'female novelist' and by your totally unjustified assertion that there aren't very many good novelists who are women?"

David and Louellen smiled while Barrett looked slightly shaken. "I'm certainly entitled to my opinion," he said.

"I suppose you're reading that male poet almost no one's ever heard of?" I continued. "Ernest something—wasn't it? How do you explain his obscurity? Good writers simply don't pass into oblivion."

Barrett rolled his eyes and said, "This is definitely beyond your comprehension. The selection of subject matter for one's dissertation has nothing whatsoever to do with popularity or personal taste. It's a purely academic decision."

"Oh, I think my little brain can comprehend that, Barrett," I replied sarcastically. "And if that's the case, then I wish you many hours of boredom reading the works of Ernest whoever, obscure and I'm sure quite third-rate **male** poet. I'll take Edith Wharton any day."

Barrett swung his legs onto the floor and sat up erect in the chair, his nostrils flaring with indignation. I knew Louellen and David were enjoying our repartee, but I just wondered for how long I could continue this verbal volley. Perhaps victory would come now if Barrett stalked off.

"On the contrary," he said, "I receive much pleasure reading writers such as Dowson and those of the late Victorian era. Until we were so rudely interrupted by that undisciplined child, I was happily engaged in the brilliance of Pater."

I was stumped. If I failed to respond now, Barrett would win. There was only one thing Walter Pater had written that stuck in my mind, but I wasn't sure how to use it against Barrett.

"But it's such a pity," I began, "that you admire the man but don't follow his advice."

"What do you mean?"

"You seem to me to be the sort of man who's always letting his **candle** go out. Didn't Walter Pater say that success in life is to burn always with a **hard**, gemlike flame?"

For a moment I was afraid Barrett would call my bluff and begin some discussion of Pater's philosophies that would be quite beyond my knowledge. Furthermore, I knew the logic of my argument was rather brittle: one could admire an artist and yet reject his tenets. All I could hope was that Barrett would interpret my words in light of his sexual impotence with Natalie and Emma. He seemed about to reply, but then he just gave me the coldest look imaginable, rose from his chair, and headed toward the registration desk.

"Yeah, Sara!" Louellen said softly in an admiring, congratulatory tone as he walked off.

"That guy is—pardon the expression—one crock of shit," David said. "Did you hear him call that little defenseless baby undisciplined?"

"Yes," Louellen replied, "as if a tiny baby can be disciplined so she won't cry!" (I hadn't even caught Barrett's description of the baby because of the pressure I'd been under to defeat him for his literary haughtiness.)

Louellen continued, "She couldn't have been more than two or three months old."

"Well, maybe a little older," David said. "I have a cousin who's got a six-month old, and that baby looked about the same size as my cousin's. Also, Louellen, I think **she** is a **he**. The kid's outfit was trimmed in blue and there was a fire engine on it."

David's perceptiveness suddenly impressed me.

"I'm sure you're right," Louellen said. "I don't know anything about babies. I hardly ever babysat when I was growing up. Tiny babies sort of frighten me. I'm not sure I ever want to have kids. I'm afraid I'd be a real basket case trying to take care of a small baby. Hopefully, the Peace Corps won't put me in charge of any nurseries!"

"Oh," I said, "I'm sure you'd learn fast. Millions of people become parents with no experience." I was thinking of Melly and Dan. Then Louellen asked the time and David told her that it was almost ten. She announced that she wanted to use the restroom, and David and I returned to our reading, although I couldn't concentrate.

"You're not laughing," David said.

"What?" I muttered, as I looked up into his intelligent dark brown eyes.

"Didn't you say you're reading *The House of Mirth*?"

"Oh," I smiled, understanding his emphasis on "mirth."

"Actually, it's not a funny novel at all." I was fairly close to finishing the book and I'd been crying over parts of it, but I didn't want David to know that.

"So what's it about?" he asked.

"Well," I began, "it's about this woman who—how can I summarize this? Well, she's very beautiful but she's getting middle-aged and she lives in an era in which it's difficult to be a woman and single and middle-aged. And she doesn't have any money, yet she's been brought up and lived under very comfortable, even opulent, circumstances."

"If she's beautiful, why doesn't she find some nice middle-aged rich man to marry?"

"That would be nice," I said, "but I don't think it's going to turn out that way."

"No prospects?"

"Well, there's one, and they'd be just perfect for each other and they even love each other, but they don't know that they do. You know, that's the way novels are."

"Unlike real life," he concurred.

During our conversation, I kept feeling we were speaking on one level and yet communicating our thoughts on a much deeper one. It gave me a strange feeling.

"Do you do much reading?" I asked.

He laughed and said, "I really don't have much time for leisurely reading. I can barely squeeze in the newspaper and *The Wall Street Journal*, maybe *Playboy* once in a while when I want some really intellectually stimulating reading."

We both smiled, and then I noticed that most of the others had congregated by the entrance, and so we walked over to them. Right away Emma told me that Natalie wanted to talk to me, so I went back to the room. She was still in her bra, but at least she'd put on her makeup and jeans. Barrett was closing her suitcase.

"Do be a dear and take that down for me," she told him. As soon as he was out the door, she said, "Sara, I need a big favor. Will you switch places with Barrett and ride back home in Pete's car? Pete said it would be no problem to drop you off in Mount Morris."

I was totally surprised by her request, but I didn't see any reason why I couldn't comply. At least then I wouldn't have to be with Rafe. "Sure, that's no problem," I said.

"Oh thank you, Sara dear!" she gushed as soon as her head appeared after she'd pulled on her sweater. "I really feel Barrett and I have something special. He's certainly the most fascinating man I've ever met."

"But remember, Nat, you only just met the guy. You really don't know him that well."

"That's why I want to ride back to Iowa with him," she replied. "Now I'm all set, so let's get going."

As we waited for the elevator, she said, "I'm sorry things didn't work out for you and Rafe. Maybe it was for the best. Emma told me he's got a girlfriend in Des Moines anyway."

This announcement shocked me. "Nat!" I exploded. "Why the hell didn't you tell me about this girlfriend?"

"I just found out," she replied innocently. "Emma says they're not really serious, and don't ball me out because Emma's the one who knew all along."

I didn't believe Natalie's nescience for one moment, but my mind was racing to the other implication of her condolence. "And so how do you know things didn't work out between Rafe and me?" I asked.

Just then the elevator came and after we got on, she whispered, although it was only us in the elevator, "Apparently Rafe must have told Bruce there weren't any fireworks last night, and you know what a big mouth Bruce has. So what if everybody knows you didn't sleep with him? Who gives a damn anyway?"

Suddenly the doors opened and I was helping Natalie out and into the lobby. I give a damn, I thought. All the girls and Barrett were in the lobby, and Susan told us that the guys were loading our luggage. Pete returned and collected Natalie's money for her share of the bill. As soon as he paid, we all headed outside. The luggage was almost in place, with the plan being for Rafe to follow Pete and to stop for gas and food early in the afternoon.

The trip back home was very boring. Marc studied or slept most of the time. Louellen and I read when we weren't talking to Susan and Emma, who conversed mainly about the wedding. I felt a little out of things because I was not going to be a bridesmaid like Emma and Louellen. Hence, all their discussions of colors of dresses and places to shop and days to meet excluded me. (Susan had asked me to be at the guestbook, but my job didn't evoke any points of conversation.)

I was surprised to learn that Susan's third bridesmaid, Frannie Browne, had dated David Woodley in college. I didn't know Frannie very well because she was two years older than I was and had left the U after her junior year to go to a fashion institute in New York City. She was from Parker, Susan's hometown, and had been her pledge mom at the house. Susan said that she and David hadn't seen each other in at least three years, and then Emma and Pete decided to place a bet on whether or not this reunion would rekindle their romance.

"I didn't know Frannie very well," Emma said, "but from what I remember she was a very striking girl—lovely auburn hair, green eyes, and a very fair complexion. Quite vivacious, loved to party, something of a flirt, right?"

"That's her," Susan said.

"Then I predict they'll get back together," Emma said. "You know I'm a romantic at heart."

"I bet they don't," Pete countered. "I'm a realist at heart. They're too far apart. He's in Chicago. She's in New York. They both have their careers. Neither one's probably ready for a long-lasting romance or marriage at this point in their lives."

"Spoken just like a man," Susan sighed.

"I seem to remember you weren't thinking of wedding bells in December, Pete ol' man," Marc kidded.

"And I suppose you'll never give in?" Pete replied. "I bet if Emma popped the question you'd be married tomorrow."

"Hell no! Emma and her mom have got to have the biggest,

most lavish wedding of the century. It'll take at least five years to plan the fuckin' thing."

I was surprised to hear Marc joke like this after our initial conversation in which he'd revealed that perhaps he didn't even want to marry Emma Aspen. Then Pete got started on his parents, who had married late. I learned that his father had been fifty when Pete was born, while his mother was fourteen years younger.

"I had this horrible complex while I was growing up," he said. "I thought for sure I was adopted and that my parents weren't leveling with me. I mean, there I was, the only 'only child' Catholic in the whole damn town. Do you know what it's like to be Catholic and an only child? The priest is constantly harping, 'Multiply, multiply,' and my parents are the only ones who aren't. After a while you figure out they're not doing anything at night. Or maybe mom's a traitor to the Pope and taking the hellish Pill? Or maybe they can't have kids and I'm really adopted and they're going to wait until I'm twenty-one to spring the news on me?" As we all laughed, he continued, "Well, all I can say is that Susan and I are not going to wait until I'm fifty to have kids."

"That makes sense to me," Susan replied, "because I'd be fifty too!"

Then Emma asked about Melly and we talked about her pregnancy for a while until the conversation somehow drifted off into sports and politics. When we stopped for gas and lunch, I found myself seated across from Rafe and David in a small booth at a typical truck stop diner. After we'd ordered our burgers, Louellen mentioned the upcoming wedding, and then David asked me if I was going to be there.

"Yes," I answered, "I'm going to be at the guestbook. Are you going?"

As soon as I asked, I felt stupid because Louellen was sitting right there, and from the conversation in Pete's car, I should have assumed David would be at the wedding.

"I certainly hope to make it back," he answered. "I'm actually rather anxious to see an old friend, Frannie Browne. She's one of Susan's bridesmaids."

"Hell, I didn't know Frannie was going to be there!" Rafe said. "Now I really feel bad that I've got that business seminar over Memorial Day weekend. I would sure have liked to have seen her again."

All this talk about the lovely Frannie Browne depressed me. Moreover, both Rafe and David disgusted me. Here Rafe had a girlfriend and yet he wanted a one-nighter with me and probably a night of flirtation with the beautiful Frannie, while David was the type of man who only dated the most attractive girls. He hadn't been interested in Natalie or Louellen or me, for that matter, because we weren't drop-dead gorgeous. For the remainder of lunch, I was deliberately quiet and uninterested in conversing. I complained of a headache and excused myself as soon as possible on the pretext of getting some aspirin.

The journey across the rest of Nebraska seemed doubly long. When we finally stopped near Omaha at a McDonald's, the decision was quickly made to eat our food while traveling. Since this would be my last time to see those riding in the van, I said goodbye to Bruce, Jenny, Rafe, and David, and I made a promise to Natalie to get together some weekend in April. "Good luck on your dissertation," I told Barrett. He merely nodded and gave a sort of grunt.

After we had gotten back into Pete's Olds, David said, through Pete's open window, "See you all in May for the big event. Remember, it's too late to back out now, Byron! Drive carefully."

The next time I saw him was at St. Jerome's in Parker. I was seated behind a small table in the vestibule. There was a tiny bouquet of daisies and baby's breath on the white linen tablecloth in front of me. All I had to do was sit up straight and greet the guests with a pretty smile and a cheerful hello or good evening. I had found a delicate Robin's egg blue dress to wear. It had a scooped neckline, and I had lain out every day since school ended, so my skin had a tanned, healthy glow. I felt pretty sexy and quite content.

He came with his sister and Bruce. They were some of the last guests to arrive and had to wait in the line which extended out the door. When I finally saw him standing near the entrance, I thought of the rehearsal dinner the night before and my meeting with Frannie Browne and her East Coast beau, Sean Sewell. The fact that she was very stylish and beautiful struck a cord of envy in me, but the appearance of her thirty-something boyfriend pleased me greatly. Just as I found myself wondering again if David knew about Sean, he looked over at me and our eyes met. He gave me a wonderfully big smile.

Bruce was the first to greet me with "Howdy, Sara!" Then Jenny and David said hello. "You look real damn good," Bruce continued as he took the feathered pen and signed the book.

"I suppose you miss school terribly," I kidded him.

"Immensely! I'm just like a lost puppy if I don't have some final to cram for or a twenty-page paper to whip together overnight."

After I congratulated Jenny and Bruce on their graduation, she said, "We'll talk to you later, Sara," and they entered the sanctuary.

After the five p.m. ceremony, there was a reception at the Parker Legion Club. I had ridden to Parker with another sorority sister, Vicki Becker. Natalie, whose liaison with Barrett Sawyer had lasted no longer than our Colorado weekend, had come with us also, and the three of us unescorted females drove to the reception together, but we were late arriving there because of pictures and because Vicki was helping with the gifts. We ended up driving first to Mr. McHenry's home and dropping off several presents that had been taken to the church.

When we got to the Legion Club, guests had begun to go through the buffet line, and there were few seats left, so we ended up sitting with two couples in their seventies who were friends of Pete's parents. While we were eating, Emma and Marc came over, and he said, "How are the three fairest damsels faring?"

"Like shit," Natalie answered. "Where the hell are all the eligible bachelors? Almost all the Sigs here are either married or engaged, and Simon won't speak to me. I never knew anybody who didn't have at least one good-looking male cousin."

"Oh, I met Pete's one cousin," Vicki said. "Unfortunately, he's married and about fifty-five years old."

"Did you meet Pete's uncle?" Emma asked. "Father Byron. He's **definitely** not married!"

As we all laughed, I noticed our elderly table companions looked aghast.

"Since age doesn't matter with you, Nat," Marc continued, "you should meet Susan's cousin. What is his name, Emma?"

"You mean the one from Cedar Rapids who's in high school? I've forgotten."

"He's about fourteen," Marc said. "He'd probably find older women very intriguing."

Then there were the sounds of tableware ringing on glasses, and we all watched while Pete gave Susan a hearty kiss.

"They're going to cut the cake pretty soon," Emma said, "so let's go back and sit down. We'll talk later, okay?"

As they walked back to the head table, I noticed how good Emma looked in her bridesmaid's dress, even though it was too frilly and prom-like for my taste. Louellen looked all right in the dress too because she looked as if she was about fifteen years old to begin with, but Frannie Browne seemed terribly incongruous in the attire.

As we were eating wedding cake, the four-piece band, relegated to a small stage, began playing dance tunes, and we watched Susan and Pete dance the first dance. Soon Susan's father took his daughter, and then Pete appeared with his mother for a partner, and after a few minutes, the two couples exchanged partners once again. Then the parents sat down, and for a few minutes there were just Susan and Pete entwined on the small dance floor. Then Simon, who was Pete's best man, took the floor with Louellen, and Marc and Emma soon appeared also.

"Time to mingle," Natalie announced, as one song ended and other couples began to fill the dance floor.

"Let's go talk to Marianne Reynolds and her date," Vicki suggested.

"But they're sitting with Hank Locke," I began my protest. "Let's avoid **him** as long as possible."

"Okay," Natalie agreed, for once being empathetic. "Then let's go talk to David Woodley and Jenny and Bruce. They're over at the head table with Frannie and Sean."

The three of us made our way there, and I introduced Vicki to David and Sean, who said to Vicki, "Yes, you're the one who's going to start med school." To Natalie, he said, "And you're working for the telephone company and taking business classes at night. And you're the teacher," this last comment being addressed to me. "See, I only just met or heard about these ladies and already I can differentiate them by occupation. Actually, I must confess, though, I've forgotten your names."

After Natalie and I told them to him, Frannie said, "Sean is utterly dreadful with names. Before the evening's over, he'll have to ask me, 'Now what's the name of the girl in the red dress with the dark hair?' or 'Who's the blonde in the navy dress?' I keep telling him he just doesn't listen when he's introduced to people."

"You know," David said, "I had a prof in law school who memorized everybody's name after just four class meetings. And there were about sixty students in the class. No assigned seats. To this day, none of us can figure out how he did it. But he called each of us by name without looking at any seating chart or class roll. Just at our faces. He must have had an incredible memory and used some mnemonic trick."

"It's rather like cocktail waitresses being able to remember who ordered what," Natalie said. "But I don't know how the hell they do it!"

"Hell no, it's easy with me, Nat," Bruce said. "They just remember Bruce: beautiful boy, Budweiser beer—all B's."

As we were laughing, Frannie said, "Oh, I've got a marvey idea. Let's come up with alliterative adjectives to describe each of us and then we'll see if Sean can remember when the evening's over. You know, like Funny Frannie—only not that because I'm not that funny."

"How about Sweet Sara," David said, and everyone agreed that was perfect for me.

Then we began making suggestions for everyone, and we finally reached the following nomenclature: Fabulous Frannie (*fickle* and *flamboyant* were rejected), Notorious Natalie, Beer-drinking Bruce, Gentle Jenny, Decent David (Bruce preferred *dastardly* or *degenerate*), Victorious Vicki (for having been accepted into a first-tier med school), and Jobless Sean (pronounced "Shobless" since he had recently left Bank of America and was looking for another job.)

After we each had our sobriquets, Bruce and Jenny went off to dance, and then Natalie shocked the rest of us by asking Sean to dance. She flashed David a big smile as they went out to the dance floor. He seemed surprised but quickly asked Frannie to dance, which left Vicki and me alone. I saw Hank Locke and another Sig heading toward us, so I immediately suggested we find the restroom.

When we returned, the coast was clear to say hi to Marianne, so we went over to her and met her date, whose name I immediately forgot, despite our discussion about remembering names. While we were talking to them, Simon came over to say hello and try to impress us with his burgeoning career. While we were listening to him explain all the wonderful opportunities in Seattle, someone sneaked up behind me, grabbed my bare arms, and whispered, "Guess who, beautiful?"

My heart sank. All I could think of was that *horrible* was too good an adjective to describe Hank Locke.

"We haven't had a chance to talk yet," he told me, and then he asked me to dance, and Simon asked Vicki. I was at a loss for an excuse, so I said I would when the next number began. It turned out to be a polka, and I thought about lying to Hank and telling him I didn't know how, but then I decided I'd get this dance over with and that would be it. As the polka ended and I told him I needed to find Vicki, he begged me for another dance.

"No," I protested, "I've got to find Vicki. I'm sure Simon's left her."

"Yeah, but she's coming out to dance with Marianne's boyfriend," he said, and as I turned around I saw it was true.

Hank grabbed a hold of me and started asking me all about how my first year of teaching had been and what I was doing this summer. As we danced, I tried to be as evasive as possible about my summer plans, but Hank kept pumping me for information. The floor was crowded and hot, and I felt perspiration on my neck. I looked around in desperation at the other couples and saw that Marc and Natalie were dancing while David was with Emma, who at least gave me a consoling look. As I was lying to Hank that I hadn't yet been assigned housing for summer school, there suddenly appeared David and Emma beside us, and he asked for an exchange of partners, with Emma adding, "I'm dying to hear what you've been up to, Hank." I knew Hank was disappointed, even at the prospect of dancing with Emma Aspen, the most beautiful girl in Parker, maybe even Iowa, but I latched onto David as fast as I could while Emma threw all of her charm into pacifying Hank.

When we were away from them, David said, "You seem rather relieved."

I suspected that perhaps Emma had said something to him and that it wouldn't do any good to pretend. "Hank Locke is not one of my favorite people," I confessed.

"I think Emma used the term *loathe* to describe your feelings."

I blushed deeply. Another song began and he took me in his arms and led us farther away from Hank and Emma.

"But, of course," he continued, "Sweet Sara is always nice and polite to everybody. Why don't you just tell the guy you're not interested in him?"

"Now you sound like Emma."

"I think it's pretty deceitful on your part to lead him on."

"What!"

"I think most guys want to know the truth."

"I don't show any interest in Hank Locke," I protested. "Even though I don't particularly like him, I can still dance a couple dances with him without leading him on."

"Okay," he said, "let's go find him and I'll turn you back over to him."

I saw him begin to canvass the floor with his eyes. While I was studying his handsome face, he suddenly looked right at me and said, "Of course, if you'd rather be with me than him, you can just say so."

His audacity displeased me, but I felt willing to humble my-self rather than return to Hank. "I'd rather be with you," I said, looking directly into his eyes.

"Good. Let's go take a walk outside. This place is too hot."

When we left the Legion Hall, I noticed that the warm after-noon air had become cool, and it felt very good at first to escape from the stuffiness inside. David suggested that we cross the street and walk on the sidewalk which defined the courthouse square. It seemed quite peaceful, the only sounds being the muffled music of the band and the indistinguishable voices of conversing guests.

As we strolled, I decided I'd let David begin the conversation, but we walked for several minutes without his saying anything. Eventually I began to get chilly, but we were only half way around the square.

"I suppose you're cold," he finally said. I told him I was and he took off his suit coat to put it around my shoulders, the warmth of his coat feeling so good. "There's a bench over there," he said. "Let's sit down for a minute."

After we sat down, he still didn't speak. We just sat on the bench and listened to the faint sounds of the reception. Once in a while a car passed on the street. The lighted marquee above the First National Bank of Parker slowly flashed 8:56, 66 F, 25 C, 8:57, 66 F, 25 C, 8:58. Just as I was about to suggest that it was time to go back inside, David said, "You're awfully quiet. You're not upset with me, are you?"

I hesitated before I spoke. "No, not really," I said, and then I quickly added, before I had a chance to contemplate the words, "I don't want to lead you on."

He leaned back and stretched out his legs. "Okay," he said, staring across the street at the shady storefronts that housed Anderson's 5 & 10, Grand's Drug, and Mac's Market. "I appreci-ate your honesty."

I felt unhappy with myself because I liked David and just moments ago he had seemed very interested in me, but now I had given him the wrong idea. I always communicated poorly. There was nothing left to say but, "Let's go back inside," and David agreed.

As we walked along the remaining side of the square, I decided to give myself one more chance. "I thought maybe you wanted to talk about something?" I ventured.

"Oh, I suppose I did," he answered. "I guess I was just feeling a little down and maybe I did want to talk to somebody."

"I'll still listen if you want," I said.

"No, it's not that important."

"Well, whatever you want," I replied, "but I am a good listener."

He stopped walking and said, "All right, here goes. I feel like a fool because of Frannie. I had all these idiotic notions that when we'd see each other again we'd fall madly in love, get married, and live happily ever after. I had no idea she had somebody and that she'd bring him home. What irks me is that we danced a couple dances together and she never told me she's living with the guy. She acted as if they're just 'good friends.' It was Pete who told me before dinner that they live together in an apartment on Staten Island. I just can't believe . . . gosh, I guess I sound pretty mad at her, don't I?"

"Well, I think that's normal."

"Did you meet Frannie's parents?" he continued, as I nodded. "I mean, these people are Mr. and Mrs. Ultra Conservative. I can't imagine her bringing Sean home to meet them."

"Makes you wonder how she handled things with them."

"Yeah, it sure does."

Then he was silent and I wasn't sure what to say. "Anyway," I began, "don't feel bad. . . ." I wanted to mention the cliché about other fish in the ocean, but I wasn't that brave.

"I still feel pretty foolish," he said. "I feel like everybody's saying, 'Oh poor David! He came all the way from Chicago to see Frannie and, boy, did she deal him a blow.'"

"Nobody's thinking that," I said. "Besides, why should you care what other people think anyway?"

"Because I'm a human being. Don't tell me that you don't give a damn about what others think of you."

I knew I was one of the worst offenders of being true to myself since I was constantly self-conscious of how others perceived me, yet there had to be worthier attitudes for attaining a healthy self-image. "Of course I care," I replied, "but I wouldn't let an erroneous assumption—namely, that everybody's laughing at or pitying me—spoil my whole evening. Besides, for the umpteenth time, everyone thinks very highly of you, David."

"Well, thanks for the pep talk. I really feel a lot better just getting all this off my chest." His eyes left mine and he looked across the street. "Look, Marc and Sean just walked outside. I guess they came out to cool off too."

My back was to the Legion Club, but I didn't turn around to acknowledge their presence. "Can they see us?" I asked. "And if so, what do you suppose they're thinking?"

"Hell, what do I care!" he said laughingly.

"Of course you care!" I teased, moving very close to him. Then I whispered, "This is what Notorious Natalie would do because Sweet Sara is too afraid." I put my hands on his shoulders and gave him a soft kiss on his lips. As his hands went around my waist, his suit coat slid from my shoulders, but neither of us bothered to prevent its sinking to the ground. Instead, his lips stayed on mine and he gave me a lingering kiss.

When we finally stopped, he said, "Why'd you do that?"

"Because I like you." There, I'd said it, but somehow I didn't feel too foolish or corny.

He took his hands away from my waist and I quickly removed mine from his shoulders, stepping to the side to pick up his coat. As I stooped down, he did so too, retrieving it first. He brushed it off, moved close to me, and put it back around my shoulders. Then he stepped back and said, "I guess I'm a little confused. But the main thing I want you to know is that I didn't take this walk with you just to get back at being jilted by Frannie. In all fairness, I concede that somewhere in my subconscious there probably was the notion that I'd show Frannie I didn't care by . . . by being interested in you, but . . . well, I just don't want you to think that's the only reason I kissed you."

"Then why did you?" As long as this was a night for self-revelation, I knew I had to take the gamble.

"Because I like you too," he said.

I returned his smile and suggested that we go back inside. As we crossed the street, I saw that Marc and Sean were still outside. Sean was smoking and Marc, who had a can of beer in one hand, flashed me a big grin and said, "Jesus Christ! I thought it was hot inside, but it looks as if there's more heat out here. What do you say, Sweet Sara?"

I found myself blushing (thankfully, it was dark) and at a loss for words.

"Teacher," Sean said as he pointed his finger at me.

"Right," I answered, and then I said to Marc, "So you heard about our new names?"

"Sure did. And by the way, I'm Magnificent Marc. Do you prefer Elegant Emma or Everyman's-Dream-Girl Emma? And say, David, I don't think Hank Locke's going to think you're a very **decent** fellow."

"So who's a decent fellow?" he retorted in a light-hearted way.

"Where are Emma and Frannie?" I asked.

"Oh, they went to help Susan use the john," Marc said. "You know, it takes a half dozen of them to hold up her dress and veil."

Then David told them we were going back inside and that we'd talk to them later. As we entered the hall, I returned David's suit coat, but before we got very far, we ran into a small group of Sigs that I didn't know very well. Simon was chatting with them, and then suddenly Jack Bindel appeared with a pretty blonde and another baseball jock whose name I thought was Steve.

"Sara!" Jack exclaimed. "I didn't know you were here!"

"Well, I didn't know you were here," I said confusedly. "I was at the guestbook at the church and I swear I didn't see you come in!"

"We didn't make the wedding," Jack began. "Debbie's cousin—Sara, this is Debbie Daniels, Debbie, Sara Keatson—her cousin got married today too and we drove over from Oskaloosa after that reception, and so we just got here a few minutes ago. Sara, do you remember Steve Braka? He played third."

I told him I did, shook his proffered hand, and then introduced David, explaining that he was a senior when we were freshmen. "Maybe you knew his little sister Jenny Woodley?" I added.

They both responded that they didn't, and then I explained to David, "Jack and Steve both played with Pete on the baseball team."

"If I remember correctly," David said, "you had a good season my senior year."

"Yeah, those were the good ol' days," Jack replied. "Well, Sara, you look real good. Are you teaching somewhere? And how are your parents?"

I told him I taught in Mount Morris and that my parents were fine, and then I asked what he was doing.

"I'm still at Richmond's in the accounting department. Debbie works there too. We're going to be married August 9th."

"Congratulations," I said warmly as she held out her hand for me to admire her ring. "I love the setting."

"Thanks," she said. "We're real excited."

David's hand went across my lower back as he said, "Well, it's been nice to meet you, Jack and Debbie and Steve. I need to say hello to a couple of old friends, so we'll see you later." Then he ushered me a few steps away to three more Sigs and their dates. After introductions were made, David talked briefly to them about their jobs. Then he asked me to dance, and we walked to the crowded floor just as a slow number began. As soon as his arms went around me, he asked, "So how many other old boyfriends of yours are here tonight?"

"What?"

"You know. There's Hank Locke. There's Jack whatever his last name is. And I think maybe even Marc White figures into the picture somehow."

"Hank Locke was never a boyfriend," I said, feeling very pleased that he thought I had had a lot of boyfriends. "We had two dates at the most."

"All right. But I forgot that Simon fellow, and how about that baseball guy?"

"Jack Bindel?"

"Yeah."

"What makes you think he was a boyfriend?"

"It was pretty obvious the way you two looked at each other!"

"What!"

"You mean you never dated him?"

I wanted to be flirtatious and accuse him of being jealous, but I was too sober and timid. "We just went out for a little while," I said. "That's all."

"So there are only two left, Simon and Marc."

"Oh, those guys were never really interested in me. We had two dates max. We just didn't click. Really, it was nothing."

"All right."

He drew me closer and I could feel his breath on my hair and smell his after-shave. I closed my eyes. David seemed very strong and sure of himself. I felt certain of his sincerity and that he wasn't using me because his dream with Frannie had not materialized.

Suddenly we stopped moving and I opened my eyes to see Hank Locke beside us. "Excuse me," he said, "if it's all right, I'd like to get my original partner back. Sar?"

"Sure, Hank," I said meekly, and he took me so quickly in his arms that I didn't even have time to give David a glance.

"I've been looking all over for you," he whispered in my ear. "Somebody said you went outside with Dave for some fresh air. You're not going with him, are you? Doesn't he live in Chicago?"

"Yes, he does live in Chicago," I muttered, knowing I couldn't tell Hank I was going with David even if it appeared as a way to escape Horrible Hank. "We're just acquaintances. He was along on that ski trip to Colorado over Easter. That was the first time we met."

"I see," he said. "Now let's pick up where we left off. I think you were telling me about where you're going to stay this summer."

Just then the song ended and a loud, fast boogie began, thankfully halting our conversation. While we were dancing, I decided that I had to tell Hank how I felt. I calculated that I couldn't endure another long slow dance with him, but that I couldn't tell him at the beginning or even the middle of the next slow number. As he swung me around, I saw that most of our crowd was at the bar and no one we knew was by the cake table, so when the number ended, I quickly asked him if he'd bring me some punch and told him I'd be waiting by the wedding cake. Once there I took a seat at the end of a nearby table at whose far end were unknown middle-aged occupants. When Hank returned he sat down beside me and said, "I'm glad we finally have a chance to really talk."

I silently thanked him for such a perfect beginning and said, "Yes, I really want to talk to you, Hank. I want to tell you that I'm just not interested in you. I like you, but I don't want to have a dating relationship with you, and I really think it's not fair of me if I . . . I construe things so that you think otherwise. Do you understand what I'm saying?"

"Of course," he said. His face showed no feelings of embarrassment or sadness or enmity.

"Good," I said, laughing nervously since I thought I'd been too cruel, "because I don't know if I know what I just said."

"You were quite lucid, Sar," he said, as he took my free hand in his and squeezed it gently, "and I want you to know that I appreciate your honesty and think highly of you for it."

I was so relieved by his graceful acceptance of my rejection that I didn't know what to say. I'd expected him to be a little crestfallen. "Well, ummm, I'm so glad you understand, Hank," I said, taking another sip of punch.

"Shall we go find some of the ol' gang?" he asked.

I nodded in agreement, and we went over to a group that included Vicki, Louellen, Emma, Marc, Natalie, and a short unattached Sig named Mel whom Nat had managed to ensnare.

"Sara, I'm glad you're here," Louellen said as soon as I walked up. "Now I can go tell Susan we're ready to sing, and then she can toss her bouquet. And then we've got to help her get changed."

Louellen disappeared and, while we chatted, I tried to look around the room to see where David was, but I couldn't locate him anywhere. Louellen returned shortly with her sister and Pete, plus Jenny, Frannie, Marianne, and several others, although not David.

"Are you gals ready?" Marc asked, and then he told Bruce and Mel to tell the band to stop playing. Almost instantly the noisy hall became still, and then Marc announced in his distinct baritone voice that Susan's sorority sisters would be singing a tribute to the newly-married couple.

After we finished singing, Marc announced that it was time for the garter and bouquet tosses. There were a few dirty remarks while Pete lifted up Susan's gown and removed the garter. Then the room's bachelors were coaxed into a group, and Pete began winding up his arm in true pitcher-style. I noticed that David was missing from the knot of fellows, all of whom were protesting their desire to be the lucky recipient. Finally Pete threw it high up in the air and some Sig I didn't know reached out and caught the circle of blue and white lace. Cries of "Scott and Liz" filled the room, and I saw the girl who must have been Liz take lots of ribbing from her friends.

Then Susan was helped to stand on a chair, and we girls were urged to congregate nearby. I stood on one edge with Vicki and Frannie on either side and hoped that the flung bouquet would go elsewhere to save me the embarrassment of catching it without having the prospect of a future husband.

"Everybody ready?" Susan hollered, with her back to us.

"Yeah, we're ready," one girl called out. "Liz is especially ready, and she's right in the middle."

Susan threw her bouquet of white and pink roses to the side away from me, and Emma, with an expression of surprise and rapture, caught it. Susan gave a cry of joy when she saw Emma with the bouquet, and Natalie, who was somewhat drunk, began calling very loudly, "Marc White! Marc White! Where'd you disappear to, you ol' sonofabitch?"

Then everyone kidded and congratulated Emma, and soon Susan and her three bridesmaids left for the ladies' room. The band resumed playing, and several couples went off to dance. Hank even found a partner in a friend of Louellen's, and I danced with Simon. When we left the dance floor, we saw Pete, now dressed in a pair of slacks and a casual shirt, and Marc, who had another can of beer in his hand and a drunken glaze in his eyes.

Vicki walked over to us and exclaimed, "Here's the lucky groom-to-be!"

"That bouquet just sailed through the air as if Fate had destined it for Emma," I added. "Congratulations, Marc."

He moved very close to me, slid his arm around my waist, and said in a drunken whisper, "Sweet Sara, will you marry me?"

"Only if you promise to give up booze and other women."

"Ah shit, this lady won't marry me if . . . goddamn, give up other women? Maybe, but booze—never!"

"I hope Emma's driving back to I.C.," Vicki said.

"Damn, Vic, I'm as sober as . . . as the Pope is—"

"Hey," Pete interrupted, "watch what you say, White."

In a lighthearted voice, he continued, "Remember who's Catholic around here."

I'd never known Pete to get bombed, and even at his own wedding he'd not drunk much all evening and hence was extremely pleasant and actually quite debonair.

"Did I hear congratulations are in order for you, Marc?" asked David as he suddenly appeared beside us.

"Well, you heard wrong, sir," Marc said, still leaning against me with his hand roaming over my posterior. "Sweet Sara won't marry me unless I give up booze and other women, and shit, that's just askin' too goddamn much, even you for, babe!" Then he gave me a hard kiss on the mouth and said, "I'll always remember the good times, kiddo, but she's all yours, Woodley ol' buddy."

As Marc moved away from me and headed in the direction of the bar, David said, "Well, Pete, it looks as if you're all set to take off."

"I just need my wife. Gee, that sounds strange."

"So if I don't get a chance to speak to you before you leave,"

David continued, "I just want to say it was a swell wedding, and the best of luck to you and Susan. Remember, I'll be looking for a visit from you. I've got my tour of Chicago honed to a really first-rate presentation. And Vicki, congrats again on medical school and good luck at Columbia. And Sara," (I held my breath wondering how he was going to say goodbye to me) "there can't be many more dances left. Will you do me the honor?"

"Sure," I replied, and after the others had said their goodbyes, he led me away.

As we danced a fast number, I had time to contemplate things. We had certainly given the others something to talk about, but what perplexed me was how it had all started. I'd come to Parker curious to see Simon and Frannie and maybe Jack Bindel and not really anxious to see David since I thought him too persnickety in his taste for women. Then Frannie had shown up with Sean, and all of a sudden David seemed to be looking at me more and more, and then he had rescued me from Hank, making me choose between Hank and himself. Now we seemed to be "an item." The kiss outside had definitely helped. What had I said? *This is what Notorious Natalie would do because Sweet Sara is too afraid.* I blushed to think how silly I'd acted. Stupid Sara was more like it. Stupid, stupid Sara! I made up my mind I'd be very indifferent to David and get away from him as soon as possible.

When the dance ended, the band began a slow number and David started to put his arms around me. "Oh, I'm really tired," I began, but then I couldn't think of an excuse to leave. It seemed silly to say I needed to keep Vicki company when she was with Pete, and besides, David seemed so appealing right now that I continued to dance with him. Neither of us spoke for several minutes, and then he whispered, "Marc is really lit." I agreed and he continued, "Did you come with him and Emma?"

"No, with Natalie and Vicki," I answered, glad that he was so concerned. "Vicki's driving, and she's sober."

"So are you all going back to I.C.?"

"Yes, I'm staying overnight at Natalie's. Nat, Emma, and I are all going shopping tomorrow afternoon."

"I'm not going back until Monday." I wanted to say, *so what?*, but I didn't say anything at all. Finally he said, "Maybe we could get together for brunch tomorrow—that is, if you don't already have plans?"

I couldn't believe what I'd heard. David was actually asking me to go out with him! "That sounds nice," I said, hiding all the excitement I was feeling.

"Great! What would be a good time? Not too early, of course. Would around 11:30 work?"

I told him that would be fine, and then he asked me if I'd ever been to Millie's Pancake House.

"Yes," I answered, "but just once a long time ago. If I remember correctly, the food was quite good."

"It still is. My parents go there frequently after church."

We danced the rest of the number in silence, with David holding me close to him, and then he said, "Since you said you were tired, would you like to find a quiet place to sit down and talk?"

"All right," I said, and we started to make our way to a relatively unoccupied area of the hall, noticing that Pete was now leading Susan, who was dressed in a shirt and pants, onto the dance floor for presumably their last dance tonight.

After we sat down, David took out one of his business cards and asked me for directions to Natalie's apartment, which I then gave him. I had just finished when Natalie came over with Mel. "I've been looking all over for you, Sara!" she said loudly. "Everybody's gettin' rice outside, and you've got to come see what Marc wrote on their car!"

So David and I went outside with them to find quite a crowd gathered around Pete's decorated Olds. But before Natalie could point out Marc's handiwork, we ran into most of our other friends, and Frannie wanted to see if Sean could remember everyone's nicknames. Then Natalie pushed our way through a group of Sigs so we could see the back window of the car. There, in large crooked white letters, Marc had written, "DELTA CUNT IS BEST!" David laughed and shook his head when he saw it.

"Can you believe he did that!" Natalie shrieked.

"Ol' Marc should know!" Mel chimed in.

"Admirin' my contribution?" Marc said in a drunken slur, as he and Emma joined us.

"I think we better wash it off before they leave," Emma said.

"Hell, no!" Marc roared. "That there is the absolutest goddamn truth! We'll all swear to it, won't we, men?"

"It's obscene, Marc," Emma said. "This is a small town. You can't have them driving around the middle of Iowa with that on the window! I'm going inside to get some wet paper towels."

"No, no," Marc protested, as he grabbed a hold of her. "Pete's gotta see it first!"

Just then there were admonitions to get the rice ready and cries of "Here they come!" David got some rice packets for us to throw, but Pete and Susan appeared so quickly that I didn't have time to get the netting on mine undone. They hopped into the car without even a glance at the back window. Marc kept shouting to Pete, "Look at the goddamn window!" But there was a lot of noise and confusion, and I was sure they left without knowing what Marc had written.

Then there seemed to be more confusion as most of the younger guests quickly scurried off to their cars to follow Pete and Susan throughout the town. As I was left standing beside

David wondering what to do, Jenny and Bruce moved over to us and announced that they wanted to leave, so David said a hurried goodbye to me and reconfirmed our date for tomorrow.

Since Natalie had disappeared with Mel, I went to find Vicki, who was inside the Legion Hall with Louellen and some other girls from the house. The reception was noticeably winding down as more and more guests left. As we helped Louellen carry gifts to her father's car, Vicki and I found ourselves mutually upset with Natalie, since we both wanted to leave.

"We'll stay ten more minutes," Vicki said, after all the presents were loaded into Mr. McHenry's car, "and if she's not back by then, we're leaving and she can find her own way back to I.C."

"You forgot I'm staying with her," I reminded Vicki.

"Oh, shit." I could tell she was tired.

Fortunately, Natalie arrived in about five minutes, and we said our thanks and goodbyes and left. We were barely in Vicki's car when Natalie said accusingly, "Sara, how could you let David use you like that!"

I was too tired to blow up at her, so I said simply, "He wasn't using me."

"Well," she continued, "it was grossly obvious to everyone but yourself that he leeched onto you just to show Little Miss Frannie a thing or two."

"Oh, do you think she was jealous of me?" I asked innocently, knowing Natalie would have no fast answer for that, and she didn't.

"Nat," Vicki said, "we're a little ticked off at you for making us wait so long while you go screw around with that little Mel. So I'd appreciate an apology from you along with some consideration. And besides, the way I saw things, David was very much interested in Sara, which I thought was neat. And talk about being used—you're the one whom Mel used!"

Natalie didn't respond and, in fact, she didn't say another word the rest of the way home.

The next day Natalie slept until eleven, and when she awoke, she announced that she had a horrible hangover. Having slept on the lumpy futon in her living room, I had gotten up much earlier, and now I was all ready for the day.

"Are you going somewhere?" she mumbled.

"I'm going out to brunch . . . with David," I said, thinking about adding, *so he can use me again,* but I didn't say those words. Natalie had enough problems without my reminding her of all the cruel things she'd said. "He's coming by here to pick me up at eleven thirty," I continued. "Hope that's okay with you."

"He's coming here!" she groaned. "In twenty-five minutes! God, I'm a wreck!"

All I could think was, *Natalie, quit focusing only on yourself. He's not even interested in you.* But instead I said, "I'll be back by two, so we can still go shopping. All right?"

"Sure," she mumbled as she closed the bathroom door, emerging in a robe with a towel wrapped around her head about five minutes before David arrived.

"You feel okay, Natalie?" were David's words of greeting her.

"I've got a helluva hangover," she announced. "Too much beer and cheap champagne."

"Take it easy today," he said, and then we left rather quickly. In the car, David said, "She didn't look too good."

"I'm glad you didn't say that to her face," I replied. "Nat definitely doesn't like to be told that she doesn't look good!"

"She's quite a character," he continued. "I don't see how you and Emma and Susan are such good friends with her."

"Sometimes I don't know either."

Brunch was nice but uneventful. David asked me a lot of questions about my family, my job, and my summer plans. I found out that he was playing golf with his father and two of his father's friends in the afternoon. He was leaving early the next day to drive back to Chicago and hoped the traffic wouldn't be too bad despite the Memorial Day weekend. I told him I was leaving Natalie's apartment later that afternoon to go see my parents and my sister and her husband. He reminded me to ask them if they knew Charlie Brown.

On the way back to Natalie's place, he surprised me by announcing, "I'm coming back over the Fourth of July weekend. It's my mom's birthday. Maybe we can get together and do something? See a movie—that is, if you're going to be in town?"

"Sure," I replied, "I'm sure I'll be around. That would be nice."

"Look, I'm running a little late to make our tee-off time," he said, "so I'll not stop in." He put his car in park and pulled a small notebook and a pen out of the glove compartment. "That's Richmond Hall you'll be staying in?"

I told him that was correct and then thanked him for brunch. As I got out of the car, I told him I hoped he'd enjoy his golf game. He gave me a big smile and I shut the door. I decided David was very easy to talk to and that I really liked him a lot. Still, I was afraid that our relationship would go nowhere because of the distance between us.

He surprised me in mid-June with a letter. It was handwritten on his firm's stationery. He told me about a case he was working on, that Pete and Susan were coming to visit in August, and that he was driving to I.C. on July 2nd for a four-day visit with his parents. He suggested that perhaps we could see a movie on July 3rd. He told me his parents were having a cook-out on the Fourth and asked me if I'd like to join them. He signed the letter, "Fondly, David."

I was busy with my classes, and before I could write him back, he called me. After we had chatted for a few minutes, we agreed to see a movie on the 3rd, and I said I'd love to join him for his parents' cook-out on the Fourth.

I was sitting on a big vinyl chair in the lobby of my dorm when he walked in. As soon as I saw him, I rose to greet him, and he looked so good. We smiled at each other but he didn't kiss me or touch me.

We saw *Annie Hall* and had a drink at O'Flynn's afterward, and then he took me back to my dorm. I had told him about my rather strange roommate, Orpah Lindberg, and so outside the door to my room, he quickly kissed me goodnight, and then he was gone.

He picked me up at five the next day. He had told me to dress casually, but I wondered if my jean shorts were too short. I was nervous about meeting his parents. I'd seen them a couple times at the house with Jenny, but I'd never been formally introduced to them.

"Do I look okay?" I asked him, regretting that I'd asked such a dumb question.

He looked at me a little strangely, and I felt so embarrassed that I blushed. I didn't want him to think I was trying to make the perfect first impression on his parents. "You did say casual, right?" I continued, hoping to conceal my ulterior motives.

"You're fine," he said. He could have said lovely or sexy or almost anything else, and I was beginning to feel as if my relationship with David Woodley was going nowhere. But at his parents' home he was very attentive and made me feel welcome and special. His parents seemed very nice, and their friends were cordial. Since Jenny and Bruce were there too, we all had an enjoyable time.

About eight, Jenny and Bruce left to go to Bruce's parents' home, and gradually the other guests left also. Then I helped his mother with some kitchen cleanup, while David and his father worked on the patio cleanup.

"Want to go to the fairgrounds to see the fireworks, Sara?" David asked, coming into the kitchen with two more dirty platters.

"Whatever you'd like to do," I said.

"Are you and dad going, mom?" he asked.

"No," she answered, "I'm too tired. We're going to stay here and finish cleaning up, but you two run along."

"Then let's go," David said, and before we left, he grabbed some insect repellent and a stadium blanket from a hall closet.

There were lots of cars and people at the fairgrounds. We parked and then walked for a few minutes before we found a spot where David spread out the blanket. "They should start pretty soon," he said. "It's dark enough by now."

Actually by now I was feeling very tired, and the ground felt really hard when I sat down. Despite the fact that I'd put on some insect repellent, I kept slapping mosquitoes on my legs, arms, and face. David had sat down beside me, but after a few minutes of silence and slapping and no fireworks, he announced, "This is really uncomfortable. Let's go back to the car and watch from there."

"Great idea," I said, getting up eagerly.

The car was stuffy, but we rolled down the windows a little, and then the fireworks started. "That one was pretty," I commented.

"Yeah," he said, and then he looked over at me. "Hey, come on over here next to me, please."

I moved across the seat next to him, and he put his arm around me, saying, "I really missed you."

Oh sure, I thought, *like there are no girls in Chicago*, but instead I said, "I missed you too."

He leaned over and kissed me hard and long on the mouth. Then he started kissing my cheek and neck, and his other hand went on my thigh, and he was stroking me so high I thought he was going to touch my panties. After we had kissed for a while, he started to unbutton my shirt and began pulling it up from where it was tucked into my jeans shorts. *This is when you say that you want to make love to me*, I thought, *and really show you care by bringing up birth control*, but of course, he was like all men and never said anything as he tried to undress me. When he started in on my belt, I knew I had to stop him.

"David," I mumbled, "I'm really not ready for this." It was a lie, but it was the only thing I was brave enough to say.

"You don't want to make love?" he whispered, while still kissing me.

"I want to make love to you, but I don't want to get pregnant," I said simply. It was the truth, for once, and I didn't feel stupid saying it.

"I've got some condoms," he said.

"They're not one hundred percent effective," I said. "I just don't think I'm ready yet."

"Okay," he said, still kissing me. "I really think I'm falling in love with you, but I can wait until you're ready." Then he drew away from me a little and we watched a few more fireworks explode in the sky. There seemed to be one or two basic configurations and about six colors. That was what I disliked about firework displays: they were boring and predictable.

"Is it okay if I pick you up at 4:30 tomorrow?" he asked finally. Earlier he had invited me to go out to dinner with his parents to celebrate his mom's birthday.

"Sure," I said. "Where are we going to eat?"

"Rick's Steak and Seafood. It's my mom's favorite. The food's actually quite good. Have you been there?"

"I think once," I replied, remembering a date with Jack Bindel.

"What do you say we head home?" he asked. "I think the show's almost over and, if we leave now, we can beat some of the traffic."

I told him that sounded like a good plan, and on the way to my dorm, I told him he didn't need to park and walk me in, so we stopped in the circular drive in front of Richmond Hall, and I slid over and gave him a quick kiss on the cheek. Swiftly he grabbed my far shoulder, pulled me closer, and French-kissed me. I didn't want him to stop, but finally I whispered, "Thanks again for a fun Fourth. I'll see you tomorrow."

The next day I had a little studying to do and also some shopping. I had put off buying a birthday card for his mother because I didn't know how my relationship with David was moving: forward into girlfriend-boyfriend-lovers-marriage? Or backward: just friends-maybe never see each other again? I didn't want to be too pushy, since I'd only met Mrs. Woodley yesterday, but I needed to acknowledge her birthday. I'd taken some cheese and a bottle of wine to their house for the cook-out, and they'd pay for dinner tonight, I assumed, so I felt I should get a little something for her, but not too much.

In the card section at the university bookstore, I looked for a future mother-in-law category, but of course there was no such heading in the birthday section. I picked out a simple card with reddish and pink roses on the front, having observed that the Woodleys had several floribundas and hybrid teas in their well-kept yard. David had told me his mom liked to garden and read, so I also got a nice cloth bookmark with a floral design, and just by chance I found a cute rose magnet. I'd noticed her refrigerator was full of pictures of David and Jenny and other relatives, as well as newspaper clippings and invitations. The refrigerator was next to a small desk which was littered with junk mail, gardening catalogues, several notepads, and coupons. In the middle was a sign which said, "Mom's Desk." I figured I could slip the bookmark and magnet inside with the birthday card. That way it wouldn't look as if I'd gotten her something large and expensive, a real future mother-in-law sort of gift.

After I left the bookstore, I went to the corner drugstore for some lipstick and shampoo. When I noticed it wasn't too crowded, I got up my nerve to find the contraceptives, and I quickly grabbed some foam. "Be prepared, be prepared" kept pounding in my head, and I envisioned a Boy Scout surrounded by boxes of contraceptives. Be prepared.

Then I had half a tuna fish sandwich and an apple for lunch. I spent most of the afternoon doing coursework. At four o'clock I changed into a yellow and white striped sundress and touched up my makeup. I put the card in my purse along with two of the contraceptive packages and my favorite lipstick color, Rosa Rosa. At four twenty-five, I went down to the lobby to wait for David.

He was fifteen minutes late, and for a few minutes I had the sinking feeling he wasn't going to show at all. But at four forty-five he rushed in, dressed in shorts and a Bears T-shirt.

"Sorry I'm late," he began. "Jenny was supposed to meet me at three at Goldman's to pick out a gift for mom, and she was late, and then we couldn't decide what to get her, and then I needed to get gas and my car washed, and the lines were so long to go through the car wash. But I'm here now. I just need to change." As we headed out the front door, he added, "You look great."

On the way to his parents' home, I asked him about the rest of his day, and we also chatted about my classes. When we arrived at the Woodley home, his parents were in the kitchen with another couple, the Wilsons, who, David told me, had been friends for thirty years. Mr. Woodley was mixing drinks, and Mrs. Woodley was looking at photos of the Wilsons' first grandchild. I wished Mrs. Woodley a happy birthday, and then I began admiring the baby's pictures too. After David had greeted the Wilsons and introduced me, he excused himself to change clothes. He was only gone a few seconds when his head popped back into the kitchen.

"Sara, could you help me a minute?" he asked. "And Mom, give Sara some scissors and Scotch tape please."

"Gee, I wonder what that's for," she kidded, as she got the items from her desk drawer and handed them to me. Then I joined David in the hallway. He had told me in the car that Jenny and he had gotten their mom a Waterford vase and a rose bush.

"Can you help me get Mom's presents from the car and then get them wrapped?" he asked. I told him I'd be glad to, and then he explained, "We didn't have time to get the vase gift-wrapped at the store."

With David carrying the rose bush and me the vase box, we quickly slipped past the kitchen, and he led me into a bedroom which looked as if it could have been his old room. There were some posters of rock bands and pennants on the walls, a navy corduroy bedspread on a twin bed, a dresser with a lamp and clock radio, and a desk with a briefcase propped open. A duffel bag was lying in a corner, and some clothes were on top of an orange bean bag chair.

"Yes, these are the remnants of my old room. My mom says she's going to redecorate in the fall," David explained. He put the rose bush on top of the dresser and continued, "This thing's a little messy." Then he pulled off his T-shirt, spread it on the carpet, and put the rose bush on top. It was boxed, but I could see where the box was dirty. The bush had two solid pink blooms and there were at least a dozen more buds which were almost ready to begin opening, although I reasoned that it could be several days before they did. My mother had rose bushes too, even more by the town house than the farm one, and I had observed that even though the bud looked ready to do something, sometimes it took days before it opened. I supposed it depended on the amount of sunlight.

David, who had studied the bush while he placed it on his T-shirt, looked up at me and asked nervously, "Do you think it's healthy? "Oh yes," I assured him, although now I was only thinking how great his chest looked. "It's just ready to be planted in a warm, sunny spot. I love its color. Is it a tea rose?"

"Yes, I think so," he said, rising and coming next to me. "You know, I think you forgot to kiss me today."

I laughed and said, "No, **you** forgot to kiss me," and then I put my hands on his shoulders and kissed him. His hands went around my back and he kissed me back. My whole body tingled while we kissed for what seemed like several minutes. Then he withdrew from me and said, "Unfortunately, I've got to get ready. Let me show you where my mom keeps some wrapping paper, and you can wrap the vase while I get ready, and then we can figure out what to do with the rose bush."

He led me to another bedroom. This one was tastefully decorated with a small couch, a TV set, and several bookcases which were completely filled. Inside the room's closet there were a waste paper basket filled with rolls of wrapping paper and a large plastic box with ribbons and bows. "Pick out whatever you think will look good," he told me and left.

I looked through everything, deciding on a pinkish floral wrap and a white bow. Since I hadn't carried the vase, tape, or scissors with me, I returned to David's room, whose door was open. I could hear water running in the hall bathroom. I took the box with the vase, sat down on the bed, and began wrapping it. I was almost finished when David, with just a pair of boxers on and holding a towel, walked back in and closed the door. "That looks nice," he said. "What should we do about the rose bush?"

"I was thinking maybe we could just put some tissue paper around it and tie the paper with some nice-looking ribbon right around the top of the box."

"Whatever you think," he said, while he finished toweling himself off. Then he walked across the room, slid his closet door open, and took out a pair of tan slacks. He walked over, put them on the bed next to me, returned to the duffel bag on the floor, and produced a white sport shirt.

I hopped up from the bed and announced that I was going to get some tissue paper from the other room.

Just as I opened the door, his father appeared. "We were wondering what happened to you two," he said jovially, but I felt as if he were checking things out, and I wondered if my lipstick was smeared.

"I'm just helping David get his presents wrapped for his mom," I said. "I'm almost done."

"Dad," David said, appearing nearer the door, still naked from the waist up, "look at this rose bush we got. Do you think mom'll like it and find a spot to put it?"

Mr. Woodley walked into the room and surveyed the bush on the carpet. "Heavens yes," he said enthusiastically. "You know your mother's flower beds keep getting bigger and bigger every year. Queen Elizabeth," he continued, reading the box. "That's one of your mother's favorites."

I left David's room and returned to the room with the wrapping supplies, quickly finding several large sheets of white tissue paper and some pink ribbon. David's door was closed when I returned, so I knocked gently. "It's me," I said, and then I opened it. David was standing with his back to the door next to the bed. Now all he had on were briefs, not boxers.

"Did you find some tissue paper?" he asked, with his back still toward me.

"Yes, I think this will work," I said, dropping down beside the bush. I put several sheets of tissue paper down and then moved the rose box on top and gathered them up. The paper's size was just a trifle too small, but I moved the sheets around so I could gather them together at the top.

"Want me to hold that while you tie the ribbon around it?" he asked, dropping down beside me. He still didn't have his clothes on, and my heart was beating fast with his almost naked body next to mine.

"Sure," I said, letting him take the scrunched top ends of the paper while I cut off a piece of ribbon. Then I quickly tied it around the top. It actually looked quite nice for improvisational wrapping. "There," I said, "it really looks pretty good. Very festive, if I do say so myself."

"Yes," he agreed, putting his arm around my waist. "Thanks so much for doing this." Then he kissed me, and our bodies fell down on the floor with his halfway on top of mine. While we kissed, he murmured, "I wish we could skip dinner."

"Your mom's birthday dinner?" I mumbled back.

"I know," he said, getting up and reaching for his shirt. "I'll be ready in a minute." I couldn't help but notice that his briefs seemed to be bulging in the right spot. As I got up, he looked over at me and smiled, "Of course, now I really do need a cold shower."

"It's quite obvious," I said smugly, and then I wished I hadn't been so blatant. "I'm going to the bathroom to freshen up," I added and quickly left.

Holding the present with the vase, David, now dressed, was in the hall when I exited the bath. "Do me a favor and put this on the game table in the family room. I'll get the rose bush," he said.

I did as he said, and he followed me with the bush. Then I slipped my card on the table too. There were other wrapped boxes there, a couple envelopes, and several cards that had already been opened.

"My parents and the Wilsons left a few minutes ago," he said. "Shall we?"

It took about twenty minutes to get to the restaurant, a Tutor-looking structure whose dimly-lit interior had dark red carpeting, silver gray walls, and lots of rustic ceiling beams. I thought it hadn't changed at all since my date with Jack.

"My eyes are going to take a minute to get adjusted to this," David said, as we scanned the dining room for our party. After we had located the other two couples at a large corner table, we sat down and the hostess lit another candle on our table. I decided we all looked pretty good in the pinkish glow of the candlelight. There were just six of us, although the table was set for eight. Jenny and Bruce were to join us later, after she got off work. They arrived while we were finishing some appetizers.

"We left some for you two," Mrs. Woodley said, sliding her small plate to her daughter.

"I was wondering why you were taking so many, mom," David kidded her.

"She knows this place serves my favorite fried zucchini," Jenny said. "Thanks, mom. Everybody looks great. I love that dress and your earrings, Sara."

"Pretty sexy," Bruce mumbled into his menu, and then winked at David. I thought I was going to die of embarrassment, but David just replied calmly, "So how was work today, Bruce? Sell any houses?" Bruce was working in the real estate office his parents owned. We'd heard yesterday from him that the market was very slow.

Bruce gave his assessment of the current Iowa City real estate market, and then Mrs. Wilson asked me, "Sara, do you rent in Mount Morris?"

"Yes, I do," I replied. "I have a small one-bedroom apartment. As you can imagine, the rent's pretty reasonable in Mount Morris."

Then we talked for a while about real estate in different towns and cities, and I found out for the first time that David was buying the unit he rented in his apartment building, which was being converted into a condominium. I thought it strange that he hadn't mentioned this before. I guessed there was still a lot I didn't know about him.

I also found out that Mr. Wilson was an insurance agent, that Mrs. Wilson used to sell real estate, that Mrs. Woodley used to be a librarian, that Bruce's birthday was in March, that Jenny's was in April, and that David's birthday was August 25th. He would be twenty-six, and he would not make it back to Iowa to celebrate with his family because of "work commitments." Mr. Woodley revealed that they were considering going to Chicago over Labor Day weekend.

After dinner when we got into David's car to return to his parents' home, the first thing he said was, "Why don't you come to Chicago with my parents over Labor Day weekend?" I must have looked pretty surprised at this suggestion because he added quickly, "I promise a topnotch tour of the Art Institute."

"That sounds nice," I said, "but I already promised my parents I'd spend the weekend with them and my sister and her husband. It's my dad's birthday on September 6th, and my mom's planning a party on the 5th. My sister will have had her baby by then, but I doubt she'll be of much help, so I've already committed myself to helping my mom, . . . but I'd like to visit you sometime."

"Come and help me celebrate my birthday then?" he implored.

"August 25th? That's the day before my school starts," I said. "I don't think my principal would be too understanding."

"Then come the weekend before, or the weekend before that. Look, Sara, I want to see you again and frequently, and we're two hundred miles apart, so we've got to make plans, or we'll just get too busy with work and . . . I don't want to wait until Thanksgiving and Christmas to see you again."

"I know," I said. "I feel the same way. It's just hard with the distance between us. But I do have a little time after summer school ends and before I have to be back in Mount Morris for the start of school there. Maybe the second or third weekend in August? You said you were going to be pretty busy for the rest of July and August, so maybe there'd be a better time?"

"I don't really know for sure exactly how busy I'll be. This partner I do a lot of work for inferred there'd be a lot of weekend work ahead, but I just don't know how it's going to be. I've still got to eat and sleep. Chicago's got some great shopping, so you could shop while I'm at work. Jenny came last November to visit and she spent a whole day at Marshall Field's and said she still didn't see the whole store. My good friend at the firm, Jake, his wife Pidgy works at Field's, and we could go out to dinner with them. They're a really fun couple. Pidgy's very artistic, so I know you two would hit it off. And besides the shopping on State Street, there's also Michigan Avenue. Have you heard of Water Tower Place?"

"No," I replied, "but it sounds interesting."

"When we get back to my folks', let's look at my calendar and see which weekend would work out the best, okay?"

I told him that sounded good, and then I thought about what I was going to tell my parents: *I'm going to Chicago to visit this guy I've only known for a few months.* Obviously there were some details to work out. Still, I was twenty-three years old, old enough to figure out exactly what I wanted to do with my life. And being with David seemed a priority now.

As we pulled into the Woodley driveway, David grabbed my left hand with his right and squeezed it tightly, then slid over to kiss me passionately. However, we weren't long in our embrace when Jenny and Bruce pulled up alongside us.

"Time for cake and ice cream," David said without much enthusiasm.

We all gathered in the family room, where Mrs. Woodley opened her cards and presents. She seemed to like my selections for her. She loved the rose bush. Mr. Woodley gave her a watch and a book of poetry. The Wilsons gave her a small bud vase and a gift certificate to Amling's Nursery. Then Mr. Woodley brought out a small cake with one candle, and I learned for the first time that she was turning fifty-five today.

After we all sang Happy Birthday, I helped Jenny cut and serve the cake and ice cream. Everyone was so full from dinner that we served very small portions. Soon after we finished eating, Bruce excused himself, saying he needed to head home, and Jenny went to see him off and then to her room. The other two couples decided it was time to play some bridge, and David suggested that we take a walk to wear off some of the many calories we'd consumed, so we excused ourselves and headed out the front door and down the block.

It was going on ten and fairly dark, but most of the homes had their outside lights on and the street lights provided more illumination. It was a very nice neighborhood of spacious ranches and neat-looking colonials, lots of mature maples, lindens, locusts, and oaks, and well-kept lawns. I decided it must have been a pretty good place to grow up and that David and Jenny had certainly turned out fine. He held my hand and we walked in silence for quite a while, listening to the night sounds of humming insects.

Finally I asked him, "What time are you starting back tomorrow?"

"Too early. About seven. I need to go into the office when I get back."

"It's getting pretty late now. I should probably go back to my dorm soon . . . and you've got a long drive ahead of you tomorrow."

"Yes," he agreed, "and one I'm not looking forward to." We turned back and walked in silence to the Woodley home. Right before we entered the house, David said, "Let's go and look at my calendar," so I followed him to his bedroom. He closed the door behind us and got an appointment book from his briefcase. Then he said, "I've got engagements scheduled for August 12th and 13th. I have to go to Milwaukee on business on August 17th. How about the weekend of August 20th through the 22nd? Do you think that would work for you?"

I moved closer to see the small calendar spread open on his desk, and his arm slid around my waist. "Yes, I think that would probably work out okay," I said, wondering when I was going to get my period in August.

"Great!" he replied. "I'll start checking on some things we can do when you visit. Maybe the Cubs will be in town." He pulled me closer to him and began kissing me. Then his fingers found the zipper on my sundress and that went down. One of his hands was stroking my lower back and the other was starting to pull one of the straps of my sundress down when there was a knock on the door.

"What now?" he muttered, and then he called out, "Yes, who is it?"

"It's Dad," came the reply, and David walked over to open the door. "We didn't hear you come in," he explained. "The Wilsons just left, and your mom and I are heading off to bed. We didn't know whether to lock up or not."

"Sorry, dad. I was just going to take Sara back to the dorm, and then I'll be sure everything's locked before I go to bed."

I had pulled my sundress strap in place, but I was standing facing the door, my dress still unzipped. "Thanks again for the lovely dinner," I added. "And please tell Mrs. Woodley good night."

"I will. We hope to see you again soon, Sara. Good night."

As he left, David walked back to me and said, "I'd really probably better get you back. It is getting late. Turn around and I'll zip you up." After he had zipped my dress, he kissed the top of my hair, and then we left.

On the way to my dorm, we talked about foreign cuisines and he told me about some great restaurants in Chicago. He asked me how I thought I'd travel there, and I said I'd either drive or fly. He told me to come in on Thursday or Friday and leave on Monday or Tuesday. When we got to my dorm, I told him he didn't need to park, but he said he wanted to walk me to my room.

After we got off the elevator, he put his hand around my bare shoulder as we walked down to my room. "I suppose your roommate's asleep?" he asked.

"Yes, most probably. You know I told you she's a little different. She goes to bed precisely at 9:30 every night and gets up at exactly 5:30. Orpah's into yoga, health food, roller skating, and studying in the library. It's actually quite nice that she doesn't bother me, except that she gets up so early. David, you know I'd want you to come in if she wasn't here, but I'm just not the sort of roommate who believes it's fair to . . . to disturb her after she's gone to bed."

"I know," he said, taking me in his arms and kissing me. "I just want you so much, but I can wait," he whispered. Finally he let go. "Call me or write me. Take care of yourself. I'll see you in a few weeks, okay?"

"Okay," I whispered back. "Thanks again, and drive carefully tomorrow. Good night."

He called the next evening from Chicago and a couple times during the next two weeks. Then he called late on a Wednesday night. "I'm desperate to see you, Sara," he said. "Here's my plan. I get Saturday night and Sunday off this weekend. Let's meet about half way. I looked things up on the map. We could do Sterling, Illinois, or if you don't want to drive as far, the Quad cities. Do you have a map in your room?"

I told him I didn't; he told me to buy one, think about what he'd proposed, and call him back tomorrow night. After I hung up, I wasn't sure I wanted to drive two to three hours just to be with David, and yet I was eager to see him. I knew he wanted to have sex, and I thought I knew I wanted to, but I wasn't sure. It was so easy to have doubts about our relationship when we were two hundred miles apart. I knew that once he had me in his arms, I'd be an easy prey to his seducing ways. There would be no dad knocking on the door, no Orpah sleeping in the next bed, no stopping this time.

I didn't sleep well that night, and toward morning I had the strangest dream that seemed so real. I dreamt that I had forgotten to lock our dorm door; someone had slipped in and was raping me. I tried to call out Orpah's name, but she didn't appear to be there. Then after a few seconds, she appeared in our doorway with her roller skates on, but the attacker was gone. Suddenly I woke up and saw that Orpah was sleeping peacefully in the bed across from me, but I couldn't shake the dream because it had seemed so real, and yet I knew it was all an illusion.

I tried to analyze it, of course, but the dream didn't make much sense. I knew David wouldn't be raping me if I wanted to have sex and I knew I wanted David to seduce me. I thought I wanted to go all the way. Emma Aspen and Natalie slept with men as if having sex were the same as having a Diet Coke. Why was it so different for me? Finally, I decided that I did really love

David and, if giving myself to him led to a future rejection by him, then I'd only be the wiser.

I got to the Holiday Inn in Sterling about five o'clock. (I had told my parents that Emma and I were meeting a friend of hers from grad school.) David had said he wouldn't arrive until six or seven, so I had a little wait. Since it was 98 degrees in the shade, I locked my car and went to the small lobby, where I sat with a magazine. I couldn't concentrate on any of the articles, though. About six fifteen, I walked to the lounge and ordered a glass of white wine. Before she served me, the barmaid asked to see my I.D., which made me a little nervous. As more and more people entered the lounge, I felt a little silly sitting by myself. I sensed two guys, cowboy types, were getting incorrect vibes from me. I picked up my magazine but was startled when they appeared in their tight jeans and cowboy boots at my table.

"Howdy, miss," one of them, with curly auburn hair said. "We was wonderin' if we could join you and buy you a drink?"

I glanced at my watch and said, "I'm sorry. I'm meeting someone shortly. Actually, I've got to leave now, so you can have this table if you want."

I quickly went to the restroom and spent a good ten minutes in there. Then I began to worry that perhaps David had shown up and couldn't find me. When I emerged, I headed back toward the lobby, and the moment I got there, David appeared in the doorway.

"Sara!"

We hurried to each other and hugged. "It's really good to see you," I told him. "Did you just get here?"

"Yes, I parked next to you in the parking lot. Let me check us in, and then we'll go find our room, okay?"

"Fine," I said, sitting down again on the other lobby chair and glancing at my watch. It was almost seven. From where I sat I could see David at the reception desk. He had on navy pinstripe suit pants and a white shirt, with his sleeves rolled up, and he was tie-less. He looked a little hot and tired, but also excited. *Probably the prospect of having sex,* I thought. *Why are all guys alike?*

I was wearing a short casual skirt, a sleeveless blouse, and newly-purchased sandals. It had been hard to know what kind of clothes to pack. I had asked David on the phone, and he had said jokingly, "Clothes! You don't need to bring any clothes!" So I had gone out and bought some sandals on sale and a new pink nightgown which I hoped was pretty sexy.

Just as he finished at the registration desk, the two cowboy characters walked into the lobby. I got up to join David, who put his arm around my waist as we headed toward the door.

"Have fun, little miss!" yelled one of the cowboys, and my face reddened.

"You know those guys?" David asked me.

"Oh, they just tried to pick me up in the bar," I explained. "Before you got here, I just sat down to have a glass of wine and they . . . well, they came over."

"They didn't know the little lady was spoken for," he joked.

"That's right, but I set them straight."

When we were beside our cars, he said, "Now we have to drive around to the right. Here's your room key. I'll meet you over there."

I got into my car and followed David around the motel. After I parked, I took my small overnight bag from the back seat and walked over to David's car. He had a duffle bag, a big briefcase, and his suit coat.

"We're in Room 218," he said. "Want me to carry your bag?"

I told him no and we climbed the stairs together, quickly finding 218. Inside the air conditioning was turned on high and made a loud humming noise. The room smelled a little antiseptic, and it was very cool and dark. After I had put my bag down, I opened the beige drapes and had a wonderful view of the parking lot.

"I'm really thirsty," David said. "I'm going to get some ice, okay?" He took the vinyl ice bucket from the dresser and left. While he was gone, I brushed my hair and checked my lipstick for the umpteenth time. Then I started to unpack by hanging up the one blouse and sundress I'd brought.

When he returned, David filled a glass with ice and water and sat down on one of the beds with his legs stretched out in front of him and his back against the headboard. I got a glass of ice water too and sat down on one of the chairs next to the large window.

"So is your job going pretty well?" I asked him.

"So-so," he answered. "We still have a lot of work to do. But even the partner on the job agreed that we all needed a brief respite. I am so looking forward to the next twenty-four hours."

I couldn't help blushing when he said that and hoped the room was still dark enough so that he couldn't tell. Then he asked, "Are you hungry? Do you want to get a bite to eat?"

"Not really," I answered, "but I'll do whatever you want to do."

"I want to kiss you again," he said. "Come over here and give me a kiss."

I slipped off my sandals and positioned myself next to him, sliding my hands around his neck and kissing him. While we kissed, he undid all the buttons on my blouse, pulling it out from my skirt. I began to panic a little, reminding myself that I didn't have on that many pieces of clothing: my blouse, my skirt, my bra, my panties. Four things.

I wanted him to say something about birth control. As he kissed my neck and undid the button and then the zipper on my skirt, all I could think was: *Say something about birth control; let me know you really care about me by saying that you want to be responsible.* But of course all he did was turn his attention to unhooking my bra. His hands were on my back searching for the hook, but fortunately I'd worn a bra with a front hook. I backed away a little.

"David," I began, "maybe we're rushing things a little bit. Let's just get things straight about birth control." I felt like a country bumpkin blurting it out, and then suddenly I remembered that I'd stopped him before on the Fourth of July. *He's going to think I'm really really weird,* I thought.

David looked right into my questioning eyes and said simply, "We'll use birth control. I was planning to. Is a condom okay?"

"Sure," I answered, adding quickly, "Can I use some foam too?"

"Fine," he said. "You know I love you and don't want to hurt you."

I smiled and said, "I know. I love you too," moving closer to him. "You've got way too many clothes on." I started unbuttoning his shirt. Then he took it off and pulled his T-shirt over his head while I took off my blouse. "My bra hook's in front," I whispered, as I bent to kiss him. He quickly undid it and suddenly my breasts were next to his naked chest, and it seemed the most wonderful feeling in the world. Remember this ecstasy, I thought to myself: remember, remember, remember. Soon my panties were being pulled down, and I began working on David's belt buckle, but I guess I was too slow because he pulled away somewhat and quickly took off everything, including his socks, so our two bodies were naked next to one another. After a few minutes of intense kissing, I excused myself to go to the bathroom, and when I returned the drapes were drawn and the bedspread was turned down. I slid next to David, and as we kissed he rolled on top of me. I spread my legs apart, and, after a few attempts, his penis went clumsily into me.

When he entered, I gave a slight moan since he felt so immense, and his thrusting motions were a little uncomfortable. With his breathing loud and rapid, he had ceased kissing me. Then suddenly he stopped thrusting, and I guessed he'd had an ejaculation. He withdrew from me and collapsed on his back. After a few seconds, he got up and went into the bathroom.

All I could think was that I'd finally done it, and it'd been okay, not terrifically great. I felt a little wet and a little sore, but otherwise I was content.

After David emerged from the bathroom, he lay down next to me, put one of his arms around me, and asked, "Are you okay? Are you hungry now?"

"Not really. What time is it anyway?"

He rolled over to look at his watch on the nightstand. "It's 8:08," he replied. "So is it okay if we just stay here, watch some TV? We could order a pizza if you're hungry?"

"No, I'm fine. But if you're hungry, go ahead and get a pizza."

"Actually, I'm not hungry at all, but I am kind of beat. I just want to stay here and hold you." He picked up the remote control and turned on the TV. "You'll forgive me if I fall asleep?"

"That's okay. I know how hard you've been working."

So we lay naked in each other's arms with the pillows propped up and watched TV, and it wasn't long before David fell asleep. When the show ended, I got up and went to the bathroom to take out my contacts, brush my teeth, and wash my face. Then I put on my nightgown, turned out all the lights and the TV, and got back into bed. It took me forever to fall asleep. I kept wondering if David had really enjoyed making love to me, if he thought I was a hopelessly inexperienced prude and he'd dump me, or if there was going to be a next step in our relationship.

Sometime during the night after I had finally fallen asleep, I felt David's hand on my hip and then it went slowly up to my breast. Part of me wanted to pretend to be asleep, but his hand returned to my hip and then my crotch, and I gave a little jerk. My stomach felt delightfully queasy. He moved closer to me and kissed me on the neck and breasts. I could feel his penis erect again, and his breathing and kissing felt wonderful. This time he came into me easier and stayed much longer, and I fell right back asleep.

We made love again in the morning, and then while we were having breakfast, he wanted to make plans for my trip to Chicago. I sensed everything was going to turn out all right.

When I had finished ironing the sampler for Georgiana's baby, I turned off the iron, walked to the hallway, unlocked the door, and picked up the Sunday *Trib*. Back in the kitchen, I sorted through the many sections: those I read, those David read, those we both read, and those that neither of us read, which I put on the trash pile in the closet. Then I poured a cup of coffee and took the Real Estate section into the bedroom. David still seemed to be asleep. I put my coffee cup down on the nightstand, propped up my pillow, and got back into bed. I had just found the "For Sale by Owner" houses when David rolled over and stretched.

"Good morning," he mumbled. "Lorenzo wants to visit."

I leaned over and kissed him on the cheek, returning his greeting. His hands went around me as he kissed me on the neck and took the straps of my nightgown down. I turned over on my back, as he sat up to pull my nightgown down over my legs. Then he began sucking and biting gently on my right breast while he was stroking my thighs with his hands. I kept my legs together for a few minutes, basking in his heavy breathing and kissing and the pressure of his body next to mine. Finally, I opened my legs wide so his fingers could penetrate me. After several exquisite moments, I slid down, undid his pajama bottoms and took them off. My tongue found his penis, and because I knew how much he enjoyed this, I stroked his thighs and sucked his penis for several minutes, pretending it was a lollipop and enjoying the small groaning noises he made. When I finally pulled away, I let my breasts linger for a moment on his penis. Then I turned the front of my body away from his, with my belly against his and my legs spread out so that his hands could reach me, as my tongue moved up and down and around his penis.

"Sara, I can't hold it much longer," he finally moaned.

I lifted my head up and turned my body around, still cradling him with my legs. I held his erect penis and gently guided it inside of me while I sat down. He slid in perfectly, snugly. He put his hands on my breasts, while I put mine on his chest.

"Oh, Sara, you feel so good," he murmured, "and you are so incredibly juicy."

After all that manual stimulation, how could I not be, I thought, but instead I said, "Lorenzo feels pretty incredibly good too."

Then I bounced up and down on him for several minutes, pretending I was riding a bucking bronco and thinking surely he would ejaculate any second, but he did not, so finally I stopped and slid quickly off him. Just as rapidly he got on top of me, slid in, and put his hands under my buttocks to make the fit tighter while he thrust and thrust and thrust, I thought maybe forever, before he finally ejaculated.

After a few minutes, David got up and went to the bathroom, and I could hear him peeing. I took a pen from the nightstand drawer and started circling house possibilities. He walked into the bedroom and said, "Do you want to shower first, or can I?"

"I was just going to get in," I answered. "Is that okay?"

"Sure, I'll shave." He headed back to the bathroom and I got up to follow him. "Did you see any good house possibilities?" he asked.

"Maybe," I said, kissing his back and noting how small and droopy Lorenzo looked after his morning workout.

After I showered, David did so, and then we both had breakfast, reading the paper and eating our cereal in silence. I finished eating first and, as I got up with my dishes, David said, "It's a good thing Jerry Brown isn't going to run for President; he wouldn't have stood a chance." The 1984 election seemed so distant that it held little interest for me. Just as I had finished putting my bowl and juice glass in the dishwasher, the phone rang, and David, who was still sitting at our small kitchen table which was closer to the wall phone, picked it up. I decided to wait a moment to see if it was for me, and if it wasn't, then I'd get dressed.

I heard David say hello and then, with surprise, "Marc!" After a few seconds, he continued, "Fine. And how are you and Emma?"

Marc White? I thought, as I headed toward the bathroom. Maybe they're coming to visit. We had talked about getting together over Labor Day weekend or maybe later in the fall in Galena. It would be fun to see Emma and Marc.

I had just finished brushing my teeth and putting on my makeup when David came to the bathroom doorway.

"There's some really bad news, Sara," he began. "There was a horrible automobile accident last night, and Pete and Susan were killed. Pete Jr. was in the car too, but he's all right. I got all the details about when Marc thinks the funeral might be, but Emma wants to talk to you. She's pretty upset."

I felt tears rush to my eyes as I hurried to the kitchen phone. "Emma?" I gasped.

"Oh, Sara," her voice choked. "It's so sad. They had everything to live for! Their bodies are so bad. They don't know if they should have closed or open caskets—they're that bad!" I could hear her sobbing, and we both just cried because I couldn't think of anything to say.

Finally I said, "At least Pete Jr.'s okay. How's Susan's dad taking it?"

"Well, we got in touch with him, sort of, this morning. God, Sara, you know he's 65 and in a rest home and the nurse aid said he's got Alzheimer's and he's usually not completely with it, so we told her and they were going to try to tell him and make him understand, but they weren't too hopeful. Pete's dad, as you know, died about a year ago, and we haven't been able to reach Pete's mom yet. Did you know she's in Arizona?" Then Emma started sobbing more loudly while she continued, "Marc was on call when they brought them in, and I've never, ever, seen him so sad and angry and full of despair. And what's so damn annoying is that the other guy was drunk and walked away without a scratch!"

"Oh, that is disgusting! But Pete Jr.'s okay?"

"By some miracle of God. Not even a scratch, as far as the doctors can tell. He's at the hospital now, but they said he could be released, but there's nobody to take him—except us! We're actually his godparents, and we have the spare key to Pete and Susan's house, but the hospital has to locate Pete's mom first, and then Marc's going to ask her and the authorities if we can have temporary custody of Pete Jr. Oh Sara, you know we've been trying for over a year to have a baby, and we were just going to start looking into adoption, and now—boom!—a baby falls right into our laps. But I don't know! I don't know what we should do. Of course, we'll have to talk to Louellen and Pete's mom and Susan's dad, but all I can think is: here's a baby for us, here's a baby for us. But it's not our baby. It's Pete and Susan's! And they're gone, and they shouldn't be! They had so much to live for."

She was sobbing harder, and I couldn't think of anything to say except to agree with her, and then finally she mumbled, "Marc said David thinks you'll be able to come. Oh please come, Sara! I need you!"

"Sure," I said hesitantly, "we'll try to."

"Marc says to get off the phone in case Louellen or the hospital is trying to get through. Bye, Sara, I hope I'll see you soon."

David was in the bedroom getting dressed when I walked in. He rushed over to me and put his arms around my bare shoulders to hug me. I still had on only my bra and panties.

"I think we should drive to Iowa City today," he said. "I'm not very busy at work, so I can easily take three to four days off. And I know Pidgy will give you a few days. After all, this is your slow month. I know you don't start dreaming up adventures for Mistletoe Bear until September."

David's attempt to cheer me up was sweet, since he knew I always looked forward to the holiday season at Field's, but now my stomach felt queasy, and my eyes hurt from crying.

"I think they need our moral support, Sara," David said. "And we can see my parents and hopefully yours. What do you think?"

"I think you're right," I sighed. "I think we should go. So when exactly is the funeral, or do they know?"

"Marc said they still haven't reached Pete's mom or Louellen, but he guessed maybe there'd be a funeral or memorial service on Wednesday or Thursday. Marc told me Pete's mom is in Arizona. Did you know she's had a recurrence of breast cancer? And Louellen's somewhere in Africa. Marc's meeting a policeman at Susan and Pete's house at 10:30, and they're going to look for their phone numbers. Marc said he wants us to stay with them, but I said we'd probably stay with my parents. He expects that he and Emma will be the ones who end up making all, or most, of the arrangements."

"Do you think they had a will?" I asked.

"Marc didn't think so. Hell, Sara, we don't even have a will and I'm an attorney."

"I know, but we don't have any kids yet."

"Well, Pete Jr.'s only four months old. They probably just didn't get around to it yet."

"I know. Oh David, it is so sad."

We held each other for several minutes, and then I pulled away and said, "I'll finish getting dressed and call Pidgy. When did you want to leave?"

"Let's shoot for eleven to eleven-thirty. I've got a few calls to make too. And I'll call my parents to say we're coming."

"Okay," I said, "but I don't know if I can take the whole week off. I'd really better be back on Thursday or Friday."

"That's fine. I can't afford to be gone all week too."

Because it was summer, it was easy to pack. I pulled out a couple pairs of shorts and tops, my nightgown and panties, a black bra. I took a sleeveless black cocktail dress, black hose, and heels in case we were able to stay for the funeral or memorial service. I tried to remember when I'd last been at a funeral, and it seemed ages ago. I'd been married and in Chicago when Sharon Thomasino killed herself, and so it seemed as if the last funeral I'd been to was when my Great Aunt Daphne died around Christmas a few years ago, and that seemed like ages ago, although I could remember that I'd worn a black wool dress to her funeral on a cold December morning.

After about an hour in the car, I got really drowsy while I was trying to read the *Trib*, so I took out my contacts and told David I was going to take a little nap. I also had a slight headache, probably from crying, although it felt sort of like the headaches

I sometimes got right at the beginning of my period, yet I wasn't due to get that for about a week.

That afternoon after I finished student teaching, there was a faculty meeting and then after that Marnie Howe, my supervising teacher, invited me to go out for coffee with her and two other teachers. As I drove back to I.C., I realized I was going to miss dinner at the house, so I swung through the drive-thru at McDonald's before I reached the campus. I took all my papers and supper up to my room and was surprised to see that the door was closed. When I opened it, there were Natalie and Emma sitting on Emma's bed with a bottle of sloe gin and a carton of orange juice on the floor. They each had a glass in their hands.

"You guys could get into lots of trouble," was the first thing I said, probably because I was so tired after such a long day. Emma picked up the gin bottle and moved it to the other side of her bed where it wouldn't be visible from the doorway. Alcohol was not allowed in our sorority house.

"Shit, shut the door," Natalie demanded. "Come on in, Sara dear. We're celebrating." She got up, took another glass from her dresser, put in some ice cubes, and walked around to pick up the gin bottle.

"Celebrating what?" I asked wearily.

"What are we celebrating, Emma dear? Hell, we're celebrating menstruation! Menstruation! Menstruation! Emma got her period!"

"Here's to cramps!" Emma shouted.

"And bloating!" Natalie cried out.

I went over and gave Emma a hug. "I am so glad," I told her.

She held up her drink and said, "Super absorbent tampons—don't leave home without 'em!"

"Here's to ruined panties and stains on clothing!" Natalie proclaimed. "Have I got a story for you kids! Come on over and sit down, Sara dear, and eat your burger and fries. Here's your sloe screw—God, I love that name. I never told you guys this because it was so embarrassing, but I think this is the right moment."

I sat down on the bed with them and got ready for one of Natalie's tales.

"Last summer," she began, "Simon asked me to go to Nebraska with him to see this Sunday matinee. One of his good friends from high school had one of the male leads. Pete knew the guy too, of course, so Pete and Susan were going to go with us, but they had to back out at the last minute because Pete's father had to have emergency heart surgery. Anyway, there was this charming little outdoor theatre along the Missouri, and when I went to the bathroom when we stopped at this rest stop on the way there, everything was fine. And then I went to the bathroom when we got there, and everything was fine. I had my period—you guys got that, right?"

"Yeah, we got that, Nat," I said.

"So anyway, at the intermission I went to the restroom and everything was fine. I come back out and sit down in the hot sun in the front row seats Simon got for us, and while I'm sitting through this interminable final act, I'm getting that feeling, you know?" We nodded. "Anyway, the play is finally over and the cast comes out for their curtain calls, and when Simon's friend comes on stage, Simon jumps up applauding like hell—you know Simon—and I'm just sitting there thinking, I've got to get to a toilet, I've got to get to a toilet. But finally I stand up too, and a few more people do too, and I'm just praying, please get me to a toilet, God! And then I feel this tap on my shoulder, and this middle-aged lady sitting behind me whispers, 'Dear, I think you need to go to the restroom.' So I'm thinking, shit, that I know, lady. How bad can it possibly be?

"So I excuse myself and practically sprint to this little john, and I have on this pale blue sundress—what was I thinking?—and I try to see the back of it in the restroom mirror, and I can see that there are several bright red globs all over the skirt part of my dress.

"So I stay in the stall for the longest time, thinking, what the fuck am I gonna do? I've got plenty of tampons, but my dress and panties are a mess. I hear other women come and go, and finally this gruff voice says, 'You ever comin' out of there, honey?'

"So I say, 'I've had an accident, and I have to take off my dress, so I'm coming out now.'

"I emerge from the stall with just my messy panties and bra on, and this two hundred pound lady looks right at me and knows what's happened. 'What can we do to help you, hon?' she asks me.

"So I start running cold water over the stains on my sundress and explain that I'm two hundred miles from home and I'm supposed to go out to dinner now with my boyfriend and one of the cast members, and she says to her daughter, who has just come out of the other stall, 'Do you still have that hair dryer in your car?'

"The daughter says yes and the mom tells her to go get it, and meanwhile a couple other ladies come in to use the facilities, and I feel so dumb standing there. The mom tells me, 'I'll finish working on the stains. You go wait in the stall.'

"So I do what she says, and the daughter returns with the dryer, and the mom turns it on high and starts drying my dress, and it's so noisy because of the dryer that she shouts to me behind the stall, 'Do you need a Kotex?'

"So I tell her no, I've got plenty of that stuff, and then she explains that her daughter is a senior in high school and throws discus and they live out on a farm and so sometimes after meets her daughter showers at school before she goes out to eat or to friends' homes and therefore she keeps a hair dryer in her car, and all I'm thinking is, thank you, thank you, thank you, God.

"Then this mom tells me that they only live 20 minutes away and were planning to go straight home and she tells her daughter to give me her underwear, so the daughter goes into the stall beside me, takes off her panties—these huge white things, the girl's pretty good-sized too—and pushes them across the floor to me, and I really want to tell them it's not necessary, but my own panties are such a mess that I take them and put them on.

"And I'm shouting at her to write down her name and address so I can mail her daughter's underwear back to her and she's telling me, 'Hon, that ain't necessary. The good Lord has always taken care of me and my family, and we can truly spare a tiny piece of cotton.'

"Then she tells me my dress is fairly dry and that I should stand out in the sun for a few minutes and it should be perfectly fine. She hands it over the stall door to me and tells me they have to leave now, and when I come out they're gone, and all I'm thinking is, there must be a God or angels or something. And the rest of the day is perfect!"

Now Emma started crying. Sometimes when she drank a lot, she tended to start bawling. "Oh, I just have this horrible feeling," she sobbed. "Like I'm so happy **now**, but like someday God is going to punish me. I don't know, I don't know."

I got up to get her a Kleenex box and throw my fast food wrappers away.

"Don't be ridiculous," Natalie chided. "We're celebrating! Pass me the booze, Sara dear!"

"I think you've had enough, Nat," I suggested.

"All right, mommy dearest," she sighed. "Hey, just remember, Sara dear, that if any guy ever says to you, 'You can't get pregnant the first time,' or 'I'm sterile,' or 'I'm allergic to condoms,' run for the hills!"

"Please, Nat," I said, "I wasn't born yesterday."

She raised her almost empty glass for one more toast, "Well, here's to menstruation! I guess we can't be female without it. Let's just pray that by the time our daughters grow up, somebody invents a condom that doesn't break!"

Emma had stopped crying to giggle at Natalie's humor, but now she said, "Hell, have I got a horrible headache! Do you have any Pamprin, Sara?"

When we stopped briefly, I ran into the gas station's restroom, popped in my contacts, and bought a bottle of Tylenol. Then I offered to drive for a while, but David said he wasn't tired and didn't mind driving. So I read the rest of the newspaper and even found a few more house prospects, including a great-sounding one in Northbrook, for what would now be next weekend's house-hunting trip to the burbs.

It was a little after three thirty when we rolled into the Woodley driveway. There was no answer at the front door, so David got out his key, saying, "They're probably still with Grams. I told them we'd be here about four."

We had decided to stay with David's parents rather than Marc and Emma, and I had decided to wait until one of us talked to Emma or Marc again before I called my parents to tell them what had happened. My parents had known Susan pretty well since we'd roomed together one semester at the sorority house, and they'd talked with Pete on a few occasions, especially at our wedding two years ago. I knew they would be saddened at such a great loss and that they would want to come for whatever sort of service was held. I always loved seeing my parents; they had been to Chicago to visit us in July. Our being together this time, however, would be bittersweet.

While we were unpacking, we heard the garage door open and David's mother called out, "Hello!" We met her in the hall. "I'm so sorry we weren't here when you arrived," she apologized. "We went to visit Grams, as we usually do on Sunday afternoon, and then we stopped at the store for a few things. The fridge is pretty bare when it's just the two of us, you know. You both look good, and we do enjoy having you, but I wish you were here for another reason." She gave me a hug, and then David one. I told her she looked good and that it was nice to be with them, even if it was under tragic circumstances.

David's father came down the hall, and after we had all hugged and kissed, his mother said, "Dad was going to put some steaks and salmon on the grill for dinner. Why don't you see if Marc and Emma want to join us?"

"That's awfully thoughtful of you, mom," David said. "I was just going to call them, and then Sara wants to call her parents."

"Well," she said, "you two go ahead and tend to your business while I get dinner ready. I'm just thankful you're here and that you've all been such good friends."

At her toasting preceding the luncheon, Melly said, "I'm so glad my little sis has so many good friends." After the luncheon on the day preceding my wedding, Natalie and Emma were in the dining room arranging gifts on Grandma Keatson's mahogany sideboard; Mother was washing her best china, crystal, and silver, while Melly, Vicki, Jenny, and David's mom were drying; and Father had taken little Mandy and Pidgy, who was North Shore all the way, out to see the old farm because, being a Chicago gal, she'd confessed to never having ridden in a pickup or having been on a farm in her entire life. Georgiana, Susan, and I were putting all the washed and dried items away. We were about done when Susan pulled me aside and said, "Let's go into the pig room. I have something I want to give you."

"You mean the pink room?" I asked.

"Oh, I thought it was the pig room because of the picture you did. Sorry, Sara."

"No problem," I said, as we slipped down the hall and into the pink room. Susan was carrying her purse, and she took out a small box and gave it to me, saying, "Let's sit down. I want to explain this little gift."

So we sat side by side on the leather sofa, and I eagerly opened the box she handed to me. Inside was a charming pin that looked as if it was very old. "Oh, it's lovely!" I exclaimed.

"Now maybe you've already been given something 'old' to wear tomorrow, but you know how I love antiques, and I just don't think we can have enough special old things in our lives, so I want you to wear my great grandmother McHenry's cloisonné pin. I wore it on my wedding day—remember way back when?— and my mom and grandmother and great grandmother before me did too. Great grandmother McHenry came to Parker, Iowa, in a covered wagon after the Civil War. She died young, at age 26, in childbirth, but her son, my grandfather, survived, so this pin is very special. You know, it reminds me about our pioneer heritage and how strong we Iowa women are, so I want you to have it, with all my love and best wishes for a long and happy marriage to David, one of the best guys I know."

My eyes moistened as I gave her a hug. "It's so thoughtful of you, Susan," I said, "but this is really a family heirloom. You should keep it to give to your daughter on her wedding day."

"Well, Sara, I've thought about that, so let's make a pact. Whichever one of us first has a daughter to get married, let's let her have the pin for her wedding day. You know with my family's history of breast cancer, and Pete's mom has had it too, I'm really praying I only have boys. Pete wants a whole baseball team, but I'll settle for about three."

"But how about a future daughter-in-law?" I asked. "Maybe you'd want her to have it?"

"Sara, you've always been the dearest friend. I've got other pieces of family jewelry, so don't fret so. Let's just make our pact, and you start praying too that I only have boy babies, okay?"

I hugged her, and we smiled at each other. All I could manage to say was, "Well, it's a deal then. Here's to sons for you and a daughter for me. And thanks so much for being such a wonderful friend."

After David got off the phone, he told us that Marc and Emma would join us, but that they had Pete Jr. now and so he'd have to come too, and they wanted us to come over as soon as we could. So, after I made a quick call to my parents, we swiftly left, with plans to return with the Whites around six thirty.

On the way there David told me that Marc had finally made contact with Pete's mom and Louellen. Mrs. Byron was flying in tomorrow, and Louellen was going to try to get on a plane today, but she probably wouldn't get here until Tuesday. Pete's mom told Marc that Pete's uncle, Father Byron, was in a nursing home for retired priests and not in good health, but she wanted a priest for a funeral mass. Even though Pete and Susan hadn't attended any church regularly, Pete's mom said she would find a priest for the funeral, which had been temporarily scheduled for Wednesday morning.

"Marc wants me to help him take the crib down at Pete and Susan's, and then set it up at their house. I guess they've been getting Pete Jr.'s things. They brought him home from the hospital about three this afternoon."

"Do you suppose Emma and Marc will ask if they can adopt Pete Jr.?"

"I dunno, hon. I guess we'll have to wait and see when everybody gets here. But in the meantime, Emma and Marc are going to take care of him."

It was hard to imagine Emma Aspen, now White, in a maternal role. Her image as one of the most beautiful coeds on campus was forever etched in my mind. And then there was Marc White, probably the most gorgeous male being I'd ever met, and over the last few months, I'd met several male models through my work at Field's.

"Hey, Sara, it's me, Marc."

"Hi. What's up?"

"I was just calling to see if you wanted to take in a movie this Saturday."

"I don't think that's such a good idea."

"Why not? You're a good friend. There's no reason we can't go to a movie together. I've heard *Three Days of the Condor* is pretty damn good. Have you seen it yet?"

"No."

"Good. I'll pick you up at eight fifteen. Bye."

I hung up the hall phone and wondered how I was going to explain this date to my best friend. I decided not to mention anything until Saturday night. That evening I said casually, "Marc wants to go see a movie," while I was putting on lipstick. Emma was in bed reading *The Great Gatsby*.

"With you?" she asked.

"Yeah, I think he just wants somebody to talk to. You know Marc. Whenever you two break up, he wants to hash it all out, and he's praying I'll tell him how miserable you are, how much you really love him, etc., etc. Hey, what do you want me to tell him? Are you out on a hot date tonight or pining away?" I was trying to be Emma's friend, but I didn't know if she was buying anything I was saying. She was silent, so I went down the hall to the bathroom.

When I returned, she said, "I can't believe you're going out with him."

"We're just gonna see a movie."

"He's using you, Sara. How can you let that son of a bitch do that?"

Because he's the most handsome son of a bitch I know, I thought, but instead I said, "Okay. I won't go. When he shows up, you can go downstairs and tell him I'm sick. Then **you** can go out with him."

"I am never, ever having anything to do with Marc White for the rest of my life!" she fumed. "And if you had a brain in your head and weren't listening to your hormones, you'd do the same!"

The house intercom suddenly interrupted us: "Sara Keatson! You have a visitor downstairs. Sara Keatson!"

"So does this mean if Marc asks me to marry him," I queried, "you won't be my bridesmaid?"

She smiled a little and then said, "Sara, be careful."

After the movie, Marc wanted to "talk," so we went to his room at the frat house. Since he was president of his house, he had his own room that semester, a small room in the middle of the second floor, which on that particular night seemed very quiet. He offered me a glass of wine and then sat down in his Lazy Boy recliner. I was standing by his desk looking at Emma's pictures. I turned the desk chair around to face him, and then I sat down and said, "She's really mad at you this time." Neither of us had brought up the subject of Emma earlier.

"Frankly, Sara, I don't give a damn. I've had it with her. We're just not right for each other. It's taken me a hell of a long time to figure that out, but now that I know we're not right, as a couple, I actually feel damn good. I feel this tremendous freedom. Do you understand?"

"I don't know," I began. "I think maybe you're deceiving yourself, but maybe it's good if you stop dating for a while."

"So what was she doing tonight? Going out with that guy Gordon from her American novel class?"

"No, she was just at the house. She was reading when I left. And I don't think she's interested in Gordon at all."

"She doesn't have to be interested in a guy to fall into the sack with him!"

"You know you're being too hard on her," I said, finishing my wine and standing up. "It's late and I've got a lot of work to do tomorrow, so I'd better get back to the house. Thanks for the movie and the wine."

Marc got up, walked over to me, and put his arms around me. "Hey, Sara, didn't you just hear me tell you that it's over between Emma and me? I want to get to know you." He bent over to kiss me lightly on the lips, and I felt my body go wild with anticipation. Then his fingers touched my face and he tilted my head up and kissed me hard. Then, while kissing my neck, he whispered in my ear, "Let's go lie down and get comfortable."

Since his arms were still around me, it was easy for him to lead me to his bed. We sort of fell down on it with him on the bottom and me on top, but then he moved to the side so I slid down on the bed.

Marc White was definitely the best kisser of any boy I had ever kissed, and he kept kissing me on the neck and mouth and blowing on my neck while his hands pulled my shirt out of my jeans. My heart was telling me to stop him, but my body wanted him to continue. Soon he was unbuttoning my shirt from the bottom, and when it was all undone, he quickly pulled his sweater and T-shirt off and began kissing my chest while pulling my bra straps down.

"Marc, this isn't right," I mumbled. "You've got to stop."

"Why isn't it right if I want to fuck you and you want it too, Sara?" he whispered back while kissing me. Now his hands had moved to my jeans belt and he was undoing that.

"You know it isn't right, Marc," I said weakly while he unzipped my jeans zipper.

"Why isn't it right if you want it?" he whispered. "I know you want me, Sara."

"No, I don't," I said with more conviction. "Maybe my body wants to have sex with you, but we don't love each other, Marc. You're trying to screw me to get back at Emma."

He stopped trying to unbutton my jeans and sat up. "Damn it, Sara! This isn't about Emma. I told you it's over between us."

"Well, what we're doing isn't about love either, Marc."

"You sure kissed me like you loved me," he shot back. "Simon's right. You're a big tease."

"I'm sorry," I said, getting off his bed and starting to button my shirt. "I have to go now."

He was staring at me. "Maybe we can go out for pizza tomorrow evening?" he suggested.

"I don't think that's a good idea. It's just not right."

"So you're not even willing to give **us** a chance?"

That was a hard question to answer coming from the most handsome guy I'd ever kissed. "I guess not," I said.

"Well, I'm here, Sara," he said, looking straight into my eyes. "We can still be friends."

"It's fortunate that we were all such close friends," David was saying as we reached the White residence, a 60's split level with red brick, white trim, and a neat lawn with pink petunias and red geraniums planted along the sidewalk and in pots by the front door. When I saw this house it reminded me that we were all no longer college students but young adults on the road to mid-dle-age maturity, a journey that had ended abruptly for Pete and Susan, one that could end as suddenly for any of us.

Emma, wearing one of her flower-child dresses, answered the door and threw her arms around me. "Thank God you're here!" she said, her voice choking with grief. Marc appeared at her side, and we greeted each other. Then Emma continued, "There's so much to do and it's all happening so fast. And you've got to help me with Pete Jr. He hardly sleeps at all and just wants to be held all the time."

"Great lawn," David said to Marc, as they led us inside to the small foyer.

"Yeah, we got a lot of rain last week, so it really greened things up," he answered, and then changed the subject. "Man, instant parenthood is pretty hard. I've already made two trips to the store this afternoon. Babies sure do need a lot of stuff."

We followed Marc and Emma into their kitchen, where Pete Jr. was dozing in a carry-cradle in the middle of the floor.

"Everybody be really quiet," Marc whispered. "He's been

asleep for twenty minutes, and that's the longest he's been out since we brought him home from the hospital."

Pete Jr.'s head was cocked to one side, with his huge pinkish baby cheek almost resting on his double chin. He had long dark eyelashes but just wisps of soft dark hair.

"He's so adorable," I whispered.

"Woodley, could we head right over to Pete and Susan's so we can get that crib over here?" Marc asked.

"You bet, but I've got to admit I have no experience with disassembling and then reassembling cribs."

"That makes two of us," Marc added.

"Got a tool box?" David asked, as they headed toward the door to the garage, and I chuckled inwardly, for it seemed as if this was definitely a case of the blind leading the blind.

After they left, Emma asked me if I wanted anything to drink, and after I declined she said, "I've got a hundred questions, so hopefully you can help me out. I feel so dumb calling the hospital. Susan was breastfeeding Pete Jr., but the hospital told me to give him Similac. Marc got both these kinds at the store." She showed me two kinds on the kitchen counter. "I used the green one and mixed up a batch according to the directions, but Pete Jr. wouldn't take any. I know he's used to being breastfed, but do you think I did it right? The stuff seems disgusting." She opened the refrigerator, took out a plastic container, undid its lid, and let me sniff the contents.

"I think it'll be okay. He just has to get used to it," I ventured. "Did you warm it up for him?"

"No, because I just made it. The hospital also told me I could give him diluted apple juice, but not too much, so I did that, and he loved it! He drank all four ounces and then cried when it was gone, but I'm afraid I gave him too much, and now he won't take the Similac when he wakes up."

"Once he gets hungry enough he'll take the formula," I said. "Don't worry so much, Emma. You're doing fine."

"Come and see the room where we'll put his crib," she said, leading me down a hall to a bedroom which was currently functioning as an office. There were a desk, two file cabinets, and Marc's old Lazy Boy recliner from the frat house. On the carpeted floor was a Hawkeye beach towel, with packages of diapers and a container of wipes nearby.

"Marc got Huggies," she said, "or do you think he should have gotten Pampers or Luvs?"

"I don't really know, but I don't think it matters."

"The hospital said to change him on the floor," she continued. "They said beds and changing tables can be really dangerous. They also said Pete Jr. has a slight case of diaper rash and to use Desitin when I change his diaper, but Marc forgot Desitin on his first trip to the store, so I haven't used it yet. The hospital said not to use powder, but I thought that would help the rash. I called my mom—she has to work tomorrow and Tuesday, but then she's going to come and stay for a few days—and she couldn't believe they told me not to use baby powder. She said she covered me with powder when I was a baby and I never had diaper rash!" Her beautiful face radiating hope, Emma smiled for the first time. I imagined she must have been a lovely baby.

"I don't know," I said. "I think I'd do what the hospital said. Remember, I'm not a pro at any of this either."

"But at least you've been around Melanie's kids," she countered. "By the way, how are she, Dan, the kids, and your parents?"

"They're all fine," I answered. "My parents want to come for the service." Suddenly we heard little cries coming from the kitchen.

"Well, we almost made it to thirty minutes!" Emma said, as we headed back to the kitchen. "Should I try formula now?

And look at all these bottles with different kinds of nipples. Marc just got one of each. They had so many different kinds, he said. But you know him, once a nipple man, always a nipple man." She smiled at her attempt at a joke while pulling one bottle out from the drainer in the sink. "I used this kind for the apple juice, and he loved that. Maybe I should use it for the formula?"

I went to pick up Pete Jr. He was a big baby. "There, there, Petey, we're here. It's okay, it's okay," I said in my most maternal voice. "First, let's change his diaper," I told Emma. Suddenly a few things that Melly had mentioned came back to me. "Keep the nipple that you used for the apple juice just for that. I remember Melanie saying that it will get stained."

We walked back to the bedroom and I put Pete Jr. down on the towel. Then I got the Desitin and wipes ready. After I had undone the snaps on Pete Jr.'s romper, Emma asked, "Did I get the diaper on right? Oh look, some of the pooh leaked out and got on his outfit!"

"The diaper was on fine," I said, as I began to clean a screaming Pete Jr. "This just happens sometimes with a big, runny pooh. The next time you get diapers, get the kind with the elastic around the leg holes. Don't worry, Petey, we're gonna get you all clean and dry. Yes, yes, you little sweetie pie." And then to Emma I said, "Gee, he does have diaper rash, doesn't he?"

"I'll say," she agreed.

"Do you have some small garbage bags, or plastic bags from the grocery store?" I asked, as I continued cleaning him off with the wipes. "Melly always put the diapers with pooh in bags and then right out into her garage trash can so they wouldn't stink up the house. And let's get a clean washcloth and pat this rash area dry before I put on the Desitin."

"Gosh, Sara, you're like a pro!"

Suddenly Pete Jr. began to urinate; a yellow stream went high into the air in a beautiful arc and dropped on the towel.

"Oh my God!" Emma exclaimed, and I giggled.

"You'd better get some more towels and washcloths to have in here," I suggested. "Little boys like to do this." I hadn't seen Carson do it, but Melly and my mother had told me about it. "And bring me another outfit to put on him," I added. "But get me a washcloth first."

"Okay," she said, rising from the floor. "Gee, I think I've only got one clean outfit left. Marc just didn't grab enough when he went over to their house. I'm going to call over there and tell him to bring some more of Pete Jr.'s clothes."

"Good idea," I said, taking off the soiled romper and then picking up his soft naked body and cradling it against me. Holding Pete Jr. gave me such a wonderful feeling; I listened to his quiet breathing and felt such a sense of calm.

"I'll be right back," Emma said, pausing in the doorway to stare at us. "Taking care of Pete Jr. with you is fun, but when I'm by myself I worry so much that I'm doing it right."

"Well, you're doing great, Emma," I said with as much conviction as I could, savoring the warmth of the tiny body against me and anticipating how marvelous it would be one day to hold my very own child.

"Thanks, Sara," Emma responded, her voice cracking with emotion. "But just think, this is the easy part. Tomorrow I've got to select the caskets and the clothes they'll wear and meet with the priest." She began sobbing. "Please help me, Sara."

I told her I would, and she disappeared down the hall.

I found out during the ride back to David's parents' home that Pete's mom had asked Marc and Emma to take care of as many details for the funeral as they could. She was flying in from Arizona tomorrow but wouldn't arrive until late in the afternoon.

"She's 61," David said sadly, "and she's had breast cancer twice. Marc says she's currently having chemotherapy. She's pretty devastated by this. And Susan's father is useless. They don't even know if they should try to bring him to the funeral. And Louellen won't get in until late Tuesday, but I understand that she and Pete's mom talked on the phone. That's when they decided to ask Marc and Emma to handle as much as they could. Pete's mom is handling the burial arrangements, but she asked Marc and Emma to pick out caskets. However, Marc has to work tomorrow, and so he asked me if we could pick up Emma at their house and go with her, and I guess the baby, to the funeral home."

"When I first talked with her today," I interrupted, "Emma had said that their bodies were pretty bad from the accident, so I'm assuming that the funeral home will be able to . . . to fix them up?"

"That's my understanding at this point. At least we're supposed to bring clothes over for them. Since we didn't have time to get their clothes when we got the crib, we'll either have to go back to Susan and Pete's house after dinner tonight or go early tomorrow. What do you think?"

"Let's see what time it is after we finish dinner and how Pete Jr.'s doing," I suggested.

"The funeral home mentioned doing a photo display for the funeral, so we'll need to find some pictures too. Are we supposed to bring shoes in addition to their clothes? And how about underwear?" David asked.

"I have no idea. I've never done this before, but I think we should just take everything over, and they can use what they need."

We pulled into the Woodley driveway with Marc, Emma, and

Pete Jr. following in their car. In addition to the crib, Marc and David had found a swing, and at my suggestion, we brought that along for the evening. David got it out of our backseat and carried it into his parents' home, while I picked up a shopping bag in which we had put baby supplies. Then I helped Emma get little Pete out of his car seat, and with Marc carrying a bottle of wine and a six-pack, we all entered the house.

While David's dad cooked steaks and salmon on the grill, we three women took turns holding Pete Jr. and getting the rest of the dinner ready. David's mom had made her famous scalloped potatoes, and there were also baked beans, fresh corn on the cob, garlic bread, and fruit salad. At my suggestion, we waited until we were ready to eat and then we changed Pete Jr.'s diaper and put him in his swing next to the dining room table.

"Let's hope this does the trick and we can enjoy our meal while little Pete falls asleep in the swing," I said, and my hoped-for plan worked. We then had one of the most enjoyable meals I could ever remember having, with everyone being witty and relaxed and laughing a lot. We talked mostly about babies and our jobs, our childhoods and our college years, and of course, the weather, because everyone in Iowa always talked about the weather. No one mentioned the funeral preparations or tomorrow's agenda or anything remotely morbid. Toward the end of the meal the phone rang, and when David's mom reappeared in the dining room doorway, she announced, "It's for any of you. Your friend Natalie from college. I told her that Marc and Emma were here too, and she said she'd talk to any of you."

"I'll just start crying," Emma told me. "You take it, Sara."

"Okay," I reluctantly agreed, rising from my chair and heading to the kitchen desk area. "Hello? Nat?"

"Oh God, Sara! I can't believe it! We—this guy I'm dating—and

I went away over the weekend, and when I got back my room-mate told me everything. She said Emma was going to call you and David, and I figured you'd come if you could. When I tried to call the Whites there was no answer, so that's why I tried David's parents. I hope you don't mind."

"Of course not," I said. "It's good to hear your voice, and we'll love seeing you. I just wish the circumstances were completely different."

"So what's going on? Where's Louellen? Isn't Susan's dad in a nursing home? Where's Pete Jr.? When's the funeral? How did the accident happen? What's gonna happen to the kid?"

"Well," I began, "the hospital, with Pete's mom's permission, let Marc and Emma have temporary custody of Pete Jr. We got in this afternoon, and David helped Marc get little Pete's crib set up at their house. Emma and I haven't really talked, but I think they'll probably ask to get permanent custody of Pete Jr. They are his godparents, you know. I mean, who else is there?"

"What about Louellen? Or you and David? I just can't see Emma and Marc being parents!"

"Well," I said quietly because Emma and David's mom were bringing dishes into the kitchen, "didn't you know Emma's been trying for quite a while to get pregnant?"

"Oh Lord! Irony of ironies!" she exclaimed, perhaps remembering a sloe screw celebration we had once had. "I just can't stomach the idea of that lecherous Marc White as a father!"

"Please, Nat," I reasoned, "David and I talked in the car on the way here, and it seems like the best option for Pete Jr., but of course Pete's mom and Louellen will have to make the final decision. And you were correct. Susan's dad is in a nursing home and he's got Alzheimer's."

"Really! Susan never told me that, but that certainly explains why I thought he was a little weird on their wedding day. Even way back then, I could tell the guy was short a few marbles. Now, how exactly did the accident happen?"

"I don't know too much, Nat," I responded. "Marc told us that Susan and Pete had decided to drive up by Decorah on Saturday to do some antiquing. They took Pete Jr. along and were going to make a day of it. You know how they loved antiques and hunting for them. It was about eight-thirty at night, and they were on their way home, and some drunk crossed the highway and smashed into them. They were killed instantly, but Pete Jr. didn't even have a scratch. He was in the backseat asleep in his car seat. And of course, the drunk walked away, perfectly fine!"

"Oh, that is **really** annoying!" she said. "That is pure shit, pure shit."

"Yes," I agreed.

"So do you know when the funeral is going to be, and has anybody called Simon yet?"

"I think so," I said, but I really wasn't sure. "We think the funeral's going to be Wednesday morning, and we're going to help the Whites tomorrow with some arrangements. Do you want to come over to the Woodleys' right now, or meet us at Emma's sometime tomorrow?" I asked, actually hoping she'd have other commitments.

"Well, I'm exhausted from being gone all weekend—no sleep, just lots of wonderful sex. My current beau is a divorced forty-two-year-old who, until I came along, hadn't done it for fifteen months, so you can imagine what he's like in bed, and I've got to work tomorrow, and I was planning to crash in front of the tube—*The Way We Were* is on TV tonight—but God, I'm dying to see you! I've got to unpack and throw a load of laundry in, but maybe I could swing by David's parents' house or Marc and Emma's for just a few minutes. How much longer are Marc and Emma going to be there?"

"Hold on a minute. Let me see if I can find out," I told her and turned my attention to the guys, who were now in the kitchen too helping with the clean-up. "Marc, David, what are our plans for the rest of tonight? It's about eight-fifty now. Are we going to swing by Pete and Susan's?"

"Definitely," Emma chimed in, "since I didn't reach the guys before they left with the crib, we've got to stop over there and get some clothes for Pete Jr. Plus I think we should get the stuff for the funeral home so we won't be rushed in the morning. Let's help with clean-up and try to leave here as soon as we possibly can. You two do feel up to coming with us, don't you? I mean, if you're not too tired from the drive here, we could sure use the help?"

"Of course," I assured her, and then I got back to Natalie, told her our plans, and asked her if she wanted to meet us at the Byron home around ten.

"Tell Nat I've got a favor to ask," Marc hollered, as he brought the swing into the kitchen. "Tell her that Simon is flying in, and I'd like her to pick him up at the airport. I'll get her all the details."

After I had conveyed this message, we hung up and I finished helping with the kitchen cleanup, even though David's mom insisted we didn't need to. "Emma," she suggested, "let me come over tomorrow with David and Sara, and I'll stay at your house with Pete Jr. while you three go to the funeral home. I just heard Marc saying that the hospital told you to call the body shop where they towed the car to see if Pete's diaper bag and stroller were left in the car trunk, so that will probably be another stop for you, and you don't need to be dragging the baby along everywhere. I'm not that old that I can't remember how difficult it was to do things with a tiny baby!"

"Thanks, Mrs. Woodley," Emma said, and to me, "You have a really great mother-in-law, Sara!"

"I know," I said. "She's the best. Let's change little Pete's diaper and then get going."

I had been to Pete and Susan's only once before. Their home was a small aluminum-sided ranch in an older section of town filled with mostly scrabbly houses. The Byron home was neat, though, and Susan had been so proud of it. Even though there weren't many rooms, she had shown me all of them. They were filled with mostly cheap furniture with a few antiques: a dry sink in the tiny dining L, an oak pie safe in the living room, a steamer trunk in the bedroom—all of these pieces providing just a glimpse into the way Pete and Susan probably envisioned their home to be eventually. There was also an antique rocker in the small bedroom which they'd been fixing up for the baby. Susan was especially proud of this room.

"I love the jonquil-yellow walls!" I'd told her. "And the crib set is really adorable with all the little teddy bears. It will go perfectly for either a boy or a girl."

"Yes," Susan had said, beaming and patting her round tummy. "So are you two thinking about kids yet?"

"Oh, probably not for a couple more years, or at least a year," I'd answered, hesitant to reveal our whole scenario, which included David's making partner. "We want to buy a house, get out of the city, you know, check out suburbia. I'd like to teach for a year. We want to have kids someday, but not for a while yet. . . ."

With no porch or yard lights on, their house was very dark, but we all managed to get Pete Jr. and ourselves up to the front door, which Marc finally got opened. Emma was holding Pete Jr., and I had one shopping bag with baby supplies, as well as two empty ones that David's mom had given us. David was holding the carry-cradle.

We entered directly into their small living room, and Marc

found a wall switch, which caused a dusty overhead fixture to come on. "Let's try to do this as quickly as possible," he said. "You girls get Susan's clothes and Pete Jr.'s clothes. We'll get Pete's. Then we'll look for some pictures and photo albums. If Nat gets here, she can help."

"This place gives me the creeps," Emma said, as we all headed down a narrow hallway to their bedroom. Marc found a wall switch and a faint overhead fixture came on. I turned on the lamps on a nightstand and dresser. It was a small bedroom with too much chunky oak furniture, a faded bedspread with orange and yellow flowers and kiwi-green leaves, a medium chair upholstered in brown velveteen. Crammed on top of the dresser was a small TV along with a lamp, a jewelry box, a pink tissue holder, a plastic valet, a container of baby wipes, one shoe horn, two dimes, and a tape measure opened to eighteen inches.

I offered to hold Pete Jr. for a while, so Emma opened the sliding door of their small closet to reveal Pete's half. There were several suits, pants, and casual shirts. The men quickly selected a navy blue suit, with our approval, and then Marc said, "Where the hell are all his dress shirts?"

"Maybe they're at the cleaners," David suggested, as he checked all the hangers once again.

"They didn't have enough money to send them out," Marc said. "They've got to be here somewhere." He slid open the door to reveal the other half of the closet, but only Susan's clothes were there.

"I think maybe they used one of the closets in one of the other bedrooms," Emma said, pulling out a dress with purplish flowers.

"And where the hell are his ties?" Marc asked. "Don't you keep your ties next to your suits, Woodley?"

"Yes, that's what I do," David replied, "but Pete evidently didn't. I'll go check around in the other bedrooms."

"What do you think about this, Sara?" Emma asked me. "Gee, it's too party-like, isn't it? I suppose we should find something black or gray or navy. I don't know what to pick. It's summer and we don't want to put her in a wool dress, do we, Sara?"

"This is hard," I said, trying to calm Pete Jr., who had started crying loudly and was turning his mouth toward one of my breasts between wails.

"Do you suppose he can smell his mother on her clothes?" Emma asked. "Oh, being here is freaking me out!"

"Don't be ridiculous," Marc said, throwing a pair of socks and underwear on the bed and continuing to open every drawer in the bedroom. "Where the hell does he keep his ties?"

Suddenly David hollered from another room, "Marc, come here and look at what I found."

"I think we need to feed little Pete," I said to Emma, while I continued to walk around the room, trying to comfort him. "Here, you hold him while I get a bottle ready."

On the way to the kitchen, we joined Marc and David in another small bedroom. "This is the only closet with shirts," David was saying, as he held up a light blue and a light pink shirt. "But this is it. These two and two white shirts that are pretty frayed around the collars."

"I would think he'd have more white shirts," I said. "Maybe they're in a laundry basket or the washer or dryer?"

"We should check there for Pete Jr.'s clothes too," Emma said. "The washer and dryer are in the basement. I know they have a laundry chute."

She went back out into the hall and immediately said, "Here it is," pushing open a small door in the wall.

"Well, I've got to fix Pete a bottle," I said, heading toward the kitchen.

"I'll go down to the basement," Marc offered. "Emma, why

don't you go get some of Pete Jr.'s things, and David, you can continue to look for Pete's ties."

"I don't want to be left alone," Emma protested.

"All right," I heard Marc say from the kitchen. "David, you go with Emma to Pete Jr.'s room, and when I get back from the basement, we'll all look for his ties."

There was a microwave on the counter in the small, somewhat messy kitchen, so I took out the Tupperware container with formula, shook it, filled a small bottle, and heated it for a few seconds. Then I rinsed the nipple with very hot water and put it on, trying to remember how I'd seen Melly do things. Then I grabbed the shopping bag and bottle and headed toward the nursery. David was cradling the baby and pacing the room, trying to quiet Pete Jr., who was still crying, while Emma was putting a small pile of clothes on top of a tiny dresser with the sampler I'd done nicely framed and hanging above it. Whoever eventually got Pete Jr. should have that sampler, I thought, which immediately seemed a stupid thought to have at this point in time.

"Here, honey," I said to David, "sit down in the rocker and see if he'll take this." From one of the shopping bags, I found an old green hand towel and placed it on David's shoulder. "After he's had a little, hold him upright against your shoulder and try to get him to burp."

Suddenly we all heard Marc holler from the basement, "Eureka! Somebody come here!"

"You go, Sara," Emma said. "I'm almost finished going through the drawers and then I'll check the closet here."

The stairs to the basement were in the kitchen, so I quickly headed there and then down. Marc was in a small dark-paneled room with lots of boxes, an old TV, a soiled sofa, three cheap bookcases, and two rusty file cabinets. He was standing beside an open file cabinet drawer looking at some papers in a file folder.

"I can't believe I found this!" he exclaimed. "Look, Pete's got everything marked: Taxes 1979, Taxes 1980, Appliances, Lawn & Garden, Insurance. And this file is marked 'Peter James Byron, Jr.' And here's a piece of paper that Pete and Susan signed, dated June 21, 1981."

I had moved across the room so that I was standing next to Marc and could read over his shoulder. "Here's what it says," he continued. "'In the event of both of our untimely deaths, we wish that our son, Peter James Byron II, be raised by his godparents, Marc and Emma White.' Earlier in the summer, he'd asked me if it would be okay if we'd be Pete Jr.'s godparents and also his guardians, in case anything would ever happen to him and Susan, but I never knew he actually put their desires in writing. They didn't have a will—at least according to Pete's mom—so I guess he figured he'd better get something in writing. What a guy!"

I felt a shiver, almost like the kind I sometimes got when I watched a scary movie, as I stood close to Marc and stared at the notebook paper on which Pete had written in his large, clumsy handwriting exactly what Marc had just read.

"Well, I don't know that much about the law, but I think this paper would hold up in court in case Louellen or Mrs. Byron would present any objections to your getting custody of Pete Jr.," I said.

"And why the hell would either one of them object?" Marc demanded insolently. "Lou's off in God-forsaken Africa doing the Peace Corps drill and we heard she was thinking about medical school. I don't see why she'd want to undertake raising a child by herself at this point in her life. And Mrs. Byron's health is so poor. I don't think she could possibly want custody."

I wanted to tell him that we all had doubts about Marc White as a father, but of course there was nothing I could say. "Any luck with the shirts?" I asked.

"The washer and dryer are in the area behind those doors," he said, pointing to shuttered doors on the far side of the room. "I haven't looked yet, so let's go see what we can find."

We walked over and opened the dusty doors, and Marc found the cord of an overhead light bulb, which dimly illuminated the area when he pulled it. The washer and dryer were against the outside wall, and an ironing board and iron were set up close to the furnace and water heater. Draped across the ironing board were what appeared to be several shirts.

"Eureka again!" Marc exclaimed, picking up the top shirt, which was white. "This just needs to be ironed."

There was an empty basket on top of the dryer whose door I opened, but it was empty. Ditto for the washing machine. There was an unpleasant, musty odor pervading the area. "Where's the chute come down?" I asked.

"I dunno," Marc said. "Maybe behind the furnace and water heater?"

I turned to head down the narrow pathway between a studded wall and the appliances when the dim light coming from the lone overhead bulb illuminated them hanging on nails pounded into the wall studs. I gasped and shrieked. My masks! My almost finished masks! My masks that had disappeared during my senior year in college! They were hanging in Pete and Susan's basement!

Marc appeared right behind me, and his hands grasped my bare shoulders. "What's the matter, Sara?"

"My masks," I mumbled.

"Oh, those are just a couple of ol' masks. They look like they should be part of a voodoo ceremony. Maybe Lou sent them from Africa. Don't let them scare you," he said while running his hands up and down my arms, as he stood so close to me that I could feel his breath on my neck. "I think we've found what smells so God awful," he continued, squeezing past me but letting his hands fall across my back and linger on my hips, before he reached a teaming laundry basket in the corner. "This is definitely where the horrible odor is coming from. I think we should just take this back to our house," he said, picking up the basket.

"You don't understand," I said, moving back to let him through. "I made those masks in college my senior year. I left them in the art building and they disappeared. I never found them or knew what happened to them. How on earth did they end up in Susan and Pete Byron's basement?"

"You're sure they're yours?"

"I'm positive."

"Well, it beats me," he shrugged. "I've never seen them until now. Maybe Simon or Nat knows something. They were awfully close senior year. God, these clothes really stink! How long do you think they've been sitting down here?"

"I have no idea, but let's take them upstairs so we can see better."

"Grab all the shirts," Marc told me, "so we can find a nice one. I'll carry this stinkin' basket."

After we ascended, we found David in the kitchen with Pete Jr., who was upright and against his shoulder, with David patting his back. "He still hasn't burped yet," David said hopelessly. "You two decide to take a vacation down there?"

"Here, hon, let me have him," I said, reaching for the baby.

Just then we heard the front door open and Natalie's voice hollered out, "Hello! Anybody here?"

"Back here, Nat," Marc called out, "in the kitchen." And then to David he said, "You won't believe what I found down there."

I was expecting him to say, "Sara's masks," but David interjected, "Looks like unironed shirts and a ton of dirty laundry."

As Natalie walked into the kitchen, we all greeted her. She was wearing tight black jeans and a sleeveless black top with a plunging neckline. One thing Natalie never forgot to do was to flaunt her large bosom. She squeezed my shoulder and said, "I'll give you a hug when you lose the kid. So what's going on?"

Marc answered, "We're getting things like clothes for the funeral, and Emma says we have to get all of Pete Jr.'s clothes because she keeps running out of clean outfits for him. I think we hit the jackpot downstairs. Help Sara look through these shirts and find a nice one. It will just need to be ironed. Now, everybody, look at this," he continued, taking the paper out of his pants pocket. "See what I found in Pete's filing cabinet. They both signed this and dated it, stating their desire for Emma and me to be Pete Jr.'s guardians in the event of their deaths."

"Well, congratulations, Marc!" Natalie proclaimed, after she gave me a funny look and patted Pete Jr. on the head. Just then Emma appeared in the doorway; she rushed to Natalie and they hugged. "I just can't believe this is happening," Natalie said. "It's like a really bad nightmare."

"I know," Emma said, as she started to cry.

"But what the hell stinks in here?" Natalie asked. "P.U. It's worse than the john at the Theta house or Mr. Keatson's hog house!" She started to handle gingerly the clothes in the laundry basket. "Didn't Susan ever do laundry?" she asked as she put one of Pete Jr.'s badly soiled rompers on the floor.

"I just think it sat all day in the basement for a few days," I ventured. "She probably would have washed today."

"I think all the rain and the dampness in the basement contributed to a little mold growth," Marc added, examining the romper with his physician-trained eyes. "Do you think this is salvageable, Emma?"

"I'll take it home and wash it with tons of bleach and we'll see," she replied, putting it back in the basket. "We need all the baby clothes we can find. This little guy seems to go through a lot of outfits in one day."

"So congratulations, Emma. You two get the kid," Natalie said, winking at Pete Jr. and giving him another pat on the head. "He looks like he's a real porker."

"All babies have chubby cheeks, Nat," Emma protested, "and we don't know for sure what's going to happen to Pete Jr., although we'd love to have him. I don't think I've told you, Nat, but Marc and I have been trying to have a baby without any success."

Marc moved over to Emma and put one of his arms around her. "Well, hon, there's been a new development that everybody here but you knows about. Look at what I found in a filing cabinet in the basement." He handed her the paper and then asked, "Woodley, do you think this would hold up in court?"

"I think so," he answered. "You'd just have to verify that those were their signatures and that they were of sound mind when they signed the paper."

After Emma had read it, she said, "Wow! I can't believe you found this!" Then she hugged Marc and continued, "I can't believe they actually did this. It's like . . . the answer to our prayers . . . except that they're gone, and that's not right, of course. They were so young, just twenty-six. It's just not right!" Then she began crying.

I felt my eyes well up, but suddenly Pete Jr. let out a big burp, and I sensed he threw up a little also. I'd forgotten to get the towel David had been using as a burp cloth, and now Pete Jr.'s spit was on my shirt and arm.

"God, Sara, his puke is all over you!" Natalie shrieked.

"Let me take him now," Emma said, rushing over to scoop up the baby. "Let's just hurry up here and get him home and put him to bed. It's so late. Sara and Nat, come in the bedroom and look at the dresses I picked out and tell me which one we should take to the funeral home. Marc and David, you put those shirts and that laundry basket and this shopping bag in the car. We can find some photo albums tomorrow. I can't bear to stay in this house another minute."

After I had wiped the formula off my shirt and arm with a wet paper towel, I joined Emma and Natalie in the bedroom. Natalie was holding a black dress with white dots in front of her. "This okay, Sara?" she asked.

"Fine," I answered.

"Okay," Emma said, still pacing the room with the baby. "Put it in that shopping bag. I've got hose, panties, a slip, a bra, and shoes in there. Does that seem sufficient?"

"How about earrings?" I suggested. "Nothing valuable. Just some costume earrings. You know how Susan loved earrings."

Nat went over to the jewelry box on the dresser, opened it, and started rummaging through the contents. "You're not gonna believe this," she said, "but there aren't any earrings in here. Only some necklaces, a couple rings, and a whole lot of cuff links. This thing looks like a rosary. Susan didn't convert to Catholicism, did she? Where do you suppose she kept her earrings?"

"Well, we don't have time to start searching for them now," Emma countered. "I just can't stay in here any longer."

"Didn't Susan use clip earrings because she never got her ears pierced?" Natalie asked. "Otherwise we could just use a pair of ours, except we all have pierced ears."

"Nat's right," I said, picking up the shopping bag, "so let's get out of here now. We can have the funeral director add earrings to the body at the last minute, can't we?" What I'd just said sounded so unreal to me.

"Oh Sara, that thought just seems so gross to me," Natalie said. "I just don't think I could bear to touch Susan's embalmed body in the casket."

"Enough!" Emma declared as she headed down the hall. "Being in this house just sends shivers up my spine." She quickly headed to the living room door, while I told Natalie I'd stop in the kitchen and turn off the lights there. When I got to the front door, Natalie was already outside but Marc had returned.

"All set?" he asked.

I turned around once more to look at the small, cluttered living room, filled mostly with cheap furniture. I spied Susan and Pete's wedding picture on wood veneer shelves holding a TV, stereo equipment, books, and knickknacks.

"Just a minute," I said, walking across the room to the shelves and picking up their picture, which was next to a Precious Moments figurine. "I think sometimes it helps the funeral home when they prepare the bodies." I was thinking about what Emma had told me on the phone that morning about the accident.

"Yeah, good idea," Marc said. "Also, it's a great picture of them. I think Pete's mom will want to have it on display during the services." We both glanced down for a second at their forever young, radiant faces before Marc hit the light switch.

When we got to the three cars, Emma had just put Pete Jr., who had fallen asleep, in his car seat, and Natalie was asking Emma if she could help by making phone calls tomorrow.

"Marc called about a dozen people earlier today," Emma was saying. "Who else do we need to call, sweetheart?"

"I'm going to have to think. I called as many fraternity brothers as I could think of today, but I know I'm forgetting people. Then there's the baseball team. Sara, do you know where Jack Bindel's living?"

"I'm sorry," I replied, "but I don't know where he is. Maybe Steve Braka would know. I think he lives here in I.C. He should be in the phone book."

"I'll try to reach those guys tomorrow," Natalie offered. "And how's Simon taking things?"

"Well," Marc said, "when I told him, he just couldn't believe it, like all of us. I think he's probably taking it pretty hard. He and Pete knew each other since they were toddlers. He's calling us tomorrow with his flight info, and then I'll let you know, Nat. It'd be great if you could pick him up at the airport on Tuesday. And, of course, Louellen and Pete's mom will also need to be picked up at the airport."

"I called Marianne Reynolds," Emma said, "and she wanted to know what she could do to help. Maybe she can help pick up people at the airport."

"Yeah, that'd be good," Marc said. "And Mel also asked what he could do to help. Jesus, sometimes the offers of help just really get to me. Hank Locke and his wife had a son in May and he's into videotaping, and he offered to get some footage of this house because he thinks that Pete Jr. may enjoy seeing the video some day when he's older. You know, it'd be one of the few things he would have other than photos." Marc's voice got softer, and I thought maybe he was going to break down, but he didn't.

It was still very hot outside, a typical August night, although the mosquitoes had not discovered us yet as we stood in a small circle on the driveway. None of us seemed to want to move or say anything for a few minutes. I was about to break the silence when Marc continued, "Hank thought maybe we could all meet here after the service and he'd shoot the house, and those of us who are here could add a little commentary, which reminds me, Woodley, I was going to ask a big favor of you. Since I'm going to be tied up at the hospital tomorrow, could you come over and mow this yard, so it'll look nice for Hank's videotaping and when Pete's mom gets here? With all the rain we've had, the damn grass is so long and it looks like it hasn't been mowed in weeks." He glanced over at the dimly illuminated lawn, whose length I had not previously noted.

"Sure thing," David said. "I'll just bring my dad's mower over."

"And Sara," Marc continued, "maybe you could help Emma pick up the house? Pete's mom indicated she was going to be staying here. You know, change the sheets, run the dishwasher, tidy up a bit. I know now's not the time to say anything about Susan's housekeeping, but frankly I think the place could be spruced up a bit. I suppose Mrs. Byron will try to put it on the market soon, which reminds me that I haven't called Bruce. I know he and Jenny aren't dating anymore, but maybe you can talk to him tomorrow, Woodley? As I recall, he's still in the real estate business."

We both said we'd be glad to do what he'd asked, and then I inquired, "Have you called Frannie, Emma?"

"I don't have her number or address in New York," she said. "Do you?" When we told her we didn't, Emma continued, "Well, tomorrow I'm going to call a high school friend of Susan's in Parker, and she can give me Frannie's parents' number. Frannie probably won't be able to come, but I think we should let her know. I especially think we should contact those people who would have to fly in as soon as possible. But of course, we've got to talk to Pete's mom first to know for sure when the funeral is going to be."

"Yeah," Natalie agreed, "and remember that I can make some calls too."

"Okay," Emma said, "we'll call you tomorrow, Nat, with any more names we think of. Marc, didn't you say there'd probably be a notice in tomorrow's newspaper?"

"I think so," he answered. "Just a short one. Not their obituaries. I think we'll have to wait for Pete's mom and Louellen to get here to compose those. God, I can't believe I just said the word *obituaries*."

Emma moved closer to him and put her arm around Marc. Then she said, "It's so late and I am so tired. And we've got to get little Pete in bed." Then she walked over to hug me, adding, "Sara and David, you'll be by about 8:30 tomorrow with Mrs. Woodley? Oh dear, do you think I'll have Pete Jr. and myself ready by then?"

"Just get yourself ready," I said, squeezing her shoulders. "David's mom can handle the baby."

"You know, I never did find any ties," David remembered suddenly.

"Heavens, we're not going back in there tonight!" Emma gasped. "We can take one of Marc's ties to the funeral home."

"Did you check the backs of doors and the backs of closet doors?" Natalie asked. "Since their house was so small, I remember that Susan was really into all this organizational gadgetry."

"No, I didn't look behind doors," David confessed.

"Well, we're not going to tonight," Emma piped in. "Tomorrow we'll take one of Marc's ties to the funeral home, and if we have time we'll swing by here and make one more check for ties—"

"And earrings," I added.

"Oh, yes," Emma continued, "earrings! I've got to start making a list. We might as well take diapers and other baby supplies that we can find. And if we can't find any ties, then Peter Byron is just going to be buried with one of **your** ties, Marc White. And if we can't find where she keeps all her earrings, then Sara and I will go out and buy a pair."

"Excellent plan, sweetheart," Marc said, putting his hand around her waist and kissing her hair. "Well, goodnight, everybody. Thank you for all your help. Let's all get some sleep, and we'll talk tomorrow."

As the Whites got into their car, David announced that he too was exhausted and wanted to get back to his parents' home. "It's after eleven," he concluded, "way past my bedtime for a normal Sunday night."

I wanted to ask Natalie about the masks in the basement, but I knew David and I were both really tired and it was too late and I doubted she'd know anything about them. Probably Simon and Louellen wouldn't know anything either. Only Pete and Susan knew, and they would never be able to tell me. It was one of those mysteries, like the tape measure opened to eighteen inches on Susan and Pete's dresser, that no one would ever be able to explain.

"Thanks for stopping by, Nat," I said, giving her a hug. "Let's plan to get together tomorrow evening."

"Sounds good," she said, and then whispered in my ear, "Promise me you and David will think about taking the kid."

I smiled weakly and got into our car. "Good night, Nat," was all I said.

As David turned on the engine, I noticed that the clock on the dashboard said 11:11.

"What a day," David said. "You as tired as I am?"

"Aaaha," I mumbled.

"You took their wedding picture?" David asked, noticing the portrait on my lap.

"Yes, I thought maybe the funeral home might find it helpful when preparing their bodies." I suddenly realized how it had gotten a little easier for us to talk about the more morbid aspects of our tasks. I thought about the probability that I would bury my parents and David's parents, that I would bury David someday, if statistics were accurate.

"You should speak for all of us at the memorial service, Sara," David was saying, "if Mrs. Byron and Louellen say it's okay. Emma asked me to try to persuade you. I guess Marc and Emma have been talking, and they both think you'd do a great job. Did he say anything to you while you were down in the basement?"

"No," I replied, remembering my masks again and Marc's hands lingering on my body. *Just because a man was adulterous didn't make him a bad father, did it?* I wondered.

"Well, you'd do the best job of any of us."

"Me? What would I say? Plus I'd probably break down!"

"Well, think about it, honey. You're the most eloquent, artistic, poetic person I know. You have a very compassionate nature, and you knew Susan and Pete really well."

As we stopped at a well-lit intersection, I glanced down at their portrait: Susan's demure face, large glasses, lacy, white wedding dress, Pete's auburn hair, long sideburns, faint freckles, light blue tuxedo, gaudy, ruffled shirt. I thought back to their wedding day over three years ago and tried to remember all the feelings of that night—clearly hope and anticipation and passion—was that when I first knew I loved David?—but also acceptance and calm, almost the same sort of serenity I felt now as David accelerated the engine and their smiling faces were engulfed in darkness.

I stared back at the dashboard, and 11:17 appeared on the car clock. Why had I checked the *Trib* today to see what time the sun had risen, when I never do that?

"These paradoxes tease me," I murmured.

"What?"

"Nothing," I said softly. "It's time to go to sleep."

Epilogue
OCTOBER 15, 1998

"*M*om! Telephone!"

"Okay!" I hollered as I picked up the kitchen wall phone while taking the plastic off a roll of paper towels. "Hello."

"Hey, Sara, this is Pidgy. I hope you've got a minute to talk. I've been trying to get you all day, but I couldn't get through on your cell phone."

"Oh, sorry. I think it needs a new battery."

"Well, I just wanted to check with you to see how the program cover is coming along. I hope you've had a chance to work on it because we have a planning meeting next Thursday?"

"Well," I lied, "I've just started working on it. Unfortunately, I haven't gotten too far yet. I've just been incredibly busy. My parents and my sister and her family were just here to visit last weekend."

"Oh," she interrupted, "how is your family?"

"Everybody's great. I can't believe my mom's seventy-seven and still painting murals."

"Oh, that is wonderful!"

"And can you believe I've got more company coming this weekend? My friend from Iowa and her son are coming in tomorrow. He's thinking about Northwestern."

"Oh, the friend who was here in June? The one with that humongous RV and those gorgeous twin girls?"

"No, that was Georgiana. But you do have a good memory. She has a son who's a senior in high school too. But the friend who's coming tomorrow is my friend from college—Emma. You may remember her from my wedding? Her son Peter is really interested in Northwestern, and we're all going to the game on Saturday."

"Now is she the one who's been married and divorced a couple times?"

"Oh no, that's Natalie," I said. "Emma is divorced, but she never remarried."

"Of course, now I remember. The really striking gal who was on Oprah? Who's really involved with M.A.D.D.?"

"Yes, now you've got her," I said, thinking of beautiful Emma giving tons on talks in auditoriums all over Iowa right before prom season.

"Well, she must have done a fantastic job with that boy if he's thinking about Northwestern. I've sort of forgotten the details, but isn't she the one who couldn't have kids of her own? And weren't the boy's parents killed in a car accident?"

"Yes," I answered, "over seventeen years ago."

"They grow up so fast, don't they?"

"They surely do," I agreed. "I just wish they'd help out around the house while they're still here! I just got home from Jewel with tons of food for this weekend, and now I'm trying to get everything put away and get the house in order. Well, you know the routine!"

"Do I ever!" she agreed. "I think even two houseguests is a lot!"

"And we'll actually have three this weekend because Peter's aunt, who's been in Bosnia, is coming to the states for a few weeks, and she'll be here this weekend too. Louellen--that's Peter's aunt--she's a physician--wants Emma to bring along a tape that I've never ever seen. It was made the day of Peter's parents' funeral. Another friend from college videotaped the gathering that was held after the funeral, and he had me stand up in the living room of our deceased friends and read the words I'd spoken at the funeral. I can't even remember what I said at the funeral it was so long ago, but Emma told me once that Peter found comfort in my words, so I'm anxious to see it. I think I quoted some poetry and said something about an antique pin, but for the life of me, I can't remember exactly what I said. It just seems like it was ages ago. But as soon as everybody leaves, I'll get busy on the program cover. An Evening in Provence? No sweat. I've got tons of ideas."

"Oh, you are a gem, Sara!"

"Well, I've got to hang up soon because I didn't get anything done this morning because I went with David to look at senior living facilities for his dad. Ever since his mom died, his dad just hasn't been the same. Talk about a depressing excursion! Of course, now David's at the club entertaining clients while I'm frantically trying to get everything together for this weekend."

"That's so typical of them, isn't it?" she commiserated.

"Look, Pidgy, I've really got to run now. I need to pick up Jonathan from soccer practice, and Susanna's hollering for help with her homework, so I've got to run now, but don't worry about the program cover. I'll get it over to you early next week."

"Thanks, and the auxiliary thanks you! You're a dear, Sara. Hope the weather's good this weekend and you all have a great time. I'll talk to you soon."

"Yes, we'll talk soon."

CPSIA information can be obtained
at www.ICGtesting.com
Printed in the USA
FFHW021708211118
49540753-53914FF

9 781977 204462